The
Zelmenyaners:
A Family
Saga

MOYSHE KULBAK

TRANSLATED BY HILLEL HALKIN

INTRODUCTION AND NOTES BY

SASHA SENDEROVICH

The Zelmenyaners: A Family Saga
By Moyshe Kulbak, translated by Hillel Halkin, with an introduction by
Sasha Senderovich

Yiddish Book Center
Amherst, MA 01002

© 2024 by White Goat Press, the Yiddish Book Center's imprint
Printed in the United States of America
10 9 8 7 6 5 4 3 2 1

Paperback ISBN 979-8-9909980-0-1

Library of Congress Control Number: 2024943589

Cover design by Kandy Littrell
Zelmenyaners family tree illustration by David Coons

Previously published in 2013 by Yale University Press / New Yiddish Library

*This book has been made possible with
generous support from Eileen Tunick*

◆◆◆ Contents

♦♦♦ *Introduction*
For Raya Kulbak

The December 1929 issue of the *Star* (*Shtern*), one of the Yiddish-language monthlies in the Soviet Union, opened with a full-page photographic portrait of Joseph Stalin, placed opposite the journal's table of contents. Congratulatory remarks on the occasion of the fiftieth birthday of Stalin, the general secretary of the Communist Party and the leader of the Soviet Union, were printed above the portrait, with the collective signatures of the journal's editorial board underneath. Listed in the table of contents were a few poems and short stories, an article about the work of proletarian writers in capitalist countries, and something entitled "From the Book *The Zelmenyaners Family* (Chapters from a Novel)" by the writer Moyshe Kulbak.[1] Set in an expanding Soviet metropolis slightly more than a decade after the Bolshevik Revolution, these chapters would later form the basis of a comic Jewish family saga called *The Zelmenyaners*.[2]

The Zelmenyaners first appeared in serial form: Part One in 1929–1930, Part Two in 1933–1935.[3] What today's reader can get through in just a few sittings took the readers of the *Star* six years, with a long break between installments.[4] In this respect, Kulbak's novel was not so unusual. Charles Dickens took a year and a half to bring out *Bleak House* in serial form, and subscribers to the journal the *Russian Messenger*—the original audience of Leo Tolstoy's *Anna Karenina*—had to wait two and a half long years to read the novel from beginning to end. A war that hadn't yet started when Tolstoy began to serialize his novel in 1875 was in full swing by the time he was finishing it in 1877.[5]

Similarly, the Soviet Union where Kulbak first set out to work on *The Zelmenyaners* in 1929 was hardly the same country once the serialization of the novel was finished in 1935. Many momentous things happened in those years, and these changes were palpable in the pages of the *Star.* The issue containing the first installment of *The Zelmenyaners* appeared just one month after Stalin's famous speech calling 1929 "the year of the great breakthrough." The first Five-Year Plan, announced in 1928, was beginning to yield noticeable results as the Soviet Union started its transition to a planned economy propelled by the modernization of its industrial complex and infrastructure and the collectivization of the agricultural sector.[6] After potential opposition to Stalin's leadership was squelched, the year 1929 also marked the appearance of what would eventually come to be known as Stalin's cult of personality.

The novel, announced in the table of contents opposite Stalin's portrait, was thus conceived, published, and circulated in an era of unprecedented social transformation. A product of its author's creative meditation on the paradoxes of political, cultural, and technological developments and their impact on a Jewish family in the late 1920s and the early to mid-1930s, Kulbak's *The Zelmenyaners* is a novel enmeshed with the heady epoch that began a decade and a half earlier in the Bolshevik Revolution of 1917 with its project of remaking human society and human nature itself. *The Zelmenyaners* focuses on the incongruities and disjunctions between Soviet rhetoric and the prerevolutionary cultural and religious mentalities that were transformed under its weight. It exploits those incongruities for comic potential unmatched in Yiddish literature since Sholem Aleichem but contemporaneous with similar literary efforts, some comic and others not, by such Russian-language writers as Mikhail Zoshchenko, Isaac Babel, and Andrey Platonov. Kulbak's novel is a masterpiece of both Yiddish and early Soviet literature simultaneously.

The Zelmenyaners is set in a specific geographic location. Though that location remains unnamed throughout Part One of the novel, the arrival of one of the protagonists in Minsk at the beginning of Part Two is accompanied by a sentence identifying that city as his home. Minsk was a fitting setting for a novel dealing with the social changes enabled by Stalin's industrialization policy. A city in which Jews made up a significant portion of the total population at the time of the Bolshevik Revolution, Minsk became the capital of the Belorussian Soviet Socialist Republic (one of the eventual constitutive republics of the USSR) in 1919. Rapid urbanization and a significant expansion of the population followed. Nearby villages and outlying neighborhoods found themselves incorporated into the growing metropolis while inhabitants of these peripheral locales suddenly found themselves to be newly minted city dwellers.[7]

More precisely, the setting of *The Zelmenyaners* is the courtyard of one Jewish family somewhere on the outskirts of Minsk. Though also a place where one would hang laundry out to dry—as in an ordinary yard or backyard—an Eastern European courtyard is primarily a space enclosed by houses along most or all of its perimeter. "Courtyard" refers both to the space between houses, where the inhabitants of the surrounding dwellings interact with each other, and, collectively, to the surrounding structures themselves together with the space between them. *Hoyf*, the word for courtyard in Yiddish, has a number of connotations. Isaac Bashevis Singer's *Der hoyf* has been translated to English as *The Estate;* in that novel about several generations of a single family, the word points to an aristocratic abode.[8] Derived from the same Yiddish word is the *shulhoyf*, a synagogue courtyard, the most famous of which was in Vilna, where several synagogues large and small were located around a single courtyard. The word *hoyf* also denotes both the physical space and the cultural institution of the court of a rebbe, a leader of a Hasidic sect. In David Bergelson's novella *Joseph Schur*, written in 1922, we read of "the court of the Rebbe of Great Setternitz," which "had been in decline for some time now."[9]

Prominent in Soviet culture, the courtyard figures particularly large in Soviet Jewish culture. Kulbak's *hoyf* emerged at the same time as Isaac Babel was setting his *Odessa Stories* in some of that city's famed courtyards.[10] The courtyard remained a focal point of Soviet Jewish experience in the work of such Russian Jewish writers as Fridrikh Gorenshteyn and Arkady Lvov and was a central setting in the internationally acclaimed film *The Commissar*, which depicts, among other themes, the story of a Jewish family during the Civil War.[11] Kulbak's novel centers on Reb Zelmele's courtyard—both the physical structures and the family institution established by the patriarch Reb Zelmele when he arrived in the vicinity of Minsk and put down roots there. (In Yiddish, *reb* is an honorific meaning "Mister"; Zelmele is a diminutive of the first name Zalman.)

As the novel opens, Reb Zelmele's widow, Bashe, still resides in her deceased husband's courtyard—where she has remained much longer than anyone could have expected. The four sons of Reb Zelmele—Uncle Itshe the tailor, Uncle Folye the tanner, Uncle Yuda the carpenter (and amateur violinist), and Uncle Zishe the watchmaker—are now the four pillars of the family, but these pillars are crumbling under the weight of the new zeitgeist despite the uncles' effort to adjust to it. The three daughters of Reb Zelmele, mentioned at the beginning, never turn up as characters: Kulbak, guided by Sholem Aleichem's use of only five of the seven daughters of Tevye the dairyman, must have concocted these three extra children in case more plot lines became necessary as the serialization went on.[12]

Much of the comic plot in *The Zelmenyaners* derives from challenges to the authority of the uncles' generation from the generation of their children (Reb Zelmele's grandchildren), who have grown up after the Bolshevik Revolution and the entrenchment of Soviet power in Belorussia. The inhabitants of the courtyard are all known collectively as Zelmenyaners even though the family's surname is actually Khvost (which in Russian means "tail" and in Soviet-speak of those days referred to those individuals and groups of people accused of being in the rearguard of social and political changes—those literally at the tail end of the revolution). The Zelmenyaners, as it were, are at once Jews who are becoming Soviet citizens and a unique species of humans whose comically exaggerated reactions shed light on the incongruities inherent in the Soviet project of modernization.

Kulbak was born in 1896 in Smorgon (present-day Smarhon, Belarus), a small town in the Russian Empire situated between Vilna and Minsk, about a hundred kilometers from either city.[13] Between the seventeenth and nineteenth centuries the town was the site of a so-called academy where bears were trained for performances in marketplaces around much of Europe. Though the "academy" was effectively defunct by 1870, when bear shows were banned in the Russian Empire, the fame of the town's peculiar trade was felt around Belorussia as late as the 1930s, when the occasional wandering Roma with a bear in tow would still be called, jokingly, "Smorgon teacher and his student."

In a 1922 poem, Kulbak drew on the strange history of his hometown:

> My grandfather's kinsman, a Jew who tamed bears,
> Performed in the market towns;
> By day his beast was confined in chains;
> At night, they danced under the stars.[14]

By recalling his grandfather, the speaker of the poem situates himself as a descendant of someone from Smorgon at the time when the bear "academy" was still active. But the poem is less about the speaker's biography than about the genealogy of his own poetic imagination. Chained by day, the bear is an object of terror and titillation; unchained by night, dancing with its trainer under the canopy of the nighttime sky, it offers up a beautiful image of the organic unity of man, beast, and nature.

This celebration of primal instincts freed by human encounter with the natural world is a unique feature of Kulbak's poetry and shows the influence of the poet's birthplace and upbringing. Toward the end of the nineteenth century, when Kulbak was born, Smorgon had become a center for tanning, logging, and other industries and agriculture-related occupations that employed, among others, Kulbak's father and numerous uncles. Growing up around peasants and in a family of Jews who worked the land, Kulbak had his childhood to thank for furnishing him with precise words for plants, trees, and natural phenomena. Many such words were lacking in the vocabulary available to Yiddish writers and needed to be imported from the region's panoply of Slavic languages.

In fact, more than any of the other Yiddish writers and poets before and of his time, Kulbak has been consistently credited with enriching the language with new organic and earthy metaphors.[15] The most impressive display of his linguistic knowhow is the 1922 poem "Belorussia," in which Kulbak invented a family of near-mythic proportions that predated the Zelmenyaners. This was a family of Jewish peasants probably not unlike Kulbak's own—a family with the patriarch working the land ("A farmer with a horse and with an ax and with a sheepskin")[16] and the matriarch giving birth to one son after another to produce the poem's narrator and his sixteen uncles, each of them a strong muscular type at one with nature:

> As common as the clay are all
> My sixteen uncles and my father,
> Hauling logs out of the forest; driving rafts upon the river.
> They toil the livelong day like ordinary peasants,
> Then eat their supper of an evening gathered around a single platter;
> And fall into their sixteen beds like sheaves of grain—together.[17]

In "Belorussia," Kulbak's Jews are different from their brethren elsewhere in the Russian Empire. They are not the Jews of the market towns who populate many pages of Yiddish literature, nor are they Jews weighed down with worry over how to make a living, or sickly yeshiva students consumed by pedantic arguments over the finer points of Jewish law.[18] Instead, they are Jews who "are known to the birds in the air [and] to the snakes in their marshes."[19] When, at the end of the 1920s and in the first half of the 1930s, Kulbak's gaze would shift in *The Zelmenyaners* to Jews who were becoming Soviet city dwellers, the touch of a poet's pen trained in organic metaphors would remain palpable through the numerous natural images that made their way onto the pages of his urban prose.

Through these same verbal images, Kulbak conveys his observations on the heady era of industrialization and collectivization that provides the novel's context. Far less triumphant than the official rhetoric of the first Five-Year Plan, which celebrated the Soviet Union's astonishing leap forward from a largely peasant society to a modern industrial one, Kulbak's observations are also far more ambivalent. In a failed rendezvous outside the city, the fiercely dogmatic Tonke, daughter of Uncle Zishe, and the uncertain Tsalke, son of Uncle Yuda, stand at the edge of a road that "stretched to the piney horizon." The narrator notes: "Far off on the horizon rose a spiral of smoke. A tractor chugged beneath it, creeping slowly along the edge of the earth without vanishing."

On a bright day, when the sun's "hot, green breath blasted the meadows," this tractor—a symbol of technological progress and mechanized agriculture—enters the pastoral landscape in order to stay there for good, to remain a part of the new reality. The image causes Tsalke to pronounce, in one breath, the blessing that thanks God for bringing forth "bread from the earth." Tsalke is not entirely wrong to do so: the tractor on the horizon is going through a field of wheat, working at bringing forth bread from the earth. Has Tsalke—an aloof amateur intellectual who serves as one of Kulbak's protagonists—attempted to join the revolution's modernizing call with his understanding of the natural world as inscribed in Jewish liturgical practices?

That is one possible interpretation of the scene, which is also reminiscent of the conclusion to Isaac Babel's contemporaneous masterpiece *Red Cavalry*. There, Babel offers the portrait of a Jewish youth who has attempted to comprehend both Lenin, the leader of the Bolshevik Revolution, and Maimonides, the medieval Jewish philosopher and religious commentator, as elements of one and the same worldview.[20] Kulbak, however, by painting an image of something organic transformed into something mechanical, also appears to hint at the devastating effects of the policy of collectivization, which led to the deaths of millions of people in the early 1930s because of forced expropriations of private farms and the confiscation of harvests. The tractor, planted into the natural landscape, disrupts a reaping process long practiced manually by peasants.

Later in the novel, when one of the Zelmenyaners' distant relatives arrives from Ukraine, whose population suffered the most in the years of forced collectivization, Kulbak's hints at the political context become more overt. The Zelmenyaners themselves are Litvaks, Jews of Lithuanian stock. The arrival of a distant relative from Ukraine is therefore very noticeable. The relative in question, we are told, smells of a village threshing floor and incessantly eats bread as the younger Zelmenyaners sarcastically inquire whether the collective farms, whose successes they have heard lauded on the family's newly installed radio, have stopped producing wheat. Accused of being a kulak—one of the class of peasant landowners that the policies of collectivization sought to exterminate— this relative may very well be, as the language here suggests, a survivor of the great man-made famine in Ukraine in the 1930s.

The question of harvests comes up throughout the novel, serialized at a time when discussion of the negative aspects of collectivization was not easy to conduct openly. But tracing the evolution of Kulbak's nature metaphors in *The Zelmenyaners* also reveals his ability to fuse nature and industry, to the point where it becomes impossible to imagine the one without the other. On the morning that Uncle Yuda leaves Reb Zelmele's courtyard on a journey that would lead him to a collective farm, "far in the east, the first fires of day bubbled up through a cleft in the snow as though from a hearth in a foundry." The image is still organic, but drawn from one of the regnant metaphors of the Five-Year Plan, which likened the project of creating the new Soviet man to the process of forging metal. Such language was already abundant at the time Kulbak was writing these lines, but he would become acquainted with it directly when later, in 1936, he was contracted to edit the Yiddish translation of Nikolai Ostrovsky's *How the Steel Was Tempered*—a paradigmatic Soviet production novel—for the Belorussian State Publishing House.[21]

Toward the end of *The Zelmenyaners*, Kulbak gives us a description of another morning in which nature has apparently been replaced by industry in Reb Zelmele's courtyard:

> In the early hours of the morning, when factory whistles sounded all over the city, the still-sleeping tanners heard their steady foghorn, discernible by its low, ample drone like a bassoon in an orchestra. . . . In early morning, as a gray dawn broke, the stars ceased their singing. In Reb Zelmele's yard, a polyphony of sirens took their place.

Here the space of the courtyard, reconfigured through the use of industrial language, itself gets reshaped by the dominant Soviet literary metaphors of production.

As a young man, Kulbak studied for a while at the Volozhin yeshiva, where one of his predecessors was the great Hebrew poet Hayyim Nahman Bialik. During World War I, Kulbak's family had moved from

Smorgon, which ended up right on the front line between the German and Russian armies, to Minsk. In 1919, Kulbak moved again, this time to Vilna, where success awaited him upon the publication of "The City"—an energetic poem full of revolutionary rhythm and force that would later be quoted in *The Zelmenyaners* by Tonke, the novel's most doctrinaire protagonist, as the work of a "Zelmenyaner poet, Kulbak."

In 1920 Kulbak left Vilna (then known by its Polish name, Wilno—a city in the newly independent Republic of Poland) for Berlin. There he spent three years living from hand to mouth while frequenting the cafés that were the meeting places of Yiddish, Russian, and Hebrew writers unsettled by the Civil War in Russia and Ukraine.[22] Between 1923, the year of his return from Berlin, and 1928, Kulbak served as a teacher in Vilna, a major Jewish cultural center and nascent laboratory of modernist Yiddish poetry, where he became an inspirational figure to the younger generation of poets. His poem "Vilna"—a hymn to the city known in the Jewish imagination as the "Jerusalem of Lithuania"— was published in 1926 and remains one of his best-known works.[23]

In 1928, Kulbak moved back to Minsk—in part because of his belief in Soviet support of Yiddish culture, in part out of the strong Communist convictions that were already apparent in his earlier work, and in part out of a desire to be reunited with his family. Like Vilna, Minsk was the home of several Yiddish cultural institutions, but in Minsk all such institutions were supported by the state in its attempt to create a new and progressive Soviet Jewish culture. In fact, in the interwar years, Yiddish was—along with Belorussian, Russian, and Polish—one of the four official languages in Soviet Belorussia: the first state-level recognition of Yiddish as an official language anywhere in the world. (The second, and last, such recognition would follow a few years later as Yiddish became the official language of the Jewish Autonomous Region in the Soviet Far East.)[24] The move to a political setting very different from Vilna gave Kulbak plenty of food for thought—and *The Zelmenyaners* could be viewed as a comic assessment of what the writer saw in Minsk after he settled there.

The dating of events inside the novel itself is implicitly clear, not simply from the fact of its serialization but from certain textual details. The author gives indirectly—albeit precisely—a date for the beginning of the narrative in the fourth chapter of Part One, which is devoted to

Uncle Folye. There we learn that the events described "happened thirty-five years ago, when [Folye] was no more than a boy of ten." In other words, Uncle Folye is forty-five years old at the time the narrative begins. A few pages later we are given a further indicator: "In 1914, Uncle Folye was thirty." When we put the two sentences together—1914 minus thirty plus forty-five, the date of the narrative's inception emerges as 1929. The very first installment of the novel, published in the *Star* in December of that year, contains both the first chapter and the chapter on Uncle Folye, numbered there as Chapter 8. Since that chapter would eventually become Chapter 4 when the novel was published in book form, we can estimate that Kulbak drafted a significant portion of Part One before the year 1929 was over.

Nineteen twenty-nine was an important year in Minsk. Local newspapers lauded the achievement of a number of the modernizing goals spearheaded by the Soviet state. Much of the city was hooked up to the electrical grid, part of an all-Union project judged by Lenin to be no less important to the success of Communism than Soviet power itself. The "liquidation of illiteracy" campaign was also advancing by leaps and bounds in Minsk, increasing the number of city dwellers who could read and write. In addition, outlying districts formerly not regarded as parts of the city became connected to the center by an urban rail network.[25]

All of these events made their way into Kulbak's novel. The introduction of electric lighting finds the older Zelmenyaners initially disgruntled by the loss of familiar shadows and hidden passageways between houses of the courtyard, where previously the call of nature could be answered out of the sight of others; an aunt comically attempts to learn how to write; family members feel the courtyard suddenly transformed into part of a larger universe as faraway radio broadcasts fill its airspace; Uncle Itshe is enthusiastic about the arrival of the trolley, enabling the whole family to ride freely from their place of residence to other parts of Minsk. When chapters of Part One of *The Zelmenyaners* are read side by side with Minsk's newspapers from the time, it becomes clear that Kulbak treated his fictional courtyard as a kind of laboratory where real events could be put to the test of comedy.

The Zelmenyaners' comic reactions to Soviet innovations have to do with their unique biological makeup, folksy attitudes, and private language. The Zelmenyaners, as a human specimen, are in turn the literary representation of Kulbak's own interest in the folkloric and the everyday. The protagonist of *Monday,* a novella by Kulbak about the effects of the revolution upon a shtetl intellectual, is said to prize not the holiness of the Jewish Sabbath but rather Monday, "the simple day, when the poor go begging from house to house."[26] In an unpublished Russian-language memoir by Kulbak's widow, Zelda, written in the 1960s, there is the following note:

> He loved to speak with workers and simple people. He used to say to his students: "One must listen to the language of the people, to idioms and sayings, to folklore." Together with older students he would go on excursions to the market. They would eavesdrop on and record the words of merchants and customers.[27]

Kulbak's novel displays a similar attentiveness to idiomatic language and ethnographic detail. As for the novel's obsession with the Zelmenyaners as a kind of separate species, its epitome is to be found in a chapter in Part Two entitled "The Zelmeniad" (as in "The Iliad"). Initially serialized in the *Star* in February 1935, it was one of the last chapters to be published. Drawing on the device of a "found text," the chapter is said to have been "compiled and revised from the notes [about the courtyard] by the young researcher Tsalel Khvost, a native of the same courtyard." (Elsewhere, Tsalel is called by his nickname, Tsalke.)

At the time he was writing his novel, Kulbak held a day job as a research associate and editor in the Jewish sector of the Belorussian Academy of Sciences.[28] In this position, he processed and revised Yiddish-language texts for publication. Within the comic frame of *The Zelmenyaners,* Tsalke's "study" is an exercise in mock ethnography, a parody of the actual ethnographic debates that Kulbak would have witnessed up-close from his position at the academy.

Tsalke's study is divided into an introduction and six parts. The introduction specifies that Reb Zelmele Khvost had founded the courtyard in 1864. This is a brief excursion recapitulating the local history already related earlier in the novel but presented here as better researched and with a date that places the local history within the context of a larger historical timeline. According to Tsalke's study, the traits that have distinguished the Zelmenyaners have been at work from the very beginning: "Set apart from their neighbors, the Zelmenyaners forged a distinctive lifestyle of their own in the course of the next generations." Each of the subsequent parts describes these specific customs and practices as they become manifest in various spheres of life, indicated in the titles of the parts: in addition to a subchapter on technological and medical peculiarities of Reb Zelmele's courtyard, there are chapters on "Zelmenyaner Geography," "Zelmenyaner Zoology," "Zelmenyaner Botany," and "Zelmenyaner Philology."

Tsalke's research categories are parodies of actual ethnographic studies being undertaken at the time. Reb Zelmele's courtyard, the smallest possible unit available for Tsalke's amateur ethnography, strikingly resembles another social unit subjected to contemporary ethnographic research and debates: the shtetl. Such research was encouraged at the time to help the Soviet government determine appropriate economic policies that would enable the Jews residing in the former Pale of Settlement—to which they had been restricted between the end of the eighteenth century and 1917—and formerly engaged in middlemen's occupations, to enter "productive" professions.[29] Accordingly, the use of social science was part and parcel of a larger preoccupation with ethnography that informed the state-building enterprise in the early Soviet period.[30]

Specifically, "The Zelmeniad" is reminiscent of a pamphlet called *Research Your Shtetl!* calling on amateur ethnographers to study their hometowns under ten predetermined categories. Among these categories are: "geographic position and appearance of the shtetl," "the history of the shtetl," "population," "the economic system of the shtetl," "education in the shtetl," "facilities and sanitary conditions," "practices and culture."[31] The pamphlet was published in Minsk in 1928 (the year Kulbak returned from Vilna) by the same institution that would employ Kulbak two years later. Tsalke's "study" in *The Zelmenyaners* takes up this pamphlet's call, as it were, and subjects it to parody.

From the beginning of the novel the Zelmenyaners have been described in language that is both organic and ethnographic:

> Zelmenyaners are dark and bony, with broad, low brows. Their noses are
> fleshy and they have dimples in their cheeks. On the whole they are quiet,

sluggish types who look at you sideways, though some of the younger generation can be loud-mouthed. At heart, however, while putting on worldly airs, they remain timid descendants of Reb Zelmele. Zelmenyaners are patient and even-tempered. They are as taciturn when happy as when glum. Yet they sometimes glow like hot iron in a special Zelmenyaner way.

Over time, Zelmenyaners have developed their own smell—a faint odor of musty hay mixed with something else.

Like Kulbak's Jewish peasants, loggers, and tanners in the poem "Belorussia," the entire Zelmenyaner clan is a breed unto itself. The Zelmenyaners' traits—their unique organic smell but also their turns of phrase and peculiar laughter—persist throughout the novel no matter how much their circumstances change. Even the younger generation— the generation bent on Sovietizing and modernizing the courtyard— remains organically a generation of the descendants of Reb Zelmele, a generation in which the Zelmenyaners' nature persists.

The fact that the Zelmenyaners are described in "The Zelmeniad" as though they are under observation by an amateur ethnographer did not escape the attention of Minsk-based critics of Kulbak's novel. Some disapprovingly focused on Tsalke's statement that "in the course of the generations the Zelmenyaners have worked up their own unique approach to life." This "unique approach" came under attack in the charged political atmosphere of the Soviet mid-1930s.

One critic, Yasha Bronshteyn, addressed the issue of Kulbak's ethnographic language in his 1934 article "Against Biologism and Folkishness."[32] Bronshteyn noted—not incorrectly—that in much of his poetry and prose, preceding but also including *The Zelmenyaners*, Kulbak was drawn to a particular type of character: a "stormy-raw," "biologically stripped," "naked nature man." The critic refers to this type as a *shilue* —a rascal, a "whippersnap"—a term Kulbak himself uses as an epithet for some of the younger Zelmenyaners. (Most likely, the Yiddish term is Kulbak's own coinage, and interestingly it appears on Tsalke's list of the Zelmenyaners' own linguistic peculiarities as reproduced in "The Zelmeniad.") Bronshteyn, however, makes the concept of *shilue* more inclusive, applying it not only to the younger generation but also to the generation of the four uncles and their wives.

All the Zelmenyaners, according to Bronshteyn, were "rascals" of sorts, a quality that was part of their problematic nature as individuals driven more by their gut feelings than by their consciousness. This category includes both those who supported the revolution and those who opposed it. What unites the two groups, according to Bronshteyn, is their reliance on instinct and emotion rather than on higher-order thinking. Here, operating within the permissible parameters of Soviet criticism, Bronshteyn takes his cue from Lenin's famous 1902 treatise "What Is to Be Done?" Departing from the traditional Marxist emphasis on class struggle as the essence of the revolution, Lenin, who doubted that the largely illiterate and uneducated Russian working class and peasantry would ever be able to organize themselves into a revolutionary force, proposed to rely instead on a "vanguard of the proletariat" driven more by consciousness than by spontaneity. As one preeminent scholar of Soviet literature has put it,

> "Consciousness" is taken to mean actions or political activities that are controlled, disciplined, and guided by politically aware bodies. "Spontaneity," on the other hand, means actions that are not guided by complete political awareness and are either sporadic, uncoordinated, even anarchic . . . , or can be attributed to the workings of vast impersonal historical forces rather than to deliberate actions.[33]

Bronshteyn's indictment of the Zelmenyaners can be understood in terms of this opposition between spontaneity and consciousness. Bronshteyn asserts that the "call of blood" and the Zelmenyaners' own "version of world history" are stronger than the effects of Soviet ideology.[34] The specific traits distinguishing the Zelmenyaners, moreover, exert a greater influence than whatever positive energy might be produced by the young generation of the family. As Bronshteyn points out, the younger Zelmenyaners, even those who would appear to be ideologically reliable, are described according to their typical external Zelmenyaner traits and spontaneous decisions, rather than from the inside and as doing what heroes of Soviet literature should be doing: undergoing a process of evolution from spontaneity to consciousness. The self-described rascals themselves—even the most ideologically progressive—are, first and foremost, typical Zelmenyaners.

A poignant example of the apparent triumph of spontaneity over consciousness among the Zelmenyaners comes in the chapter about electrification. The idea to extend electricity to the courtyard occurs to Bereh the policeman, Uncle Itshe's son, randomly. The critic Bronshteyn is dismayed by this: by, that is, the fact that the silent Bereh would be entrusted with implementing Lenin's electrification plan. Electrification in the Soviet Union cannot be portrayed, according to the critic, without showing the leading role played in this enterprise by Communist ideology and "consciousness." Instead, here too, the reflexes of the Zelmenyaners prove stronger than the supposedly transformative power of ideology.

According to another Minsk-based critic, A. Damesek, these same reflexes are what turns their bearers into passive characters: for example, the older Zelmenyaners resist electrification because it is in their nature to resist such innovations. Damesek does single out one character for displaying consciousness, but it is the kind of consciousness antithetical to the proper aims of a Soviet novel. Damesek's conscious character is Tsalke, and the case study of his "incorrect" consciousness is "The Zelmeniad." This chapter was at the center of Damesek's 1936 attack on The Zelmenyaners in the pages of the Star.[35]

Damesek describes Tsalke's practice of collecting his family's curiosities as "an actively hostile force that manifests itself all the more because it senses its own proximate and absolute demise."[36] That is, Tsalke is impelled to do what he does precisely because he senses the inevitable disappearance of Reb Zelmele's courtyard and its unique ways of life. As an amateur ethnographer, he consciously and deliberately occupies himself with interpreting the material in his collection. Such motivations and consciousness are absent in the other Zelmenyaners, whose reactions to Soviet modernization are driven purely by gut reactions. And yet, instead of aiming his consciousness at some socially useful task, Taskle devotes himself to recording the unique and undesirably reflexive traits of his kin.

Tsalke's mock ethnographic text, "The Zelmeniad," writes Damesek, "occupies itself with the specificity of Jewishness with the purpose not just of preventing it from becoming part of a museum display, but of transforming it into a folk tradition, an exalted national form."[37] Damesek fears that Kulbak is using the figure of Tsalke not to ridicule and satirize the Zelmenyaners' anachronistic ways, as he should have been expected to do, but rather to perpetuate and enshrine them. Damesek here joins the ranks of other critics who chastised Kulbak for his insufficient use of satire. Tsalke's activity, in these critics' eyes, is doubly dangerous: not just a reflexive but a positively deliberate counterreaction to Soviet modernity. At a time when technological innovation driven by Soviet ideology is destabilizing the courtyard for the better (according to this view), Tsalke, acting as the lone motivated figure in the courtyard, has attempted to salvage what he can.

To a great extent, the critical attacks on *The Zelmenyaners* by Bronshteyn (in 1934) and Damesek (in 1936), among others, need to be understood within the context of the changing conventions of Soviet literature. On the surface, Kulbak's novel may have seemed to be telling the story of a Jewish courtyard's gradual dissolution and the integration of the Jews into the Soviet metropolis through the force of different ideological and technological innovations. This, at any rate, was exactly what the text *should* have been about in the eyes of the critics; but, as one critic wrote, to take this narrative at face value would have been a mistake. The untamed independence of the novel's protagonists made it unclear whether they were, in fact, absorbing the lessons of the revolution.

It may be useful to recall in this connection that Kulbak began serializing his novel in 1929 and finished it only in 1935. Roughly halfway through Part Two, a watershed event occurred that quite likely changed the author's attitude toward his own text.

At the First All-Union Congress of Soviet Writers, held in Moscow in August and September 1934, all literary production in the Soviet Union was centralized through the introduction of the concept of Socialist Realism, henceforth proclaimed to be the only acceptable mode of creative expression. Though the buildup to this moment had been ongoing throughout the early part of the 1930s, the promulgation of Socialist Realism—that is, the depicting of "reality in its revolutionary development"[38]—as the only acceptable style of Soviet literary production marked an official turning point in the subordination of art to Soviet political and ideological ends.

Kulbak heard the news directly as a member of the Belorussian delegation at the congress.[39] Whether by coincidence or by design, the chapter entitled "Bereh and Uncle Folye Fight for the New Man" was initially serialized in the issue of the *Star* devoted to reports about the proceedings in Moscow. In this chapter, Bereh, expelled from his work at the police station for some unspecified ideological shortcoming, is sent to work at a leather goods factory so that he can prove his credentials as a reliable Soviet citizen by undertaking socially important work (in this case, ratting out the state's ideological enemies, one of whom turns out to be his own relative).

Having already begun the serialization of Part Two with a prologue about Bereh, Kulbak appears to have seized on the new literary directive as requiring a clear central protagonist in the process of evolution from spontaneity to consciousness. Such an evolution, according to the tenets of Socialist Realism, could not be accomplished on one's own but required the help of a mentor. Since, aside from the courtyard itself, *The Zelmenyaners* does not really have a central protagonist, Kulbak appears to have tried to invent one after most of the novel was already written.

In the prologue about Bereh, serialized in the *Star* in March 1933, Kulbak had already planted the seed of this idea by dispatching Bereh to participate as a soldier in World War I and the Russian Civil War, where he could presumably have earned some military distinction. There, a non-Jewish officer named Porshnyev befriends Bereh and, by asking promptly whether he belongs to any party, establishes himself as a figure who will later be presented as Bereh's ideological mentor.

But Kulbak must have judged this initial chapter insufficient to establish Bereh's credentials as the novel's main protagonist. In October 1934—one month after the codification of the doctrine of Socialist Realism—he published an additional chapter about Bereh's experience during the war. As if modifying the utterly nonheroic Bereh of the prologue, Kulbak now presents him (albeit with a satirical edge) as something of a hero. Returning to those earlier events, the new chapter informs us that Bereh had been taken in by a Jewish baker who wants to arrange a match for his daughter. But, declining the settled life of a family man, Bereh runs away and undergoes his wartime experiences as he continues on his journey home—experiences that come as close to the heroic as a comic novel will allow (and that mimic the scene in Homer's Odyssey where Odysseus rejects Calypso in favor of making his way back to Ithaca).

When the second half of *The Zelmenyaners* was published in book form in 1935, this later chapter was included, out of its original sequence, as Chapters 3 and 4 of Part Two. In this we can see Kulbak's attempts to grandfather the entirety of his novel into the guidelines of Socialist Realism by introducing Bereh, very belatedly, as a potentially passable protagonist who journeys from spontaneity to consciousness. Evidently aware of the artificial nature of this enterprise, Kulbak also introduces another detail: the discovery of an autobiography written by Bereh as part of his application for a job at the police station—where his boss will be none other than Porshnyev, his ideological mentor and wartime companion. Such autobiographies were indeed required of Soviet citizens seeking employment in the 1920s and the 1930s, when anyone not from a desirable class (with aristocratic roots, for example) would have had trouble getting hired.

By narrating his own adventures during the war, Bereh passes off his youthful exploits, such as they were, as a proper Soviet biography. It is clear, however, that Kulbak was still undercutting his own apparent efforts to conform to the requirements of a proper Soviet text. Bereh's autobiography is found and scrutinized by the pedant Tsalke, who, comparing the place names mentioned in the document with the route Bereh would have realistically followed in returning home from the war, judges the autobiography to have been concocted out of thin air.

Midway through the novel, at the beginning of Part Two, the family and their courtyard are in decline. In the early chapters of Part Two, then, Bereh emerges as a kind of messenger from the "Promised Land" of Communism—someone who could turn the family's fortunes around. This image of a messenger from the Promised Land had arisen before in Yiddish literature. Sh. Y. Abramovitch's classic satirical novel *The Brief Adventures of Benjamin the Third*—a harsh critique both of life in the shtetl and of the messianic dreams that make life only more difficult for their Jewish dreamers—includes the following episode:

> Once, it so happened, someone arrived in Tuneyadevka ["Lazy Town"] with a date. You should have seen the town running to look at it. A Bible

was brought to prove that the very same little fruit grew in the Holy Land. The harder the Tuneyadevkans stared at it, the more clearly they saw before their eyes the River Jordan, the Cave of the Patriarchs, the tomb of Mother Rachel, the Wailing Wall.[40]

Here, the Promised Land, which exists as an imaginary construct in the minds of Tuneyadevka's Jews, suddenly acquires a more realistic status in the form of date fruit. Kulbak unquestionably has this scene in mind when, during Bereh's adventures on the road, someone delivers to the Zelmenyaners an apple rumored to have come from Bereh himself:

> The apple lay for a few days in a place on the table. It was a red, winter-storage apple with a thick peel, a short, thick stem, and a winey smell that filled the room. Everyone touched its cool peel and lifted it by the stem while thinking of Bereh and his exploits on the battlefield.
>
> For those few days, the whole yard dreamed of him. Suddenly he was seen as the rising star of the family, which had seemed headed downhill.

In many ways, Part Two is built on applying these hopes for the family's revitalization to the realities of the political and cultural context in which the Zelmenyaners find themselves. If Bereh is the bright hope of the family, someone who can help the family become integrated, this hope comes with an underside of betrayal: Bereh will need to turn on his family in order to establish his credentials as a trustworthy Soviet citizen, thereby earning the admiration of the political mentor who has helped him complete his journey from spontaneity to consciousness.

The entirety of *The Zelmenyaners* was serialized through the most transformative years in Soviet history. Perhaps, in deciding to publish it, the censors read the novel as a proper Socialist Realist story of the disintegration of a traditional Jewish family and its integration into Soviet society. As we have seen, however, critics of the time did indeed perceive the degree to which Kulbak's insistence on the family's unique and persistent traits made the Zelmenyaners odd candidates for the perfect Soviet narrative. In 1971, interestingly enough, when the book was reissued in the Soviet Union long after its initial publication, a number of passages that had not been excised earlier fell victim to the censor's knife.

In September 1937 Kulbak was arrested on charges of spying for Poland. Such charges were pervasive in Minsk during the heyday of the Stalinist purges because of the city's proximity to "bourgeois" Poland, where many of Minsk's Jewish cultural figures had connections that were now suddenly suspect. Kulbak, given his travels throughout the 1920s, enjoyed extensive professional and personal associations in Vilna, then known as Wilno, Poland. After a brief trial behind closed doors, he was executed on October 29, 1937, at the age of forty-one. Kulbak's wife, Zelda, whom he had met and married in Vilna, was also arrested in 1937 and spent eight years in a labor camp in Kazakhstan designated specifically for wives of "enemies of the people." In 1942, Kulbak's elder child—his son, Elya—was killed shortly after the German invasion of the USSR. His younger child—his daughter, Raya, born in 1935—survived the war and was reunited with her mother after the latter's release from the camp in 1946.

Both Zelda, who was born in 1897 and died in 1973 in Minsk, and Raya, who emigrated to Israel in 1990 and now lives in Tel Aviv, spent many years trying to acquire correct information about Kulbak's arrest and execution. Zelda had been told in the 1950s that Kulbak died in 1940 from natural causes in a labor camp. As with many other purged artists, such as the writer Isaac Babel, the state for a long time tried to create the impression that its victims had died naturally some time after their arrest rather than being shot almost immediately. Raya eventually succeeded in establishing the truth. As with other victims of the Stalin era, Kulbak was posthumously rehabilitated in the 1950s after the dictator's death.

Kulbak could hardly have known his fate when he moved to Minsk in 1928 to rejoin his family and partake in the great opportunities presented by state-level sponsorship of Yiddish culture. The world into which Kulbak moved upon his relocation to Minsk was hardly a place whose evolution could have been predicted from the outset, and it would be unseemly to criticize his and others' decision to relocate and remain in the Soviet Union.

The Zelmenyaners, the novel that Kulbak was writing during almost the entire time of his stay in Minsk, is as good a testament as any to the unpredictability of the political situation in the Soviet Union during that period: a brilliant laboratory of reactions to an ongoing drama of social and cultural experimentation.

Despite the fact that nearly six years had passed between the novel's first installment and the last, the end of *The Zelmenyaners* comes thematically full circle. The first chapter contains the text of Reb Zelmele's will, in which a request is made that the family continue living in the courtyard. In the novel's last chapter, it becomes clear that this core provision will not be heeded: the family is in the process of leaving the courtyard, which is itself being destroyed to make way for a new factory. Yet the text of the will in the first chapter and the list of possessions that the Zelmenyaners salvage from their houses in the last are somehow similar. The novel is bracketed by these two sets of details outlining the family's inherited and remaining material possessions.

The lists get an additional gloss at the end of Part Two. During what is ostensibly a show trial—another institution of the Stalin era—Tonke, the most dogmatic of all the Zelmenyaners, testifies in court against the family and its purported uniqueness. In her testimony, as if channeling the negative commentary of the novel's real-life critics, she makes her case by citing the same list of material possessions and character traits. In this respect, Tonke is the opposite of her cousin Tsalke, for whom the collection of lists, linguistic items, and family curiosities had formed an amateur ethnographic project to salvage the traces of a disappearing culture. But though Tonke appears to have the final word, thus seemingly casting the entire novel as a narrative fitting the imperative of Soviet literature, Kulbak's mastery of details challenges any such impression.

From the very beginning of the novel's serialization, Kulbak has prepared his reader to understand *The Zelmenyaners* as a narrative not about disappearance but about transition and transformation. Reb Zelmele's will, which opens the novel, contains a curious detail. It is dated not by the secular day and year but by an indication that it was written in the week when the scriptural Torah portion of *B'shalakh* is read during Sabbath morning services. (The Jewish year is also given, counted from the moment of the world's creation, but, we are informed, with its last two digits "erased.") *B'shalakh*, spanning Exodus

13:17–17:16 and covering the crossing of the Red Sea by the Israelites escaping Egypt, the giving of manna in the desert, Moses's drawing water from a stone, and the battle with Israel's enemy Amalek—is the first of the scriptural narratives dealing with the multiyear wanderings of the children of Israel on their way toward the Promised Land.

Leaving his property and possessions to the Zelmenyaners as a bequest, Reb Zelmele taps into the metaphors implicit in the Torah narrative. A Soviet Yiddish critic was thus correct in chastising Kulbak for not creating ideologically reliable characters but instead populating his novel with protagonists who were all part of "the generation of the desert" (*dor hamidber*).[41] The courtyard itself becomes a site of wandering, with a Soviet "promised land"—of electricity, radio, bigger buildings, and revolutionary pathos—slowly taking over this space as its inhabitants, each in his or her way, try to engage with the new reality.

The significance of Kulbak's novel lies not in its description of what once was and what no longer is but rather in its preservation, in great detail, of the rapidly shifting meanings of what appear to be stable objects, concepts, and words. On the last page of the novel, as the Zelmenyaners' courtyard is knocked down to make way for a candy factory, the family members forage through the remains of their home, picking out household items that could be used in the new quarters where they are being resettled. As pots, pans, shoes, and inkwells are uncovered, someone unscrews a mezuzah from the entryway in the hope that it can later be installed at the entrance to a new apartment. The critic Yasha Bronshteyn took this concluding scene as one final example of the family's "biologism": another sign, manifested in the desire to cling to outdated possessions, of their inability to become fully Soviet.

But there is a different way to read these same details. The objects that remain of the courtyard are turning into displaced markers of a family that is becoming both Soviet and Jewish. They acquire a transitional status: no longer meaningful parts of a functioning household, they must now be viewed separately from the larger system of which they had formerly been a part. Unmoored from their natural contexts, the remnants of the Zelmenyaners' courtyard await their reinterpretation and recontextualization in the family members' new apartments, persisting beyond the old home's physical disappearance but with their final meaning deferred.[42]

Set in the Soviet Union in the late 1920s and early 1930s, *The Zelmenyaners* collects and preserves the structure of a Jewish family's courtyard together with the process of its transformation and all the changing rituals, practices, idioms, words, and objects that this process entails. Because of Moyshe Kulbak's imaginative genius, the resulting novel, synthesizing a changing world in compelling comic prose, becomes a space through which we, in turn, gain access to that world in the very moments of its metamorphosis.

NOTES

I am grateful to the late Joseph Sherman for introducing me to Kulbak's novel; to Robert A. Rothstein for sharing his extraordinary expertise in linguistics and folklore; to William Todd for teaching me how to approach serialized works of literature; and to Paul Hamburg for helping me find the materials I needed. I'm indebted to perceptive commentaries on this essay by Svetlana Boym, Gregory Carleton, Amelia Glaser, Liora Halperin, Galit Hasan-Rokem, Anna Wexler Katsnelson, Mikhail Krutikov, Harriet Murav, Gabriella Safran, Naomi Seidman, Jonathan Wilson, and Ruth Wisse.

1. M. Kulbak, "Funem bukh 'Di mishpokhe zelmenyaner,'" *Shtern*, no. 12 (1929): 6–15. Unless otherwise indicated, translations are my own.

2. For the study of Soviet Jewish culture in the interwar period see Anna Shternshis, *Soviet and Kosher: Jewish Popular Culture in the Soviet Union, 1923–1939* (Bloomington, IN: Indiana University Press, 2006).

3. In book form they appeared as Moyshe Kulbak, *Zelmenyaner: Ershter bukh* (Minsk: Tsentraler felker farlag fun F.S.S.R, 1931); Moyshe Kulbak, *Zelmenyaner: Tsveyter bukh* (Minsk: Melukhe-farlag fun vaysrusland, 1935).

4. Soviet Yiddish periodicals like the *Star* and books like this novel circulated outside the Soviet Union as well, and so Kulbak's novel was reviewed by non-Soviet Yiddish critics in addition to those inside the Soviet Union. For example, Nakhmen Mayzel reviewed both parts of the novel, as they were published in book form, in the Warsaw-based peri-

odical *Literary Pages:* Nakhmen Mayzel, "Dos bukh vos ikh hob akorsht ibergeleyent: Moyshe Kulbaks 'zelmenyaner,'" *Literarishe bleter,* no. 14 (413) (April 1, 1932): 224–225; Nakhmen Mayzel, "Moyshe kulbaks 'zelmenyaner,'" *Literarishe bleter,* no. 11 (670) (March 12, 1937): 174.

5. William Mills Todd III, "Anna on the Installment Plan: Teaching *Anna Karenina* through the History of Its Serial Publication," in Liza Knapp and Amy Mandelker, eds., *Approaches to Teaching Tolstoy's Anna Karenina* (New York: Modern Language Association of America, 2003), 53–59.

6. Stalin's speech was published in all major newspapers, including Minsk's main daily Russian-language newspaper the *Worker* (*Rabochii*), which is where Kulbak would have most likely read it: I. Stalin, "God velikogo pereloma," *Rabochii* (Minsk, November 6, 1929).

7. I am thankful to Elissa Bemporad for allowing me to read prior to publication chapters of her book *Becoming Soviet Jews: The Bolshevik Experiment in the Jewish City of Minsk, 1917–1939* (Bloomington, IN: Indiana University Press, forthcoming). See also: Elissa Bemporad, "Behavior Unbecoming a Communist: Jewish Religious Practice in Soviet Minsk," *Jewish Social Studies* 14, no. 2 (Winter 2008): 1–31; Andrew Jay Sloin, "Pale Fire: Jews in Revolutionary Belorussia, 1917–1929" (Ph.D. dissertation, University of Chicago, 2009).

8. Isaac Bashevis Singer, *The Estate* (New York: Farrar, Straus and Giroux, 1969).

9. David Bergelson, "Joseph Schur," in *A Treasury of Yiddish Stories,* ed. Irving Howe and Eliezer Greenberg, trans. Leonard Wolf (New York: Penguin Books, 1989), 527.

10. Isaac Babel's "The King"—one of the stories of his *Odessa Stories* cycle— opens with the following sentence: "The wedding ceremony ended, the rabbi sank into a chair, then he left the room and saw tables lined up the whole length of the courtyard." Isaac Babel, *Isaac Babel's Selected Writings,* ed. Gregory Freidin, trans. Peter Constantine, Norton Critical Edition (New York: W. W. Norton, 2010), 261.

11. Fridrikh Gorenshteyn, *Berdichev: Izbrannoe* (Moscow: Tekst, 2007); Arkady Lvov, *The Courtyard,* trans. Richard Lourie (New York: Doubleday, 1989).

12. Sholem Aleichem published his first Tevye story in 1894; the last one was published in 1914. Sholem Aleichem, *Tevye the Dairyman and The Railroad Stories*, trans. Hillel Halkin (New York: Schocken Books, 1987).

13. For a detailed biography, see Robert Adler Peckerar and Aaron Rubinstein, "Moyshe Kulbak," in *Dictionary of Literary Biography*, ed. Joseph Sherman, vol. 333 (Detroit: Thomson Gale, 2007), 121–129.

14. Moyshe Kulbak, "Ten Commandments," trans. by Leonard Wolf, in Irving Howe, Ruth R. Wisse, and Khone Shmeruk, eds., *The Penguin Book of Modern Yiddish Verse* (New York: Viking, 1987), 386.

15. One of Kulbak's students in Vilna, writing about his teacher's penchant for organic metaphors, gives this among a number of his favorite examples: "mokhike neshomes" ("moldy souls"). Shlomo Beylis, "Gezangen tsum erdishn (notitsn vegn Moyshe Kulbak)," *Di goldene keyt*, no. 105 (1981): 106.

16. Moyshe Kulbak, "From *Byelorussia*," trans. by Leonard Wolf, in Howe, Wisse, and Shmeruk, *The Penguin Book of Modern Yiddish Verse*, 388.

17. Ibid.

18. R. Beriozkin, in an introduction to the Belorussian edition of Kulbak's selected works, paraphrases an unattributed critic on this point: "In Yiddish poetry before Kulbak, a Jewish peasant was a myth; for Kulbak, he is real." Maisei Kul'bak, *Vybranae* (Minsk, 1970), 8.

19. Ibid., 398.

20. "The Rabbi's Son," *Isaac Babel's Selected Writings*, 175–176.

21. Nikolai Ostrovskii, *Vi shtol hot zikh farkhatevet: Roman in tsvey teyln*, ed. M. Kulbak (Minsk: Melukhe farlag, 1937). This Yiddish translation of Nikolai Ostrovskii's paradigmatic Soviet novel, *How the Steel Was Tempered*, lists Moyshe Kulbak's name on the title page, referring to the text having been "edited" (*baarbet*) by him; the name of the translator is not listed. In fact, the text was translated into Yiddish by Khatskl Dunets, who had been purged by the time the translation must have been nearly finished, in 1936. In the minutes of a meeting of the Party committee of the Belorussian State Publishing House (Belgoslitizdat) from March 17, 1936, there is a discussion of the danger of assigning translation of texts to ideologically unreliable translators: "It is inconceivable for [the editorial board] to have assigned the translation of Ostrovskii's *How the*

Steel Was Tempered to Kh. Dunets, who had been expelled from the Party as a bourgeois nationalist." National Archives of the Republic of Belarus, f. 238, op. 8, d. 27, l. 55.

22. For recent scholarship on Jewish literary and cultural figures in interwar Berlin, including Moyshe Kulbak, see Gennady Estraikh and Mikhail Krutikov, eds., *Yiddish in Weimar Berlin: At the Crossroads of Diaspora Politics and Culture* (London: Modern Humanities Research Association, 2010).

23. Moyshe Kulbak, "Vilna," trans. by Nathan Halper, in Howe, Wisse, and Shmeruk, *The Penguin Book of Modern Yiddish Verse*, 406–411.

24. Gennady Estraikh, *In Harness: Yiddish Writers' Romance with Communism* (Syracuse: Syracuse University Press, 2005), 102–110. On Soviet Yiddish culture, see also David Shneer, *Yiddish and the Creation of Soviet Jewish Culture, 1918–1930* (Cambridge: Cambridge University Press, 2004).

25. The electric trolley in Minsk became operational on October 15, 1929. "Tramvai poshel," *Rabochii* (Minsk, October 15, 1929).

26. Moyshe Kulbak, *Monday,* in Joachim Neugroschel, ed., *The Shtetl: A Creative Anthology of Jewish Life in Eastern Europe,* trans. Joachim Neugroschel (Woodstock, NY: Overlook Press, 1979), 490.

27. I thank Raya Kulbak for sharing with me her mother's handwritten memoir and many other unpublished documents about her father from her home archive in Tel Aviv.

28. A document from the Academy of Sciences of the Belorussian Soviet Socialist Republic confirms Kulbak's employment as a "research associate" ("nauchnyi sotrudnik") from December 1, 1930 until 1937. The confirmation was issued posthumously on May 22, 1957, at the request of Zelda Kulbak, who was at the time seeking a pension on behalf of her late husband after his posthumous rehabilitation in 1956 (Central Archive of the National Academy of Sciences of the Republic of Belarus, f. 2, d. 3682, l. 6). A separate document, reconstructed on the basis of notes of the meeting of the presidium of the academy on November 29, 1930, confirms the order to appoint Kulbak as a stylistic editor of Yiddish publications of the academy ("na dolzhnost' stil'redaktora evreiskikh izdanii Akademii nauk BSSR") beginning December 1, 1930

(Central Archive of the National Academy of Sciences of the Republic of Belarus, f. 2, d. 3682. l. 5).

29. Deborah Yalen, "Red Kasrilevke: Ethnographies of Economic Transformation in the Soviet Shtetl, 1917–1939" (Ph.D. dissertation, University of California, Berkeley, 2007), 4.

30. For a seminal discussion of the role of ethnographers and ethnography in the early Soviet period, see: Yuri Slezkine, *Arctic Mirrors: Russia and the Small Peoples of the North* (Ithaca, NY: Cornell University Press, 1994), 219–263. For an assessment of the role of ethnographic knowledge as part of the Soviet state-building effort, see Francine Hirsch, *Empire of Nations: Ethnographic Knowledge and the Making of the Soviet Union* (Ithaca, NY: Cornell University Press, 2005).

31. H. Alexandrov, *Forsht ayer shtetl!* (Minsk: Institut far vaysruslandisher kultur—yidisher sektor, 1928), 10–16.

32. Y. Bronshteyn, "Kegn biologizm un folkizm (vegn Moyshe Kulbaks literarish veg fun 'shtot' biz 'zelmenyaner,'" in *Farfestikte pozitsyes* (Moscow: Emes, 1934), 158–185.

33. Katerina Clark, *The Soviet Novel: History as Ritual* (Chicago: University of Chicago Press, 1981), 15. For a reading of the consciousness/spontaneity paradigm in Soviet Yiddish criticism in the early 1930s, see Mikhail Krutikov, *From Kabbalah to Class Struggle: Expressionism, Marxism, and Yiddish Literature in the Life and Work of Meir Wiener* (Stanford: Stanford University Press, 2011), 253–56.

34. Bronshteyn, "Kegn biologizm un folkizm," 174.

35. A. Damesek, "Der realizm fun kulbaks 'zelmenyaner,'" *Shtern*, no. 7 (1936): 80–95.

36. Ibid., 92.

37. Ibid.

38. Quoted in the charter of the Union of Soviet Writers in the minutes of the First All-Union Congress of Soviet Writers: *Pervyi vsesoiuznyi s'ezd sovetskikh pisatelei, 1934. Stenograficheskii otchet* (Moscow: Khudozhestvennaia literatura, 1934).

39. A brief article by Kulbak was published on September 18, 1934, in the Minsk Russian-language daily the *Worker* as part of the larger report by the members of the Belorussian delegation upon their return from the

First All-Union Congress of Soviet Writers in Moscow. Kulbak wrote about the necessity of translating Soviet Yiddish literature into other languages spoken in the Soviet Union.

40. Sh. Y. Abramovitch, *The Brief Travels of Benjamin the Third*, trans. by Hillel Halkin, in Sh. Y. Abramovitch, *Tales of Mendele the Book Peddler: Fishke the Lame and Benjamin the Third*, ed. Dan Miron and Ken Frieden (New York: Schocken Books, 1996), 307.

41. Damesek, "Der realizm fun kulbaks 'zelmenyaner,'" 83.

42. Kulbak's novel was masterfully translated into Russian by the Yiddish poet Rokhl Boymvol (who knew Kulbak from his time in Minsk) and published by the Soviet Union's main publishing house in 1960. According to anecdotal accounts, the entire run of thirty thousand copies was sold out right away—a fascinating piece of evidence about the persistent relevance of Kulbak's novel as a compendium of Soviet Jewish culture more than two decades after its initial publication. Moisei Kul'bak, *Zelmeniane*, trans. Rakhil' Baumvol' (Moscow: Sovetskii pisatel,' 1960).

THE ZELM

Reb Zemele

(His Wife) .... Uncle Folye

Uncle Zishe

Aunt Gita ....

Mottele

Khonye

Tonke

Sorke (Sonke)

NYANERS

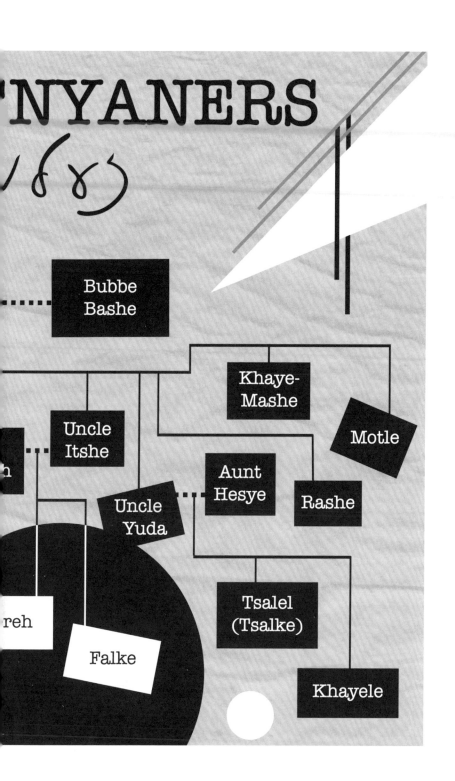

Bubbe
Bashe

Uncle
Itshe

Khaye-
Mashe

Motle

Uncle
Yuda

Aunt
Hesye

Rashe

reh

Falke

Tsalel
(Tsalke)

Khayele

◆◆◆ *Part One*

♦♦♦ *Chapter 1*

THE ZELMENYANERS

That's Reb Zelmele's courtyard that you're looking at.

An ancient, two-story brick building with peeling plaster and two rows of low houses filled with little Zelmenyaners. Plus stables, attics, and cellars. It looks more like a narrow street. On summer days, Reb Zelmele is the first to appear at the crack of dawn in his long underwear. Sometimes he carries a brick or furiously shovels manure.

Where did he come from, Reb Zelmele?

The story told in the family is that it was from "deep Russia." One way or another, he married Bubbe Bashe—who, younger than she is now, began at once to have children.

Bubbe Bashe, they say, bore children with reckless abandon, one after another without stopping to count. Each child to leave her womb was tall, dark, and broad-shouldered, a true Zelmenyaner. Reb Zelmele took charge of the boys. Not being a wet nurse, he soon apprenticed them to a trade.

One, Folye, was placed with a tanner at the age of ten because of some business with a horse.

No one paid much attention when Reb Zelmele's children began having children of their own. Reinforcements arrived, sons- and daughters-in-law of varying degrees of fertility who soon crowded out the neighbors. The rooms bulged with black and rust-colored little

Zelmeles. Blonds, mostly girls, were infrequent, a thin, pale, barely noticeable veneer. In recent years, however, a growing number of them have turned up. No one knows where they've come from.

♦ ♦ ♦

Zelmenyaners are dark and bony, with broad, low brows. Their noses are fleshy, and they have dimples in their cheeks. On the whole they are quiet, sluggish types who look at you sideways, though some of the younger generation can be loud-mouthed. At heart, however, they too, while putting on worldly airs, remain timid descendants of Reb Zelmele. Zelmenyaners are patient and even-tempered. They are as taciturn when happy as when glum. Yet they sometimes glow like hot iron in a special Zelmenyaner way.

Over time, Zelmanyaners have developed their own smell—a faint odor of musty hay mixed with something else.

It's been known to happen that, in a railroad car packed with Jews all yawning at a frosty morning, someone opens his eyes and asks a passenger:

"Excuse me. You wouldn't happen to come from N_____, would you?"

"As a matter of fact, I would."

"You're not a grandson of Reb Zelmele's!"

"To tell you the truth, I am."

The Jew tucks his arms into his sleeves, and the train rattles on. He has smelled Reb Zelmele's odor in his sleep without realizing it. No one is consciously aware that the Zelmenyaners have their own smell.

Something else is special about them too, especially the menfolk. A Zelmenyaner likes to sigh by holding his breath and letting it out through his mouth in a soft snuffle of content such as is heard only among horses munching oats in a stable.

Which proves that Reb Zelmele hailed from the countryside.

In sum, a Zelmenyaner is no more complicated than a slice of bread. There has never been a barren woman in the family, nor an early death apart from Aunt Hesye's.

As for baldness—you're no descendant of Reb Zelmele's if you show the least sign of it, even though you smell like a hayloft.

♦ ♦ ♦

By the time a fourth generation had begun to sprout, Reb Zelmele was ready to take his leave. He wrote his will on the inside cover of a prayer book, hung around a while longer for no apparent reason, and died.

He was a simple man. His will was in a Yiddish full of Hebrew words that not everyone understood. Since it is lying around uncared for, it's best to make a copy:

> Monday, the week of the Torah reading of *B'shalakh,** in the year of the Creation 56. . . . [The last two numbers are illegible.]
>
> Here's how I reckon on dividing my goods when I've lived as many years as I have to live. My children can go on staying in my *khotser.*† I own a plot of *karke*‡ that will fetch 400 rubles and my seat in the synagogue is worth 150 and there's 1,000 in the oven, under the sixth brick to the right. Split it like this: 50 rubles *livni*§ Itshe, because I gave him, my son Itshe, 150 *ad lekheshbn*‖ in my lifetime. 200 *livni* Zishe and 200 *livni* Yuda and 200 *livni* Folye and 100 *leviti*# Khaye-Mashe and 100 *leviti* Matle and 100 *leviti* Rashe. I owe 150 plus 20 to Hurvitz, who lent it to me for Itshe's *ad lekheshbn*. Make sure he gets it. 25 rubles go to charity and the rest are for my expenses in leaving this world. The household belongings go to *ishti*** Sore-Bashe. When my *ishti* has lived as long as she has to live, let my three daughters divide them and give two pillows to Itshe's *bsule*†† Khayke. My sons can have my *malbushim.*‡‡ Whoever wants my lambskin coat can take it. If there's more than one of you, draw lots. Just don't fight. I want it all done proper. And don't let strangers take what I haven't given them. Let

---

* **B'shalakh** (Torah portion), usually read at the end of winter, corresponding to Exodus 13:17–17:16. Reb Zelmele follows the custom of dating events by weekly Torah portion readings.

† **Khotser** (Hebrew)—courtyard.

‡ **Karke** (Hebrew)—land, a plot of land.

§ **Livni** (Hebrew, contraction of "laben sheli")—to my son.

‖ **Ad lekheshbn** (Hebrew)—as a loan.

Leviti (Hebrew, contraction of "labat sheli")—to my daughter.

** **Ishti** (Hebrew, contraction of "isha sheli")—my wife.

†† **Bsule** (Hebrew)—virgin, unmarried daughter.

‡‡ **Malbushim** (Hebrew)—clothing.

everyone be happy with their share and enjoy it, that's what I wish with all my heart. And after I've lived as many years as I have to live, don't forget me. Remember to say kaddish* when you can.

Yours,

Zalman-Elye, the son of Reb Leyb Khvost.†

♦ ♦ ♦

Bubbe Bashe outlived her husband by many years. In a manner of speaking, she's still doing it. Not that she sees so well or hears so well or walks so well, but you can't deny she's still alive. She's just more like an old hen than a human being and doesn't realize that everything has changed.

Bubbe Bashe lives in a world all her own. If she has any thoughts, they're very strange. They must be made of a special material.

Sometimes, at nightfall, she bumbles about in the dark. Suddenly she asks a red neckerchief:‡

"Mottele, why aren't you in synagogue?"

Mottele, dark-haired and smelling faintly of hay, goes over to her, lifts the kerchief from her ear, and shouts:

"Grandma, I'm in the Pioneers!"

Bubbe Bashe nods. "Yes, yes. He's already said his prayers. In which synagogue did you say it was?"

She will depart this world in age-old serenity. The yard, as far as she is concerned, is exactly as Reb Zelmele left it. Each year brings forth another batch of dark, quiet Zelmenyaners

In summer, Bubbe Bashe steps outside. She sits on a stoop and basks in the sight of little Reb Zelmeles spilling from every doorway like black poppy seeds.

---

* **Kaddish**—prayer for the dead.

† **Khvost** (Russian)—tail (of an animal). The family's actual last name. Kulbak will continue punning on the meaning of this word throughout the novel.

‡ **Red neckerchief**—worn by Pioneers. The Young Pioneer Organization of the Soviet Union (also known as Lenin All-Union Pioneer Organization), founded in 1922, was a mass youth organization for children between the ages of ten and fifteen.

A huge sun shines on a new crop of them.

That's Bubbe Bashe.

♦ ♦ ♦

The second generation of Zelmenyaners branched out in three great rivers and several smaller streams. The pillars of the family were, and continue to be, Uncle Itshe, Uncle Zishe, and Uncle Yuda.

Uncle Folye is a special case. Uncle Folye has gone his own hard way in life. He has nothing to do with the other Zelmenyaners, by whom he believes he was insulted as a child. He's a big eater with a weakness for potato pudding, and no one knows what he thinks because he keeps his thoughts to himself.

The rest of the family are smaller fry. Their bloodlines matter less, although they too have Reb Zelmele's stamp and go around with his smell.

A place of honor goes to Uncle Zishe, who is considered a cut above the others. A heavyset watchmaker with a four-cornered brow and beard, he is, or pretends to be, frail.

It was once the custom to ask him to read official notices. Uncle Zishe then unscrewed his watchmaker's lens, asked the visitor to have a seat, and read aloud what was given him. Afterward, he could repeat it word for word

He had a good head on his shoulders.

The high point of these sessions was Uncle Zishe's inquisitive mind, which enabled him to give advice on important matters.

He was said to have hidden powers.

Uncle Zishe's wife, Aunt Gita, bore him two daughters in difficult deliveries such as Zelmenyaners frequently have. One, Tonke, is a Zelmenyaner through and through. The other is a melancholic, a trait that Aunt Gita, though she is not to blame for it, smuggled into the family. Everyone agrees it isn't her fault, since she comes from a long line of rabbis.

Uncle Itshe is a prince of paupers. That's why he couldn't wait for his inheritance money and had to ask his father for an *ad lekheshbn*. He's a tailor, a needle pusher. His tall, thin, bizarre-looking sewing machine clatters all day.

It's quite deafening.

The many Zelmenyaners sired by Uncle Itshe are of the purest type. Some say he even outdid Reb Zelmele himself.

Apart from his family traits, Uncle Itshe has one all his own. He sneezes like an explosion.

Once a sneeze of his caused a neighbor to faint.

In the days of the Civil War, Uncle Itshe's sneezing was unnerving. Finally, Uncle Zishe went to have a talk with him.

"Itshe," he said, "do you realize that each sneeze of yours could cost someone his life?"

What was Uncle Itshe to say? He sneezed with an explosive shriek.

Various proposals were made. The most practical was Aunt Malkaleh's. Whenever Uncle Itshe felt the urge to sneeze, she told him, he should hold his nose and jump into bed. She then threw a pillow on top of him and sat on it—or else, if she was occupied, had one of the children do it. Beneath the pillow, Uncle Itshe could sneeze to his heart's content. When he was done, he brushed off the goose down and went back to work.

After the war, the danger passed.

Now Itshe can sneeze all he wants.

It's an early summer morning. Half the yard is still in shadow. Already washed and dressed, Uncle Itshe sits by an open window, clattering away on his machine. Suddenly he lets out a sneeze. With it comes an ominous howl, a shriek like a dying man's. The yard wakes with a start. Sleepers rub their eyes and jump from bed.

"What happened?"

"It's nothing," someone says. "Uncle Itshe just sneezed."

"It's nothing, nothing." The word goes around.

Windows and transoms are opened. All manner of dark-haired, rumpled, early morning heads appear. From everywhere come shouts of:

"God bless you, uncle!"

"A long life to you, uncle!"

"God bless you! A long life! To your health, uncle!"

Uncle Yuda is a different story—and a strange one. He's a carpenter, a thin Jew with a short, shiny beard and spectacles on the tip of his nose, over which he peers grumpily whenever he needs to see something. Most likely they're strictly for appearance's sake, a matter of dignity. He works and eats with them, though there is no reason to believe that he sleeps with them.

Uncle Yuda is a philosopher and a widower.

His wife, Aunt Hesye, was killed by the Germans at the side of the kosher slaughterer. It wasn't a nice death at all.

Uncle Yuda spent the week of mourning in the synagogue. He took a seat behind the stove and refused to get up again, having resolved to renounce all worldly affairs and devote himself to pure thought—an honorable occupation, if truth be told. Yet public opinion was against him and forced him to return to his carpentry shop.

Just how did Aunt Hesye die?

Our town was under an artillery bombardment. Housewives up and down the street locked their homes and took refuge in Reb Zelmele's cellar. All of a sudden, Aunt Hesye had a craving for chicken soup. This came from staring so long in the crowded cellar at Reb Yekhezkel the slaughterer that it was all she could think of. Aunt Hesye grabbed a hen, Reb Yekhezkel reached for his knife, and they went outside to slit the bird's throat

Just then there was a huge explosion. The yard burst into flames. Not a window pane was left in place.

After a while, a neighbor knocked on the cellar door and asked that someone come out. Pale and peaceful, Aunt Hesye lay on the ground as if nothing had happened. Next to her, its beard sticking up in the air, was the slaughterer's head. The rest of him, knife in hand, lay by the wreckage of a fence.

The hen stood philosophizing.

Although Zelmenyaners are taciturn even when happy, Uncle Yuda's silence is morose. It's his one departure from the traditions of Reb Zelmele, to which he has generally adhered.

It's also in Uncle Yuda that the love of nature, so pronounced in the family, reaches its height. He once gave his geese the freedom of the vestibule (the hen has already been spoken for) and he traps rainwater in a barrel. Every spring he puts aside urgent work to gather sorrel for soup. His passion for wooden planks and boards comes from the same love of the outdoors. When Uncle Yuda planes a piece of wood, he does it ecstatically. He is devoted to carpentry and frightfully fond of fiddles, songs, and all things musical.

Uncle Yuda has children of various degrees of importance. Two alone concern us: his daughter Khayaleh and his son Tsalke.

♦ ♦ ♦

Finally, a word needs be said about one of the younger Zelmenyaners, Uncle Itshe's eldest son, Bereh Khvost.

Young Bereh is a man among men, a tanner of few words. During the Civil War he was awarded the Order of the Red Banner* for his heroic Zelmenyaner sangfroid in the fighting around Kazan.

He also took part in Marshal Gai's† march on Warsaw.

He was almost killed there. Taken prisoner by the Poles,‡ he miraculously managed to escape and make his way home on foot.

When Bereh appeared in the doorway, there was a great commotion. The whole yard came running, even Uncle Zishe. Bereh sat down, slowly pulled off his boots, and said to Aunt Malkaleh:

"Mama, give me something to eat!"

He sat chewing his food with savage haste while staring at the ceiling. Uncle Yuda spat in disgust and walked out. Gradually, everyone else left, too. Bereh finished eating, put on his boots, and returned to the war.

* **Order of the Red Banner**—a military honor in the Red Army established during the Civil War.
† **Gai Dmitrievich Gai** (pseudonym of Hayk Bzhishkyan, 1887–1937)—Red Army military commander during the Civil War and the Russo-Polish War of 1920. Gai was arrested in 1935 on the phony charges of terrorism against the Soviet state, and executed in 1937.
‡ **The Poles**—the reference is to the Russo-Polish War of 1920.

♦♦♦ *Chapter 2*

IT'S SOME WORLD!

All is quiet in the yard.

Apart from Aunt Hesye, who died foolishly for some chicken soup, the war and revolution passed safely.

The Zelmenyaners returned from the front in stiff army greatcoats and tattered fur hats. At first they prowled the yard like wolves, gulping down whatever came to hand. Slowly they were lured back into their homes and gently talked to until they reverted to their former selves. The greatcoats were draped over doors to keep out the winter cold, and the hats languished in corners behind the stoves. Sometimes, in a bad frost, Uncle Itshe grabs a hat from the dusty back of a stove, yanks it down over his head as far as his beard, and goes to fetch Aunt Malkaleh a load of firewood.

That's all that is left of the war.

♦♦♦

The most stubborn of the Zelmenyaners is Uncle Folye. He never says a word, having been insulted as a child. Not that anyone wants him to say one.

Uncle Itshe's Bereh comes a close second. He's a character, Bereh, a policeman in the Second District, which is no cause for worry in the yard because he's never around. He only comes home at night to sleep on his father's plank couch.

As a rule, when the young folk spout the latest nonsense, they get a friendly talking to. A word is all it takes to put the whippersnaps in their place—or, if worse comes to worst, a box on the ear.

"It's time you had the foolishness beaten out of you," Uncle Zishe says.

"It wouldn't hurt you to be a human being," says Uncle Itshe.

Uncle Yuda declares: "What I want to know is, how much blabber do I have to put up with?"

◆ ◆ ◆

Uncle Yuda must be thinking of Khayaleh. It's no secret he wants to marry her off to a nice Jewish boy. Lately, he's put down his carpenter's plane and gone looking for a bridegroom in the synagogues. He'd prefer a kosher slaughterer, someone with a bit of Jewish education.

They say the following actually happened.

Once, Uncle Yuda arranged for Khayaleh to meet a highly eligible bachelor on a street corner at the far end of town. That night a blizzard struck. Khayaleh went to the corner and waited as told. Although no one, not even a bachelor, would have ventured out in such weather, she was so desperate for a husband that she huddled against a wall and resolved to stick it out to the bitter end. It's anyone's guess what she had in mind.

Lying in bed late that night, Uncle Yuda suddenly remembered her, ran across town, and brought her home more dead than alive.

"You'd think she'd have realized," it was said in the yard, "that not even a bridegroom gets married in a snowstorm."

There is one Zelmenyaner who would gladly marry Khayaleh even in a snowstorm. He's not so young any more, thirty-one if a day, a taciturn type who comes home at night to sleep on his father's plank couch. But while it might not seem a bad match, Khayaleh's love for him is unstoked by the heat of passion. That's why she continues to try her luck at blind dates.

Uncle Yuda is opposed to the match for the following reasons:

1. Zelmenyaners don't like Zelmenyaners.
2. The young man isn't Jewish enough.
3. The young man sneers at the yard.

And so he does. Just the other day he went and played such a dirty trick on his mother, Aunt Malkaleh, that it shocked the older Zelmenyaners to the core.

Just what, you ask, did he do?

Aunt Malkaleh went to visit him at the police station. "Bereh," she said, "how come you never smile? A person might think all kinds of things about you!"

As Aunt Malkaleh tells it, Bereh chose that exact moment to smile. Whether he did or not, he then sat sniffing while staring at his mother in her many layers and wraps. Finally he asked:

"Mother, do you have enough to get by on?"

Malkaleh's husband Uncle Itshe was a merry Jew who didn't think getting by called for much.

Bereh sighed, let out a soft Zelmenyaner snuffle (see Chapter 1), and added:

"I hope you realize, mama, that you can't even read or write."

As a matter of fact, she didn't. In no uncertain terms, he advised her to join the anti-illiteracy campaign.[*]

He even picked up the phone and registered her with the teacher's college.

♦ ♦ ♦

It was February. Aunt Malkaleh went home freezing and thinking:

"The less I see of that Bereh, the better."

The yard couldn't believe its ears.

♦ ♦ ♦

The next morning a teacher turned up, a young man with a tousle of hair sticking out from under his cap.

Aunt Malkaleh's heart began to pound. Thoroughly flustered, she washed, put on an apron, and sat down at the table. Terrified of what lay in store for her, she gave the teacher a worried look. The young man, being new at this too, blushed beneath his cap.

---

[*] **Anti-illiteracy campaign**—known in Russian as "likbez" (short for "likvidatsiia bezgramotnosti," literally "the eradication of illiteracy"), the obligatory campaign to educate all Soviet citizens between the ages of eight and fifty was launched by Lenin's decree in December 1919.

Since the pens and pencils of all the young Komsomol* members—
that is, the whippersnaps—were locked away in their drawers, Aunt
Malkaleh found an old inkwell that had only flies and blew into it until
assured by the teacher that this would not create any ink. A pen was
produced from behind a mirror, and the cobwebs were brushed from
it. When advised to test its nib on his fingernail, the teacher discovered
it was a prerevolutionary antique.

Aunt Malkaleh believed in testing pens on fingernails. She thought
it was a sign of cultivation.

Uncle Itshe was nervous, too. Opening a small compartment in his
sewing machine, he took out a rolled-up notebook to which a pencil
was attached by a string, flattened it on his knee, and handed it trem-
ulously to the teacher.

The whole yard came running. A crowd formed. For a while it
watched in astonishment, then gave a puzzled shrug.

"It's some world!" Uncle Itshe blurted.

Uncle Yuda peered angrily at him over his spectacles and said:

"Better six feet deep!"

He was thinking of Aunt Hesye, to whom the new literacy laws did
not apply.

Uncle Zishe alone remained unruffled. Standing off to one side, he
pulled a hair from his beard and smiled.

"A fine bunch of young folk!" he said.

♦ ♦ ♦

It took some getting used to. The teacher came every evening. No one
could deny that Aunt Malkaleh was making progress. She had a head
on her shoulders, undeniably lazy though it was.

"I just can't put my mind to it," she would say.

On the whole, she behaved like a third-grader. Given her brains, this
was difficult to comprehend.

Once, when she had played hooky again, the teacher lodged a complaint with Uncle Itshe.

* **Komsomol** (Russian, abbreviation of Kommunisticheskii soiuz molodezhi, or the
Communist Union of Youth)—a youth wing of the Communist Party established in
1918 for children and youth older than those in the Pioneer Organization (mainly
between the ages of fourteen and twenty-eight).

"Your wife," he said, "is intelligent, but she doesn't apply herself."

"She doesn't?" Uncle Itshe was shocked.

He gave Aunt Malkaleh a talking-to.

"You know very well," he said, "that this is costing us money."

Aunt Malkaleh blushed and didn't know what to say. Then she thought of something:

"I don't have any books to practice with."

This was already too much for Uncle Itshe.

"What are you talking about? The house is full of books! I suppose you know them all by heart."

Thwarted, she took another tack.

"I can't see properly. There's a lens missing from my glasses."

Let it not be thought, however, that Uncle Itshe was always so strict with Aunt Malkaleh. Their love, after all, was an ancient one of forty-two years. Besides, he sympathized with her.

The following happened, too.

The teacher was due to arrive. Aunt Malkaleh was hurrying to depart for town before he did. All at once, Uncle Folye's dark little Mottele came running and said:

"Auntie, the teacher is here!"

They say Aunt Malkaleh was so discombobulated that she crawled into bed with her coat, boots, and shopping basket. It was Uncle Itshe who discovered her there. He folded his arms on his chest, cocked his head to one side like a true Zelmenyaner, and said sorrowfully:

"My wife is indisposed. Just sign the attendance chart, Comrade Teacher. We'll make up for the lesson another time."

Nevertheless, Aunt Malkaleh is definitely making progress.

♦ ♦ ♦

A midwinter night. The windows are coated with snow. All the young comrades have gone to their activities. Aunt Malkaleh, spotted with ink, is plying her pen. There's an old No. 8 kerosene lamp* on the table, the kind tailors use. The wind whistles down the chimney. Uncle Itshe

---

* **No. 8 kerosene lamp**—known in German as *Acht-Linienbrenner*, a kerosene lamp manufactured in Germany or in Russia based on the German design; "No. 8" refers to the thickness of the wick.

sits on one side of the table, ripping out seams and resewing them. Aunt Malkaleh sits on the other, surrounded by piles of paper. The pen scratches away. Beaming, she hands Uncle Itshe a piece of paper. He holds it up to the lamp. Uncle Itshe has to read at arm's length.

Aunt Malkaleh has written:

"i feel gud wen u get upp go too the stov and put upp the ketel and weel hav tee yor beeluvd wif malkeleh khvost."

Uncle Itshe smiles with satisfaction. Over tea, however, he has a serious talk with his wife. The little mistakes don't bother him. It's her style of expression.

"You shouldn't write like that," he says. "It's all right for talking, but writing needs to be more refined."

Aunt Malkaleh is crestfallen.

"Here," he says. "You wrote 'I feel good.' That's not the proper way to put it."

"What should I have said?" asks Aunt Malkaleh.

Uncle Itshe shuts his eyes. "You should have said, 'I am in the very best of health.'"

Aunt Malkaleh realizes he's right.

"Get yourself an old copybook," he says. "No one writes worth a damn any more. You have to read the old books. That's what makes a person smart. There was once a writer named Shomer,* you could learn a lot from him. Just keep away from the modern kind. They're all stardust and moonshine."

Outside, in the dark, the winter is a cold silver bowl.

◆ ◆ ◆

The cold is fierce—thirty-five below. The white roofs keel to the ground. At night the snow glistens and the blue air burns like alcohol.

The streets are already empty, though the night is still young.

Who is that couple out walking on an evening like this? Why, it's

---

* **Shomer** (pseudonym of Nokhem Meyer Shaykevitch; 1849?–1905)—a Yiddish writer of sentimental novels, which were widely popular with readers. Shomer's name became synonymous with *shund* (trashy) literature.

Uncle Itshe's Bereh and Uncle Yuda's Khayaleh! They've slipped away down the slope at the back of the yard and out to the street.

It's high time they did. Bereh doesn't mind the cold. Khayaleh pulls her collar up around her neck and stomps in her high boots as if bound for the gallows.

What kind of young lady, asks the yard, goes out with men only in frosts and blizzards?

Aunt Gita, the rabbinical blue blood, breaks her customary silence to tell no one in particular:

"She'll give birth to a water carrier, that girl!"

♦ ♦ ♦

Bereh and Khayaleh walked in silence. He kept a step ahead of her, the better to concentrate. It was easier at the battle of Kazan.

"Khayaleh, do you like me?"

Uncle Yuda's Khayaleh was expecting such a gambit. With a smile she answered:

"That's no way to ask."

"Why not?"

Now he smiled, too. The winter, like a silver fish, flip-flopped in Khayaleh's heart. She had the Zelmenyaners' love of nature.

"Do you like me?" she parried cunningly.

Bereh smiled and smiled.

Now what?

Suddenly, Khayaleh seized Bereh's head with a thick, frozen hand and kissed him all over the lips, the nose, and the hard pockets of his cheeks.

That's what.

Things were now clearer. The strangest part of it was that they went on standing in that crazy cold and kissing. It was so cold that an old man walking down the same street that night ended up with frostbite in one foot.

They walked on and on while it got colder and colder. At last they reached a corner with a streetlamp. Shivering coachmen stood in a pool of electric light, trying to warm themselves in the hot breath of their horses. It was as quiet as a meadow.

Bereh glanced at his watch and ordered a sleigh. "There's still enough time to get to the marriage bureau,"* he said.

For Uncle Yuda's Khayaleh, this was a bit too much. The evening was already full. She wanted to go home, lie down in her warm, quiet bed that smelled of her father's wood shavings, and reflect. Love was pounding in her brain. Her thick Zelmenyaner blood needed to digest it.

Yet the sleigh pulled up beside them.

Bereh helped his betrothed into it and covered her with an ice-cold blanket. With a lurch they set out down the broad street. Khayaleh nestled against Bereh with Zelmenyaner directness, his broad, cold shoulder as solid as an oak tree.

◆ ◆ ◆

Uncle Yuda's Khayaleh headed home. All around her, the frost was as green as old glass. Her solitary footsteps rang in her ears. She walked up the street to the yard and let herself in. In the first house, Uncle Itshe was still up with Aunt Malkaleh, sipping tea while discoursing learnedly.

"You should use a copybook. Letters need to look stylish. You can make a neat loop on a *C* or an *F. L*'s can be done something with, too. Do you remember, Malkaleh, the letter I wrote you before we were married? I hope whoever read it to you showed you my handwriting. What a pity," he sighed, "that I haven't held a pen in my hands for years."

---

* **The marriage bureau**—marriage in the Soviet system had to be performed before representatives from the Bureau of Registration of Acts of Civil Status (ZAGS).

Chapter 3

THE GREAT TO-DO

In the morning, there was a great to-do. The yard seethed like an anthill. Despite the icy cold, the Zelmenyaners ran from room to room in their slippers. They talked all at once without bothering to take a seat.

"Just think of it, in Reb Zelmele's yard!"

"Without a rabbi, yet!"

"Why does it always have to happen to us?"

The elder Zelmenyaners went around with their beards jutting out, sighing and shrugging. The young whippersnaps peered from beneath their caps, sniffing the charged air. Uncle Yuda, beside himself, stood chewing his beard at home. In the next room lay Khayaleh, red with shame. Uncle Yuda blew on his carpenter's plane and worked feverishly while grumbling to a plank:

"The silly cow! What was the big rush? Why kick over the traces?"

Uncle Yuda was one of a kind, a widower and a philosopher. All at once he laid his plane on a bench and stood glumly reflecting that, since the time of Reb Zelmele, weddings had been celebrated with music.

His fiddle hung on the wall. He took it down, went to the plywood partition beyond which Khayaleh lay, and tuned the instrument. Then, smoothing his glossy beard, he shut his eyes and played.

This was meant to be Khayaleh's wedding march.

Or rather, it started out that way. Soon, however, as if played in a graveyard, it turned into a requiem, a heartbreaking prayer for the dead—namely, for Aunt Hesye, who had departed before her time without living to see her daughter's wedding. The tears streamed from Uncle Yuda's eyes, and his wet lashes glistened through his spectacles. In thrall to the melody within him, he played the song of Aunt Hesye's unseemly death.

Of the hen's, too.

He might have fiddled forever if not for a quiet whimper from the other side of the wall, a muffled sob that grew stronger. Khayaleh, choked by tears, had thrown herself on her pillow.

Uncle Yuda filled a dipper with water and went to her room. Khayaleh was weeping. Sitting up weakly, she took a sip from the dipper and collapsed on the pillow again. Uncle Yuda stroked the bride's hair to let her know her tears pleased him and returned to his carpentry shop.

He reached for his saw and plane and labored all day, putting the ill-advised match out of his mind. Only when evening came did he realize he had made, not the trousseau chest he had planned on, but a bench, a plain bench.

Bereh had the next day off.

How did he make that known? By removing his boots, which meant he was on vacation. Only without them was he ever relaxed. He strolled barefoot around the kitchen in baggy pants, sampling the pots on the stove, filching a potato pancake from Aunt Malkaleh's frying pan, dipping it in sauce, and tossing it down his gullet. Then he read the newspaper standing up, sat on the hard couch with his feet tucked beneath him, and strummed on his balalaika.

Bereh's repertoire consisted of a few dour songs brought back from the front that inhabited a cellar inside him from which they were sometimes dredged up. His baritone voice came from his belly and filled his eyes with rapture when he sang.

To tell the truth, his musical delivery was rather strange.

Not that he was too transported to be practical. He was quite capable of breaking off in the middle of a song to say something like:

"Mama, there's butter on sale at the Central Workers Cooperative!"

After which he returned to his poor balalaika more rapturously than ever, crooning while it screeched.

Hail to the Zelmenyaner troubadour style, unrivaled in musical history!

♦ ♦ ♦

Bereh is still barefoot on the couch, plucking away at his balalaika. It's a sign that the groom is enjoying the wedding feast. His shirt is open, and his oaken voice booms from his stomach through puffy lips.

> As I was riding to Rostov-on-Don,
> I took along a loaf of bread.
> As I was riding to Rostov-on-Don,
> I left the bourgeois bastards for dead.

In the yard, voices said:
"Wives they want, the whippersnaps? A fever they'll get!"
"Since when does a jackass need a wife?"
Uncle Yuda went to Khayaleh's room.
"What are you lying there for?" he asked. "Don't you want to listen to your husband the rabbi give a Torah lesson?"
Bereh boomed like a kettledrum and left. He didn't breathe a word to anyone about having gotten married.

♦ ♦ ♦

That evening, after a heated debate, Aunt Malkaleh went to see Bereh at the police station. Known as a creative thinker, she had been entrusted with coaxing him to attend his own wedding party, which was to be celebrated with honey cake and vodka.

Just because you were no longer a Jew didn't mean you couldn't still act like a human being, did it?

She had to walk down many cold, dark corridors to find Bereh's room. Between two pushed-back tables, the newlywed, flushed and soapy, was mopping the floor.

Aunt Malkaleh was stricken with shame. "What kind of work is that for a policeman?" she scolded. "You should find someone else to do it."

Bereh wiped his mustache with an elbow, said he was sure he would get the hang of it, put down the mop, and welcomed his mother with Zelmenyaner cordiality.

Aunt Malkaleh settled slowly into a chair, taking her time. She picked up a pen from the table, tested it on her fingernail, and asked:

"Bereh, isn't this nib too sharp?"

"No. What's new with you, mother?"

"Nothing you don't know about," she said. "I've been learning to write—a little Yiddish, a little Russian . . ."

They beat around the bush for a while.

You mustn't think Aunt Malkaleh had forgotten her mission. Not at all. But there's an art in talking to people—and it was no accident that clever Malkaleh had been chosen for the job, even though Uncle Yuda would gladly have taken it on himself, as he declared that afternoon, to beat the living daylights out of his new son-in-law. In fact, not only had Malkaleh not forgotten, she had the gumption to declare that a government marriage license meant nothing to her. She didn't give two hoots for it.

Bereh smiled.

Aunt Malkaleh chose that moment to invite him for honey cake and vodka. "Don't worry," she told him. "There'll be no religious ceremonies. Nowadays, we're all a bit modern, Komsomolish . . ."

♦ ♦ ♦

Preparations were under way in the yard for a quiet wedding.

Mouth-watering smells came from the ovens. Braided breads lay on the tables, as in the good old days. Aunt Gita, with the help of a secret recipe, had made the honeyed dough balls relished by her rabbinical ancestors. An odor of cinnamon and saffron hung in the air.

Only Uncle Yuda, stepping into the cold air to shake out his sand-colored caftan with its leathery, brown satin collar, looked glum.

But let's have a look at Uncle Zishe through his window. If you see a four-cornered beard held by one hand and combed against the grain by the other from bottom to top, you can be sure there's a special occasion.

Yes, there it is in the window.

Tsalke brought a bottle of wine. The yard came alive. Uncle Itshe had been up and about since dawn, strutting like a pigeon. Like silence incarnate, he eavesdropped on every conversation while doing his best to avoid Aunt Malkaleh's glance.

Why would he want to avoid it?

He would want to avoid it because he had a way of drinking too much at parties and kissing all the women. This was generally put down to his being none too bright.

The day drew to a close with a cloudless sunset. The yard was spic-and-span. The polished candelabrum that hung like a strange piece of machinery from Uncle Yuda's ceiling gleamed brightly. A smell of fresh pine boards mingled with the odor of the long-gone geese that had once laid their eggs in the vestibule.

Uncle Yuda's beard glistened with cold water. In his stiff old caftan he looked like a village priest who had blundered into the Zelmenyaners' yard by mistake. After him came Bubbe Bashe, dressed like a medieval queen, the black beads on the cape around her shoulders twinkling with a thousand dusky colors. A whole flower garden was growing on her head. Next to appear was Uncle Itshe, his beard trimmed with scissors and his hair well shampooed, followed by Uncle Zishe and Aunt Gita. Uncle Folye, needless to say, did not show up, having been insulted as a child. Last to arrive was Uncle Yuda's schlimazel of a son Tsalke. Too educated to do anything but read, he was the kind of modern young pedant who's always asking you to repeat what you've said so that he can write it down in a notebook. He was fond of passing his time in the company of Bubbe Bashe, who was even less representative of the younger generation than he was, and he had the habit of occasionally taking his own life—which is, however, another story.

All took their places at the table with Zelmenyaner sangfroid and awaited the entry of the groom.

♦ ♦ ♦

As soon as Bereh crossed the threshold, there was a most un-wedding-like hush. Eyelids blinked rapidly. Not liking the festive looks of what he saw, Bereh got right to the point.

"Something tells me," he said, "that I've walked into a wedding celebration." He glanced at Khayaleh, who, all made up, was seated on a cushion at the head of the table, higher than anyone else. "Have I guessed right?"

"You tell us," Uncle Yuda answered crossly. "Does it look to you like there's anything to celebrate?"

Uncle Yuda's sarcasm showed that he lacked the social graces.

Bereh took out a newspaper and began to read. By now it was clear that things would end badly. Only Uncle Itshe, a string tie around his collar, remained eagerly seated in expectation of a toast. Suddenly his knee was pinched sharply. Informed beneath the table of Aunt Malkaleh's anxiety, he looked around nervously.

Bereh finished reading the newspaper, let out a Zelmenyaner snuffle, and regarded the candles on the ceiling as he was wont to do at such times. He apparently meant to sit through his own wedding party without a word.

Not that this was such a great accomplishment. Still, it took some doing. Bereh managed it by staring with a heavy silence that weighed on everyone like a woolen coat while looking as bored as if he were in the waiting room of a train station. Ten minutes of this had the guests on the verge of a nervous collapse.

It was inhuman, the way he sat there, his cold eyes cutting like a frost.

The first to break the silence was Uncle Yuda. Hunched over the table, his dark eyes glowering above his spectacles, he said:

"Would it be too much, my dear son-in-law, to ask you to say a few words?"

Uncle Itshe, his face pale, came to Yuda's assistance.

"You better speak up, you imbecile, because this is your wedding party!"

"What have we done to deserve this?" Aunt Malkaleh wanted to know.

To which Bereh replied in a lazy drawl:

"Don't bother me. I'm thinking."

"And what," Uncle Yuda asked, unable to restrain himself, "might you be thinking about?"

"I'm thinking," Bereh said, "of how to electrify the yard."*

The Zelmenyaners looked at one another as if in a bad dream. They were not in the habit of making improvements in the yard, and even if these needed to be made, now was not the time to contemplate them. This was tactfully explained by Uncle Yuda, a man not given to long silences.

Bereh rose and told Khayaleh to put on her coat, and the newlyweds departed.

♦ ♦ ♦

It was no small scandal. The family sat crestfallen, staring at the table-cloth. Suddenly Uncle Yuda lost control, grabbed the bottle of wine, and smashed it on the floor. Then he clutched his beard as if intending to yank it out by the roots.

There was a commotion. Everyone made for the door. Uncle Zishe alone remained calm, the twinkle in his eyes spreading over his face. He pulled a single hair from his beard and declared:

"A fine bunch of young folk!"

Uncle Yuda spun around like a turned screw and shook a finger at him.

"Just you wait, Zishke! You haven't seen anything yet. You have daughters of your own."

"I can assure you," Uncle Zishe answered, unruffled despite the pallor of his nose, "that Zishe the watchmaker's daughters will have proper Jewish weddings."

Aunt Gita stood beside him, holding on to his sleeve. Although Uncle Zishe had a frail constitution, he didn't shut his mouth that quickly once he opened it. His brother Yuda, he advised, should worry about his own daughter. With such a talkative catch for a husband, Khayaleh had better see to it that she didn't lose the power of human speech.

But why was Uncle Zishe's nose so pale?

---

* **I am thinking of how to electrify the yard**—inspired by a widely propagated slogan, attributed to Lenin, that "Soviet power equals Communism plus electrification," the electrification campaign was one of the major undertakings of the Soviet government to modernize the country's infrastructure.

◆ ◆ ◆

Uncle Zishe returned home silently. The hour was late. Silvery star darts pierced the little blue windows. He opened the door to the back room.

An oil lamp gave off its light. Uncle Zishe's daughter Tonke lay in bed, reading a fat book while nibbling on a crust of bread.

Uncle Zishe smoothed his beard in the semidarkness, uncertain how to begin. He turned to his wife, who was standing beside him as always. "What do you think, Gita?

"I think something's the matter with her," Aunt Gita said. "There's a whole pot of stew in the oven."

"What I want to know is, how long will this Komsomol business go on?"

Tonke looked up at her father. "You wouldn't happen to be talking about me, would you?" she asked.

"And if I am?"

"I wonder if you're aware, papa," Tonke said, propping herself up on bare, brown Zelmenyaner arms, "that on the 25th of October, 1917, one-sixth of the globe took part in the first great proletarian revolution."

"So?"

"So that's what I wanted you to know." She smiled to herself and went back to her book.

Uncle Zishe looked at his wife. "Did you hear that, Gita? That means Itshke's Bereh is now a big shot."

"Would you be happier," Tonke asked, "if the big shot were Tsar Nicholas?"*

"And what if he were? What makes you think, you ninny, that the Jews were worse off under Nicholas?"

Tonke spat, threw her bread on the floor, put out her kerosene lamp, turned her head to the wall, and pulled the blanket over it.

It was dark and still. You could hear a pin drop between the slow ticks of Uncle Zishe's many clocks, pitter-pattering in the next room like a heavy rain. It was so dark you couldn't see a thing.

---

* **Tsar Nicholas II** (Nikolai Aleksandrovich Romanov)—the last emperor of the Russian Empire, executed by the Bolsheviks along with the entire royal family in 1918.

"That's honoring your father for you, eh?" The words rumbled up from the depths.

He and Aunt Gita groped their way out of the room, calling to each other in dim, bleary voices. Uncle Zishe, so it seemed, was none too keen on the New Order.

♦ ♦ ♦

Just what sort of a fellow was he, Zishe the watchmaker?

To begin with, a sickly one. Soon after his marriage he had made this known to the world, which took due note of it. Some chicken soup or a slice of lemon was sometimes needed to revive him. All the watches he fixed, to tell the truth, never brought in much. It was Aunt Gita who made ends meet by peddling thread to the sewing cooperatives. Yet she, too, was far from healthy. Of her various illnesses, two were inherited from her rabbinical ancestors and four others she had cultivated on her own. Assured by the doctors that she hadn't long to live, she had learned to keep careful records. She never left a sewing shop without writing down what was owed her, so that her heirs would know whom to bill.

What sort of a woman was Aunt Gita?

Tall, thin, and bony, she buttoned herself up to the neck. When she spoke, it was in a man's voice. Although overall she talked even less than the other Zelmenyaners, her silence had a special quality—a melancholy, fine-as-silk, true-blue rabbinical texture. Whereas Bereh's, for example, could kill a man, several hours of Aunt Gita's made you feel you were listening to a violin.

♦ ♦ ♦

In the middle of the night, Uncle Zishe raised a sleepy, four-cornered head from its pillow and woke his wife.

"Has Sorke come home? I'm asking if Sorke's come home!"

He was referring to his older daughter Sonya, who worked at the People's Commissariat of Finance.*

---

* **People's Commissariat of Finance** (Narkomfin)—Soviet government-level ministry in charge of the country's economic affairs.

Chapter 4

UNCLE FOLYE

Uncle Folye goes his own hard way in life.

He is thrice silent, once because he has nothing to say, once because he looks down on the yard, and once because he was insulted as a child.

This happened thirty-five years ago, when he was a mere boy of ten. Not only was he treated vilely, he was beaten within an inch of his life.

In those days Reb Zelmele, still a newcomer from "deep Russia," was eking out a living by trading in calves. His sons Zishke, Yudke, and Itshke the Goat went from yard to yard foraging for bones, leaving their brother Folye at home.

"We're not taking that nitwit with us," they said. "He's bad luck."

Uncle Folye went about in silence, planning nasty surprises for his family. He prowled through the neighborhood yards and rummaged in the garbage pails without turning up an honest bone. All alone, he thought his dark thoughts.

To tell the truth, he had been a loner since infancy.

One evening he went for a swim. In a pit by the river lay the carcass of a skinned horse. Uncle Folye stood staring in the still darkness at the gutted belly and flayed legs. A monstrous thought made him tremble.

So many bones could make you rich!

Almost in tears, he ran home to fetch a sack.

For three days he labored, bringing home bits and pieces of horse on his back and cramming them behind the stove.

Reb Zelmele was off in the countryside. Arriving home early one morning, he stepped inside and clutched his nose.

"Soreh-Bashe, there's a bad smell in the house!"

Over breakfast he was more explicit:

"Soreh-Bashe, it reeks of dead horse in here!"

Bubbe Bashe opened the windows, emptied the chamber pot, had a look at the henhouse, searched under the beds, and found nothing.

Before long a Jew stopped in the street and shouted:

"Neighbors! Shut your windows! You're stinking up the world!"

Needless to say, this was an exaggeration. As the story goes, however, Reb Zelmele, despite his good nature, lost his temper. He grabbed his collar as if about to heave himself through the window and roared:

"I want clean air *now!*"

Bubbe Bashe grabbed a mop, splashed water on the floor, and began to scrub away while the children blew their noses and combed their hair. Yet before the air had gotten any cleaner, there came a yell from Uncle Itshe (that's Itshke the Goat):

"Papa, I found it!"

"What?"

"The whole horse!"

Uncle Itshe appeared with a blackened joint of horse on one shoulder. The house went berserk. Reb Zelmele hurled putrid horse meat from behind the stove as though working in a butcher shop, screaming in an inhuman voice:

"I'll skin the culprit alive! I'll tear him bone from bone!"

The horse was quietly buried behind the stable.

Splattered with gore and grime, his beard awry, Reb Zelmele returned to the house, reached for the broom, and pulled out a handful of hard bristles. Then, gathering his bespattered sons around him as ceremoniously as if about to conduct a sacred rite, he said:

"All right, you hellions! Who gets down on the bench?"

Uncle Folye stepped wretchedly forward and said:

"I do, papa."

Bubbe Bashe grabbed her kerchief and rushed outside.

A solemn hush came over the room. Uncle Zishe and Uncle Yuda held the nitwit's arms while Uncle Zishe pinned his legs. The lashes started at a leisurely pace and grew fiercer.

Uncle Folye lay mute as a board. He didn't let out a peep until, all at once, he lunged for Reb Zelmele's knee and sunk his teeth into it as though it were made of dough. By the time he let go of it, his mouth was full of blood.

Then he took to his heels.

For several weeks, Uncle Folye lurked in the neighbors' late summer gardens, sleeping behind the fences. Uncle Itshe brought him secret slices of bread from Bubbe Bashe.

Reb Zelmele put hot poultices on his knee and said nothing while mulling things over. The horse struck him as a providential sign of what needed to be done with his son.

One evening he sent the cleverest of the boys, Uncle Zishe, to tell the young outlaw to come home because his father's wrath had abated.

Folye agreed. First, though, he demanded to be fed all the food he had missed during his absence. The request was granted, and everyone helped bring it to the table. Pot followed pot, accompanied by as much bread as Uncle Folye could show what he was made of by eating. As he was polishing off the last of it, Reb Zelmele said with fatherly love:

"Go to sleep now, my child, because at the crack of dawn I'm bringing you to Mende's tannery."

And so Uncle Folye became a tanner, the first in Reb Zelmele's family.

♦ ♦ ♦

His isolation grew. Before long his nails were as brown as strips of copper. He no longer talked to a soul.

One Friday night, he went to a tavern in honor of the Sabbath and drank a whole bottle of vodka. Befouled and drunk as a sailor, he was carried home more dead than alive. Subsequently, he learned to hold his liquor and became the tanners' best boozer. He liked to drink quietly, in a corner by himself.

In those days the rumor spread that even the peasants would soon start wearing boots, making all the tanners rich. Uncle Folye was delighted by the prospect of such sweet vengeance. Yet even then, knee-deep in the dark vats full of tree pulp, he had an aggravating thought:

"He could have apprenticed me to a tailor! And if I was being punished for the horse, why not to a shoemaker?"

♦ ♦ ♦

Reb Zelmele passed away.

Although you couldn't say his death disturbed the Zelmenyaners greatly, a few tears were undoubtedly shed. Uncle Folye strolled around the yard with his hands behind his back, yawning and complaining:

"How long will the corpse go on lying here?"

Nor was that the worst of it.

Smack in the middle of the seven days of mourning, he brought home from somewhere a small, dark, doleful little wife. To Bubbe Bashe he declared that, being old enough to have one, he saw no point in waiting any longer.

This little wife, it so happened, was immediately disliked. All her protests notwithstanding, she was said to be none too clean. Zelmenyaners don't easily change their minds.

Just as quickly, however, she began to give birth at a miraculous rate. The children tumbled out of her so fast that she took to putting on airs, which led to her acceptance by the family.

With one exception, all her children looked like pumpkins, short, plump, and round-headed. This was dark Mottele, who took after Uncle Folye. After supper, when fathers sat on the front stoops with their children in their arms, Folye bounced Mottele on his knee and lovingly tweaked his nose. His little wife's children had the odd, inexplicable trait of uttering as their first word (and always quite distinctly) not "papa" or "mama" but the single syllable "more."

Given a slice of bread with a pickle, or a radish and a bowl of sorrel soup, they gulped it down and cried:

"More!"

One of them, Khonye, even cried "More!" after swallowing a bar of soap. Naturally, no one paid him any attention.

♦ ♦ ♦

In 1914, Uncle Folye was thirty.

One morning he went tearfully off to war and vanished without a trace.

His doleful little wife took her children and went around the yard begging from door to door while grieving eloquently, even melodiously, for her husband. After a while, she went to ask the rabbi's advice about bringing home a new breadwinner for her orphans.

It's always the woman, come to think of it, who's worst off.

Five years later, Uncle Folye came home unannounced from being a prisoner in Austria. Standing in the doorway, he informed his wife that he had eaten frogs. This was all he had to tell her. Nor, in point of fact, did she ask him too many questions.

Uncle Folye shut himself up with his doleful wife for three days and was restored to his old self with the help of the hard, dark pancakes that she kept bringing to the table. In the end, he regained all his lost faculties.

He went back to the tannery. It wasn't Mende's anymore. It had a different owner, someone no one had ever managed to lay eyes on.

While Uncle Folye was cleaning the stables of a pockmarked German lady in the Tyrol, a revolution (if only he knew what that meant) had broken out and the working class (the devil knew since when workers sat in classrooms) had seized power. However, the bourgeoisie (that was, the rich) were recalcitrant (which was at least a word he understood, though it wasn't easy to pronounce). The hardest thing for him to grasp was that the revolution, so it seemed, was partly the work of a girl he had known named Donya and a skinny smoke-and-mirrors friend of hers who went about before the war stuffing people's pockets with leaflets that looked like the incantations against evil spirits hung on walls, the only difference being that you could go to jail for them.

He, Folye, had never bothered with such damned things. Now, though, he was curious to know what would come of it all.

"The working class is no Mende!"

Now what was that supposed to mean?

Meanwhile, he went on eating all he could.

♦ ♦ ♦

One day a Party member came to the tannery to commandeer an unused boiler for another factory. The tannery put up a fight. A veteran worker, lame old Trokhim from the village of Novinki, began to shout:

"Cut the crap! We're the bosses of this country now!"

Trokhim pointed at himself and at Folye standing beside him.

Uncle Folye was alarmed. He wanted no part of it.

"Don't look at me, comrade," he told the Party member. "I'm no boss."

Afterward, though, walking slowly home with a smile on his big mustache, he felt something burrow in him like a worm.

He didn't sit right down to eat as was his custom when he came home. Pacing his three dark little rooms, he rubbed the stiff brush of beard on his chin and ordered his wife:

"Go tell the yard that Folye's become a Bolshevik."

The doleful woman, as usual, said nothing. Obediently, she did as she was told.

Uncle Folye stood by the door. For the first time in his life, he was experiencing a spiritual upheaval. It felt like a nobler kind of drunkenness that affected not the stomach but the heart.

To make a long story short, the little woman (her name was Khyene or Henye—no one was quite sure) went and spoke to a few people. Folye was waiting on the front steps when she returned.

"So? What happened?"

"I told them."

"What did they say?"

"They laughed," was the doleful answer.

Uncle Folye let out a sigh and went home, silent, brooding, and feeling black as coal.

Later, slurping from the big bowl in front of him, he reflected that the Zelmenyaners were best kept away from. The young varmints were even worse than their parents.

He hated their guts.

Chapter 5

ELECTRICITY

One day Bereh turned up in the yard. An unseasonably warm glow coated the world, glazing the storm windows with an unexpected spring sheen. He walked slowly down the dark footpath, followed by a worker of some kind. They surveyed the roofs, tapped the walls, and pointed at the sky.

A wave of unrest swept the yard.

"We're in for a new disaster!"

"What's he up to this time, the genius?"

Aunt Malkaleh took it as a sign to break out her primers and copybooks and spread them on the table.

Bereh proceeded to have a look at all the rooms. He checked the walls and ceilings and went away.

At no time did he say a single word.

That evening it got around that he was planning to electrify the yard. They would all have to trade in their kerosene lamps for electric current.

At first no one knew what to make of it or realized how serious it was. Some even thought it a good thing. Hats and coats were donned, and all ran to Uncle Zishe to see what he had to say. Zishe proclaimed that things looked bad for two reasons:

1) No one knew what to do with electricity once you had it. 2) It wasn't for common folk like them.

"I'm all for it," Uncle Yuda declared, "as long as it's in someone else's house."

"Take my word for it, he'll be the death of us all!" Uncle Zishe told his beard as he paced back and forth in his room.

Only Uncle Itshe blinked and asked:

"What's the big deal? Doesn't the synagogue have electricity?"

Uncle Zishe stopped pacing, as if suddenly bolted to the floor. "Listen to the know-it-all!" he said to the womenfolk who were present. "The synagogue also has a prayer stand. Does that mean we need one in the yard?"

Bubbe Bashe took it the hardest. At first, thinking that Bereh was planning to dig a well in the yard, she remembered with a pang that this had been Reb Zelmele's great dream. It hadn't come to pass. Condemned to drink the water of strangers all his life, he had died with it unfulfilled.

Finally grasping the truth, however, she exclaimed with all her wits about her:

"Mark my words. No one is breaking down any walls around here as long as I'm alive!"

♦ ♦ ♦

That night the elder Zelmenyaners assembled in the dark yard and waited for Bereh to come home. The sky was sprinkled with a few small stars. They stood wrapped in their scarves and kerchiefs, collars up, breathing heavily. It was close to midnight when Bereh turned into the yard from the street. At once they assailed him.

"Listen here, you bandit! What are you doing to us?"

"Why can't we live out our lives with our old lamps?"

"You can have your electricity! We don't want it!"

"Get off the backs of us plain working folk, brother!"

Bereh stood there saying nothing, his neck stiff as an oak beam. The cool rays of the moon glanced off his cheeks and off the Zelmenyaners' homespun shoulders.

♦ ♦ ♦

The next morning a worker knocked on Uncle Itshe's door and asked to borrow a ladder. In short, it had begun. Tools and spools of wire lay scattered around the yard. The workers set to work without mercy.

The Zelmenyaners walked about in dismal silence as if someone were critically ill, glancing timidly around them.

Uncle Zishe sat by his watchmaker's table and refused to step outside. He seemed to consider this a fitting riposte. Uncle Itshe, on the other hand, stuck his nose into everything, whether it was welcome there or not, until the workers had to shout at him from their ladders.

Elderly Jews gathered to observe the proceedings and discuss the subject of electricity. It struck them as unjust to turn Reb Zelmele's yard upside down for no good reason. Circles of them kept forming all day long.

That evening a Jew with a cat skin on his head that passed for a fur hat explained the logic and benefits of electrification so profoundly that no one knew what he was talking about.

He was obviously not a gifted teacher.

Suddenly, Uncle Yuda loomed in the darkness. A born philosopher, he began to expound electricity's secrets.

"Numbskulls, what don't you understand? Haven't you seen that building with the chimneys by the river? It pumps in water, boils it up into electricity, and sends it out through wires."

The Jews still didn't get it.

"Idiots, what don't you get?" Uncle Yuda was growing exasperated. "When you boil water, you get steam, don't you?"

"You do."

"Well, what's steam? It's the same as smoke, and where there's smoke, there's fire."

"Presto, electricity!" the man with the cat skin jeered.

Uncle Yuda took one look at him over his spectacles, clasped his hands behind his back, and walked off. It was beneath him to quarrel with nincompoops.

♦ ♦ ♦

A few days later, at supper time, the electricity came on. A sudden jolt cast a thin, strange glow over the houses of the yard, flashing through windows and leaving everyone aghast.

Thousands of little shadows that had always clung to the corners were dislodged as though by a broom. The rooms looked bigger.

It wasn't easy to get accustomed in one's old age to the new, long, spindly shadows now crawling on the walls.

Take Uncle Itshe's, for example. All winter long it had lain with its feet on his sewing machine and its head by the stove. Now the stove looked newly whitewashed and Itshe's shadow was gone. It made one's heart sink. Only after a long search did he find it forlornly cringing beneath the couch.

Aunt Malkaleh stood for a long while in the middle of the room. Hands pressed to her chest, she regarded the cold threads of electricity running from her new lamp, let out a sigh, and declared:

"If we have to see each other by electric, it wouldn't hurt to look a few years younger!"

Uncle Itshe was too preoccupied with his shadow to respond. He turned his sewing machine this way and that, rearranged the benches, and finally stuck the electric lamp in a chest of drawers and covered it with a newspaper. Clearly, the man was unhinged. Putting on his jacket, he ran into the yard. It was lit from end to end, even though not a single Zelmenyaner was standing there. With filial devotion Itshe hurried to Bubbe Bashe, arriving in the nick of time to find her dumbfounded. Wrapped in her winter furs, she was staring blankly at a lamp. Seeing a human figure appear by her side, she remarked:

"This isn't for me. It's time I joined your father."

Uncle Itshe was so befuddled that he protested:

"Now, in the middle of the night?"

From that day on, if truth be told, Bubbe Basha was not entirely of this world. Perhaps she had really taken too long to die.

♦ ♦ ♦

Uncle Yuda was a different case, a widower and a philosopher. A sly Jew, he pretended not to notice how bright the house had become. All day long, while busy in his carpentry shop, he left the electricity on. Then, quitting work, he lit the kerosene lamp and sat down to read, pushing his glasses up on his nose to let everyone know that electric light was worthless.

Say what you will, no one was going to force it down Yuda's throat.

Surveying the scene from her little room, Khayaleh, Uncle Yuda's daughter, wondered what had made him pick up a book after so many years. Her annoyance grew as he went on coolly reading and grimacing, entirely lost in the higher spheres.

Finally, she couldn't take it any longer. Falling on her father like a madwoman, she put out the kerosene lamp and screamed:

"You crazy Jew! Can't you see there's electricity?"

Uncle Yuda shut his book calmly, laid it on the chest of drawers, and strode around the room humming a Hasidic melody.

♦ ♦ ♦

The electric revolution had taken place.

Beneath its rows of illuminated windows, the yard lost its nighttime look. Blue carpets of snow gleamed in its once dark corners. The long finger of electricity stabbed at the walls, probed mute recesses, and invaded crannies that for years had breathed quietly in the darkness without glimpsing a ray of light.

♦ ♦ ♦

Uncle Itshe stepped outside, glanced around to see if anyone was looking, and headed for the quiet space between Uncle Yuda's and the stable. Once it had been pitch-black. Now it was bright as day, making Itshe realize that a sanitary convenience had been lost forever. Angrily he turned back toward the yard, disgruntled at the new-fangled world.

Sluggish spring rivulets flowed from the melting ice and ran downhill to the street with a chill tinkle. From his place in the shadows, Uncle Itshe noticed Uncle Zishe heading toward him. Someone else, a third man, coughed by the stable.

The night was still, so still you could hear the electricity buzzing on the cobblestones. Bright stripes of light lay sheathed in the darkness like slaughterers' knives in their scabbards.

The three Zelmenyaners wandered about the yard, trying to avoid the electric cables that lay on the ground like strips of bandage on the wounds of Reb Zelmele's estate. They blew irritable noses and from time to time emitted the delicate snuffle that was a family trademark.

Meeting beneath Uncle Zishe's balcony, they stood there for a while, stroking their beards in silence.

At last, unable to restrain himself any longer, Uncle Itshe said:

"It's some world, eh?"

Uncle Yuda regarded him crossly over his spectacles. "Six feet deep would be better," he replied.

He was thinking of Aunt Hesye, who was deep in the earth.

Uncle Zishe alone was unfazed. Pulling a hair from his beard, he declared with a sad smile:

"A fine bunch of young folk!"

Uncle Folye slipped out of bed in his underwear, drank three dippers of water, and went back to sleep.

Chapter 6

MORE ABOUT ELECTRICITY

Electricity won the day. Could Reb Zelmele have revisited his old home, he might have walked right by it thinking it was a government office building. Its long, narrow rooms flared each evening with a cold blaze that shone in the sickly gold windowpanes like a patient breathing through an oxygen mask.

There were rumors that here, on the outskirts of town, they were getting the electricity's dregs, second-class goods from the bottom of the boiler. This upset the Zelmenyaners greatly, as indeed it should have. After all, if you're going to give someone electricity, give him the best! It was even agreed upon that Aunt Malkaleh should go to Bereh and give him a talking-to. For once, however, she put her foot down. "Why does it always have to be me?" she wanted to know.

♦ ♦ ♦

There followed a kind of electromania. Inspired by Bereh's exploits, the younger Zelmenyaners installed the light bulbs called "Lenin bulbs"* in every room and scaled moldy walls and roofs to bang in nails

---

* **Lenin bulbs** (in Russian, "lampochka Ilyicha"—"Ilyich bulbs"—named after Lenin's patronymic, Vladimir Ilyich)—a regular electric bulb usually mounted from the ceiling without a lampshade.

and hang wires as if they were building—pardon the comparison—a holiday sukkah.* The yard was electrified to its foundations. Zelmenyaners ran around with hammers in their hands, screws in their pockets, and bits and pieces of cable. Uncle Itshe's son Falke presided over it all. Electricity shone in every eye.

In the black nights on the outskirts of town, whose kerosene-burning homes were soaked by the first rainstorms of spring, the yard was lit like a railroad station. Staring wide-eyed at its windows, the neighbors marveled to their children:

"Just look, darlings, what some people manage to make of themselves!"

♦ ♦ ♦

The yard was buzzing with electricity. And no wonder. Uncle Itshe's Falke was driven like a dynamo. It was said he could live on bread and electricity alone.

Falke shared crowded quarters with Uncle Yuda's Tsalke. Thanks to him, the whole yard was soon rigged with the very best electricity from top to bottom.

It's worth saying a bit more about these two young men.

♦ ♦ ♦

Who was Uncle Itshe's Falke? He was a student at the Workers Faculty.† Long pig bristles of hair stuck out from under his cap. All in all he was a fine young fellow, as was made clear at the time of his birth, when he entered the world with a shout. Six months later he was still screaming so hard that it gave him a hernia. At the age of five he was scalded by a hot samovar. At thirteen someone split his lip. Now, a book under his arm, he went around all day in Bereh's beat-up army greatcoat, setting the world on fire. He had his finger in more pies than did all the other Zelmenyaners together. In a chest in his room were hammers, screws, chisels, and all kinds of odds and ends. He mended old

---

* **Sukkah**—a temporary booth-like structure erected in the celebration of the autumn harvest festival of Sukkot.

† **Workers Faculty** (Russian, *rabfak*)—a vocational school for adult education.

shoes, repaved the yard by himself, could change a broken window-pane, and even installed a new roof. His latest project involved broken beer bottles. Collecting them in his room, he filled them with a blue liquid into which he stirred strips of copper, chunks of coal, and scraps of iron.

And who was Uncle Yuda's Tsalke?

Uncle Yuda's Tsalke was a cultivated type. He liked to read, had a cowlick of hair combed to one side like a badly made wig, and wore glasses on his nose.

Every now and then, after Tsalke had been in Tonke's room, Uncle Zishe would ask uneasily:

"What was that young man doing in there?"

Uncle Zishe, so it seemed, had forgotten Tsalke's name. He didn't want a Zelmenyaner for his son-in-law. (Zelmenyaners don't like Zelmenyaners.) "It's enough for me," he said, "to see my Gita living with such crude characters."

Tsalke, as has been mentioned, had the annoying habit of sometimes committing suicide. No one knew where it came from, since Zelmenyaners commonly lived to be a hundred or more. Not even the idleness of Reb Zelmele's last years had caused him to die any sooner.

It was anyone's guess where Tsalke had picked it up.

♦ ♦ ♦

The little apartment in which the pair lived had two bare, empty rooms. The front room had a pair of corduroy pants on the wall. This was Falke's. The back room had a table, a shelf with books, and a teapot. A chamber pot, too. This was Tsalke's.

The chamber pot once led to a fierce quarrel. We might as well relate that, too.

It was a moonlit night. Fast asleep, Tsalke heard someone making use of his private property. He sat up with a start, jumped out of bed, saw Falke standing in his underwear by the chamber pot in the chill light of moonbeams, and fell on him with a choked cry:

"Pithecanthropus!"

This meant that Falke was a primitive ape with no culture. Falke, for his part, kept his wits about him and shot back, spittle flying from his mouth:

"Petty bourgeois!"

Which implied that Tsalke had reactionary tendencies.

They made up the next day. Tsalke wasn't a bad sort. Their midnight spat had been occasioned by purely hygienic concerns.

Not that the two had much in common.

Now and then, a strange gleam in his eyes, Tsalke furtively brought a tattered copy of some old rabbinical tract to his room and sat devouring it all night until dawn. Running his fingers over its thick, mildewed pages, he pleasurably traced letters, words, and sentences that no ordinary Jew could make heads or tails of.

At such times Falke would be sprawled on his bed in the next room, his blanket kicked off, whistling accompaniments through a chronically stuffed nose to his dreams of roofing houses in Leningrad or of spanning the Dnieper with electric cables.

Sometimes he cried out in his sleep.

♦ ♦ ♦

With due apologies, these two philosophers were one day asked to evacuate their quarters, which they had occupied for no apparent reason, so that Khayaleh could raise a new generation of Zelmenyaners there. She had even purchased a bed, a teapot, and a mop with this in mind. In exchange, they were given her little room at Uncle Yuda's.

Falke gathered his broken beer bottles, nails, screws, and corduroy pants and moved. Then he came back for Tsalke's bookshelf.

At first, life at Uncle Yuda's was uncomfortable. The fierce way he stared at them over his spectacles, his carpenter's plane in his hand, gave them goose pimples.

It seemed to say, that stare:

"Schlimazels! How long will you go around doing nothing?"

Or else:

"Blockheads! Do you think I don't know that's what you are?"

The two tried being on their best behavior, averting their eyes to avoid Uncle Yuda's sharp glance. Yet one evening when the electric lights came on, Falke's cheeky look was too much for him. Coming to the door of their room, he shouted:

"I suppose you morons think that electric's the only way to be!"

♦ ♦ ♦

The story with Uncle Folye is this.

At first, believing the electrification of Reb Zelmele's yard to be a Bolshevik initiative, he was happy that someone had cut the Zelmenyaners down to size. He didn't doubt that the order came from high up, since electric wires had porcelain insulators that looked like big teacups and porcelain was for the upper crust.

Uncle Folye made sure the electricity was turned off when he went to work. The secrets of electric power were not for a woman's brain. Dark Mottele alone was allowed to flick the switch in his father's presence, since Uncle Folye loved him and thought him a gifted child.

"Come visit," he told lame old Trokhim at the tannery. "We'll turn on the electric and live it up."

"Get a load of him!" Trokhim marveled. "Where did you get electricity?"

"What do you mean, where? From high up!"

The tannery had a good laugh at Uncle Folye's expense. Coming home in a black mood, he set about interrogating his wife. The electricity, it turned out, had been installed free of charge by Bereh. For weeks now Uncle Yuda's Khayaleh had complained that he was wasting his time on it while reducing her to penury.

Uncle Folye ate his supper by the light of a kerosene lamp.

For several days, he went around plotting in silence. Looking out his window at the yard, he thought:

"Those Zelmenyaners won't live to see the day when Folye owes them!"

His whiskers quivered like a hungry cat's.

That Sunday, the first day off from work that spring,* when all the Zelmenyaners were lounging outdoors in their summer clothes, he climbed a ladder propped against his window and began cutting the

---

* **The first day off from work that spring**—during the period of industrialization in the Soviet Union, days off did not fall on fixed days of the week. Depending on the type of employment, a worker might get, for example, every fifth day off—regardless of which day of the week it happened to fall on.

electric wires. Then he smashed the porcelain insulators. Despite the hue and cry, no one wanted to tangle with a madman. In the end, Uncle Itshe's Falke came running with a revolver.

"You wrecker!"* he yelled. "Come down or I'll shoot!"

Uncle Folye refused to come down. Falke didn't shoot.

"I'll see to it you rot in jail!" Uncle Itshe shouted up at the ladder.

Uncle Folye didn't even turn to look down. Perched on the ladder with his back to the yard, he cold-bloodedly hacked away at the electricity, determined to erase every trace of the Zelmenyaners' triumph. Uncle Zishe ran outside, knocked on a window, and shouted:

"Do something! Go get Bereh!"

"There'll be blood!" a voice warned from within.

Uncle Zishe thought it over and said he didn't care. Someone ran to get Bereh.

The women quietly made the rounds of the yard, getting rid of every rock and sharp rod. Whoever's blood was shed, it would be a Zelmenyaner's. Someone ran into the street to see if the inevitable crowd was already gathering.

Uncle Folye alone remained aloof from it all, looking vaguely around as if the commotion had nothing to do with him. With an air of detachment he finished ripping the last connection from the walls, climbed slowly down from his ladder, and surveyed his work from below to make sure it was complete. Then he joined in waiting for Bereh. He even had his wife tell the yard to look for him in Kitchen No. 9, where he might be having lunch.

♦ ♦ ♦

Bereh strode into the yard with his hard head thrust forward, advancing with the slow, rolling gait of a man wading out of a swamp. He had never been observed to walk like that before.

---

* **Wrecker**—a politically charged Russian word, *vreditel'* signified intentional "wrecking" of state property and "sabotage" of industrialization efforts. The term received wide circulation in the wake of the Shakhty Trial in 1928, in which a number of engineers in the mining town of Shakhty were accused—on trumped-up charges—of intentionally "wrecking" state property.

Uncle Folye, knowing exactly what this meant, unbuttoned his jacket as if in his sleep, let it drop to the ground, and stood calmly waiting by a wall. Bereh headed toward him without a word. As though meeting by accident, they were soon face to face, flushed neck against flushed neck. With a crack, their heads came together.

"Stop!" the women screamed. "Stop!"

It was too late. The two men were already butting each other with their foreheads, hands groping for the best way to break each other's bones.

All at once Folye let out a groan, and the two toppled to the ground. They were too far gone to feel the blows. Blood ran from one of Bereh's ears. He lay on Folye like a log, fists pounding the body beneath him. It wasn't clear how much of his uncle remained.

It went on for quite a while. More and more of Uncle Folye's back showed through his ripped, bloodied shirt.

Finally, Bereh stood up.

Uncle Folye got to his feet with a battered face, one purple eye the size of a fist. Taking his time, he picked up his jacket, flung it over his shoulder, and shook a finger at Bereh.

"That's the last electricity you install around here, you son of a bitch," he said.

Vindicated, he returned to his rooms.

Aunt Malkaleh came running with a broom to sweep up after the near Zelmenyanercide, and that was the end of it.

Chapter 7

EARLY SPRING

It happened in the yard in early spring.

Uncle Zishe's Sonya from the Commissariat of Finance brought someone home, a big, burly fellow who walked with heavy Belorussian steps and barely fitted through Uncle Zishe's low front door. He said a friendly "good morning" in Belorussian and followed Sonya into the back room.

Uncle Zishe removed his watchmaker's lens, turned slowly to Aunt Gita, and regarded her with angry consternation. Aunt Gita, buttoned to the neck, was sitting by the window in the middle of her afternoon silence, a hand on her heart. There followed a wordless exchange.

Uncle Zishe began it by declaring:

"Gita, I don't like what this daughter of yours is up to one bit!"

Aunt Gita said nothing, her usual response.

Uncle Zishe continued:

"I want you to know, my dear wife, that you're to blame for it all!"

Aunt Gita said nothing. That was her usual response.

Uncle Zishe went on:

"Tell me, how can a mother not notice what's happening under her nose?"

He gave Gita a proper dressing-down.

Next, he went out to the yard to inspect his property, whose windowpanes, he thought, especially in Sonya's half of the house, might need new putty. Running a proprietary hand over the shutters, he gave the windows a worried look, long enough to ascertain that Sonya's guest was a far cry from being a Jew.

Sonya was not a little embarrassed by her father's behavior. Yet since she and her guest were good friends, they amused themselves by poking quiet fun at the insatiable nosiness of the petite bourgeoisie.

Silent and enraged by the world, Uncle Zishe put his watchmaker's lens back on and resumed peering at the innards of a dust-encrusted mechanism while making snorting sounds through his nose.

♦ ♦ ♦

The yard had no secrets. Aunt Malkaleh put a finger to her lips, screwed one eye tight, and turned the other on Uncle Itshe, who rose quickly from his sewing machine. His first thought was that Tsalke, whom he tried keeping in sight nowadays, had, God forbid, killed himself again.

Uncle Itshe ran out barefoot to the yard.

The wives of Zelmenyaners, new offspring of Reb Zelmele in their wombs, stood whispering in the doorways with knowing sighs.

"No question about it. A real goy!"

"Now how," asked barefoot Uncle Itshe, who liked to joke with the women, "would you ladies know a thing like that?"

Sticking his needle in his vest, he hitched up his trousers and took a turn around the yard. A crowd began to form. Black Mottele swung on the window frame, giving Sonya an impudent wink to let her know that he knew what her big boyfriend was doing in her room.

Everyone waited for the two to reappear. Before they did, however, Uncle Zishe stepped out on his balcony. His hands trembled as he said in a pleading voice:

"Can't you fools let a decent young man visit this yard?"

Poor Uncle Zishe was putting on a brave show. His heart was full of a great bitterness.

♦ ♦ ♦

That night he didn't try to sleep. Half-undressed, he sat waiting on his bed for his fine daughter. As soon as Sonya tiptoed into her room late at night, he jumped up.

"Listen here, damn you!" he said. "You're not bringing any more goyim to this house, is that clear?"

He was just warming up.

"You slut!"

Just then he felt a nervous palpitation in his heart. His nose pointing upward like a dead man's, he collapsed, stiff and yellow, on the bed.

Tall Aunt Gita sprang from under her blanket, looking like a scarecrow in a field. She was so frightened that she actually talked in her man's voice. She boiled pots of water and brought hot compresses while Sonya ran for the doctor.

Uncle Zishe lay sprawled like a drunk at a wedding with his yellow chest bared and his four-cornered beard in the air. A heavy eyebrow lifted slowly as if to ask:

"What? They think they're going to revive *me*?"

♦ ♦ ♦

Next morning the birds sang their simple song.

It was high spring. The days were hot and clear, as though forged on an anvil. The sun glowed like molten iron in the yard, its rays flashing darkly in the windowpanes. There wasn't a sound. Whoever wanted to could have heard the nettles growing by the walls. (Not that anyone wanted to.) Reb Zelmele's yard was the hottest place on earth. The sun baked it with a hard clang.

How is Uncle Zishe after his dizzy spell?

Everyone knows you can't knock and ask. You can't look through his window, either, because the curtain is drawn. Draped in silence, it's the only window in the yard with nothing to say.

♦ ♦ ♦

The spring is on fire. Hot voices crisscross the yard. Through the open windows, strange things can be heard.

Voice No. 1:

"The controls are in Cabin 6. 8 marks the drive shaft, which is powered by a steam engine. 9 marks the pulleys. The frame is soft steel, 28 meters by 11.5."

Voice No. 2 (if this is Aunt Malkaleh's, she hasn't made much progress):

"Mira is next to the machine. Next to the machine is Mira. Mira is a mother. Emma is next to Mira."

Voice No. 3 (which is Tonke's):

"The prime factor in maneuvering a naval fleet, as any armed force, is firepower. All battles are fought on this basis. A fleet's main weaponry is its heavy guns. Their range and caliber are the major determinants."

Voice No. 4:

"Swinging into action, the European Pioneers organized a boycott of the pacifist congress of Social Democratic children's organizations in Vienna and of the militarist Boy Scout Olympics due to take place in Liverpool."

Black Mottele leans out a window in his birthday suit and screams into the yard:

"Tonke! Are you deaf or what?"

"What is it?"

"Where's Liverpool?"

From another window Falke answers:

"Mottele, get it into your head once and for all that electric power needs a diesel engine! A diesel engine! A diesel engine . . ."

◆ ◆ ◆

It was study time in Reb Zelmele's yard. No one noticed the jeweled day that lay gleaming like a piece of polished crystal. No one noticed anything.

The sun throbbed like a diesel engine, a diesel engine, a diesel engine.

Rays of light, each so solid you could touch it, nailed the yard to the earth.

Reb Zishe's window alone kept aloof. Its curtain drawn, it was the one mute mouth in Reb Zelmele's yard.

A new breed of little Zelmenyaners squatted in the dry gutters as though in kneading troughs, sucking their stubby brown toes.

(Ah, what irresponsible fraud has scattered his redheaded genes among the Zelmenyaners?)

Even the cobblestones gleamed in the light.

Chapter 8

TSALKE AND TONKE

At exactly twelve noon, Uncle Yuda's Tsalke crossed the yard to Tonke's room. Uncle Zishe, his lens screwed to one eye, was bent as usual over a watch, poking in its innards. His bent neck was cross with the world.

Tsalke wasted no time on Uncle Zishe. He had come to see Tonke, who was in the next room.

While Tonke sat smoking a cigarette on her old sofa from which the springs stuck out, Tsalke was at his wits' end. Why? No one was quite sure. He was suffering, it was said, from a hay fever that hurt like a toothache.

Uncle Zishe saw things from a watchmaker's perspective. At first he had been of two minds. Now, after Sonya's latest visitor, he was ready, despite the risk of her being widowed at a young age, to marry Tonke off even to a schlimazel like Tsalke.

Tsalke belonged to the new generation of scholars. Having communed all night with the venerable souls of the dead Jewesses who had prayed from the women's book of devotions sold him by an antiquarian dealer, he was tired and sleepy. His mind wandered from Rebecca the daughter of Besuel in the Bible to Tonke the daughter of Zishe sitting across from him. He felt equal love for both. His sole desire was to lean back in his chair, stretch out his legs, and take a vacation from thinking.

All at once Tonke jumped from the sofa and grabbed his thick mane of hair.

"Come on, you big herring," she said. "Let's go for a swim."

♦ ♦ ♦

The river was a mile or two from town. There wasn't a bit of shade on the way. It was a hot July day. They were exhausted by the time they reached the first fields of potatoes, in whose cool greenness they rested before walking on.

Trailing behind, Tsalke remarked wearily:

"What a night! You wouldn't believe it, but I found an old copy of *Tsena-Rena** without its title page. It's a seventeenth-century edition, printed in Metz by Shimshon Zimle."

Tonke took her time to reply.

"Herring! What does your discovery mean for socialist construction?"

Tsalke cleared his throat.

"In that case," she said, turning to face him, "you may as well go back to sleep!"

Sticking out her foot like a wrestler, she sent the young scholar sprawling in some wheat.

"You moron!" he shouted, pawing the ground for his glasses. "You're the biggest moron I know!"

Tonke was already at the far end of the field, doubled over in a semblance of laughter with one hand on her knee.

Zelmenyaners never laugh. They only grin, which is mistaken for laughter by the uninitiated.

The road stretched to the piney horizon. Between the low shadows of the potato fields, the burning wheat rippled in big, rectangular brass beds. A hot, green breath blasted the meadows. Bright streams of sunlight flowed all around, cascading from field to field until one's eyes felt drunk.

Far off on the horizon rose a spiral of smoke. A tractor chugged beneath it, creeping slowly along the edge of the earth without vanishing.

---

* *Tsena-Rena*—a book of paraphrased Bible stories in Yiddish directed at female readership often unfamiliar with Hebrew.

Tsalke said:

"BlessedartThouOLordourGodKingoftheUniverseWhobringethforth bread fromtheearth!"

♦ ♦ ♦

Tonke took off her blouse and ran the rest of the way to the river.

From a distance, Tsalke saw the sparkling ribbon of water into which she plunged, her bronzed body a blinding flash that made him wince, her cry blending with his pain. Lying down in the grass, he chewed on a blade of it while a confusion of thoughts came and went.

Tonke splashed in the water, spraying cold fireworks at the glowing sun. All at once she stood, her wet body glistening, and called:

"Tsalke, look! Am I beautiful or not?"

♦ ♦ ♦

They took a shortcut back through the fields. The ears of wheat were full. Nothing stirred. Bright swallows swooped low and long over the fields, the sun a flaming bonfire overhead. They threw themselves down in the wheat. From time to time Tonke's red kerchief shone against the fiery brass like a big drop of blood. She sang in Belorussian:

Okh-tsi, mnie, okh!
Na balotsie mokh,
Khlopets pa dzyiauchyntse,
Sem gadou sokh,
Sokh-ta ion, sokh,
Vysakh, iak garokh. . . .
Okh-tsi, mnie, okh!*

Tonke sang and Tsalke accompanied her wanly like a noonday shadow. He was thinking:

"Tonke, you treat me as if I were anyone. A person might even say

* **Okh-tsi, mnie, okh!** (Belorussian)—"Oh my, oh my! / The swamp is covered with moss. / For seven years / A guy has been pining for a girl. / In his pining he dried up, / Turned all dry like a bag of peas . . . / Oh my, oh my!"

you were cold to me. And that galls me, because I think I'm a little bit in love."

He let out a stifled sigh—a sure sign, as everyone knows, of hay fever.

♦ ♦ ♦

They reentered the city from another direction. The heat pouring off the parched tin roofs was thick and dense.

♦ ♦ ♦

The newly dug-up street looked like the floor of a factory. All along it, naked to the waist, stood workers with shovels and crowbars. They were laying rails for an electric trolley.* The slanting sun glanced off the burnished mirrors of their strong backs. Two hundred tanned torsos, brown shoulders forming a dark mural, moved to the easy rhythm of the work. Their muscles rippled like living creatures in a wave that ran down the street as though in a strange brown sea. Acetylene welders joined the rails together, their ovens glowing bloodred in the fiery air. Now and then sparks shot up from the half-naked figures with a crackle, little stars of phosphorescent blue fire. A thin vapor rose from their wet, sweaty bodies, which looked fresh from a steam bath. They worked in incandescent silence. Two rows of hard, dark rails ran down the street to a second bare-chested cluster of men who buffed the welded steel.

"Isn't it a gorgeous sight?" Tonke asked.

"Yes. The beauty of human toil." Tsalke could have been quoting from a textbook.

Tonke said:

"There's a Zelmenyaner named Kulbak who wrote a poem I can't stop thinking about:

And driving them on,
The bronzed young,

---

* **Electric trolley**—the first two lines of the urban rail network opened in Minsk in October 1929.

Is the will
To still
The anger
Of years
In arrears."*

"Yes. It's a fine poem." Even Uncle Yuda's Tsalke had to agree.

They walked on wearily, moodily. When Tonke teased him by asking whether he too belonged to the race of beautiful toilers, Tsalke replied:

"I happen to think that what molds the body is the spirit."†

"You don't have much choice, Tsalke, do you?"

He felt depressed. What had made him get involved with this bird-brained, arrogant woman too narrow-minded to talk to? He was beginning to think his love was a childish blunder, not in keeping with his twenty-six years. That's how bad things were.

As Tsalke was turning into Uncle Yuda's, Tonke reached out, gently gripped his unshaven chin, and asked:

"You haven't fallen in love with me, pussycat, have you?"

* **And driving them on**—a stanza from Moshe Kulbak's own poem "The City" ("Di shtot"), written in 1919.

† **It's the spirit that builds the body**—a line from Friedrich Schiller's *Wallenstein's Death*.

Chapter 9

MORE ABOUT TSALKE

Tsalke wandered around the yard in a daze like a sleepwalker, tie twisted to one side.

Uncle Itshe, who kept watch over Reb Zelmele's yard from his window, left his sewing machine. For some time he had been following Tsalke's behavior with suspicion. Now, assured of its causes, he sallied forth to sound the alarm.

His first stop was Uncle Yuda's. It so happened, however, that Uncle Yuda was in an unusually expansive mood. Grabbing a stick, he drove his concerned brother back into the yard.

"Just listen to Itshke the Goat!" he shouted. "This time he's gone too far!"

It was all Uncle Itshe could do to jump back through the door, slam it shut, and lean against it to keep the madman from pursuing him. From his side of it, he regretted getting involved.

"It's no skin off my nose. They can all go hang themselves and jump in the river!"

Uncle Itshe went back to his sewing machine and said no more.

He decided to keep out of it.

♦ ♦ ♦

Although the summer day was ending everywhere, its dark brown blaze still lit each corner of Reb Zelmele's yard. Zelmenyaners sat on their front steps in their shirtsleeves, clueless to what was happening under their noses.

In the middle of the night wild, terrible screams were heard. They came from Uncle Itshe. The yard woke in a fright. Undressed Zelmenyaners ran outside. Women in long nightgowns and rumpled men shone palely in the darkness. The screams were coming from above, from the direction of Uncle Yuda's attic.

Uncle Folye's doleful little wife poked him in the ribs.

"Get up! There's a murder in the yard. Folyo, for pity's sake, get up!"

Uncle Folye turned angrily on his side and grumbled into his mustache:

"The hell with them! I have to go to work in the morning."

But his wife wouldn't leave him alone and pulled the pillows from under him. In the end, half-asleep, he climbed the ladder leaning against Uncle Yuda's attic, taking it a few steps at a time.

The screams stopped.

The crowd below held its breath, craning its necks for a look at the attic door.

The Zelmenyaners' teeth chattered. "We'd better get Bereh," someone said. "He's the only one who can deal with this."

Uncle Itshe's Falke came running, armed for the occasion with his revolver, a flashlight strapped to his chest. He followed Uncle Folye to the attic.

"Tell us what's doing up there, you two characters!"

Soon Falke's flashlight flickered through the attic door and he called down, swallowing his words as usual:

"It's nothing, nothing. Tsalke hanged himself."

"Again?"

"Is he dead?"

"No. It's the usual. The same as always."

♦ ♦ ♦

Uncle Itshe had indeed kept out of it. He had gone on sitting in the dark on his windowsill, waiting to see what would happen. Late at night he saw Tsalke leave his room without a jacket, take the ladder from the stable, and scale it with uncharacteristic agility. Like a man possessed, he disappeared into the attic.

One might ask at this point:

Did Uncle Itshe do the right thing by climbing after him?

The informed opinion in the yard was that he did. Otherwise, he couldn't have grabbed Tsalke in the nick of time.

Tsalke, on the other hand, was so weary of the world that he stuck out a foot and began kicking Uncle Itshe in the head. This gave Itshe a great fright. How could a hanged man be kicking him?

That was when he started to scream.

At that point Tsalke gave up the struggle and hung there like a herring on a string.

♦ ♦ ♦

Uncle Folye slung Tsalke carefully over his shoulder and carried him back down to his room, handling him with caution as though he were made of fine china. The hanged man was undressed and laid onto fresh sheets, and the Zelmenyaners gathered curiously to watch him breathe, slowly open his chilled eyes, and shut them again.

"Bring some jam!"

"He's weak! He needs jam!"

Tsalke turned to the wall. Aunt Malkaleh, who had been waiting for this moment, fell on his clothes and turned them inside out as though searching for a secret document. A pants pocket yielded two bone buttons and the apparent remains of a handkerchief. In a vest pocket was a wrinkled note.

Uncle Itshe ran to bring Aunt Malkaleh her glasses.

The elder Zelmenyaners gathered silently around her. She read the note painstakingly aloud, down to its last lines, which puzzled everyone

They were:

"*Umme*—the large liver (in butchers' talk).

Gudegarde (?)

Serkhele—a stinker, from Hebrew *sarakh*.

Fideldemonye—money (in some dialects).

Tshevekhtsh (?)

'To love' vs. 'to adore': a matter of nuance.

Do I love Tonke or adore her?

Tonke. Ton-ke. . . ."

The Zelmenyaners furrowed their brows over this note for a long while. Then Uncle Zishe thought it best to appropriate it, and they returned to the hanged man.

♦ ♦ ♦

Some jam made the would-be corpse feel better. It even smiled at its family, as if to say:

"How do you like that? Just when things are looking up, I go and pull such a stunt!"

Uncle Yuda went about softly, as if in stockinged feet. Although he must have been pleased that Tsalke was still alive, this was not at all evident in the little whites of his eyes, which were as irritable as always.

The yard calmed down. If anyone was a reason for concern, it was someone else entirely—namely, Khayaleh, whose condition, assuming Aunt Malkaleh's arithmetic was correct, brooked no sudden frights.

Khayaleh reassured them.

"Don't you worry. I'm not about to lose any sleep because of him. My baby comes first."

♦ ♦ ♦

The elder Zelmenyaners sat around at Uncle Yuda's, drinking tea, stroking their whiskers, and recovering from the excitement. Uncle Folye, who kept to himself, was out in the yard in his underwear.

What a summer night!

If Uncle Folye ever had any thoughts, now was the time to have them, it being that kind of night, a night for end-of-summer reckonings.

♦ ♦ ♦

It was late when Bereh came home from the police station. He walked slowly and contentedly, chewing pumpkin seeds and spitting the shells at the sky as if the world were in his pocket. Seeing Uncle Folye strolling none too steadily about the yard, he stopped suspiciously in his tracks.

"Been drinking?" he asked.

Uncle Folye turned to look at him. "What if I have? I'm as good a Bolshevik as you."

Bereh came closer. "Hitting the bottle again, eh?"

"What if I am? I work for a living while you walk around like a uniformed doorman."

Bereh could smell his breath.

"You've had one too many."

"What if I have?" Uncle Folye made two fists. "Berke, I'll have you chucked out of the Party!"

Folye wouldn't stop. Bereh decided to drop it and walked off.

Strangely, every house in the yard was lit. Uncle Yuda's front door was open. Bereh stepped through it and saw the good news at once.

The Zelmenyaners stared at the ground as if they were to blame for Tsalke's latest escapade.

Bereh leaned against the foot of Tsalke's bed, thoughtfully shelling pumpkin seeds while staring at the guest of honor. After a while he emitted a soft, heartfelt Zelmenyaner snuffle and said:

"Shmintselgessel!"

Aunt Malkaleh nodded in sorrowful agreement.

◆ ◆ ◆

The yard slept soundly. Uncle Itshe's Falke, who sometimes cried out in his sleep, had been moved to Reb Zelmele's old room to avoid disturbing the convalescent.

A silent moon glided over the roof.

Tsalke lay with his eyes open. He felt infinitely hopeless, as though adrift a thousand miles from the nearest shore. Never had he been more frightfully awake. He could even hear the drip of moonlight on the shutter.

All at once the door opened slowly.

Uncle Yuda's voice said:

"Tsalel, are you sleeping?

"Not yet."

Uncle Yuda slipped sideways into the room and sat quietly on the bed. For a while he perched there, tugging at his beard as if wanting to say something of great importance. Then he coughed gently and said in a reprimanding voice:

"Tsalel, you should learn from others. There's a big world out there.

Why spend your whole life with your books? You're foolish not to become a Bolshevik, too. Think it over. Become a Bolshevik! . . . To tell you the truth, you'd be doing your father a favor. No one lives forever. A Jew wants a son who can say kaddish for him—that's not a crime, is it? . . . I can understand wanting to kill yourself once. Why not? I can even understand it twice. But all the time? You can see for yourself that you're not meant, God forbid, to die young. You should ask yourself, Tsalel, Why go on fighting with God and the world?"

Uncle Yuda fell silent. He glanced at a shaft of moonlight piercing the shutter and resumed in quieter, more confiding tones:

"You think I have a low opinion of them? Look here, that isn't so. The Tsar had to go, that's for sure. He was one big nothing. A man like that isn't fit to be an emperor. But for them to begrudge us the little Jewishness we have left—it isn't right, it isn't right at all! In fact, it's downright nasty . . . Look here, a Jewish wedding should be a Jewish wedding, a circumcision should be a circumcision; a Jew should pray now and then, too. Why not? What's so wonderful about not praying? What harm did prayer ever do them? . . . Listen, Tsalel. If only I could have a word with them, I'd straighten things out. They're modern types, they even know foreign languages, but they're missing the point. Am I right or not? . . . And the way they pick on the rich—between you and me, it's plain foolish. It's the rich, after all, that let a man earn a living. You don't make any money from tailors and shoemakers . . . Look here, if they had any sense they'd patch it up with them. There are some fine rich people in this world, always good for a bit of advice or a friendly word. Am I right or not? Are you sleeping, Tsalel?"

"Not yet."

"Listen to me. A young man shouldn't go it alone. *Al tifroysh min ha-tsibbur,** it says . . . You can be a Bolshevik, march with the flag, say what you're expected to, and still help a fellow Jew here and there. People would only think the more of you. You're an educated young man. God knows you're handy with a pen, a writer. You're good at explaining yourself . . . Why not set them straight, eh?"

Uncle Yuda let out a sigh.

* **Al tifroysh min ha-tsibbur** (Hebrew)—"Do not cut yourself off from the community."

"You know, sometimes I look at a light bulb and I think: the only God left in this world is electricity. You tell me, though: can a light bulb be God? Can it punish the wicked and reward the just? Who gave Moses the Torah at Mount Sinai, a light bulb? And suppose I take the bulb and smash it, does that mean there's no more God? That the world is a jungle and you can do what you like? I wish I knew what's happened to people's brains. Tsalel, are you sleeping?"

"Not yet."

"You'll have to forgive me." Uncle Yuda was getting worked up. "But you're a man of culture, and I'd like to understand. What's going on? Doesn't anyone have eyes or ears? Maybe you can explain to me why Jews who should know better, grown men with beards, go around desecrating the Sabbath in public. What's going on? . . . Comrade Lenin is a great man, of course he is. But what does he know about religion? He can be the Jews' best friend, so what? Does that mean Moses is nothing? King David nothing? The Vilna Gaon nothing? . . . You know, Tsalel, there are times when I feel like going off to a synagogue, sitting on a bench behind the stove, and forgetting about everything. Tsalel, are you sleeping?"

"Yes. I'm falling asleep."

Uncle Yuda sat hunched on the bed, looking like a lost priest. Drops of moonlight glittered on a lens of his glasses and on his slightly sunken cheek. He rose and stood with his back to Tsalke, thinking. Then he turned and asked:

"Would you like me to play my fiddle? I haven't touched it for ages."

"If you'd like."

Uncle Yuda stood by the bed in the darkness and played as though coaxing Tsalke's soul out of him, not with a hangman's rope, but with a sweet, age-old lament that sounded like the smell of a graveyard. Uncle Yuda's melancholy had blossomed and opened like the sticky flower of a water lily. His melodies trembled and gasped for air. They were as weirdly broken and dead as a blind eye that keeps blinking and trying to see.

The room was dark.

Next he fiddled for the hen. Now his tears were different. They fell for the distant, uncaring orbits of the constellations that remained forever unmoved.

Chapter 10

RADIO

In our region, summer breathes its last in September. It's all done discreetly, with great delicacy, but in the end it's like losing your lungs. In our region, therefore, September makes a man thoughtful. The most hard-bitten types, who are more common among us than elsewhere and are not normally given to sentiment, shake your hand more firmly when saying goodbye in September and sometimes even do it with a smile.

It's a matter of climate.

The old people spend more time in their rooms, sipping tea from a glass and thinking.

In the windows it's gray.

♦♦♦

The yard has been quiet for quite some time. It's September. There's a feeling that something is about to happen. But where does the danger lurk? Not where you might expect. It lurks in Uncle Itshe's Falke, that's where.

♦♦♦

Everyone knows that by the time he was six months old, Falke had screamed his belly button out. It (the belly button) was treated by weighing it down with big ten-kopeck coins until it returned to its place.

With such a start in life, not much could be hoped for.

More recently, Falke had taken to collecting broken beer bottles, filling them with a blue liquid, and stirring in strips of copper.

For days on end, deep in thought, he sat in the downstairs room at Uncle Yuda's, surrounded by bottles, pieces of rubber, lengths of wire, and all kinds of scrap metal. After much blowing of his nose and consulting of books, he arrived at an understanding of the true nature of conductivity. Then he went to Bereh with a plan for hooking up Reb Zelmele's yard to radio waves.

It was a brilliant concept.

The idea was to intercept the most ethereal high-altitude waves by mounting antennas on balloons. With the help of electric batteries made from beer bottles and one-hundred-percent-copper grounding against lightning, the reception would be good enough to get America.

Bereh was sitting in front of a big watermelon, carving cold slices with a knife. He listened carefully and said:

"Let's have the radio without the balloons."

"But what about proletarian ingenuity?" Falke blurted.

"First make a plain radio," Bereh said. "Then we'll see."

"My way is cheaper. What about cost effectiveness?"

"First make it, you dunce—then we'll see!" Bereh's old dislike of his starry-eyed brother was aroused again.

Falke emerged from his meeting with Bereh beaming. Now that he had the green light, he was all set to snag the most elusive waves with his antennas and flood the yard with concerts, violin music, and the voices of broadcasters. All he needed was some money.

Drawing up a list of the most progressive elements in the yard, Falke went from door to door to collect a radio tax.

The furor was understandably great. Electricity had at least saved the cost of kerosene. This, though, was for a lot of tra-la-la—and at a time when no one was in the mood for it. Worse yet, Falke swallowed his words when he talked, so that it was impossible to know what he was saying.

Aunt Gita, for instance, thought at first that he meant to climb onto the roof, sit there singing, and charge the listeners below.

"He's just looking for an easy job, the whippersnap," she said.

Falke was undaunted. He didn't even mind that Uncle Zishe, sipping tea, looked at him as though he were a spider when he declared:

"Electricity is the basis for modern industry, radio—for modern intellect!"

He drove the yard to distraction with his enthusiasms, Falke did.

Within a few days he had collected twenty-five rubles and set to work.

♦ ♦ ♦

The first thin, slanting autumn rains began to fall. Beneath them the silent summer, its myriad colors squelched and soiled, was snuffed out in the gardens. Disconsolate beet leaves with hard, purplish veins lay cast between the vegetable beds. Dirty yellows, oranges, and browns were trodden silently underfoot.

On days like that you didn't need an antenna to hear distant cries.

A dirty drizzle was falling when Falke went to ask his father to help erect the main antenna. Uncle Itshe threw on some tattered clothes that would have suited a beggar, and the two crawled onto the roof through the attic.

Uncle Itshe had not been on the roof for forty-two years and found it hard to believe that the hundreds of buildings and scaffolds glimpsed through the dull bronze of the autumn trees belonged to the same city he had seen then. Yet he had no time to stroke his beard and stare, because Falke was already at his side with a long wooden pole, his pants weighed down by the hammers and nails crammed into their pockets.

Uncle Itshe brimmed with excitement. Even when Falke sent him running from one end of the roof to the other, you couldn't say he didn't enjoy it. He was never cut out to be a tailor. How often does a man have the chance to stroll on rooftops without owing anyone an explanation?

The dirty drizzle was still falling when, stretched out on the wet roof among the chimneys, they drove the last nails into the antenna.

Falke asked:

"Do you believe in Soviet power?"

"How's that?"

"Then why not shave off your beard? It's dripping wet."

"To tell the truth," Uncle Itshe said, "that might make me look younger. But people would talk."

"Once a petty bourgeois, always a petty bourgeois," Falke told the roof.

"To tell the truth, I've been trimming it little by little. Here a bit, there a bit—you can't do it all at once."

They came down from the roof, leaving a pole sticking into the sky to trap the most melodious airwaves. As soon as Falke's crystal condensers filled with electricity, a flood of music would pour down like rain from a cloudburst.

So Falke thought.

Yet the days went by and Falke's earphones picked up nothing but the hoarse moaning of far-off winds. He had tuned in to the autumn weather of the European continent.

More days went by, and he was crestfallen. He ran in and out of rooms, climbed back up on the roof, dug holes beneath the windows to check the grounding, and licked it with his tongue.

Things only grew worse when the enemy bared its ugly claws.

♦ ♦ ♦

One day Uncle Zishe remarked during mealtime that Falke would never get anywhere with his radio even if he stood on his head. When all was said and done, nothing worked without a pendulum.

"I'm a watchmaker," he said. "You can't teach me about such things. You may think a watch runs by itself, but it's not like that at all. It needs a pendulum."

That was all Uncle Zishe said. Yet so great was his authority that overtures were made at once to get Falke to consider a pendulum.

"Don't be stubborn," he was told. "Put up a pendulum."

"What harm can it do? Sometimes you have to listen to your elders."

Falke was beside himself. He flung his hammer on the ground and began to scream.

"Where am I supposed to hang a pendulum, from the sky? You

think that old tinker is going to teach me about radios? Let him study physics before he decides he's the new Marconi!"*

This was already too much for Uncle Itshe. Savagely hiking up his pants, he said without mincing words:

"You're going to put up a pendulum this minute, do you hear? This minute!"

The yard, so it seemed, had been peaceful for too long.

It would be safe to assume that anyone but Falke would have put up a pendulum. But Falke took orders from no one. Not only that, he turned out to be right. Just when his project was teetering on the brink and the yard was having second thoughts about Soviet power, black Mottele ran outside one night screaming that balalaikas were playing in his crystal set.

The yard came alive. A few intrepid souls actually jumped through the windows in their hurry to get to Uncle Folye's. Sure enough, balalaikas were strumming in Mottele's radio. Then they stopped and a far-off voice called:

"Hello! Hello! Hello!"

Falke ran in a frenzy to all six radios installed by him in the yard. At long last, he had tapped the music of the spheres. Granted, it was only folk music, but he had cathode tubes that would, he hoped, net violin concertos too, let alone all the political speeches wandering indefatigably through the stratosphere.

Afterward, Reb Zelmele's yard grew as quiet as the inside of an ear. Everyone formed circles around the crystal sets and listened in wonderment with eyes big as a bird's to a lecture on grain procurement† in the Belorussian Soviet Socialist Republic. The earphones were passed from hand to hand while Falke scurried between the rooms, giving directions like a symphony conductor.

---

* **Guglielmo Marconi** (1874–1937)—Italian inventor, best known for his development of a radio telegraph system.

† **Grain procurement**—requisitioning of grain from the countryside to increase the food supply in urban centers, along with forcing independent farmers and villagers into collective farms, was widespread during the campaign to collectivize Soviet agriculture, which was launched in 1928.

Uncle Yuda took to radio with a passion. Turning on all the electricity in his home, he shut his eyes and sat listening. No one dared touch his radio set. While the tears ran down his cheeks, Tsalke ran to Uncle Zishe's to find out what it was about.

A cello was playing in Moscow.

Everyone gathered at Uncle Zishe's, presumably to consult with him. Khayaleh came downstairs to ask whether she could listen to radio without harming her baby. Although Falke scoldingly assured her that the laws of physics precluded music's having intrauterine effects, Aunt Gita broke her rabbinical silence to declare that it would, all in all, be better to wait until after the confinement.

Falke's triumph was complete. Not even Uncle Zishe could say anything against it. There were none of electricity's undesirable side effects.

One morning Bubbe Bashe noticed the pole on the roof and went around inquiring fearfully whether Falke was planning to raise pigeons. Tonke, who was fond of her grandmother's company, sat her down that night by a radio and placed a pair of earphones on her shrunken little head. But Bubbe Bashe, alas, heard nothing and understood less.

She thought the crystal set was a grandfather clock.

♦ ♦ ♦

September. Clear days and cool white nights. A smell of wet, empty fields. Gray windows. In the cool yellow translucence of the season, Falke's imagination knew no bounds. He perfected his radio to the point that it could get nearly all of Europe. He studied Morse code and practiced being a shortwave operator.

In the cool, silver nights, when electric sparkles played over the cobblestones of Reb Zelmele's yard, its little windows shot up and Zelmenyaners called out to each other:

"Hello! Hello! Hello!"

"Berlin!"

"Moscow!"

"Warsaw!"

"Bucharest!"

Chapter 11

UNCLE ZISHE'S SONYA

What's with Uncle Zishe's Sonya, who works at the People's Commissariat of Finance? Is she for real?

They say she is.

But why is she always so cold? What makes her sit cuddled on the sofa, self-absorbedly wrapped in a shawl?

It comes from Aunt Gita, who smuggled frigid rabbinic blood into the family.

Sonya's skin is too pale for a Zelmenyaner's. In the dark, the whites of her eyes have a blue gleam that is highly thought of at the commissariat.

Men thirty-five years and over are quite fond of her.

Sometimes, leaving work, she is followed by five officials at once. She smiles self-absorbedly at the first, at the second, at the third, at the fourth, and at the fifth, and they all go their separate ways for lunch.

Although Reb Zelmele's yard may be fond of Sonya, too, no one has much to do with her. There is something foreign, un-Zelmenyanish, about her. It's enough to scare anyone off. Even Tonke, who sleeps in one bed with her, finds her strange. They don't talk much because they go to sleep at different times. At most a drowsy voice exclaims in the middle of the night:

"Ouch! Move your cold feet!"

Every morning, Uncle Zishe's Sonya performs her toilette. On a bench beside the bowl and water pitcher she sets out her soaps, brushes, and powder puffs. She takes her time, which amounts to precisely one hour.

Uncle Zishe takes a dim view of all this chrome-and-nickel foolishness. Yet since that's how the world is nowadays, he keeps it to himself. He just can't help wondering what the point of it is.

Uncle Zishe's Sonya is too busy to enlighten him.

She's as

> quiet as

> > a mouse.

On her days off, she sits on the sofa doing her nails. Then she wraps herself in Aunt Gita's warm shawl and cuddles up with a book.

Toward evening her burly Belorussian comes for her. He sits on the sofa, too. In the blue-tinged darkness, they talk and laugh a bit. Or else they're silent.

"*Turgenyeva chitaesh?*"* he asks, rebuking her in friendly fashion for reading a bourgeois author. "*Ostav!*"†

Uncle Zishe's Sonya thinks Turgenev is a fine, painterly writer. "*Prekrasno pishet,*" she says. "*Chutie kakoie! Kakaia garmoniia krasok!*"‡

As the windowpanes grow bluer and the furniture against the walls turns to shadows, Uncle Zishe's Sonya leans back with her hands behind her head and has a sultry daydream that makes her skin crawl with longing. Her heart begins to pound. Beside her sits Pavel Olshevsky (that's his name: Pavel Olshevsky), his phlegmatic face as cloudy as a Belorussian landscape. He sits in a chair with his head thrown back, feeling that he too has lost his equilibrium.

He lights a cigarette to calm himself.

Pavel Olshevsky loves Uncle Zishe's Sonya for her Jewish stillness. He's a lover of Jewish stillness, Pavel is. Or so at least he once told a

---

* **Turgeneva chitaesh'?** (Russian)—"Are you reading Turgenev?"

† **Ostav'!** (Russian)—"Drop it!"

‡ **Prekrasno pishet. Chutie kakoie! Kakaia garmoniia krasok!** (Russian)—"How beautifully he writes. What artistic flair! What wonderful harmony of colors!"

friend of his, the head of the Sultanov village soviet.* He loves the stillness that flows bountifully from Aunt Gita's inner being to her daughter, giving tongue to his impassioned peasant heart in the green evening light.

They sit there.

The plain Belorussian evening sounds its notes as though on a shepherd's flute. The light streaming through the windows is the violet color of the homespun cloth of Belorussian villages. Thin shadows parade through the room. On the sofa glow two warm, backward-arched arms and the bluish whites of excited eyes.

As a rule, this is the time for the door to open and Uncle Zishe to ask why the lights aren't on.

"Pochemu ne zazhigaete lampu? Eto zhe elektre."†

With a strange, tense smile he asks Sonya in a Yiddish full of Hebrew to keep Pavel Olshevsky from guessing its meaning:

"Kamo pe'omim haven't I told you not to bring *oreylim* to this *bayis?"*‡

After which, in proper Russian, he offers the Comrade Guest some tea:

"Tovarishch, moya zhena mozhet vam postavit' samovar, pozhaluista!"§

In the wake of this friendly reception, the couple leave the room in all haste. Sonya does not come home till late at night. Crawling quietly beneath the blanket next to Tonke, she lies there with her eyes wide open.

"Ouch! Move your cold feet!"

Sonya lies with open eyes until dawn. She is thinking, in the dead of night, of something important. She lies in bed, unable to decide.

---

* **Village soviet**—a council, in this case a local governmental body.

† **Pochemu ne zazhigaete lampu? Eto zhe elektre** (Russian mixed with Yiddish)— "Why not turn on the lamp? This is electricity after all."

‡ **Kamo pe'omim** (Hebrew)—how many times; **oreylim** (Hebrew)—non-Jews, literally: noncircumcised males; **bayis** (Hebrew)—house. Here Uncle Zishe, following a common practice in Yiddish, is employing Hebrew terms that substitute for words derived from the Germanic or Slavic components of Yiddish, in order to make them incomprehensible to Gentiles.

§ **Tovarishch, moya zhena mozhet vam postavit' samovar, pozhaluista!** (Russian)— "Comrade, my wife can put on the samovar for you, if you'd like!"

And then, making up her mind one night, she shuts her eyes and falls peacefully asleep.

Hail to the Zelmenyaner talent for making important decisions in bed and falling asleep at once!

♦ ♦ ♦

A few damp days later, Uncle Zishe ran outside with his coat unbuttoned. He was limping badly, like a sparrow with a broken wing, and he was in a hurry to get to town.

A watery wind hobbled through the front door he had left open. Aunt Gita did not bother to shut it.

Once again the yard filled with people.

"Have you heard the latest about the Zelmenyaners?"

"Some family!"

"You call them Jews?" This was from the man with the cat skin that passed for a hat. "They're Khazars!"*

"Why Khazars?" someone asked.

"They sure keep the pot boiling!"

The yard was as hushed as after a funeral. The Zelmenyaners went around dazed by a new disaster that they could neither acknowledge nor deny.

"Why does it always happen to us?"

♦ ♦ ♦

Falke came to Bereh with a suggestion. They should undertake to explain Sonya's action to the older generation and put it in proper perspective.

"So what do you propose to do, hold a town meeting?" Bereh asked.

"Exactly."

Falke didn't get an answer.

Bereh had watched the affair from the side without getting involved. From his vantage point on the autumn yard through his frosty window,

---

* **Khazars**—a people of Turkic origins with a kingdom in most of what is now southern Russia who converted to Judaism in the seventh century C.E. and lived according to Judaic law thereafter.

he didn't think much of Sonya. Sleeping with a peasant didn't make her a proletarian. He felt closer to Folye—who, coming home from work with his empty pot of lunchtime potatoes, was more to his liking.

Bereh opened the window.

"Folye, come on up. Let's have a glass of tea!"

Uncle Folye gave his bony head a toss. He couldn't believe his ears.

"Pshh! Get a load of him. He even drinks tea like the rest of us . . ."

"Cut it out, you ass. I want to talk to you for your own good."

Folye gave his head a bigger toss. "You just wait, Berke. I'll show you who's boss in this yard!"

♦ ♦ ♦

Uncle Zishe returned at nightfall. Pale and silent, he entered his house without a word, kicked over the stool by the stove, and sat on the floor. With a finger he signaled Aunt Gita to pull off his shoes and sit beside him in mourning for his daughter.

Aunt Gita responded with a sob, deep, dry, and tearless, in her throat. Then she pulled off Uncle Zishe's shoes and stiffly settled her long, thin body alongside his. For a long while they crouched by the dark stove saying nothing.

One by one, other Zelmenyaners stealthily joined them, all looking as if they had just happened to drop by in search of a place to warm up.

Uncle Zishe crouched as stiffly as a butcher block, his eyes staring blindly ahead of him. The disgrace was so great that he did not notice anyone at all. He was wondering whether the Zelmenyaners, vulgarians who understood neither him nor his gifted daughters, were not to blame for it all.

Old shadows flitted over the walls in the light of a No. 5 lamp, their heads protruding above a rafter like rags hung on a laundry line. At floor level, the mourners wrung inconsolable hands.

Oddly enough, no one had a kind word to say to Uncle Zishe, the family's head since the death of Reb Zelmele. This showed how hard it was to be a leader, even of a domain as small as Reb Zelmele's yard.

They all sat there saying nothing.

♦ ♦ ♦

Late at night, Uncle Yuda opened Uncle Zishe's door. He stood on the threshold peering over his spectacles at the dark stove, beside which his devastated brother sat blankly demanding justice from the world. Uncle Yuda, whose sharp little eyes smote like iron rods, looked so like a chastising rabbi that Uncle Zishe buried his face in his hands uncontrollably and burst into powerful sobs. Uncle Yuda said quietly:

"You vain man, you! Who are you hiding from?"

It was not the most appropriate remark. The startled Zelmenyaners gaped with open, toothy mouths. Uncle Zishe was too crushed to answer or remove his hands from his face. His hat toppled into Aunt Gita's lap, and he fainted dead away to let it be known that he was beyond all comforting.

This was Uncle Zishe's usual manner of doing things. When there was no other way out, he fainted and became the aggrieved party.

A bit of Zelmenyaner shrewdness!

♦ ♦ ♦

But Uncle Yuda, what's eating Uncle Yuda?

As the Zelmenyaners were heading for bed, Uncle Yuda stood on his autumnal, silver-sheened balcony, adjusted the spectacles on his nose, and said to no one in particular:

"So what's so terrible, you barbarians, if someone marries a goy? I'll be damned if a goy isn't better than a Jew. Just don't tell me you're afraid of God." He glanced up at the starry sky. "This is for God!"

He gave the sky a big carpenter's finger.

The yard was aghast. In the perfect stillness of the night, it spat and went to bed.

"What can anyone say? The man is crazy as a loon!"

Uncle Yuda, it must be admitted, was a strange fellow.

Chapter 12

REB ZELMELE'S YARD DEMONSTRATES

Word had it that a division of the Red Army would be passing through the city on maneuvers.

The trade unions prepared to give it a grand welcome. The red banner flew over Reb Zelmele's yard.

One evening Uncle Itshe came home from the Artisans Club with fresh news from the political front. Aunt Malkaleh was the first to hear it. Although she, too, read the daily paper, Uncle Itshe was better versed in politics, in which he dabbled from time to time. World imperialism, he informed Aunt Malkaleh, was about to launch an attack on the USSR. "We have to strengthen our defensive capabilities," he told her. The artisans would do their share by participating in a demonstration for the Red Army.

"Look here, Malkaleh," Uncle Itshe said. "I'll need a pair of good woolen socks to keep from catching cold in this weather."

"You're some hero," Aunt Malkaleh mocked, "to be going to war in just a pair of woolen socks."

"Don't be silly." Taken down a peg, Uncle Itshe almost lost his temper. "Everyone has to look out for his health. And who do you think Bereh learned to be a hero from, you?"

"I suppose it was you!"

"I want you to know, Malkaleh, that Bereh is the spitting image of me."

Aunt Malkaleh yielded while sticking to her opinion that Uncle Itshe was no great shakes of a warrior. Long years of living with him had taught her that, although he might be king of the roost in his own home, he was hardly that anywhere else.

This wasn't something she could tell him to his face, though.

◆ ◆ ◆

Strains of military marches drifted over the city. The red banner fluttered above the yard. The Zelmenyaners busied themselves in their rooms, striving to look their best. Small groups of workers, late for the festivities, gathered on street corners, hurrying to join their trade unions in time.

Uncle Folye washed his mustache after lunch and appeared in the yard with a pair of shiny boots and a disdainful stare for his ragtag brothers, who did not strike him as sufficiently presentable for a holiday of the proletariat. The sad sacks, he thought with a smile, would have looked more in place in a synagogue than at a demonstration for the Red Army.

Uncle Folye's pride made him overstate the case. The fact was that Uncle Itshe had been circulating since dawn in his new woolen socks and had snipped off more of his beard, which was now so diminished that some of his peers had begun to look askance at it.

There were grand preparations.

The real cause for wonderment, however, was Uncle Zishe, who had been keeping out of sight while aging greatly. Putting on his good overcoat, he took his heavy walking stick and said to Aunt Gita:

"I may as well go, too. After all, I've paid my dues more than anyone."

Only three of the womenfolk stayed behind: Uncle Folye's doleful little wife (whose name, it seems, was Khyene, not Henye), Aunt Gita, and Bubbe Bashe.

Not that Bubbe Bashe, by the way, is doing badly. The past months have witnessed her rejuvenation. She stands all day long like a bird in a cage, peering out the window while pecking at a piece of bread.

◆ ◆ ◆

Heavy marching bands drummed in the distant streets. The pensive metalworkers, the big, dour tanners, and the merry tailors had already paraded to the railroad station. Now was the turn of the industrial unions. From a side street, singing as they marched, burst the students of the Workers Faculty, tousled hair sticking out from under their caps and red neckerchiefs flaming like fireworks.

Soviet youth! Soviet youth! Soviet youth!

Uncle Itshe's Falke, the eternal student, marched in their midst with long strides while reading a book.

Next, tin helmets glinting, came the fire department.

Behind it marched the artisans with their Jewish beards, long faces, and stooped shoulders. A forlorn, antique-looking band with a patched drum and a rusty trumpet trudged in front of them, bleating away.

Uncle Itshe (never had he felt more excited!) walked directly behind the band. He held his head high and carried a bouquet of flowers, a gift for the Red Army. To tell the truth, he really did look like Bereh.

The artisans walked slowly, raising and lowering careful feet like hammers in their workshops while talking politics and enjoying their outing. Midway in their small phalanx, in a world all his own, strode a gloomy Uncle Zishe, planting his dignified walking stick in front of him while stopping to open the top button of his overcoat and catch his breath. The poor fellow wasn't used to marching in lockstep with the proletariat.*

♦ ♦ ♦

From somewhere in the distance, in the front ranks of the demonstration, came a big, booming hurrah, like the rumble of an avalanche,

There was a hush. The artisans moved aside to make way for the approaching cavalry units.

Nowhere had Uncle Zishe heard such silence before except in synagogue on Yom Kippur.†

---

* **Marching in lockstep with the proletariat**—a common phrase in the early Soviet period, which refers to members of various nonproletarian social groups (such as artisans like Uncle Itshe, who were not considered part of the proletariat) joining in the progress of the proletariat as a class.

† **Yom Kippur**—the Day of Atonement, the holiest day in the Jewish religious calendar.

Suddenly, the patched drum broke into a violent cough. Faraway hoofbeats were heard. The thousand-eyed street erupted in a frenzy of red color, trumpet blasts, and gay laughter. A powerful wave swept them all toward the city center.

Uncle Zishe had never witnessed such pandemonium.

Carried along by the crowd, he too raised his voice to cheer. For a moment, he even imagined himself a Bolshevik. He was marching with the red flag! The thought first thrilled and then frightened him. Shaken, he escaped to the sidewalk, smoothed his rumpled beard, and made his shamefaced way into a side street.

Uncle Zishe looked around to see if he had been spotted in his disgrace by anyone respectable. Then, his back stooped, he made his way home through the empty streets, leaning on his dignified walking stick.

He had indeed aged greatly.

More power, then, to Uncle Itshe, who kept his wits in the thick of things and excitedly joined in the chorus. In a fit of enthusiasm, he even kept time to the music with his hands, leading his less gifted comrades in singing revolutionary songs with a cantorial quiver while keeping order in the ranks around him. He was undeniably the hit of the demonstration.

Later, when the first frenzy had died down, he pushed his way forward, his bouquet held over his head, and presented it ceremoniously on behalf of the artisans to a laughing cavalry officer:

"*Da zdravstvuet sovetskaia vlast'!*"*

Uncle Itshe's excitement surged again.

The officer dismounted, plucked a flower from the bouquet, and deftly placed it in Uncle Itshe's lapel. Uncle Itshe almost burst into tears. He snapped to attention like a soldier and proclaimed in a trembling voice:

"*Moi syn Berke tozhe bolshevik!*"†

The officer gave him a friendly slap on the back, remounted his horse, and rode off, still waving from a distance to thank the spokes-

---

* **Da zdravstvuet sovetskaia vlast'!** (Russian)—"Long live Soviet power!"
† **Moi syn Berke tozhe bolshevik!** (Russian)—"My son Bereh is also a Bolshevik!"

man of the artisans in the name of his division, whose foaming horses smelled of the steppes, Russian rye bread, and the warmth of peasant huts.

♦ ♦ ♦

The day drew to an end. Strips of demonstrators peeled off and crumbled away. Empty spaces yawned between the columns. People spoke again in everyday voices. The marchers turned up their collars against the cold and hurried home.

All evening Uncle Itshe sat sweating in his shirtsleeves by the table, swallowing glasses of tea from the samovar and boasting of his exploits to Aunt Malkaleh: how he had saved the demonstrators from sundry dangers, how he had made a great impression on an officer, and how the latter could not bear to part with him. Then he lectured Malkaleh far into the night on the right way to fire a machine gun, position artillery, conduct a naval battle, and maneuver tanks. He was still going strong when the two of them crawled into bed.

And yet Aunt Malkaleh stuck to her opinion that Uncle Itshe was no great shakes of a warrior. He might be king of the roost at home and even sometimes still in bed at night, but he was hardly that anywhere else.

♦♦♦ *Chapter 13*

WHIPPERSNAPS

The (young) whippersnaps like to go around with peasant blouses and tousled hair. They like to carry revolvers in their back pockets. They like to stuff their mouths with bread and sausage and sit around the table poking fun.

At whom?

At Dovnar-Glembotsky,* the old professor who tells them in his lectures at the college:

"I want you all to know that I've been a Marxist since the First Congress!"

Borovke says:

"Dovnar-Glembotsky writes books as if driving a fire engine."

"*Pravil'no!*"†

"That's why he has no time for something as trivial as scientific method."

---

* **Dovnar-Glembotsky**—an altered name of Mitrofan Dovnar-Zapolskii (1867–1934). Dovnar-Zapolskii was a Belorussian historian, ethnographer, folklorist, and economist who was among the founders of Belorussian national historiography, promoting the concept that Belorussians were an independent national and cultural group rather than part of the Russian people; he fell under ideological criticism in the 1930s for this work.

† **Pravil'no!** (Russian)—Agreed!

"Listen, the revolution ruined his career. He could have been the superintendent of a school district."

"Did you pass topography, Borovke?" asks nearsighted Nyute.

"I did, I did."

"Glembotsky's *People's Will*," Tonke says, "is an attempted justification of right-wing Cadetism in the guise of writing history."*

"Go ask your mother for some more sauerkraut, Tonke," Yoshke the redhead tells her. "It's time for dessert."

The whippersnaps, it seems, like sauerkraut too.

♦ ♦ ♦

It's nine p.m. They (the young whippersnaps) like to sit around at such an hour on Tonke's sofa, seven or eight of them at a time, arms and legs all tangled together, dying of laughter.

"Get your bourgeois jacket out of my face! Is this a leather goods store?"

"You kulak,† keep out of the people's fields!"

"Shut up, Jewboy!"

Nearsighted Nyute begs to be helped to her feet. She has a weak heart. Who wouldn't help Nyute? She's helped all the time, during paramilitary training, too. Borovke carries her rifle and pulls her out of mud puddles that no one else gets into.

Nyute is a good girl. What would the college do without her? Out comes her needle and thread, someone hands her his jacket for mending, and new buttons are sewed.

Ah, no buttons fall off like the young whippersnaps'!

The (young) whippersnaps, the (young) whippersnaps, the (young) whippersnaps!

---

* . . . . **an attempted justification of right-wing Cadetism in the guise of writing history**—Cadetism refers to the liberal Cadet Party represented in Russia's parliaments between 1905 and 1917.

† **Kulak** (Russian)—originally, the word referred to affluent independent farmers who emerged from the peasantry as a result of the agrarian reform in the early 1900s under Pyotr Stolypin, the Russian Empire's chairman of the Council of Ministers. In Marxist-Leninist thought, kulaks were seen as class enemies of the peasants. The policy of collectivization of farms under Stalin sought to destroy kulaks as a class.

They have lots of pockets and are always sticking things into them: Papava's *History of the Party,* Blonsky's *Pedology,* Mueller's *English Dictionary.*
The (young) whippersnaps hang out together and study.

♦ ♦ ♦

Uncle Zishe is not home. Lately, he has been obsessed with his misfortune. Others have become involved in it too, especially a cousin of Aunt Gita's, a flour dealer. Things have taken, as they say, a turn for the better. There's talk of Sonya and her husband getting a divorce. Uncle Zishe and the flour dealer stroll down quiet streets and come to a belly-to-belly halt to bite their nails, stroke their beards, and consider their next move.

Some say that Uncle Zishe's son-in-law has agreed to part with Sonya and is holding out for more money. Others claim, on the contrary, that Olshevsky is a decent chap and is asking for nothing, the obstacle being Uncle Zishe himself, who is demanding several hundred rubles for mental suffering.

None of this is known in the yard, however—certainly not to Aunt Gita. For days on end she sits by herself in her rooms, having her silences by the gray, autumnal window.

♦ ♦ ♦

Today Tonke passed her last college exam. She has been assigned, so they say, to a job in far-off Vladivostok. The youngsters seated on the sofa at Uncle Zishe's are jealous.

It's dark at Uncle Zishe's. No one has turned on the electric lights. How come? Because it's time for some heartfelt words to Tonke before her departure.

"I'm telling you for the last time, Tonke, that Stepanov considers quality a subjective category."

"How can you have subjective idealism with an objective material world?"

"I suppose you prefer Deborin's* position that abstractions are objective, too!"

---

* **Deborin** (pseudonym of Abram Ioffe, 1881–1963)—a Soviet Marxist philosopher, a Menshevik who supported the Bolsheviks after the 1917 Revolution but was eventually accused of "Menshevik idealism" for insufficiently crediting the Bolsheviks for their role in the revolution.

"You damned metaphysician! How many times do you have to be told that abstractions can't be reified from sense impressions . . ."

♦ ♦ ♦

A tall, silent shadow, Aunt Gita enters Tonke's room. She bears the message that Uncle Yuda's Tsalke is waiting in the front room. Perhaps Tonke should go out to him.

Tonke jumps up from the sofa.

He's in a bad way, Tsalke is, however you look at it. He's standing in the front room with his collar turned up, smoking a roll-your-own cigarette.

"Are you busy?" he asks Tonke.

"What is it?"

"Are you in a hurry?"

"Well? What?"

It's like this. Tsalke has a plan. Now that Tonke has graduated, they'll go together to Odessa. They'll rent an apartment by the sea, a villa— that's what everyone does. They'll sit on the terrace, each doing his or her work. They'll buy a kettle, make Turkish coffee at night, read the young poets, and have a good time. Why not?

"Do you have a cigarette?"

Tsalke offers to roll her one.

Tonke answers him.

It's like this. First of all, she doesn't smoke roll-your-owns. And as for a villa in Odessa, it doesn't appeal to her in the least. She's not used to living in villas. Drinking coffee and reading poets aren't for her, either. To tell the truth, she can do without poetry altogether.

"Fair enough. So what do you suggest?" Tsalke asks.

As if Tonke owes it to him to suggest anything!

"I suggest nothing. As a matter of fact . . ."

He removes his roll-your-own from a mouth full of spittle and says: "Maybe I should ask your Yoshke."

She gives him a disgusted look and goes back to her room.

♦ ♦ ♦

He's in a bad way, Tsalke is, however you look at it. It's said that his hay fever has grown worse and made him take to bed. He lay there for a few days, sighing musically.

Music is good for whatever ails you!

Yet since no one can lie in bed forever, Tsalke has taken to roaming the streets. He even went for a walk to the river in which Tonke swam last summer. Alone by the leaden water, between wilted fields, he only felt more desolate. A few last storks flew overhead through the low fog.

Back from the river, Tsalke said to Aunt Gita:

"You know, Aunt Gita, I'm beginning to dislike that Tonke of yours."

"How so?" It saddened Aunt Gita to hear that.

"It's the way she behaves. Her friends."

"You don't think they're honorable types?"

"Wait and see. She'll come to no good end."

Tsalke flushed brightly.

What could anyone do? Although Aunt Gita thought Tsalel a fine young man, not like the other whippersnaps, she was not about to interfere. Silence does as silence is.

◆ ◆ ◆

The (young) whippersnaps, the (young) whippersnaps, the (young) whippersnaps!

Tonke sits with her tousle-haired friends, her blouse half-unbuttoned. She's on the sofa at Uncle Zishe's. She laughs. She flexes an arm and says:

"Borovke, look. Is this a muscle or not?"

"How about mine?" asks nearsighted Nyute.

"How about mine?" asks Entshe.

"Comrades," Borovke tells them, "those aren't muscles. They're pure anthracite coal."

"Stainless steel," says Yoshke the redhead.

"Of Kursk* they are," Borovke puns.

They, the (young) whippersnaps, laugh.

Tonke looks out the window and sees a moon in the sky.

"Come on," she says. "There's a moon out."

---

* **Kursk**—the Kursk Magnetic Anomaly was a site of large deposits of iron ore near the city of Kursk. Both "stainless steel" and "anthracite coal" are references to reports about various achievements in the industrialization efforts that Tonke and her friends must be reading about in newspapers.

The front room is half in darkness. Uncle Yuda's Tsalke is leaning on the table, smoking a roll-your-own. He watches eight whippersnaps laughingly push

each

    other   out

                                       the

                                          door.

♦♦♦ *Chapter 14*

MAKING UP

Exactly how Uncle Zishe's Sonya made up with her father is unclear. There are different versions. One, the source of which is Aunt Gita, has it that lengthy negotiations with her cousin the flour dealer ended in Pavel Olshevsky's swearing before witnesses to become a Jew on his first day off from work. Yet how far from the truth this is can be gauged, first, from the fact that Olshevsky, an ex–Socialist Revolutionary* who has been in every jail in Russia, is opposed to all religions, and second, from the physical ordeal for the male of the species, on which there is no need to dwell, of becoming a Jew.

More accurate, it would seem, is a second version, according to which Uncle Zishe wrote a long letter about his daughter to a rabbi in Moscow and received a postcard in return. For the time being, the Moscow rabbi wrote, it was best to accept God's chastisement with love, even if religion had its clear laws. In tiny Hebrew letters, the rabbi reassured Uncle Zishe that this wasn't the first time. Jewish daughters had gone astray in the days of Ezra and Nehemiah too, there being

---

* **Socialist Revolutionary Party**—a major political party in early twentieth-century Russia and an important player in the Russian Revolution. The party won the majority of seats in the Constituent Assembly following the revolution, in 1918, but was quickly destroyed and outlawed by the Bolsheviks.

nothing new under the sun. Meanwhile, seven days of mourning were recommended.

Uncle Zishe, who had little use for the other Zelmenyaners, first broke the news of this wondrous postcard in the synagogue—where, ever since Sonya's misbegotten love match, he had been in regular attendance. Word reached the yard only later. Uncle Yuda reacted by declaring it was all one big lie. Once, as Uncle Zishe was taking the air on his balcony, Yuda even sought to prove it by opening his window and shouting into the yard:

"Zishe, how would you like to show me that postcard from Moscow?"

Uncle Zishe, unruffled, replied:

"It's in Hebrew. If you can read it, roosters can talk."

"How about just a quick look?"

"It's an ordinary-looking postcard," Uncle Zishe replied coolly.

Perhaps there really was a Hebrew postcard from Moscow and perhaps there wasn't. The only thing certain was that Uncle Zishe's Sonya kept coming to see her father and sometimes emerged in tears.

What went on in those vain rooms was anyone's guess.

Uncle Itshe did his best to keep tabs on it through his window and dropped in on Uncle Zishe often to ask what time it was. A gloomy silence prevailed in Uncle Zishe's home, broken only by the ticking of dark walls.

There's no keeping a secret from Uncle Itshe.

One evening he noticed that Uncle Zishe had closed his shutters earlier than usual. For a while, debating, he rambled around the wet yard. Then, peering through a crack in a shutter, he saw a strange sight. In the large room, seated around a lit table, were Uncle Zishe, his daughter, and his son-in-law. They were drinking tea. From this Uncle Itshe deduced that Uncle Zishe and Sonya were reconciled.

It didn't take long for Aunt Malkaleh to reach the same conclusion

♦ ♦ ♦

Although at first the yard kept aloof from these developments, it ultimately rose up in arms because of a minor incident that once again, it must be said, could be blamed on Uncle Zishe.

A Zelmenyaner, as is known, is as simple as a slice of bread. He takes what comes his way and moves on. This was true of Sonya's marriage, too. The yard actually grew to be fond of Pavel Olshevsky. He, for his part, was willing to embrace the entire family without exception. It was Uncle Zishe who ruined things by refusing to share him.

He wanted Pavel Olshevsky for himself.

One day word got out that Pavel was planning to invite all the Zelmenyaners to the movies. He had discovered, so it seemed, that there were elderly Zelmenyaners who had never seen a movie in their lives.

You would think that Uncle Zishe would have been delighted by such magnanimity on his son-in-law's part. In fact, however, he laid down the law and sternly told Olshevsky to stay out of the yard's affairs if he wished to get along with his in-laws.

"They're the sort of people," Uncle Zishe told him, "that you want to keep your distance from."

It was impressed on Pavel in no uncertain terms that he had married into Uncle Zishe's family alone. To prove the point, Uncle Zishe ordered Aunt Gita to put on her best dress, and they trooped off by themselves to the movies, leaving the rest of the yard behind.

♦ ♦ ♦

It was a slap in the yard's face. Not since Reb Zelmele founded the family in 1864 had such an outrage been perpetrated.

"It's not the movie," the yard fumed. "It's our honor!"

Aunt Malkaleh, incensed, took Uncle Itshe in tow and went to the movies with him by herself. Uncle Folye took his five or six children. Best of all, Uncle Itshe's Falke announced that he would save them all the cost of buying tickets by showing movies in the stable. Lately, Falke was feeling so creative that he had even taken to biting his nails. It was then that Tonke approached him with an unexpected proposal.

"If you'd like," she said, "you can come with me to Vladivostok."

Falke stopped biting his nails and went to Vladivostok with Tonke.

Ay! Uncle Zishe had shamed the yard. Nothing but a movie in the stable could have set matters aright. And on whom had it depended but a whippersnap, a pifflehead, a vulgarian, an empty bag of hot air!

♦ ♦ ♦

They say Aunt Gita kept silent for several weeks after going to the
movies and then found the right moment to comment with bitter irony
on the modern world.

"They turn out the lights," she said, "to keep you from seeing the
swindle."

She wouldn't see a movie again for a million rubles.

The rest of the yard thought otherwise. Some said the movies were
the best thing yet. Uncle Itshe, needless to say, was one of them. Once,
when Aunt Malkaleh accidentally spilled their supper all over the stove,
he sought to take advantage of her humbled spirits by suggesting:

"Malkaleh, if we had any gumption we'd go to the movies right
now."

Alas, nothing came of it. Uncle Itshe had to make do with once again
recalling the Arctic seas with their polar bears that had flashed before
his eyes on that magical night in the cinema. He continued to go
around in a trance, envisioning strange sights and keeping his ears
open for any mention of the movies.

"There's nothing like them," he said to Aunt Malkaleh.

At night, while stitching a pair of quilted pants, he thought wistfully
of the snow-white bears, those wanderers on the frozen ice for whom
quilted pants would have been just the thing. He had long ago forgiven
Uncle Zishe his offense and even went to him to make up.

"To my mind," he said, "the movies beat radio and electricity."

"I didn't know you had a mind," was Uncle Zishe's rejoinder.

♦ ♦ ♦

Uncle Zishe is a hard man to get along with. He's a sufferer. In addition to more ordinary ailments, his afflictions include vanity and pre-
tentiousness, and there's reason to believe he's pretending now too.
The story of the Moscow postcard is an outright lie. First he spreads it
around, then he eats himself alive for it. It doesn't look as if he's any too
happy with Sonya's marriage, either. One night, lying in bed, he said
out of the blue to Aunt Gita:

"So, Gita. We've married off our eldest daughter Sorke!"

"Yes," Aunt Gita answered. "We can wish ourselves a mazel tov."

"And what's your opinion of the match?"

Before Aunt Gita could think of a fitting reply, Uncle Zishe turned out the light and said in the dark:

"To tell you the truth, things couldn't be worse."

Outside, a frost was setting in.

♦♦♦ *Chapter 15*

MARAT

A heavy snow had fallen. Sloping banks of it lay beneath the window sills. Reb Zelmele's yard was buried so deep that all you could see were patches of wall with their frosted window panes. The white roofs sagged lower. The wet, snowy corners of the yard looked smeared with whitewash.

In the middle of the night Bereh rose sleepily, made his cautious way, barefoot in galoshes, to Uncle Itshe's window, and knocked. Soon the curtain was opened and Aunt Malkaleh's broad, frightened face swam toward him as though through deep water and pressed against the pane. Bereh was at a loss for words. He mumbled into his mustache and pointed up toward his rooms.

Aunt Malkaleh understood at once. "It's Khayaleh?"

Bereh nodded.

♦♦♦

It was to be a long, hard night for Bereh. First, Aunt Malkaleh sent him for a sleigh. When he returned with it, both women insisted that he accompany them to the maternity clinic. Naturally, he didn't want to. Naturally, Khayaleh got back into bed with her coat on. Between one contraction and the next, she screamed that a stone would make a better father than a Bolshevik. It was beginning to look as if she might refuse to give birth altogether.

91

Suddenly Uncle Itshe appeared out of nowhere. Flying into one of his tempers, he threatened to take a strap to Bereh. "Nincompoop!" he yelled. "Is it your child or isn't it?"

"What's all the fuss about?" Bereh answered with a smile. "As if you took mama to a clinic when I was born!"

"Moron! What does that have to do with it?" Uncle Itshe was only growing more outraged. "I was a penniless tailor. You're a Bolshevik. It's your clinic, you imbecile!"

In point of fact, Bereh was mistaken, his birth having taken place in quite different circumstances. Aunt Malkaleh, the story goes, had gone to the river to do the wash and gave birth near a hole in the ice. A peasant drove her and her baby home in his cart, after which there was no need for any clinic.

Hard though it was to believe, Bereh gave in and went with the two women.

On the way, Aunt Malkaleh rubbed it in a bit by making Bereh stop at every pharmacy that they passed in order to buy an assortment of home remedies that she alone knew about. The sleigh filled with herbs, salves, and unguents. Bereh was as silent as a fish. Just once he turned to his wife and asked:

"Khayaleh, where did you put the key to the cupboard?"

Khayaleh pressed a hand to her spine and vented her wrath on the husband who cared more for cupboards than for her. Bereh retorted that having babies was not a man's business. In general, it was a mistake to get involved with women.

"You should have realized that before!" Khayaleh wailed.

Bereh refrained from comment.

"What about a circumcision?" asked Aunt Malkaleh, who had worries of her own.

"Stop right there!" Bereh said. "You're not foisting off any more circumcisions on anyone."

They rode the rest of the way in silence.

◆ ◆ ◆

The town lay under deep, warm snow. It was as quiet as an attic. One hundred thirty thousand people, not counting newly hatched tots, had been lying beneath their warm blankets for hours. Dream production was in high gear. Dreams of all kinds, cut from every possible cloth: old Civil War fabric, big bolts of new hopes, and loud patterns of class struggle were taken down and unrolled behind the shutters. Underneath a feather quilt, the dreams of a NEP-man* were being woven. Long columns of electric digits blinked on and off in the sleep of employees of the State Planning Commission.†

In the entire city one person alone, Uncle Folye, slept as dreamlessly as steel. Lying in bed by his wife, he snored into her ear like a steam engine.

♦ ♦ ♦

At exactly six a.m., just as a major blizzard struck, a brand-new Zelmenyaner was born. The excited doctor gave him a good smack on the rear. The little creature had a black, furry cap of hair and broad shoulders and gave off a slow smell of hay mixed with something else. (See Chapter I.)

Bereh sat dozing in the dark corridor. When Aunt Malkaleh nudged him awake with the news, he sighed with relief.

"Well, then," he said, "I guess I can go home."

He went home, put up the samovar, and had fifteen glasses of tea with jam.

♦ ♦ ♦

Later that morning, Aunt Malkaleh appeared in the yard with the good tidings. She gave big kisses to all the Zelmenyaners and to everyone

---

* **NEP-man**—someone employed in one of the semiprivate enterprises temporarily allowed under the New Economic Policy (1921–1928). By the time in which Kulbak's novel is set "NEP-man" has become a derogatory term for someone still making a living off private enterprise when the Soviet economy was being collectivized and restructured.

† **State Planning Commission** (Gosplan)—a Soviet government-level committee tasked with planning the country's economic development. One of the main duties of Gosplan was the development of the Five-Year Plans (Kulbak's novel is set during the first Five-Year Plan, launched in 1928 to succeed the period of the New Economic Policy).

else she met on her way. A circumcision, it now was obvious, was out of the question. Such things were a lost cause. The one hope left was to salvage the child's name.

Uncle Yuda and Uncle Itshe went to Bereh with the anxious request that the boy be named Zalman. Then, like two down-at-heel relatives, they stood waiting for a reply.

Which was:

"I still haven't made up my mind about the name, but it certainly won't be Zalman. I believe Grandpa Zelmele was a kulak. Where did he get the money to build this courtyard with?"

"You tell us. Where?" They edged closer to him. "Are you insinuating that our father picked pockets?"

Bereh refrained from comment this time, too.

♦ ♦ ♦

The next day, Khayaleh informed the clinic of her historic decision to name the child Zelmele. The air smelled of gunpowder. Although Bereh remained grimly silent, his jawbones stuck out sharply—a sure sign that the battle had been joined.

The (young) whippersnaps prepared to charge.

Once again, so it seemed, it had been quiet in the yard for too long.

The old folks stayed home and played innocent, making believe they didn't know what was going on while watching the foe from the corners of their eyes. The sewing machine clattered, the plane planed away, and Uncle Zishe's old clocks went on ticking.

That perfectly ordinary day in Reb Zelmele's yard, Uncle Itshe sang a little song that went:

All day I make stitches
In warm winter britches
For Mishkas and Grishkas
And Evskys and Itches.

All night I sew pantskies
For Russian peasantskys,
For Fedkas and Khvedkas
And Olskys and Anskys.

He winked like a thief to Aunt Malkalehh and remarked:

"You know something! Our daughter-in-law, thank God, has turned out well."

♦ ♦ ♦

Evening. Aunt Malkalehh was at the clinic when Bereh took her aside and told her to inform the new mother that her son's name would be Marat.

"If Khayalehh doesn't like it," he said with a tug at his mustache, "she can go marry a cantor."

Uncle Itshe hitched up his pants and prepared to fight. "You can tell that big ox," he said, "that I'll tear him to shreds."

Uncle Yuda shouted up at Bereh's window:

"Just where does a jackass like you get off spitting on my father's grave?"

Uncle Zishe, too, stepped into the yard and told the women (it's anyone's guess why it's always them he turns to):

"I've thought it over and I say that this business of the name is an eternal blot on our family honor."

Uncle Yuda glared over his spectacles.

"And I suppose your son-in-law, Zishke, is not a blot?"

Uncle Zishe replied coolly:

"In the first place, I wasn't talking to you. Second, I have permission from a rabbi in Moscow. And third, anyone but an ignoramus would know that such things already happened in the days of Ezra and Nehemiah and there's nothing new under the sun."

It was all said without fainting even once.

There was an uproar in the yard. Aunt Malkaleh barely managed to convene the warring parties in her home. She was frantic. There was in fact reason to believe that it was she who had quietly egged on the uncles in the pro-Zelmele party. Nor was she wholly blameless in the matter of Khayaleh's decision.

Which may have been why, coming back from the clinic late that night, she felt obliged to go from room to room and declare:

"Imagine! The whole clinic is oohing and aahing over Bereh's little Marat!"

She found some excuse to summon Falke to Uncle Zishe's, where the brothers were drinking tea. What, they asked him, could he tell them about Marat—not Bereh's, but the other, mysterious one. Was he a decent type? Where did he stand on the Jews? All other subjects were forgotten.

Falke assured them that Marat was the very soul of decency. He related his role in the French Revolution; explained the conflict between the Jacobins and the Girondistes; went on to the Paris Commune; criticized its gross tactical errors; and ended with a paean to the October Revolution.

That evening the elders of the tribe learned some history.

♦♦♦ *Chapter 16*

THE DEATH OF UNCLE ZISHE

Uncle Zishe was smiling.

By all reports, he felt fit as a fiddle that last winter evening and even joked with Falke and Aunt Malkaleh about the fine bunch of grandchildren the Zelmenyaners were having nowadays. (Sons-in-law were not mentioned in his presence.)

Who would have believed that twenty-four hours later he would no longer be among the living?

It now seems obvious—anyone could have seen it—that his tenderness that night was the tenderness that comes before dying. He sat looking at the Zelmenyaners with the yellowish whites of his eyes, and they, brainless as sheep, never realized he was saying goodbye.

Who can doubt he felt death approaching? He was like all old watchmakers, who deal in their way with living organisms. When it suits them, they patiently assemble a watch and make it go. When it doesn't, they screw on an eyepiece and gruesomely pull out the cogs and springs until nothing is left.

♦♦♦

That morning, Uncle Zishe awoke and blessed the new day. There was a biting frost outside. He got the samovar going and then, in the snow-blue light that rapped on the windows, said his morning prayers. When he was done, still wrapped in his prayer shawl, he brought a glass of hot tea to Aunt Gita's bed.

A chill ran down Aunt Gita's spine. Seeing a prayer shawl emerge from the shadows, she was sure her hour had come. She barely had time to put on a kerchief before Uncle Zishe said lovingly:

"Have some tea, Gita. All my life you've made me tea and I don't know what I've done to deserve it."

Aunt Gita was too astonished to answer. Whatever was happening couldn't be good.

She stood by the stove in the dawn light, casting sideways glances at Uncle Zishe bent over his watch dials and knowing from the tilt of his back and the angle of his neck that his time was up. When it came to the Angel of Death and his affairs, no one was a bigger expert than Aunt Gita.

♦ ♦ ♦

Uncle Zishe died a few hours later—all because of a trivial incident.

A country sleigh pulled into the yard, still smelling of the cold of midnight fields. From under its cover of straw, entangled in their wraps, crawled a peasant and his wife from Saltanov, their noses like hard potatoes. They had asked for Zishe the watchmaker and been shown the way.

At first Uncle Zishe thought they had brought him a clock to repair. Alas, they were soon revealed to be, not just peasants from a village, but his own in-laws, Pavel Olshevsky's father and mother. The marriage, they thought, entitled them to a place to park their horse when they came to market.

Uncle Zishe, naturally, broke into a cold sweat. He felt like grabbing hold of Aunt Gita and sitting down with her to cry. He barely heard what his visitors were saying. Yet as if to spite him, the drab peasant kept asking in wonderment:

"So you're really Zishke the watchmaker?"

"Yes," Uncle Zishe snuffled through his pale nose, looking out the window to see if anyone was aware of his misfortune. Uncle Itshe, needless to say, was already pacing suspiciously on his balcony. The scoundrel might come at any moment to ask what time it was. Uncle Zishe rose, dragged himself to the door, and stepped outside.

"Itshke," he said weakly, "I suppose you're wondering what time it is."

"Of course," said Uncle Itshe with a dig at his brother. "That's all I ever think about."

"It's a quarter to twelve."

Uncle Zishe turned heavily, let out a sigh, and pitched forward into the black snow.

The yard remained calm. It had been waiting for Uncle Zishe to faint. How else could he get rid of his unwanted visitors?

Imagine the surprise, then, when he turned out to be dead.

It was galling. All his life Uncle Zishe had fooled the world with his fainting fits—and now, so it seemed, he had purposely died in a hurry in order to fool it again.

You couldn't help wondering what had gotten into him.

♦ ♦ ♦

Uncle Zishe was dead. He lay annoyingly still in an unmade bed in the corner, his belly a stiff plateau and his cold beard pointing at the ceiling. Aunt Gita sat by the head of the bed, her bony arms like drooping wings. With round, dry eyes, she watched the condolence callers poke their heads in from the street.

The peasants from Saltanov were hurriedly escorted out. Impatient for them to be gone, Uncle Itshe threatened to take a broomstick to them.

You couldn't blame Uncle Itshe. A tried-and-true brother, he was more thunderstruck than anyone. Standing in the middle of the room, he held a handkerchief to his fat tears and blubbered like a spanked baby. He had to be asked to show some consideration, since no one could think straight with all his bawling.

Uncle Yuda, on the other hand, kept away. It was whispered that, offended by Uncle Zishe's death, the madman was staging a protest. This indeed would have been senseless, since Uncle Zishe had died perfectly properly.

Uncle Yuda finally came late that evening, when the corpse had been lowered to the floor. By now the younger generation was home from work, and Bubbe Bashe was sitting by the dead man. Even Uncle Folye was there, dozing on his feet by the stove. Uncle Yuda adjusted his spectacles, bent over the dead body like a doctor, and uncovered its face. Everyone awaited his judgment. He remained silent for a long while, shaking his head. Then he said:

"Zishke, you lived like a vain fool and you've died like one!"

And straightened up.

No one bothered to contradict him.

♦ ♦ ♦

The whole family hadn't been together like this in years. The Zelmenyaners exuded calm and tranquility, the raw smell of deep Russian earth. No one wanted the intimate evening to end. Even Uncle Folye would have liked it to go on forever.

Bubbe Bashe swallowed whatever she was chewing and said:

"It's no fun to die in a frost."

She was talking to herself, presumably convinced that someone her age deserved to die in better weather.

Everyone looked at her with the same worrisome thought. Bubbe Bashe's brains were addling without her knowing it.

The whippersnaps poked each other in the ribs, and even the disconsolate Sonya, sitting in her bonnet and gloves while inhaling from the little bottles that Pavel Olshevsky kept handing her, couldn't help smiling. The mood was turning disrespectful.

Uncle Itshe, hot under the collar, exclaimed:

"You whippersnaps, what do you think this is? The theater? A movie with polar bears?"

In the sudden silence, Uncle Folye's bony guffaw behind the stove sounded like a rattle of stones. Everyone turned just in time to see him tighten his pants, as though to belt in his laughter.

Shamefaced, Uncle Folye departed.

♦ ♦ ♦

Uncle Itshe sat crossly by the corpse, reciting psalms. The whippersnaps took off. Tonke had to take part in a tax raid on the Central Workers Cooperative that brooked no delay. She promised to be back by morning and asked that the funeral wait for her. Falke hurried off by her side. Since deciding to travel together to Vladivostok, the two were inseparable.

♦ ♦ ♦

A hard white night, its stars a hundred different colors, could be seen through the open door, left ajar to air the smell of the corpse. The frost was as dry and clear as a block of ice. All was empty. All was still.

♦ ♦ ♦

As he was leaving the yard, Pavel Olshevsky curiously asked the wife nestled against him why, as though there were a secret reason, the surviving brothers hadn't donned prayer shawls and phylacteries and blown the shofar. Sonya answered that the old folk weren't what they used to be, and in any case, the shofar was blown only on the holiday of Shavuos* to commemorate Abraham's taking the Jews out of Egypt.

♦ ♦ ♦

Aunt Gita and Uncle Itshe were left alone with the corpse. With a sigh of relief they lit the brass candlesticks by the dead man's head, turned the pictures to the wall, covered the clocks and mirrors, and set about planning the funeral.

Aunt Gita even went over to the corpse and said in her bass voice:

"Zishe, don't worry. With God's help, we'll give you a proper Jewish burial."

Uncle Zishe didn't bother to answer.

In the middle of the night they were joined by Uncle Yuda, refreshed by a few hours of sleep. Ignoring them both, he recited psalms in dry, wee-hours-of-the-morning tones. The night turned gray outside the window. It was good of Uncle Yuda to have gotten out of bed in the middle of the night in order to help a brother in need.

Aunt Gita would never forget it.

♦ ♦ ♦

The whippersnaps returned in the morning, bringing back the dullness of an ordinary day. There was a mad rush to get ready for the funeral.

"That's enough weeping and wailing, you women!" someone shouted. "Let's go!"

* **The holiday of Shavuos**—a confusion of Pentecost with Passover, when in any event the shofar is not sounded.

Bereh turned up from somewhere with a black coffin, and before the women could finish putting on their wraps and felt boots, Uncle Zishe was on his way. They had to run to catch up with him. Needless to say, the funeral was nothing to brag about. In fact, it was laughable. Aunt Malkaleh had to turn to Bereh and say angrily:

"You bandit! Are you going to allow us to cry or not?"

"Go ahead," Bereh said. "Just make it quick."

They had a good cry. The loudest was Uncle Itshe's. In a sopping-wet voice he said to Uncle Yuda:

"It's some world, eh?"

Uncle Yuda regarded him crossly over his spectacles and said:

"Better six feet under."

He was thinking of Uncle Zishe and Aunt Hesye.

Only Uncle Zishe wasn't there to pull a hair from his beard and say with a smile:

"A fine bunch of young folk!"

By the time the Zelmenyaners returned home, it was late. A gray evening was dropping. The yard lay in shadow. Not an electric light shone; not a stove was lit. Everyone felt empty, chagrined at having buried a first uncle.

Unfairly had Uncle Zishe been accused all his life of malingering, too vain to admit nothing was wrong with him. It was now clear that he had been a man of honor. He had been sick and had died young on the up-and-up—younger, at any rate, than the leading candidate in Reb Zelmele's yard.

♦ ♦ ♦

Two skinny Zelmenyaners stood by the stable with their faces to the wall. They were peeing in the snow. In the gray evening, they too looked pale, worried, and disheartened.

"Mottele, will we die too?" asked Lipa, who was in kindergarten.

"Not so soon," Mottele answered. "First we'll get married and go to war. Then we'll bring in a bumper crop."

"What kind of crop?"

"A bumper one."

They looked at the lines they had made in the snow.

"Listen," Lipa said. "I'm so big I have a callus on my foot. Do you know what Tonke says?"

"What?"

"She says a callus on your foot is fine for a Pioneer but a Komsomol needs one on his hands. That's harder."

Lipa backed away from the wall. "Which would you rather be when you grow up," he asked, "a Bolshevik or a Communist?"

"I'll be a 1905 Communist," Mottele said with a superior glance.

"And I'll sit behind a big desk."

"You're full of it!" Mottele had no patience for such a low level of political consciousness. "I can't talk to a baby like you."

◆◆◆ *Chapter 17*

A ZELMENYANER MISCELLANY

Among the major events in Reb Zelmele's yard after the death of Uncle Zishe were the following:

I.

Going to the stable to look for a board, Uncle Yuda found a postcard stuck into a roof beam. On one side of it was an inky Moscow postmark. On the other were some lines in Hebrew. Uncle Yuda took it home and managed to read:

> 22 Elul, the year of Creation 5681.
> To His Excellency Zisl the son of Reb Zalman, may his light shine.
> Peace to the near and to the far and to you t . . .

The writing was in tiny, rabbinical letters. Uncle Yuda stood holding it crossly, thinking with an angry glance at the stove:

So it's true! Zishke wasn't lying after all.

The postcard, it later turned out, must have troubled him greatly, for he even went to Uncle Zishe's grave to beg for forgiveness. You say that's making too much of it? But Uncle Yuda was feeling so low that he went around looking crestfallen, which may have had to do with his disappearance in the middle of the night, when he lit out like an escaped prisoner and wasn't heard from again for a long time. On the other hand, some thought he absconded for a different reason.

The real cause was said to be this:

After the death of Uncle Zishe, Uncle Yuda, wan and irritable, spoke to no one. He was at his most ornery. One fine day he climbed the stairs to Bereh's in a bellicose mood, stood outside the door, and called:

"Good morning!"

"A good morning to you," Bereh answered.

"I was wondering," Uncle Yuda said, "how little Zelmele is doing."

Bereh answered evenly:

"You must be mistaken. There are no little Zelmeles here."

Uncle Yuda stuck his beard in his mouth and said nothing. After a while he asked:

"So what's your darling boy's name?"

"My darling boy's name is Marat," Bereh said.

That was the end of their conversation.

According to Khayaleh, Uncle Yuda stood by the door for at least another half an hour. Then he departed in silence, carefully shutting the latch as if leaving a sickroom, descended the stairs, and went home and didn't come out.

2.

The trolley line was inaugurated.*

It was a sight for sore eyes. Starting from a central station, the trolley sped through the streets. Its cars were brand-new, its windows gleamed, it had lots of chrome, and even its passenger straps still smelled of the factory. Its windows were crowded with passengers. It raced uphill and down all the way to the outskirts of town.

The day began with the Zelmenyaners hearing an unfamiliar bell ring near the yard. The first to run to it was Uncle Itshe, who loved novelties. He returned home late at night, and was so embarrassed to tell Aunt Malkaleh where he had been that he said it was at a friend's house.

"What friend?" Aunt Malkaleh pressed him.

"A friend."

This was hard to believe, since Uncle Itshe hadn't left Aunt Mal-

---

* **The trolley line was inaugurated**—the first two lines of the urban light rail network were in fact launched in Minsk in the fall of 1929.

kaleh's side since their wedding day. His only friend from his bachelor years, Ora the tailor, had died long ago.

The next morning, Uncle Itshe urged Aunt Malkaleh to take a trolley ride. There was nothing like it, he said.

"How do you know?"

"Trust me."

He didn't tell her he had spent the whole previous day riding around town and wasting no small amount of money.

♦ ♦ ♦

From then on, the Zelmenyaners took the trolley often. A favorite route was riding to the central station and walking back on foot. Better even than the ride itself were all the people and the things one heard from them. Aunt Malkaleh liked to sit with a smile and instruct out-of-towners on proper trolley behavior. She was an expert at getting change from the conductor and felt as close to her fellow passengers as she did to the Zelmenyaners in the yard.

The following happened to Uncle Folye.

Seated on the trolley one day, Uncle Folye, realizing he didn't have ten kopecks for the fare, turned his face to the window and stared at the street. Asked for his ticket, he pretended not to hear and went on looking out the window. Only when a policeman grabbed him by the sleeve did he coolly get to his feet and say:

"*Eto tvoi tramvay?*"*

Which was his way of declaring that, the trolley being the property of the working class, he had the right to a free ride now and then.

3.

Tonke and Falke left for Vladivostok.

Six days later a postman arrived in the yard with the telegram:

STILL ON WAY STOP HAVING FUN STOP TONKE FALKE.

Aunt Malkaleh went with the telegram from room to room, asking:

"Maybe you can tell me what's so much fun?"

Piffleheads!

---

* **Eto tvoy tramvay?** (Russian)—"Is this your [familiar] own electric trolley?"

4.

In the end, Uncle Folye and Bereh became good friends.

It happened on a winter day when both were off from work. Bereh had been home all morning in his bare feet and riding britches, munching bread and reading the newspapers. After a while, he tucked his feet beneath him and tuned his balalaika. He was in fine fettle. Finding his singing voice (it had been in his stomach all along), he broke into a rendition of

As I was riding to Rostov-on-Don,
I took along a loaf of bread;
As I was riding to Rostov-on-Don,
I left the bourgeois bastards for dead.

He could see the yard through the window. Crisscrossed with electric lines and radio wires, it looked like an old pot in which a stew of beardless, uncircumcised, heathen Zelmenyaners of the new generation was simmering.

A hunchbacked crow balanced on the antenna. You could tell from how it opened and shut its beak that it was crying "Hurrah." Or more precisely:

"Hurrah! Rah-rah! Rah-rah-rah!"

Uncle Folye was out in the yard, grinning and tugging at his whiskers. Could he possibly have been a bit drunk?

Bereh ran downstairs in his bare feet. Through the window you could see him take Folye by the sleeve and talk to him. At first Folye balked. Then the two of them climbed the stairs together.

♦ ♦ ♦

Glumly, they sat without talking in Bereh's apartment. Then they drank some tea in silence. Uncle Folye stared dully at the floor. They drank more tea and were silent some more. Suddenly Uncle Folye rested both brooding arms on the table and asked unabashedly:

"Tell me, Berke. Are you a real Communist?"

"What makes you ask?"

"I need to have a man-to-man talk with you."

"Shoot."

Uncle Folye's eyes were damp with emotion. "You're a good fellow, so listen. Sometimes I'd like to give a speech. You know what I mean? It's no crime for an old workingman to get up at a meeting and say something. People like us are listened to. Have you ever done it?"

"I'm not much of a speaker myself. But when you have to, you do it."

"Look here. That's not my problem. I speak well enough. I just don't have anything to say."

Uncle Folye bowed his head sadly. As much as he sympathized, Bereh couldn't help thinking that Folye was not cut out to be an orator.

Khayaleh brought a fine-looking potato pudding to the table.

5.

Uncle Itshe shaved off the rest of his beard.

6.

Marat had a tummyache. It was nothing serious.

♦ ♦ ♦

Minor incidents aside, these were the main events in Reb Zelmele's yard after Uncle Zishe's death.

Chapter 18

UNCLE YUDA

At three a.m. he lit the lantern that once served the vestibule's long-gone geese. In the windows, the winter night was murky and gray. He poured some water from the bucket, washed his hands and said the blessing for it, took down an old sack from above the stove, and packed a few things: his prayer shawl and phylacteries, his fiddle, a pound loaf of bread, and some onions—all that a man needs for the road.

The too great silence of the night signaled a frost. To be on the safe side, he wrapped a kerchief around his ears and tucked his wet beard inside his collar. Then he shouldered the sack, cast one last damp, irritable glance over his spectacles at the yard as if looking for someone to thrash, and slipped silently away.

♦♦♦

The cloudy night sprawled over the dark snow. There was no above or below, no sky, no earth, no anything. Uncle Yuda knew the way. Taking a right turn outside the yard, he headed along the packed crust of the narrow, unpaved streets to the Dolhinov highway.*

* **Dolhinov highway**—an old road originating in Minsk and leading in the direction of the village of Dolhinov (Dolginovo), about fifty miles to the west. At the time in which the novel is set, Dolhinov was in fact located outside the borders of the Belorussian State Socialist Republic, in the territory of Poland (based on the boundaries between Poland and the USSR in the years 1921–1939).

His eyes grew accustomed to the darkness. Charred by the black silence, the dim shapes of houses, stoops, and fences loomed in front of him. Further on, the snow-blue vastness of the fields swam into view. Suddenly Uncle Yuda felt a sweet peace flow through him, cooling the fevered brain beneath his hat.

Can there be late wintry nights in which it is sheer happiness to be alone in the fields with a pack on your back, waiting to see what the world will do next, like a bird on a branch that looks here and looks there while feeling and understanding nothing?

Can a simple Zelmenyaner have moments of uplift like a crow?

The path crunched beneath his feet, climbing and dropping to the frozen, piney horizon.

Suddenly, it grew even darker. Then, off to the right, dawn began to break. The pale snow turned paler and streamed with a cold whiteness. He had walked twelve kilometers when, far in the east, the first fires of day bubbled up through a cleft in the snow as though from a hearth in a foundry.

All that walking was wearing our wanderer out.

The road ran uphill. Where it started down again, he knew, lay a large farm where he had done some carpentering one summer as a young man. (Uncle Yuda had seen a bit of the world when he was young.) Soon he saw its snow-covered orchards. To the left, a path lined with birch trees ran to the farmhouse, whose red roof rose above a stand of poplars.

Nothing stirred.

◆ ◆ ◆

Uncle Yuda entered a large, rundown farmyard that smelled of horses and warm manure. A bull bellowed in a distant barn. He brushed off the snow and headed for the two-story house whose wooden colonnade made it look like an old synagogue.

A large stove was lit in a gloomy room. Pots were cooking on it. The corners of the room still lay in shadow. Sleepy-looking women moved about in the dim light, holding crying babies, peeling potatoes, and scrubbing pots.

Curious glances took his measure, as though he portended no good.

Uncle Yuda threw down his pack, sat on the edge of a bench, and gazed irritably over his spectacles at the strange women. The women glanced at each other, uncertain what manner of fellow he was. It seemed best to send, discreetly, for a man.

From the farmyard came a sturdy little Jew in high boots. He had a short, curly beard like an ink blot and scented the wintry room with a smell of apples.

The Jew's name was Khaim.

Khaim lit his pipe from the stove and asked:

"And where might a Jew be coming from?"

Uncle Yuda thought it best to play dumb. It seemed the most sensible thing for a stranger to do. He mumbled some words that Khaim failed to make out. When Uncle Yuda didn't want to be understood, he was quite good at it.

Not that it took much intelligence to realize that he was a hungry Jew who wanted some breakfast.

Since no one with an empty stomach had turned up at the Red Plow Kolkhoz* in a long while, he was allowed to stay on.

♦ ♦ ♦

That afternoon, Uncle Yuda strolled around the yard and looked it over. A collective farm, he was beginning to think, was not a bad thing. What he did next showed his professional skills off to advantage.

What did Uncle Yuda do next?

Poking in a small barn, he found a sad-looking hen. Uncle Yuda was an expert on hens. He examined this one and saw her leg was broken. Taking her to the farmhouse, he asked for a knife and went to work. By evening the hen was walking on a wooden leg. It tapered downward like the leg of a bench and was clearly the work of a carpenter. A carpenter was something the Red Plow Kolkhoz could use.

That evening, the members of the collective assembled in the big

---

* **Kolkhoz** (Russian, abbreviation of *kollektivnoe khoziaistvo*)—a collective farm. During collectivization, when Kulbak's novel is set, individual farmers and villagers were forced to give up private ownership of their land and join such collective farms.

room, the men around a large table, the women on cots and by the walls. They were there to appraise the newcomer, which wasn't easy. Uncle Yuda played coy.

"Say, mister, maybe you've worked with cows?"

"Uncle, tell us, what do you know about chickens?"

Mind you, Uncle Yuda knew everything and could even have given the children a Bible lesson on the side. It was just as well, however, that no one wanted one, because he was also something of a freethinker. His cogitations about God were unusual, a mixture, in the spirit of the times, of Hasidic legend and electricity. What he wanted most was to care for the hens. When summer came, he would dig for horseradish roots, pick sorrel for soup, gather mushrooms—anything but carpentry.

All at once he had an idea:

"Would you happen to be in need of a fiddler?"

He took out his fiddle and played for them.

The kolkhozniks, it turned out, liked fiddling. They even understood a thing or two about it and licked their fingers with pure pleasure. Uncle Yuda was so carried away that he played the song of the hen.

Which hen was that, you ask?

Uncle Yuda played the song of the long-dead hen, the hen of once upon a time, when our town was under an artillery bombardment. Housewives up and down the street locked their homes and moved into Reb Zelmele's cellar. All of a sudden Aunt Hesye had a craving for chicken soup. This came from staring so long in the crowded cellar at Reb Yekhezkel the slaughterer that she couldn't think of anything else. Aunt Hesye grabbed a hen, Reb Yekhezkel reached for his knife, and they went outside to slit the bird's throat. Just then there was a huge explosion. The yard burst into flames. Not a windowpane was left in place. After a while a neighbor knocked on the cellar door and asked that someone come out. Pale and peaceful, Aunt Hesye was lying on the ground as if nothing had happened. Next to her, its beard sticking up in the air, was the slaughterer's head. The rest of him, knife in hand, lay by the wreckage of a fence.

The hen stood philosophizing.

♦ ♦ ♦

And so, in midwinter, Uncle Yuda joined the kolkhoz and went around with a leather apron and hay in his beard. He learned the ropes quickly. A harder worker than anyone, he patrolled the yard with an ax and a pole, here hacking out a doorstop, there giving a goose a bath, somewhere else concocting a salve for a pregnant woman's rash.

It's well known that women on collective farms conceive frequently because their husbands work in the fresh air. They also get rashes, for which Uncle Yuda had various ointments and incantations. This won him a following. He did his healing early in the morning, using a burning ember and a Belorussian chant that went:

Rash, rash, at break of day,
Go, go, go away!

Although it was all done discreetly, however, two young Komsomol members found out about it. This put Uncle Yuda in a difficult position. In no uncertain tones he was told:

"Look, pal, we don't want any quacks around here."

Luckily for him, the women took his side. He was let off with the promise that he would stay away from them and stick to his poultry.

Soon after this, the farm's dairyman returned from the city with a full account of Uncle Yuda's true history—to wit, his being a Zelmenyaner, a carpenter, and a widower. This set matters right again, especially the part about the carpentry.

The dairyman, it seemed, also brought Uncle Yuda a letter from Tsalke in which his son wrote about himself and Uncle Zishe's younger daughter Tonke, now living a debauched life in Vladivostok. Not only was she a disgrace to the family, Tsalke wrote, "but to make matters worse, Uncle Itshe's darling son Falke is gallivanting around with her. They write shameless letters and there's reason to think they've gotten married. I'm simply devastated," Tsalke wrote. "I don't know what to do about it."

Uncle Yuda stuck the letter in his pocket for a rainy day.

The dairyman also brought the report that Bubbe Bashe was not in the best of health. (Strange to say, she wasn't dead yet.)

The women of the collective formed a circle around Uncle Yuda and waited for him to admit the truth. Uncle Yuda, though, denied everything. It was all a big lie, he said. He had nothing to do with the Zelmenyaners and could prove it. Halfway through all this he grew so upset that, though no one had said an unkind word, he stalked furiously off to his hens.

With the hens he got along idyllically. It was said that he even talked to them. It was also said—though this was hard to believe—that he sometimes played his fiddle for them. Most remarkable was the absurd claim, repeated everywhere, that they liked his music so much that they kept asking for more.

♦ ♦ ♦

Winter. A hungry wolf has been sighted in the plains. The peasants have dug a trap for him. Yet the wolf is seen only at night on the horizon, lurking for hours behind a snow bank before vanishing into the black cutout of the forest.

The Red Plow Kolkhoz lies amid snowy orchards, breathing through its barns and stables with the warm manure of goitrous cows and the milky sourness of wet sheep.

A luminous silence, vast and glittering, congeals for miles around.

Snow, snow, and more snow.

Sometimes Uncle Yuda goes to the nearby village. The villagers know him as the new collective farm member, the one with the fiddle. He walks down the street with his hands behind his back, peering nearsightedly into the peasants' yards like a man who knows his own worth. He feels at home. He has even made friends with an old peasant, a potter.

♦ ♦ ♦

They sit in the warm cottage, Uncle Yuda and the potter, by the blue windows, talking about the world.

"In Moscow," says Uncle Yuda, "they're making live chickens out of cotton wadding."

"I don't believe it," says the old potter.

"They have a special machine," Uncle Yuda tells him.

"And what do they make the chickens' souls from?" the peasant asks.

Uncle Yuda knows the answer. "Electricity."

"No chicken like that is ever crossing my threshold," says the peasant.

"There's nothing wrong with it," Uncle Yuda retorts.

Snow, snow, and more snow.

Uncle Yuda and the potter are like two radishes wintering under the snow. They're frightfully fond of each other. Sometimes the potter visits Uncle Yuda. They sit in the henhouse, petting the hens.

It's a good way to relax.

In general, Uncle Yuda is feeling chipper these days. He gives the potter a big smile when he comes to visit. It's quite a sight. His eyes shut tight, his whole face crinkles, and all you can see when he opens his mouth is one dirty tooth in his gums.

You can tell by his smile that Uncle Yuda is finally at peace. Unfortunately, it won't last long. An unforeseeable mishap will make him turn gray overnight.

♦ ♦ ♦

There was a celebration in the village. Uncle Yuda was asked to play the fiddle. The potter came to the farm to help him get ready, and they set out.

Not that it's nice to poke fun at them, but the two friends trudging along looked like a pair of old brooms.

Uncle Yuda was in fine form that night. He played like a house on fire, fiddling his wailingest tunes. After a while he was lifted onto a table and fiddled from there.

Then he had a few glasses of vodka.

The potter, as always when he had something to drink, fell asleep at once. Uncle Yuda went on playing. The peasant couples danced, as usual, first in the room, then in the vestibule, and finally the devil knows where.

Uncle Yuda played with a vengeance. Seeing that no one was left in the room, he went outside and fiddled in the street.

Snow, snow, and more snow.

The snow was brighter than fire. A moon swam out from under it. Silence. The neatly ruled white fields were immaculate. In the pure snow stood a cross, and beside it, its small, trim shadow. A star, the coldest and fattest in the sky, hung above the frozen fields.

Uncle Yuda cavorted and fiddled. The moon beat down on his hat.

Suddenly he slipped. Everything spun upside down, and he went sprawling in the snow.

At once Uncle Yuda sobered up. He turned and groped for his spectacles, feeling the frozen earth. Two phosphorescent eyes were moving in the black night, accompanied by a strong smell of fur.

What did Uncle Yuda make of that?

Little by little, in a patch of darkness, he made out a wolf standing on its hind legs.

In the morning he was dragged from the wolf trap, his beard turned gray.

Chapter 19

Uncle Yuda, needless to say, was dead.

♦♦♦ *Chapter 20*

A LETTER FROM VLADIVOSTOK

Dear Parents,

Forgive me for not writing sooner. There simply hasn't been time. Tonke and I have been so busy that we've forgotten all about you, my dears. From now on, we'll try to write more often.

Now that we've become, as you say, man and wife, I've gotten to know Tonke better. She's an interesting girl, devoted body and soul to socialist construction. There's hardly a trace of petit-bourgeois individualism left in her. I'm convinced that she'll settle down even more as our work progresses, so that we'll soon see in her a more consistently class-conscious activist on the economic front.

My dears, the enthusiasm of the working class is great! One encounters it in all aspects of one's work. Yet at the same time, it must be admitted that the workers' initiatives are not always properly carried out, with the consequence that millions, if not billions, are lost to the state.

You ask what I'm doing and whether I've managed to save any money. My poor, innocent parents: what can you be thinking of? I haven't traveled all this way from home to make money. I've come to take part in one of the most momentous fronts of the campaign—the cultural front. The avant-garde of cultural construction in our Soviet Union, as in socialist construction in general, is and always will be the proletariat. The Party's task is to help the proletariat gain control of all aspects of cultural life. On the one hand, the proletarian content of our culture depends on this. On the other, it strengthens the proletariat's influence on the peasant masses.

Tonke, my dear parents, is off at a meeting right now. She'll probably come home late at night. I'll light the stove for her and make her a pot of tea. She has, this girl of mine, heavy responsibilities. But it's not just her, because we're all pushing ourselves to the limit. No one has any illusions about the many obstacles still in the way of the victorious road to socialism.

Recently we had an interesting meeting regarding the antiwaste campaign. Tonke presented an audience of a thousand workers with a fascinating series of facts and figures illustrating our negligent attitude toward our domestic resources. I haven't encountered such clarity of thought in a long while. The waste in our economy is estimated at hundreds of millions of rubles. 200,000 tons of metal end up as scrap every year. 1.5 million bricks are unnecessarily used because we continue to build thick walls by old methods. The produce lost in the food industry alone amounts, roughly speaking, to 200 million rubles. And the situation in agriculture is even worse. We could increase yields 20 percent by switching to more selective sowing. We also economize falsely in the battle against field pests, greater investment in which would more than pay for itself. In the R.S.F.S.R* alone, rodents eat 45 million rubles' worth of wheat annually. Locusts cost us another 30 million, wheatworm 60 million, weevils 172 million, etc., etc.

Tonke made brilliant use of these statistics. Until now the experts looked down their noses at her, but now Tonke Zinoyevna is considered the last word on economic matters. It's grand fun being with her. We have lunch together every day at the workers cafeteria, where we have such a fine time arguing, laughing, and playing pranks that we sometimes have to be chased out. Mornings and evenings I devote to housekeeping. Tonke says she hooked up with me so that I could take care of such things, but don't think, my dears, that she gets away with

---

* **R.S.F.S.R.**—Russian Soviet Federal Socialist Republic, the largest republic of the Soviet Union.

it. I have the willpower to be independent and I'm not under anyone's thumb, even Tonke's. Say what you will, I'm no tail wagger!*

What's new with you? How is my papa, my mama, the radio? Be sure not to put tea on the receiver or leave any food near it, because even a few drops of soup can ruin it. The antenna needs to be raised. Papa can do it himself in the following manner: take two poles, run parallel lines between them, saw them into four 35 to 70 cm sections, depending on their length, drill holes in one of the four, insert the others into them, and fasten them with metal bands. I'm attaching an illustration. You'll find all the tools you need in my chest in the attic. Just make sure to put everything back in place. And please, papa, send me a book of mine that you'll find on the shelf mama dries cheese on. It's called *Glauber's Salt*† *in the Kara-Bogaz Gulf*.

Yes, my dears, one must work, work, work. I'm not much of a philosopher. It's necessary to think dialectically and grasp things in process, and I admit that my mind is too dull for that. Sometimes Tonke tries to teach me, but she has no patience. If I don't understand everything at once, she loses her temper, grabs her coat, and runs off. After that she doesn't talk to me for days. As I see it, it's the last traces of her individualistic psychology. We both come from petit-bourgeois homes. The self-employed artisan finds it hard to think intelligently. But she's still young. As she comes in closer contact with the industrial proletariat, she will, I hope (as will I), iron out the petit-bourgeois wrinkles.

Yes, we still have a lot ahead of us!

Your Falke

P.S. As for your question, mama, about cinnamon and saffron from the workers kitchen, they're probably available, but believe me, I have no

---

* **I'm no tail wagger**—a play on Falke's last name, Khvost, which in Russian means tail. "Khvostizm" at the time of industrialization was a politically charged accusation against those who were not in the forefront of socialist construction but at the tail end of society.

† **Glauber's salt**—also known as *mirabilite* or *sal mirabilis*—salt deposits found near the Kara-Bogaz Gulf in Central Asia (on the territory of present-day Turkmenistan). This mineral has a range of chemical and industrial uses; until the late 1920s, it was gathered by the local population, but an industry was built around it in the late 1920s and early 1930s.

time to ask. Let me know what's happening in the yard. Has Grandma died? If she has, write whether she's buried with Grandpa and our uncle or somewhere else, and tell us about her last days. If she hasn't, give her my and Tonke's best regards.

♦ ♦ ♦

My dear mama,

I'm taking advantage of this opportunity to thank you for having given birth to me in such great and interesting times. As Falke is now my husband, you needn't worry that I'll be an old maid. He really isn't a bad type. Kisses, kisses, kisses!

I'd like to ask you, mama, to tell Yoshke the redhead (Khonye the shoemaker's son from the next yard) that I'll answer his letter one of these days. I don't understand his state of mind. Tell him they're not making the right demands. Here, the trade union campaign has been conducted with the greatest enthusiasm. The workers have come forth with hundreds of suggestions. If he looks around him he'll realize that it's a matter of better educational work.

Tell him, too, mama, that Borovke and Nyute were here for a few days. They were sent as delegates from the All-Union Fish Association to take part in the Kamchatka fish harvest.

Your Tonke

♦ ♦ ♦ *Chapter 21*

BUBBE BASHE

Frosts. Days that glittered like moonlit nights. A yard turned to cold porcelain. Heavily wrapped Zelmenyaners gathered to talk in whispers. About what? Bubbe Bashe had finally taken to bed. It seemed this was it, because she had also stopped eating.

Aunt Gita stepped out of Bubbe Bashe's room with her usual look of rabbinical silence, threw a knowing glance at the yard, and remained standing by the door. Aunt Gita is an expert on such things. She was surrounded at once on all sides.

"I reckon," she said, trying to sound like her father, the rabbi of Sola, may his righteous memory be a blessing, "that her soul will pass on to the World of Truth sometime tonight . . ."

"What's taking her so long?" asked the disgruntled Zelmenyaners.

Aunt Gita gave a shrug as if to say: I'm not responsible for everything.

♦ ♦ ♦

The pillars of the family were falling. Gone were the two uncles, seasoned leaders who for years had put their shoulders to the grindstone of Zelmenyaner history. Gone were the great Zelmenyaners who could with a glance put each family member in his place. Now the family groped in the dark. Bubbe Bashe lay behind the stove like a plucked goose, and there was no one to take things in hand. Alas, no one even knew when to shed a tear.

"We're alone as a stone!"

The man who said this would have resembled Uncle Itshe had he had a beard. Two fat tears ran from his desolate eyes. He was so distraught that, trying to brush them away with his sleeve, he wiped his nose instead.

♦ ♦ ♦

At sunrise, the news from Aunt Gita met with exasperation.

"How can that be?"

Bubbe Bashe was still alive and feeling better. Everyone flocked to her bed and stood around it. Aunt Gita surveyed her carefully, probing her with her sorcerer's eyes. After a while she declared:

"She's a tough nut. But it won't be long now."

Bubbe Bashe lay without moving, her shorn head on a dirty pillow, a little bundle of bones corroded by time but still breathing. She was a pitiful sight. Uncle Itshe felt heartsick. Leaning tenderly over the pillow, he asked:

"Mama, does it hurt?"

She opened two tiny, muddy eyes like a bird's, and that was all.

♦ ♦ ♦

In the evening Bereh and Folye arrived. They were now close friends and went together to clubs, meetings, and assemblies. Bereh ordered a bed with fresh sheets to be made for Bubbe Bashe in the main room, her transfer to which from behind the stove appeared to revive her. She even groaned and opened the slits of her eyes, which were filled with a bitter comprehension. They roamed around the room, taking in everything as though she were perfectly lucid.

Seeing what a faithful grandson Bereh was, the women came to his aid:

"She needs jam!"

"Bring her jam, she's weak!"

Bubbe Bashe listened attentively. She was clearly trying to summon what strength she had left in order to say something. Uncle Itshe stood closest to her bed. With her final breath, she asked for a favor. Would someone please turn off the electric light because—so Bubbe Bashe declared—she couldn't die in all that glare.

Uncle Itshe looked around desperately (there was an ideological principle involved), but Bereh gave the go-ahead:

"Don't argue with her. Turn it off!"

A kerosene lamp was lit. Silently the Zelmenyaners sat around the bed to await the soul's departure, which could now take place without hindrance. Bubbe Bashe was in her death throes. Ashen faced, she straightened her feet beneath the blanket.

"She was a fine woman! She never took a hair's worth of anything from anyone."

The lamp was smoking. Its feeble, lifeless glow lit only the bed and bony Zelmenyaner faces. The entire room lay in darkness. All at once Bubbe Bashe gave a powerful shudder and threw back her head. There was a hush. Was she still alive? Just then she opened her eyes and said clearly:

"I'm starving!"

She wanted to eat one more time before she died.

His usual noble self, Uncle Folye got irately to his feet, spat, and left the room with a slam of the door. It looked like trouble was brewing.

Aunt Malkaleh knew just what to do. Grabbing a knife, she sliced some bread and brought it to Bubbe Bashe. The dying woman opened her mouth a little wider than necessary and even tried to chew, but it was too much for her to get down.

She was late for her own last meal.

♦ ♦ ♦

A while later, she died for good.

Aunt Gita performed the last rites, shutting Bubbe Bashe's eyes and snatching the bread from her gums before anyone could laugh. Everything was done according to custom. As soon as Bereh went to sleep, the women had a good cry so as not to hurt the corpse's feelings. Their emotionless tears fell as dully as raindrops on a windowpane.

That's how Zelmenyaners cry.

♦♦♦ *Part Two*

♦♦♦ *Chapter 1*

A PROLOGUE CONCERNING A SPOON

What he went through in the Great War went unrecorded. In the long, dark trenches, as in the freedom of the rear lines, he could be seen—generally in the vicinity of the nearest field kitchen—waiting expectantly, a hairy soldier in a stiff greatcoat and a ragged fur hat. Although he had more than once lost his rifle, he was never without the wooden spoon that he kept tucked into his bootleg, his most precious weapon of the war.

He acquired it early on, on a hot summer day in 1914.

One after another, packed troop trains pulled out of the railway station of the large city. Military berets bobbed across the platforms in waves like flocks of locusts, swarming through the white underpasses and clinging to the roofs and buffers of the cars.

Vast, faceless, incomprehensible masses of men crowded the long, steadily departing trains.

Suddenly he spied through the window, standing in a corner, a peasant selling wooden spoons. A sixth sense told him to jump from the car, pick out the largest spoon, and tuck it into his boot.

It might come in handy one day.

Such simple, practical thoughts were second nature to him.

At the first rest stop, stuck without a cup, he drank his tea from the spoon and stared with cold scorn at the men laughing at him while thinking the same simple thought:

It might come in handy one day.

Far from the front, in a peaceful railroad station, before the first engagements with the enemy had taken place, he was already schooling himself in the ways of war.

You had to give him credit.

During the long years of the war, he came to love his spoon. He loved it the way a man loves a valuable tool that has gotten him out of many a tight spot. By the time it was old and black and broken at the handle, no bigger or cleaner than the palm of his hand and hardly still a spoon at all, it had done more for him than any spoon in the world had ever done for anyone.

He had raked potatoes from campfires with it. He had eaten snow with it. He had belted his army pants with it when their last button fell off. He had scratched his back with it beneath his shirt collar. He had spooned castor oil, vodka, and plain water down his throat with it. He had dug trenches with it. Once he had even rented it out for a single meal in exchange for a thick slice of bread.

And it had introduced him, his black old spoon, to his closest buddy.

One night he was sitting exhaustedly in a trench. He sat with his back against the damp earth, head slumped forward, counting what might be his last moments. Suddenly, a soldier jumped into the trench with a bowl of hot soup. Gripping it between his knees, he began to eat hungrily.

The owner of the spoon dipped it into the bowl, too.

It was a dangerous and dramatic moment. In stubborn silence he bore the unnaturally long, bemused stare of the soldier with the bowl. Then they went on eating together.

Afterward, the soldier asked in a deep, quiet voice:

"What's your name?"

"Bereh Khvost," was the answer.

It was indeed our Bereh, Reb Zelmele's grandson. Had he not bought the spoon he would never have met Porshnyev, his future friend and mentor.

When the soup was finished, Porshnyev carefully took Bereh's spoon from him and tossed it aside. Then he took out some tobacco and laid it in Bereh's lap.

"Have a smoke. Are you a worker?"

"Yes. A tanner."

"Do you belong to a party?"

Chapter 2

BEREH IN REB ZELMELE'S YARD

The Red Army cavalry, having advanced far ahead of the infantry in a bold maneuver, was now operating behind Polish lines in a region of heavy swamps. The enemy had no answer to its sudden, demoralizing attacks.

The cavalry was well trained for mounted engagements. Yet it disliked fighting on foot and was poor at it, especially in large formations on broad fronts. It had no stomach for night fighting, either, having had little experience at it, and its men were poor marksmen who preferred closing with cold steel on horseback.

Which was why its commanders preferred marching at night and fighting by day.

Nights were spent on the move.

Once, after falling asleep in its saddles, a Red division unexpectedly turned up seventy miles behind the front. This explained the weak resistance met by the main Russian army along the old eastward-facing German trench line, since every rumor of Bolshevik cavalry sweeping down from the north forced the Poles to shift their forces to meet it.

These night marches ended in groggy battles. They would never forget the attack on Swiêciany or their foray into the streets of Vilna.

It was then that Bereh learned to ride and sleep at the same time.

♦ ♦ ♦

A man rides in darkness through unknown countryside. The horse beneath him rocks softly and warmly. The reins held loosely in one hand, he sits in his canvas saddle, carefully shuts his eyes, and feels the thrill of knowing he is asleep.

Sometimes a deep, familiar voice, Porshnyev's, says quietly:

"Berke!"

"What?"

"Are you sleeping?"

"Yes."

And a mile later, more softly yet:

"Have you been sleeping all this time?"

"No. Only since we passed the mill."

Afterward, in the cold dawn, he awakes with a start and feels rested. His mild Zelmenyaner eyes open wide and take in the distances around him. Pale shades of white and rose gleam through a foggy spring morning. Nearby, in a dewy bush, a bird lets out a chirp, having also, so it seems, slept upright all night on its branch.

♦ ♦ ♦

The Zelmenyaners went off to war and disappeared there. Some were quietly given up for dead. About others there were different opinions. Eventually, they too were forgotten.

Uncle Folye was forgotten the soonest, since no one doubted his death for a moment. This made him irritable in the first days after his return from Austria.

As for Bereh, his fate was hotly debated. Uncle Itshe's family was sure he was alive. Uncle Zishe's maintained that he was, sad to say, no longer in this world.

Stroking his beard, Uncle Zishe would declare:

"Enough weeping and wailing! It's time to get over him."

It was a slow, patient battle, conducted without acrimony in low tones and empty phrases, its real points made with a glance or an eloquent wave of the hand.

♦ ♦ ♦

Winter.

As if carved from the icy air, the buildings of the yard stood etched against the snow. The sun was setting, its cold, rosy rays glancing sharply off the snow from the blue gleam of a frigid sky. The pure light streamed through the frosty windows into the rooms, as calm and serene as a Zelmenyaner's stare.

The winter day gripped the yard like a door latch.

A frozen Aunt Malkaleh walked in on Uncle Zishe as he was relaxing with his disassembled watches.

It was as quiet as a watchmaker's generally is. The hands of the clocks on the walls told the time. The pendulums ticked off the silence.

Aunt Malkaleh informed Uncle Zishe that Yankev Boyez's daughter-in-law, while visiting her parents' graves in Kremenchug, had seen Bereh enter a tall building.

Yankev Boyez's daughter-in-law ran to the building and shouted up the stairs:

"Bereh, regards from home!"

The reason Bereh didn't answer, Aunt Malkaleh was sure, was that he was already inside some room. She gave Uncle Zishe's rectangular face a stern look. Did he or did he not admit that regards were regards?

Uncle Zishe listened coldly with the placid mien of a Zelmenyaner, resolving for the umpteenth time to hold his tongue. In spite of himself, however, he couldn't help asking pointedly:

"Why would he enter a tall building?"

♦ ♦ ♦

Winter. The black beams of the houses protruded from the heavy snow like old bones. The snow had a rosy rinse.

The cold winter day gripped the yard like a door latch.

Uncle Itshe hurried in from the street with the latest news:

"Bereh's in Mozyr!"

Some coachmen there had seen him on a horse.

"Why would he be on a horse?" asked a wintry Uncle Zishe.

Preoccupied, he turned back to his eyepiece, struggling to maintain his fatal theories of whose accuracy he could no longer be sure.

Uncle Zishe, if truth be told, was a watchmaker. Like all watchmakers, he had many thoughts while examining his watches. Nor did he trust Itshe or his family, least of all Bereh, who didn't strike him as the type to get through a war by dodging bullets.

Soon after this, Uncle Zishe came back from synagogue with news of his own.

Signaling Uncle Itshe with a wink through the window, he made him promise to keep it a secret before informing him that Bereh had been hanged.

Uncle Itshe ran his hand over his face and bit the heel of it, the tears gushing as from a fountain. He was obliged to cry silently, for Uncle Zishe wagged a stern finger at him and said:

"Keep your promise, Itshke, keep your promise!"

Bereh was now the late lamented.

Uncle Zishe instructed the yard to keep the news from Aunt Mal-kaleh, it being customary to make mothers wait a decent interval before informing them of their sons' deaths. Uncle Itshe went along with this. All winter he walked around with damp eyes and a scraggly, foolish-looking beard that he alone knew was meant to be a mourner's.

Once, seated listlessly beside Uncle Zishe, he asked:

"But Zishe, what did they hang him for?"

Although Uncle Itshe's only motive for asking was despair, Uncle Zishe threw him a suspicious look. Convinced that someone had put his needle-pushing brother up to it, he shrugged and said nothing.

Yet the swindle couldn't last forever.

One night in late winter, when the yard was sopping wet from the first spring rains, Velvel the Hebrew teacher's son knocked on Uncle Itshe's door. He had come to bring regards, he said. He had run into Bereh the night before in the railroad station in Smolensk and had even been given a red apple by him.

Uncle Itshe stood in the yard amid a circle of Zelmenyaners and related:

"It's like this. Velvel the Hebrew teacher's son was sitting in the Smolensk station, smoking a cigarette. Suddenly he saw Bereh stand-ing there, eating an apple. Of course, he ran to him. 'Bereh,' he said, 'is it you? Everyone thinks you're dead.' Bereh had no idea why anyone would think that." (This was a swipe at Itshe's brother the watchmaker.) "He was thrilled to get news of us and asked about everyone, and then he took an apple from his pocket, a big one, and told Velvel:

"'This is for my papa and mama!'"

Uncle Itshe was uncommonly excited.

The next morning, it was settled for good. The dark, wet beams of the low rooms were still soaking up the first drops of spring sunshine when Uncle Zishe stepped out on his balcony with his eyepiece, took a look at the warm, cheerful sky, and conceded defeat.

♦ ♦ ♦

The apple lay for a few days in a plate on the table. It was a red, winter-storage apple with a thick peel, a short, thick stem, and a winey smell that filled the room. Everyone touched its cool peel and lifted it by the stem while thinking of Bereh and his exploits on the battlefield.

For those few days, the whole yard dreamed of him. Suddenly he was seen as the rising star of the family, which until then was headed downhill.

But what did Uncle Itshe care about that?

One rainy night Itshe, not being a man of vision, said thoughtfully to Aunt Malkaleh as the two of them were sitting alone:

"What do you say, Malkaleh? Shall we eat the apple?"

At first Aunt Malkaleh had her qualms.

"Don't you think it would be a shame, Itshe?"

Nevertheless, she brought a knife, and Uncle Itshe sliced the apple into two equal halves.

♦ ♦ ♦

That same night a regiment of cavalry rode through town on its way to the Polish front.

It was pouring rain. In the darkness, Bereh's squadron was barely able to cover the last three miles of the Dolhinov highway. Off to the left, the horizon was dotted with thousands of city lights.

Bereh sat on his horse, hunkered down inside his collar, gazing at the glowing arc of the city. The only sounds were the clop of hooves in the warm mud, the deep snorts of the horses, and a familiar voice to his right that said quietly:

"Berke!"

"What?"

"Are you sleeping?"

"No."

And a while later, more softly yet:

"How come?"

Bereh muttered something beneath his wet mustache. A man of frightfully few words, he said nothing about having been born in the city they were passing or about his old parents who still lived there, to whom he had just sent regards and a big winter apple from Smolensk.

Chapter 3

ADVENTURES ON THE ROAD WITH BEREH

The cavalry traveled on foaming horses.

It traveled with greatcoats smelling of smoke, with tousled hair singed by fire.

It spent the night riding through the Grodno Forest. Silhouetted on the hilltops along the horizon were the pointed helmets of its reconnaissance patrols, their bayonets frosty against the starry sky.

Grodno was taken.

The beaten remains of the Polish forces retreated down the foggy, birch-lined roads in their wagon trains. Gray peasants stood by burned-out huts, sucking on their pipes while regarding the havoc wreaked on their world with a morose and sleepy tedium.

The Russians' "mounted infantry" roamed everywhere. It surged suddenly from forests, galloped through city streets, forded rivers, hacked like a sword at the enemy's left flank.

The wretched strip of land between the Dvina and the Vistula with its forests, swamps, and rivers now glittered with the icy glint of the cavalry's sabers.

The countryside crawled with thousands of soldiers, army vehicles, and long, slow wagon trains that crept as though out of the earth.

Gray peasants watched from burned huts, recalling with a morose and sleepy tedium their warm stoves that had gone up in flames.

His regiment had nearly reached Bialystok. At a railroad station outside a small town, Bereh's squadron stopped to rest.

♦ ♦ ♦

Who knows what made Bereh go into town?

You might blame Porshnyev, a heavy smoker who thought Bereh might find some tobacco there. Presumably, the squadron retreated in good order when the town was retaken by the Poles (Porshnyev even salvaged Bereh's horse), because it was later decorated for an assault on Polish infantry positions beyond Lomza.

Bereh was so freakishly trapped behind Polish lines that it happened before he knew it.

He had walked into town down a birch-lined road in such a good mood that he nearly burst into song. He wandered through the marketplace, had a look at the shops, and decided there was still time for a haircut.

The town barber happened to be deaf. In the gathering dusk he cut Bereh's hair, shaved him, and plastered hot, wet towels on his face.

He was too deaf to hear time pass.

By the time Bereh rose to go, the town had fallen into a deep stupor, as though shut down behind lock and key.

Everything was so quiet and withdrawn that even the houses stuck too far into the streets.

Down a street leading to the railway station trotted a Polish patrol.

Bereh ducked into an alleyway, knocking on shut doors in the hope that one of them might open.

Suddenly, nearing a corner, he heard the slow, massive drumming of hooves. The enemy was approaching.

Without stopping to think, he gave the first gate a push. It opened and he found himself in a yard.

♦ ♦ ♦

The yard belonged to a baker. Through a small, grimy window, Bereh saw a flickering fire and a little Jew in an apron bending to slide loaves into an oven.

It was clear at once that the baker was a shrewd one. You could see it in the way he put a finger to his mouth to silence his wife and daughter. Taking Bereh by the sleeve, he let him to a dark stable.

"Young man," he said, "if they find you here, I knew nothing about it."

Bereh was now a fugitive in the stable.

In the darkness, he smelled roosting hens. Growing accustomed to the gloom, he made them out in a corner, huddled on a horizontal pole. The drowsing birds emitted little peeps as if talking chicken talk in their sleep.

Everything was dark and musty.

It was nighttime when the baker's daughter entered the stable.

"Here, have some bread."

In the morning she brought him a pot of soup. He ate it gratefully and sat waiting for his lunch, left forlornly alone with the old roof beams and the speckled hens that pecked at his boots. Lying on his stomach, he plucked hairs from his mustache and thought of Porshnyev, the carefree young soldier who rode on his right.

—Berke! Are you sleeping?

On his stomach in the stable, Bereh missed his friends.

An autumn night in the fields. The rain pours down from low clouds. The wet horses stand in the darkness. They sit, the whole gang of them, around a campfire: Krivosheyev, Porshnyev, Mitrosian, Andrey, and the others. Potatoes are baking in the coals. After a while, Porshnyev begins to sing. They huddle around him, the rain running in rivers down their sleeves, dripping from their whiskers and wild hair . . .

Bereh missed them.

Toward evening, he heard the baker puttering in the yard. The Jew checked his locks and latches and fiddled with the shutters. The sounds made the musty silence, broken only by the peeps of hens, even thicker.

Late at night, the baker, bare chested (only now, so it seemed, did he have time to leave his oven), appeared in the stable with a bundle of clothes.

"Here, young man. Put these on and come to the house."

Soon Bereh was seated at a brightly lit table in a faded jacket that was too small and a corduroy cap like those worn by well-off Jews to Sabbath services.

The oven bathed half the room in a golden glow. The little baker was tending it again, sliding trowels and baking boards in and out.

"Here, have a bagel to chew on, young man!"

Bereh chewed on a hot, brown bagel that he took from a pile while glancing furtively at the baker's daughter. Seated at the table, she smelled of caraway seed.

"Make yourself at home, young man . . ."

"Young man, have a glass of tea . . ."

After a while, the baker turned to his daughter:

"Leitshe, why aren't you reading?"

Leitshe went back to her book.

The fire crackled in the oven. Dirty streams of sweat ran down the baker's dark beard to his bare chest. His reedy voice sighed and sputtered, lamenting the looted shops in the marketplace while the boards and trowels flew in and out. A town full of Jews reduced to penury by the Poles!

A sputtering sigh of a baker.

Suddenly, as if to make sure he wasn't wasting his time, he gave Bereh a sideways look. In a less ingratiating tone, he asked if the young man had a wife.

Bereh sipped his tea, stared at the saucer, and held his tongue like a true Zelmenyaner.

The baker slid another trowel of bagels into the oven.

"What's keeping you? You must have a father and mother, no? And they must have a little nest egg put away for you, no? And am I wrong to suppose you have a bit of schooling and can say a blessing in Hebrew?"

Bereh nodded.

"I suppose you can make a living, can't you? Tell me, young man, what is it that you do?"

"I'm a tanner."

"A tanner, are you? Well, what's keeping you? You must have a few rubles salted away somewhere, no? You won't end up without a shirt on your back, will you? With God's help you'll return from the war in good health and want to start a family, isn't that so? So what's keeping you? May we all live a long life, but might I ask how old you are?"

"Thirty-two."

"Thirty-two?" The baker slid a trowel into the oven. "You're the right age, in your prime. My Leitshe is exactly ten years younger. For shame, young man, for shame! At your age I was an old married man . . ."

Nevertheless, Bereh slept in the stable that night, too. (An odd fellow, the baker, housing his future son-in-law in a stable!)

In the morning, he was invited for another glass of tea.

His future mother-in-law was wearing a new kerchief. Bereh sat by the samovar, facing Leitshe. Their minds were blank. Leitshe felt faint. She knew she should say something but didn't know what.

Just then the sleepy-faced, rumple-bearded baker jumped back from the oven. Holding up his long underwear with one hand, he danced around the room and declared:

"What do you call this? A young man sits with a young lady, two unmarried children—you'd think they'd laugh or joke a bit, the way it's done nowadays. Not that I know anything about it, but they say the young folk sing together, chew sunflower seeds, even smooch a bit . . ."

He opened the curtain on the window and peered out.

"Why don't you two go for a walk? It's a nice day. You can sit on the grass and talk about books, or the birds and the bees, the way it's done nowadays, all lovey-dovey. You're young, act your age!"

That afternoon, Bereh and Leitshe went for a walk out of town. Leitshe, smelling fragrantly of soap, walked pressed against him with hot cheeks, spinning a web of love. Around them the rosy air flowed down the sandy road all the way to the green fields below them.

They stopped on a wooden bridge that crossed a river, leaning on its birch-branch railing while looking at the water. Leitshe pulled a handful of sunflower seeds from her pocket.

"Here," she said. "Have some."

He smiled at her warmly, taking her in with his quiet Zelmenyaner eyes, which only now noticed how close she stood. It was early summer. With Zelmenyaner sangfroid, he took some sunflower seeds and asked:

"Do you know where this road leads?"

"To Volkovisk."

"And from there?"

"To Slonim."

"And from Slonim?"

"To Lida."

"It runs all the way to Vilna, doesn't it?"

"Yes. To Vilna."

He gazed thoughtfully at the river. The water was clear all the way down. A silver perch hovered in it peacefully, as though nailed to one place.

Leitshe asked:

"Have you ever had a love affair?"

"No."

"Then you can have one now."

She said it in an oddly soft voice, frightened by her own words. He gave her a quick, meaningful, sideways glance.

"Well?"

"Well what?" he asked.

"Why don't you kiss me?"

♦ ♦ ♦

Toward evening, they walked back into town. Leitshe leaned on his arm, like a wife on a new husband. All of a sudden he said:

"I'm heading out tonight."

"What?"

"Tonight," Bereh said. "I'm heading out."

The sun set, gilding the pickets of the fences and the little windows of the houses. A lamp was lit in one of them. Ruvn the baker (that was his name, Ruvn) stood by the front gate, stroking his beard impatiently.

He was thinking lovey-dovey thoughts.

As soon as the young couple appeared in the street, he ran to greet them, a smile on his pitifully anxious face:

"Had a good time, eh?"

♦ ♦ ♦

Late that night, before Bereh left town, there was a bitter quarrel at the baker's.

The baker claimed Bereh was running out on him and demanded a public explanation. The neighbors were barely able to rescue the hapless Zelmenyaner from his blows.

"Let her tell her story!" Ruvn screamed. "Leitshe, speak up!" But Leitshe ran from the room and refused to say a word about Bereh's advances. In that case, the baker insisted, his wife would bear witness. A woman knew about such things.

Leitshe's mother, however, was quite incapable of saying anything that made sense.

Bereh didn't stop to catch his breath until he was on the other side of town. Still wearing the corduroy cap, he wiped the sweat with his sleeve as though he had just fought a fierce cavalry engagement.

◆ ◆ ◆

It was a vast, black night.

From somewhere along the road came the sound of water gurgling over rocks. A warm breeze brushed the branches. The earth breathed freely. Even the sand, the moist, sandy road, smelled good.

The creak of a branch crossed the fields like a sigh.

Bereh followed the road, his feet sinking into the sand. Dim shapes emerged from the darkness: fences, bushes, trees. By the roadside, an oak tree stood sketched in ink against the sky like its own black shadow. Beneath it, someone stood without moving.

Bereh knew who it was.

"Leitshe."

She took a bag from the shawl she was wrapped in

"Bereh, here. Take some bagels for the road."

Then he was gone, swallowed up in thick darkness.

♦♦♦ *Chapter 4*

MORE ADVENTURES WITH BEREH
ON HIS WAY HOME

Getting anyone to talk about Bereh's journey home isn't easy. It remains a gap in his biography. Zelmenyaners, as is known, don't speak to one another, so that anything gleaned is tenth-hand information.

Bereh himself keeps mum.

Nevertheless, a form he filled out on joining the police tells us that he followed the highway to Grodno, and from there to Vilna and Molodechno before doubling back through Radoshkovich to Minsk. A copy of this document was discovered by Uncle Yuda's Tsalke while searching for old amulets behind one of his late Uncle Zishe's eternally ticking clocks.

Uncle Yuda's Tsalke is one of the new breed of scholars. His special interest is old religious texts. If you ever come across anyone hanging from a shelf beneath the ceiling where women's prayer books have been left to molder, it's sure to be Tsalke. He's such a bungler that they say about him in the yard, "Well, it figures. Every time he spits, it lands on his face."

Uncle Yuda's Tsalke retrieved the document from the back of the clock and ran to his room like a dog slinking behind a fence with a bone. Then he went over it with a fine-tooth comb.

Bereh had written:

". . . in the stable. When the baker wanted me to marry his daughter, we fought all night. That same night I left for Krinitsa. From Krinitsa it was a day's walk to Buczacz. From Buczacz I walked to Nozerovo. From Nozerovo I walked to Diatly. From Diatly I walked to Hayduchok. From Hayduchok I walked to a village named Drozdovo. From Drozdovo I walked to Bistrich. From Bistrich I walked to Ivye. From Ivye I walked to Sokolka. In Sokolka I went to see my mother's uncle, who lives on the main street and deals in horses. I had no food but the bagels given me by the baker's daughter Leitshe and in Drozdovo I ate the last one. And so I went to ask my uncle for something to eat, but he drove me away. Not that I minded, because he acted like a kulak. From Sokolka I walked to Radom. From Radom I walked to Pilnevo. After leaving Pilnevo I was very hungry and came to a field where a peasant was plowing. He gave me some bread and a big piece of lard and pointed out a stream I could drink from. From Pilnevo I walked on a full stomach to Zhetl. From Zhetl I walked to Damir. After Damir I reached the city of Grodno. In Grodno I worked for two days chopping wood and walked to Novaredok. From Novaredok I walked to Voronovo. From Voronovo I walked to Landvorovo. It was raining heavily there. From Landvorovo I walked until I saw Vilna in the distance. A red-headed boy was driving a wagon full of bricks and I asked him who controlled the city. He said it was the Whites, which made me so mad that I walked through town without talking to anyone, even though I was starving. From Vilna I walked to Vileyka. (There are two Vileykas— this was the crazy one.) From Vileyka I took the paved road to Kena. From Kena I walked to Gudogai. From Gudogai I walked to Soly. I walked to Oshmia. . . . [Illegible]. . . . walked. . . . Smorgon. From Smorgon I walked to Mikhnevich, where I ran into you. As you know, we walked from there to Zashkevich. From Zashkevich we walked to Perevoz. From Perevoz we walked to Logovoyo. There, while we were swimming in the Viliya, you told me how you charged the Poles to rescue my horse, which was tied to a fence. In Logovoyo we joined up with our forces and the commissar sent me to Molodechno. From Molodechno . . ."

That was all.

Night after night, Tsalke sat studying this document. A lengthy investigation revealed that Aunt Malkaleh had no relations in Sokolka and that her only cousin, Uncle Ora, lived in Ekaterinoslav* and was a butcher, not a horse dealer. Moreover, not all the towns that Bereh mentioned were where they should have been. Further research suggested that the entire document was unreliable.

Tsalke removed his glasses from his nose, wiped the lenses thoroughly, and said out loud to himself:

"Nothing adds up. It's all one big bluff."

Everyone knew that Uncle Yuda's Tsalel had a good head on his shoulders. If given half the chance, he could have disproved his own existence.

Actually, the document added up well enough, the proof being that Bereh had turned up again one summer day in Minsk.

He walked right into the yard. There was a great outcry when he entered his parents' home. Everyone came running, even Uncle Zishe. Bereh sat himself down, slowly pulled off his boots, and said to Aunt Malkaleh:

"Mama, give me something to eat!"

He sat there wolfing it down with savage haste while staring at the ceiling. Uncle Yuda spat and walked off. Gradually, the others drifted away, too. Bereh finished eating, pulled on his boots, and went back to fighting the war.

---

* **Ekaterinoslav**—unlike all the Belorussian and Polish towns mentioned in Bereh's travelogue, Ekaterinoslav is in faraway Ukraine.

♦♦♦ *Chapter 5*

THE POND

Bereh found a job with the police. First, though, he came home from the front, crawled onto his parents' hard couch, and spent several months sound asleep like a sloth beneath his tattered army coat.

Next, without warning, he married Uncle Yuda's Khayaleh and brought her two buckets of water a day, balanced on a shoulder yoke, in return for a peaceful life. Apart from him, Khayaleh acquired some domestic skills and a cat.

Bereh's life was indeed peaceful.

It was at about this time that the pillars of Reb Zelmele's yard began to totter. Subsequently, they crumbled and collapsed. Throughout those wretched years, Bereh hounded the poor Zelmenyaners like a stranger.

What happened in the yard in those years? Actually, nothing at all.

Perhaps the yard was already dead. Nothing new happened in it. All it did was suck in rumors like air, gnawing on them like a man without an appetite.

The death of Uncle Zishe turned out to be the yard's last important event. Now it lay as still as a riverbed whose waters have been diverted. The revolution had passed it by, taken whom it needed and discarding the rest like broken eggshells.

To what might the yard have been compared?

The yard might have been compared to a stagnant old pond. A green scum covered it beneath the drooping branches of trees. The air was dank and malarial. Even the golden carp that sometimes wriggled in the slime left only a fleeting wrinkle in its thick, green crust.

♦ ♦ ♦

There wasn't much point, then, in Tonke and Falke's coming home one starry dawn from their far city.

What on earth made them do it?

The yard welcomed them sadly with a jammed window, a caved-in section of roof, and an empty bottle of kerosene.

All that morning, the formerly eloped whippersnaps wandered about the yard full of wonder. Remote and silent, their faces creased by the wind, they stared at the bearded Zelmenyaners as though at the remnants of an ancient race. Although it may only be gossip, Tonke was reported to have exclaimed:

"Don't tell me you're all still alive!"

The Zelmenyaners, it seemed, should have died long ago.

The yard burned with curiosity. The bearded elders went about on tiptoe, glancing at the whippersnaps from under shaggy brows, waiting for them to shower their poor cousins with the gifts and gold coins that they must have brought back with them.

It didn't take long to discover that the two of them, glory be, were flat broke. To make matters worse, they were living in sin. Their much-discussed announcement of their marriage had been a hoax, a joke played on the cobwebbed notions of Reb Zelmele's yard, which still expected such things of its children.

And yet while the hoax, it was said, had been Tonke's idea, Falke, that big nothing, was so taken by it that he actually offered to pay alimony for the child Tonke had had by another man.

"God! You could die just thinking of it!"

The tiny child that Uncle Zishe's Tonke brought back from afar that starry dawn was indeed most un-Jewish-looking. Falke was haggard, with the blank stare of a man who has seen too much. On an arm like a convict's was tattooed a ship's anchor entwined by a snake.

This tattoo led to wild surmises. At first it was said that Falke had killed someone. Then the story made the rounds that he had gone to sea. Anyone asking him was told:

"Mind your own business!"

Or else:

"Keep your nose out of this!"

The yard was so shocked that it stopped talking. That's Zelmenyaners for you. Then the talk began again in low voices. Tongues dying to wag waited for a hairy ear, cupped by a comic hand, to press against them. The grim facts about Uncle Zishe's daughter were whispered:

"No woman ever got pregnant, uncle, from saying her bedtime prayers."

A few days of such rumors and several near strokes was all it took for the truth to sink in. Tonke smoked too much, drank too much, and spawned bastards. As for Falke, the big nothing had a shameful love affair with a certain Kondratyeva to account for.

◆ ◆ ◆

Uncle Yuda's Tsalke roamed the yard, eager to launch a thorough inquiry into the story of Tonke's child. Thin as a board from unrequited love, he went from room to room making sure no kind word was said about his beloved. He didn't even shy from spending an entire evening with Aunt Gita, quietly drumming it into her:

"You'll see. Tonke will come to no good end."

Or:

"She's in thick with the Bolsheviks. You'll see."

Aunt Gita didn't hear a word Tsalke said. She sat mumbling her evening prayers.

Tsalke wasn't at all nice to Tonke. Perhaps he deserved to be forgiven, having earlier that spring torn up the yard's paving to plant a flower garden. Everyone knew it was a memorial for the summer day when he and Tonke went for a swim in the river.

All summer long Tsalke sat in his garden on a low bench and thought. From their windows, the Zelmenyaners pointed mocking fingers at him.

"What a birdbrain! All because Zishe's daughter won't give him the time of day."

"Just look at him! It all comes from too much education."

Tsalke brooded. He tagged after Falke, the official father of Tonke's child, trying to worm his way into his good graces. He spent whole evenings at Aunt Gita's, shrouded in the smoke of his own cigarettes while rocking a stranger's baby as though it were a remedy for heartbreak.

Finally, standing with Falke by the window in the quiet of dusk, Uncle Yuda's Tsalke made some headway. The two had a long, man-to-man talk. Most of it was conducted by breathing silently while tracing patterns with their fingers on the windowpane.

"Did Tonke ever say anything about me?"

"No."

"Never?"

"Not as far as I remember."

"Try remembering more."

"There isn't any more."

It was late autumn. The heavy, gray days had a muffled sound, like a cracked jar when it's tapped. The last blood-drenched colors of the vanished summer glanced dully off the windowpanes.

Tsalke took a walk, making his way past the narrow streets of the city and following the plowed earth to the river where once, at summer's end, Tonke had gone for a swim. Amid faded fields, by the dull, foggy river, he felt mournfully uplifted. Raising an arm toward the flowing water, he exclaimed:

"Don't think I'm not still in love!"

The whites of his eyes darkened. In the misty fields, he was careful not to mention Tonke's name. Who knew whether he might not say something bad about her?

Afterward, dead to the world, he lay for weeks in his crazy father's empty room. Across from him, a large nail stuck out from the dusty wall. Carved in the dust, as if still hanging there, was the shape of Uncle Yuda's fiddle.

Tsalke lay in bed sighing. The dull autumn light barely pierced the grimy windowpane. All evening, in a hoarse, devout voice, he warbled love songs that he knew by heart from a volume of Heine.

Uncle Yuda's Tsalel, it appeared, had fallen ill. He floundered in the half-light like a golden carp in a stagnant pond, burning with fever. Suddenly, he sat up in bed and wondered:

"Can it be she thinks me politically unreliable?"

Tears came to his eyes. Sitting in his nightshirt with his hands hugging his knees, he burst into sobs.

Afterward, he went to the window to see if the green-shaded lamp at Aunt Gita's was lit. The lamp was Tonke's. Its green glow in the window meant she was at home, carrying her baby back and forth or standing by the table, bent over a pile of papers on which she drew lines and wrote little figures.

The lamp wasn't lit.

♦ ♦ ♦

What might the yard have been compared to?

The yard might have been compared to a stagnant old pond. A green scum covered it beneath the drooping branches of the trees. The air was dank and malarial. Even the golden carp that sometimes wriggled in the slime left only a fleeting wrinkle in its thick, green crust.

Chapter 6

THE UNCLES: THE FOUR PILLARS OF
REB ZELMELE'S YARD

UNCLE ZISHE

Newly deceased. Although sometimes he still appears to Aunt Gita in her dreams, she too is of the opinion that he is no longer in this world. All things point to his having passed on for good.

UNCLE YUDA

Uncle Yuda was a philosopher, and his thoughts, like those of all philosophers, were born from sorrow. When Aunt Hesye, the love of his life, was killed suddenly, the shock drove him to cogitate. Yet the less said about Aunt Hesye the better, as her death was not a nice one.

Naturally, Uncle Yuda began his philosophizing by reflecting on divine providence. That's what philosophers do.

One night soon afterward, while holding forth from Uncle Zishe's balcony, Uncle Yuda made an obscene gesture at God that turned the entire yard against him. Subsequently, he quarreled with the Zelmenyaners and even spurned the Soviet Union's electricity. One thing led to another until he absconded from the yard one winter night and disappeared.

Thus it was that the Zelmenyaners lost their last contact with Pure Reason.

◆ ◆ ◆

This happened during the great collectivization campaign. After some hard wandering, Uncle Yuda found a job as a night watchman in a small kolkhoz, to which was added something else that bore no official title. It was a new line of work, halfway between a kolkhoznik's and a small-town rabbi's. Although Uncle Yuda smelled of hay and was now nearly a collective farmer, he was still, as it were, a bit wet behind the earlocks.

You might have called him a kolrabbi.

In a word, after some hard wandering, Uncle Yuda became the night watchman of a little kolkhoz. There he was taken under the wing of Reb Yankev Boyez, a frail, burgherly Jew who had moved from the city with his equally refined relatives, all of whom joined the kolkhoz.

They took an instant liking to Uncle Yuda.

"A Jew like us!" they proclaimed. "Let's shove over and make some room for him."

At the three young comrades who protested, they shouted:

"What do you want from him? He's a worker. He's had a hammer in his hands all his life."

Although it was hard to say why, Uncle Yuda took to his new job with determination, being still wet behind the earlocks.

Once, while making his nightly rounds and gazing at the stars, he cautiously experimented with some new thoughts about divine providence. Much to his surprise, the experiment went so well that he resolved to pursue it further.

All night long, Uncle Yuda patrolled the barns and stables. When morning came, he sat on a log at the entrance to the kolkhoz, puffing on his pipe and sending coils of smoke into the air while admonishing the kolkhozniks on their way to the fields:

"Khaim! It looks like you've skipped your morning prayers again."

"Just a minute, Khontshe! What's the big idea of a Jew working on the Sabbath?"

"Kalman Gittels! Are you aware that that fine son of yours in the Komsomol isn't doing the Jews any good?"

In a word: a kolrabbi.

Quietly, in the moonlight shining down on a little kolkhoz on the banks of the Svisloch River, a centaur with a carpenter's head and a rabbi's feet had crept out of the water.

From now on, Uncle Yuda did all he could to act dignified. He walked with his hands folded over his stomach, took his time in the communal bathroom, and once, passing the barns and stables, imagined for a moment that he was the famous Maggid of Kelm.*

He even halted and said to himself with great reverence:

"Rabbi, why don't you sit down and rest?"

Unfortunately, Uncle Yuda's Hebrew was none too good. Having read a few slim Yiddish books in his life didn't qualify him for a kolrabbi's position. When the time came for him to lead the Yom Kippur prayers, some of the older kolkhozniks spat in disgust at his mistakes. This was a bitter blow. Uncle Yuda stopped praying and stood dumbstruck, his bent back turned to the congregation. The thought crossed his mind that he might have to appeal to the carpenter he had been to rescue the rabbi he was not.

Just then, though, white as chalk, Reb Yankev Boyez cried out in a voice frail from fasting:

"Jackasses! Who did you think you were getting for a cantor, the Vilna Gaon?"

The learned Jews quieted down. Yet it was still hard to accept the old carpenter as the last hope of Judaism, especially since, with his spectacles perched on his nose, Uncle Yuda looked like an absent-minded priest.

As matters turned out, he never reached the end of the service. A band of kolkhozniks, red-necked Jews who wouldn't and couldn't have prayed on Yom Kippur if they had to, gathered outside Reb Yankev Boyez's and demanded to know why prayers were being said on a kolkhoz. Just as Uncle Yuda was hitting his soulful stride again, a head was thrust through the window. Centered there like a flowerpot, it asked coarsely:

* **Maggid of Kelm** (an honorific of Moyshe Yitskhok ben Noyekh, 1828–1899)—a famous Torah commentator from Lithuania who resisted the Jewish Enlightenment (the Haskalah) and preached the study of Torah and holiness. The word "maggid" means preacher.

"Reb Yankev Boyez, do you think that sitting there on your ass is going to rebuild the Temple?"

"Riffruffians!" shrilled Reb Yankev Boyez. "Go to the devil!"

But Uncle Yuda's spirits flagged. His mood of sweet ecstasy was gone. Always a touchy type, he began to bolt the Hebrew syllables angrily, mumbling them at breakneck speed. By the time he stepped down from the lectern, a black pall (why hadn't anyone realized what a crazy Jew he was?) lay over everything.

Later, as the fasting kolkhozniks flew home in their black-and-white prayer shawls like a flock of old storks, they snapped at one another:

"We should have known better! Not everything is for a carpenter."

Uncle Yuda, however, kept groping his way in his new vocation.

He might have risen still further—to the rank of High Kolrabbi, for example, or even to that of the wisest of men, Aristotle—had not misfortune, which lies in wait for us all, cast him down and left only his boots as a memento.

UNCLE FOLYE

And what's with Uncle Folye?

Uncle Folye is enjoying the second, Soviet half of his life. After work he sits by his window looking out at the world, strokes his thick mustache, and thinks he's the top Zelmenyaner.

The revolution has washed away all his enemies and their annoying habits. He sits by the window taking revenge on the world and wondering what more pleasant surprises are in store for him.

Uncle Folye is a mean customer. With a quiver of his whiskers he can see right through anyone. Once, a cousin of Aunt Malkeleh's, a bricklayer from Ekaterinoslav, came to stay with her for a while. Uncle Folye's whiskers quivered at first sight, and he took an instant dislike to him.

Uncle Folye is something of an original, a thinker without thoughts. No matter what line you take with him, you're wasting your time. Not only doesn't he understand a thing, he's proud of it.

Pity the poor young comrade who once tried teaching Uncle Folye the ABCs of politics. "Just give me a chance," he said to his friends at work, "and I'll make a new man of him."

The young Komsomol member set to work on Uncle Folye as if curing an old piece of leather. But though he tried talking Folye up and talking Folye down, Folye just sat there on a stool as though at the barber's, fingering his mustache and waiting for the pifflehead to stop.

In the end, the young comrade ran out of patience and told the whole factory what a dunce Uncle Folye was. It was all water off a duck's back. Grinning from ear to ear, Folye said to his old buddy Trokhim:

"So I'm not a shmintellectual, so what? I'm a worker and always will be,"

Uncle Folye is as cold-blooded as an angel. He even has time on his days off for a bit of culture, after first eating and stretching.

In his room, under the ceiling, is a shelf. On the shelf is a book. Uncle Folye takes down this moldy volume, bangs it against the floor to shake off the cobwebs, and sits by the window to look at the illustrations. His whiskers quiver, a sure sign that his mind is hard at work.

The book has a pretty picture. It's of a big fish squirting water in the ocean. Uncle Folye reads loudly and clearly:

"W-h-a-l-e!"

He is seized by a great joy. He wets a finger and turns the thick, moldy pages enchantedly until he comes to some old, bearded tsars in fur hats topped by crucifixes.

Uncle Folye sits there in a trance. He stares at the tsars, makes a funnel of his fist, and examines them through it from all angles. Then he says:

"Got your asses kicked good, didn't you?"

♦ ♦ ♦

Tonke and Falke's homecoming was the talk of the yard. Uncle Folye alone kept aloof from it and spent his evenings at the sports club. French wrestling was all the rage then. Young workers preened their handsome bodies like teenage girls while two-hundred-pound grapplers with low brows, big bellies, and double chins disdainfully regarded the half-baked tyros with beady eyes.

These were famous pros who had tussled on mats all over the world. A hush descended on the gym each time one of them planted his full girth in the middle of the ring, wheezing like an ancient machine, while some strapping youngster, the sweat pouring off him, struggled in vain to budge the behemoth from his place.

"You can do it, kid! He's over the hill!"

"Stop wheezing, you tub of lard!"

Great was the chagrin each time the kid who could do it ended up with his head in the tub of lard's arm lock. A minute later the young contender was flat on his back, his shoulders pinned to the mat in accordance with the laws of the implacable French science.

On this particular evening, the old pros were on the rampage. Having polished off the entire younger generation, they strutted up and down the ring challenging and hooting at the crowd.

That's when it happened.

Uncle Folye got to his feet, a tall, pale man with thick, bristly whiskers. After being taken to the dressing room, where he shed his clothes for a jockstrap, he was ushered up a ramp into the spot-lit ring.

Picture Uncle Folye if you can: a hairy, bony-chested, pigeon-breasted man with long, pincer-like hands. He stood there without moving, one hand on his hip, his whiskers quivering.

The match began.

The old pro tucked in his overflowing belly and lunged at Uncle Folye like a young lion. Uncle Folye, looking half-asleep, reached out with his pincers, seized his opponent by the shoulders, and sent him reeling back.

Uncle Folye, we have said, was a cold-blooded angel.

The old pro let out a roar, grabbed Uncle Folye's cranium, gave it a sharp twist, and prepared to administer the last French rites.

With a sigh, Uncle Folye slipped free.

"Wake up, Folye! You'll catch up on your sleep later!"

"Smash him in the puss!"

"Better to poke his eyes out!"

"Kill the bastard!"

Uncle Folye's long, knotty arms began to revolve like the blades of a windmill. The old pro's shoulders twitched with annoyance. The crowd burst out laughing.

All at once Uncle Folye sprang forward, threw the two hundred pounds of meat to the mat, and crashed down on top of them like a fallen roof beam.

The old pro was pinned.

It was useless for him to protest loudly from underneath Uncle Folye that Folye didn't know what he was doing. Everyone could see he was beaten fair and square.

Uncle Folye dressed, went home, and did his best to keep it a secret.

His mood was grim. Getting into bed, he pulled the blanket over his head as if to conceal the whole matter.

His doleful little wife, ignorant of male psychology, tried to rouse him by repeating:

"Folye, get up and eat something! Folye!"

Folye just lay there with his bones sticking out from under the blanket like the skeleton of a mammoth. He couldn't forgive himself for getting so worked up at the sports club that he risked his neck for a bunch of young whippersnaps.

♦ ♦ ♦

Nevertheless, Uncle Folye stepped into the yard the next morning with every intention of enjoying the world while waiting for the first Zelmenyaner to appear. At last spying Uncle Itshe, who had aged greatly, he strode over to him and declared:

"Listen here, Itshke. They say that your daughter-in-law is ... ahem ..."

Folye tapped his throat in sign language for Tonke's drinking habits.

At first Uncle Itshe hung a bewildered head in shame. However, he recovered quickly. With a fury only he was capable of, he grabbed his brother by the lapel.

"You dumb mutt! I'll have you put in irons!"

The insult to Itshe was a double one. In the first place, Tonke was not his daughter-in-law, even if she and Falke had hung out for a while. And second, ever since Uncle Zishe's death Folye's insolence had become unbearable.

"The man has no fear of God!"

Following this exchange, Uncle Itshe sat down at his old sewing machine, threaded the bobbin, and cursed and spat as he sewed.

The low-ceilinged room was stuffy. It smelled of poverty and disrespect for Uncle Itshe's old age. The family's last pillar, he now had to put up with its joining forces against him. No one came to buy the clothing he clattered away at on his machine, nor was poor Aunt Malkaleh in the best of health.

Aunt Malkaleh stood all day by Uncle Itshe, staring thoughtfully through the window at the street. Her cast-iron pots hung above the stove, their clean white insides facing the room. The cat lay curled in the oven. Aunt Malkaleh listened in silence to the advice that came from all sides.

"Let him get a job at the garment factory!"

Uncle Itshe had never believed he would be treated so shabbily in his old age.

"You old fool!" he was told. "It's time you joined the working class."

♦♦♦ *Chapter 7*

ON TONKE'S CHILD AND
A CERTAIN KONDRATYEVA

After several years of mournful silence, voices were again heard at Aunt Gita's.

In the starry hours of the early morning, Uncle Zishe's Tonke had returned from Vladivostok. She filled the room with a cold draft, bundles, and a baby carriage, at the bottom of which lay a swaddled infant that didn't look Jewish at all.

Fresh air streamed through the opened windows into the stuffy, melancholy room that had ticked softly with the sound of Uncle Zishe's eternally running clocks. Water splashed from a basin onto a female body, and tartly scented young men and women came and went through the glass-paned doors as if in and out of a railroad station.

Aunt Gita kept up her vigil by her curtained window at which, after Uncle Zishe's death, the rabbinic lineage of the Zelmenyaners was wasting away in her.

If not for Aunt Gita, what would still be Jewish around the yard?

Silent, she wielded a male authority. Now and then she was asked about some point of Jewish law, which was understandable considering the dearth of rabbis.

She was old now, with sallow rabbinical lines on her face. The voices in her melancholy room only made her feel feebler than ever.

After a few days, when all the visitors were gone and only Tsalke remained in the quiet room, Aunt Gita rose and took stock of her surroundings as if seeing them for the first time. With growing desperation, she fingered Tonke's bundles.

"Daughter, where are the pillows?"

"I sold them in Vladivostok."

"And the mattress?"

"I left it in Moscow."

The blow was great.

All hope gone, Aunt Gita turned her eyes on Uncle Yuda's Tsalke—or rather, on the child nursing from a bottle in his arms.

"And whose is this?"

"Mine."

"Are you married?"

"No."

That evening Aunt Gita sat by her silent window, wrapping herself in a new layer of dark, pious silence composed of pillows and a stranger's child.

It was her end-of-day farewell to Uncle Zishe's squandered estate and her cold welcome to all the unwanted grandsons who might yet arrive from God knows where to dwell beneath her roof.

♦ ♦ ♦

Tonke went off somewhere.

Watching her leave through the gray window, Uncle Yuda's Tsalke felt a twinge of hate.

He asked himself:

Would the revolution be any the worse off if Aunt Gita were to cash in her last rubles without knowing that Tonke had sold her pillows in Vladivostok?

Those were his thoughts. He was beginning to believe that his beloved was a viper who bit anyone getting in her way and looked down on those less poisonous than herself.

On Tsalke, for example, who more than once in an attic, or clutching a bottle of iodine, had been ready to cash in his last rubles, too.

♦ ♦ ♦

Uncle Yuda's Tsalke carefully put down the sleeping baby and went out to the yard. Half-heartedly, he made the rounds to see what more could be learned about the Vladivostok affair.

Ever since the whippersnaps' return, the workaday yard had ground to a halt. Even the chimneys had stopped smoking. Silent, bearded Zelmenyaners sat with their old wives around plain kitchen tables, idly waiting for more news of the Kondratyeva and Tonke's child.

Uncle Itshe went restlessly from room to room, a piece of thread in his mouth to let it be known he was working. He didn't fool anyone, except perhaps his own wife, Aunt Malkaleh, who was worried, needless to say, about her Falke.

"What good is a cow," she asked, "that dies on you just when you need milk?"

The yard was obsessed with the Kondratyeva. She struck it as a most peculiar creature. One theory even had it that she was a man in disguise, but this was the wild surmise of a crude Zelmenyaner who was not to be taken seriously.

He said it just to get even.

Not that there was any lack of information. The Zelmenyaners extracted memories from Falke like loose threads from a tattered coat. It was just that most of what he told them was already public knowledge, while the mystery of Tonke's child went unclarified.

To tell the truth, Tonke was not well liked.

Some Zalmenyaners were even afraid of her. The short, thin, brooding bricklayer for one, Aunt Malkeleh's newly arrived cousin from the Ukraine, a Jew who liked to eat and who kept a steamer trunk beneath his bed. Spying Tonke for the first time through a window, he stopped chewing long enough to ask:

"Who is that piece of goods in the yard?"

And enveloped in the steam from a large bowl of boiled potatoes, he said with a bitter sigh:

"I don't like the looks of her one bit."

♦ ♦ ♦

What was known about the Kondratyeva?

It was known that somewhere far off, in the cities of Asia, Uncle

Itshe's Falke had taken up with a sort of countess with that name. This Kondratyeva was said to be an ex-aristocrat, or else the daughter of one. When Tonke refused to put up with her, Falke threatened to walk out and pay alimony.

Just what kind of threat paying alimony was, no one could say.

"*Ti mnye nadoyela,*" Falke had said to Tonke, meaning: I've had quite enough of you.

Crimson with indignation, Tonke snapped back—and in Yiddish:

"Say that again!"

"You're a provincial woman."

Tonke lunged at him and gave him two slaps. The poor fellow covered his face with his hands and turned to the wall to await more blows, just as he had done when spanked by Aunt Malkaleh for stealing a cube of sugar as a child.

Ah, Falke, Falke! He had left the yard a hotshot, with a wild mop of hair, an embroidered peasant blouse, and a nose that was always stuffed. Two years later he was back with a tattoo on his arm and the drained look of a man who has seen too much. The first thing he did was wash up in the vestibule. No one could believe it when he rolled up his sleeves. On one arm, slightly above the wrist, were a black anchor and a snake with Russian writing beneath them.

Aunt Malkaleh seized the tattooed arm and wailed:

"Tell me, Folinka, what is this supposed to be? A mother has the right to know."

He yanked it away from her.

"It's a tattoo," he shouted. "What does it look like?"

He also, it was said, had Russian proverbs inscribed all over his body. Most thought it the work of the Kondratyeva. She had thoroughly besotted him.

And to think he had been expected to set the world on fire! He had collected bottles, studied at the Workers Faculty, won a gold medal in the broad jump, been a tailor, a typesetter, a barber, and an electrician. Now, in a funk, he sat in his room stubbornly rocking the baby—for which, like a fool, he paid alimony.

The only person who declined to believe in Falke's downfall was

Uncle Folye's little wife. She stood by her window, holding a pot from the stove and laughing at the gullible Zelmenyaners who couldn't see the hellfire burning inside him.

"Mark my words," she said. "We'll have a bellyful from him yet!"

But who was she, the Kondratyeva?

She was an acquaintance of Tonke's, a forty-plus machine operator from Siberia who had told Falke she was only twenty-seven. It was through Tonke that he met her.

The Kondratyeva, it was agreed, was tall, powdered her face, had pale hands and crow's feet in the corners of her eyes, went all year 'round in a tatty karakul coat, and smelled of paraffin and eau-de-cologne.

The Kondratyeva loved the Jewish people for giving the world the Prophets. Encountering in Falke an offshoot of this noble race, she fell in love with him too.

On the ottoman in her little room, draped in a thousand faded scarves and exuding a thousand scents of cloves, body lotion, rubbing alcohol, and valerian, she had bewitched Falke with her charms until he was mad with insatiable desire.

"What do you think of Zinaida Gippius?" she had asked.

Although Uncle Yuda's Falke had never heard of the Russian symbolist poet, being a Zelmanyaner he answered through his stuffed nose:

"Ochen' nravitsia!"*

"Yes, she's quite a woman," said the Kondratyeva, bowing her pensive old lioness's head until it nearly touched her pale, no longer young arms.

She sniffed a little bottle. The Kondratyeva had a habit of sniffing bottles. For her frequent headaches, she also rubbed her forehead with a little white stone. (Just don't ask me what it was called.) Once, sitting at the table, she also rubbed Falke with it. Although afterward he had trouble opening his eyes, it made his stuffed nose run.

Thus it was, in her fragrant little room, that Falke fell in love, too.

♦ ♦ ♦

* **Ochen' nravitsia!** (Russian)—here: "I like her very much!"

It took a few months for the yard to piece the whole story together. Whether this was really what the Kondratyeva was like was hard to say. Yet be that as it may, so she was imagined by Reb Zelmele's yard and so she was dreamed of during the long winter nights that were haunted by her exotic figure.

The yard nearly vanished beneath mountains of snow. Blizzards swept the city. Night after night, the dry flakes fell like dust from a deep black sky. Snagged on the corners of the houses, the wind grumbled a painless, tuneless complaint.

At such times, you could hear a sleepy voice say to no one in particular:

"Would you believe how she took that pumpkinhead for a ride?"

It was the voice of an elderly Zelmenyaner warming his old bones by the stove while thinking of the countess, the Kondratyeva, who was by now as much part of the Zelmenyaners' lore as Uncle Zishe's clocks and Uncle Folye's doleful wife.

Chapter 8

DEATH AND ILLNESS IN THE YARD

The current of events, having flowed downstream with Uncle Zishe, was now shunted by his vanity into a bog of illnesses. He himself, it has been related, was compelled to end his life by dying.

The yard was beset by death and diseases of all kinds. Until then the Zelmenyaners had gone about departing the world as though performing a simple chore. They had even coined their own expression for it, namely, cashing in one's last rubles.

It was Uncle Zishe who threw a disagreeable kink into this trait, which was then handed down to others in the family. Although no one could say whether she would inherit his peculiar manner of taking leave, his poor health soon reappeared in his daughter Sonya, whose many symptoms testified to its increasingly sophisticated nature.

The sole Zelmenyaner to have had a true talent for dying was Reb Zelmele himself, whose passing, however, left no permanent mark. It might just as well have been written on a slate and erased. Although everyone knew Reb Zelmele had once existed, no one could recall how his existence had ended.

Bubbe Bashe died differently. There was something to be said for her method, too.

For one thing, her death caused no heartbreak. For another, she made it seem as easy as pie. It was like the soft sigh of someone lying down to rest, and if anything was still left of her soul, its departure was no more noticeable than a wisp of smoke from a chimney.

Still, there were those in the yard who thought it a disgrace to have let Bubbe Bashe die so soon when she could have lived longer.

This was the opinion of Uncle Folye's silent little wife, whose long spate of childbearing was followed by an eruption of garrulousness.

Folye's little wife had her own version of Bubbe Bashe's death. Bubbe Bashe had died, she said, not from natural causes but from falling off a table—an act equivalent at her age to jumping from a skyscraper.

Bubbe Bashe, according to Folye's wife, had always liked to tipple. Especially in her later years, her favorite pastime had been lying beneath her blanket while guzzling from a big black flask. That night, the last of her life, she rose from her bed, groped her way in the dark room, searched the drawers in vain, and climbed with her last strength onto the table, from which she managed to open the top compartment of the cabinet. There she found a round demijohn that Reb Zelmele had never gotten around to emptying.

Before she knew it, Bubbe Bashe had fallen from the table and died.

Uncle Folye's wife's account was not uninsidious, since she knew it would not redound to the Zelmenyaners' credit.

Aunt Malkaleh listened in silence, shaking her head as if to say:

"The smaller the heart, the bigger the mouth."

Uncle Itshe, for his part, declared:

"With a bitch for a wife, who needs a long life?"

♦ ♦ ♦

It behooves us to record for future generations a few of the more memorable Zelmenyaner deaths.

There was, for example, a Zelmenyaner named Bendet. He lived not far away, in a village called Krizhenetz, and died highly irregularly. It was wintertime, and Uncle Bendet keeled over in the snow and froze stiff as a board.

Aunt Nekhe, Bendet's wife, was so frightened by this that she moved to the city. Subsequently, she spent her time pondering the paltriness of human life, which led her to befriend Aunt Gita.

Another noteworthy death, a schoolteacher's, occurred on the same street. The man's wife had passed away, and one day he instructed his little charges:

"Children, go tell your fathers to give your tuition money to my daughter."

"Why?" asked the children.

"You'll soon see."

He died as soon as they left the schoolroom. Their fathers saw to his funeral and gave the tuition money to his daughter. This was Esther the penmanship teacher. She too was a friend of Aunt Gita's.

Does no one care that the yard is dying out? That Uncle Yuda's roof is covered with green moss?

The yard is dying out bit by bit. Here a beam, there a wall, there a rafter in the attic.

♦ ♦ ♦

Poor Uncle Zishe ended badly.

Death laid him low like an ax felling a tree. It leaped on him and threw him facedown in the slush. Stretched out to his full length, he lay fanning a dismal graveyard breeze that sent a shiver through everyone.

This was Uncle Zishe's last inconsiderate act.

The worst of it, though, was the smell of the medicines left behind by him. They caused illnesses to crawl out of the woodwork. Even Uncle Folye came down with a toothache.

The first to follow in Zishe's footsteps was Sonya. A true child of her father, she embarked on a via dolorosa of fainting fits while discovering maladies she never knew she had.

♦ ♦ ♦

Shortly after Uncle Zishe's death, Sonya began taking to bed. Her husband Pavel Olshevsky, that rarest of men, used the telephone in the People's Commissariat of Agriculture,* where he worked, to rush doctors to her on house calls.

---

* **People's Commissariat of Agriculture** (Russian: Narkomzem)—the name for the government-level Ministry of Agriculture in the early Soviet period.

The opinion in the yard was that this was a feminine wile, a sure sign that Sonya was spoiled. A closer investigation bore this out.

Sonya, however, let it be known that her fainting fits were no passing episode and derived from a frail constitution like her father's. She also disclosed that she had thrush in her mouth, which aggravated her condition.

These fits had a beauty of their own, a quiet, languorous charm. Each time they made Pavel Olshesvky think that he was about to lose his wife for good. Yet while this was all the more reason for her to swoon in his presence, he couldn't help wondering whether it was all quite genuine.

It was Uncle Itshe, though having enough troubles of his own, who took it upon himself to keep the yard posted on Sonya's health. Going from door to door, he would say with a hitch of his shoulder:

"She's done it again, that flapdoodle!"

Uncle Zishe's Sonya worked at the People's Commissariat of Finance. If truth be told, there was some doubt there whether even thrush in the mouth required so many days of sick leave. Nor, for all her self-absorption, was Sonya able to demonstrate to the doctors' satisfaction that her condition was real. Yet while their skepticism only made her sicker, she went on hoping that her path of sorrows would one day lead her to the professor who would understand what ailed her.

Meanwhile, she was understood by her husband alone. Pavel was gradually acquiring the knack of treating her. It was best done by means of psychology.

This was why, to her chagrin, he forbade pouring cold water on her when she fainted. Tucking her into bed, he gave her a whiff of smelling salts and whispered adoringly into her ear until she came to.

At which point, her condition took a curious turn.

Opening her pale, prominent eyes one day as she regained consciousness, she was so overjoyed to find herself alive, or else so grateful to Pavel, that she grabbed his head in her marvelous hands and remained glued to him in a passionate kiss that lasted forever. Anyone present would have had nothing to do but stare at the wall and smoke a cigarette before dashing out into the street and swearing never again to cross the threshold of a house inhabited by two people suspected of being the least bit in love.

Once, passing Sonya's window at such a moment, Uncle Itshe was made to feel so queasy that he stopped eating for a week.

Another time in Sonya's room, so it was whispered, Uncle Itshe had the fight of his life. It happened while the Zelmenyaners were gathered there to welcome her back from one of her attacks. Suddenly, someone wanted to know why Itshe didn't work in the garment factory.

You may ask what that had to do with Sonya. But in Reb Zelmele's yard, such quarrels broke out unexpectedly, like local thunderstorms.

Uncle Itshe, of course, defended himself tooth and nail. He fought like a panther until in the end he spat with rage and stalked from the room.

Chapter 9

THE LAST TAILOR

Yet one winter night, Uncle Itshe's stubborn resistance was finally broken. Little by little, he was forced to accept the idea of working in the factory.

They were all sitting in the small, warm room—Tonke, Falke, Bereh, and Aunt Malkaleh.

Outside was a frost. Pale heaps of blue snow, as though frozen solid while trying to scale the roof, glittered through the window.

They sat hunched over the table, sipping hot glasses of tea and exchanging terse sentences:

"Join the working class, you silly old Jew!"

"It's time you gave up your tradesman's psychology,* uncle!"

"You've patched old clothes long enough!"

"Nincompoops!" Uncle Itshe retorted. "Can't you see it's all a big swindle? I'm older than you and I've never heard of tailors working in factories."

---

* **Tradesman's psychology**—Uncle Itshe is a self-employed tailor, working as a small tradesman and artisan. Under the New Economic Policy (1921–1928), private enterprise, including small-scale self-employed tailoring, was allowed, only to be replaced by statewide efforts to centralize all spheres of the economy. This class of small-scale tradesmen was then driven to join factories and other outlets of the new centrally planned economy.

"What about America?" asked Falke, berating Uncle Itshe for his ignorance.

"I suppose you've been there! What do you know about America, you imbecile?"

"Why drag in America?" Tonke said. "Go see for yourself. If there's no factory in town, you can tell us we imagined it."

"There's nothing for me to see," Uncle Itshe said with Zelmenyaner obstinacy.

Aunt Malkaleh intervened cautiously. "Are you trying to tell us," she asked, "that you're the only one here with any brains?"

Uncle Itshe turned pale. The campaign against him had gone on for so long that he had run out of clever rejoinders. A little too stubbornly, he had retreated into an elegiac silence for the once majestic trade of tailoring that was declining from day to day. Helplessly searching the room for a sympathetic face, he saw only the black chimney of the factory that was about to swallow and digest him.

"What harm would it do anyone," he asked, "if one old tailor were left to work at home?"

He threw a last, pleading glance at Aunt Malkaleh, who said nothing. Or rather, who went on betraying him by declaring:

"It can't be that you're right and the whole world is wrong."

Without a word he rose darkly, fetched his iron and heavy tailor's shears, emptied his vest pockets of their thimbles, and laid it all on the table.

"It's yours, you bandits!"

With tears in his eyes, he turned to his wife.

"From you, Malke, I never would have expected this."

And with that Uncle Itshe clenched his jaws and lapsed into one of those frightful family silences that recalled the bitter stillness of the winter steppes. The contribution of Reb Zelmele, this must indeed have been brought from far off, from somewhere in "deep Russia."

♦ ♦ ♦

A golden star twinkled above the chimney.

At the crack of dawn, Uncle Itshe left for the factory. A place was waiting for him. Assigned to a conveyor belt, he was told to extract the basting from the parts of coats that came by. Uncle Itshe put on his spectacles and spent the day disdainfully peering over them at his surroundings while pulling out threads with a wetted finger.

The factory occupied a huge floor a thousand yards long. Bright projectors lit even the space beneath the work tables. A single needle on the ground was as coldly conspicuous as it would have been in the palm of a hand.

In a far corner, heavy presses let off steam. Bare-armed workers operated the gray, industrial machines, which heaved with soft, fabricky sighs.

Uncle Itshe's nose twitched in their direction. They, at least, gave off a good, tailorish smell.

Everything else on the floor was strange. Sleeves, collars, and midsections swam along the conveyor belt, presumably to become coats at some indiscernible point. Warily, he watched them lifted jerkily from the conveyor belt, as if snatched by thieves, by hundreds of long, bony hands with squared-off tailor's nails

Could it be, he wondered, that it was all just a show put on to fool an honest man?

Uncle Itshe pondered the matter. By closing time he had come to firm conclusions, phrased in the form of questions like:

Do these people really call themselves tailors?

Is that any way to turn a hem?

If this is socialism, what good does it do the poor?

Back home with Aunt Malkaleh, he remained in a grim mood, ridden by doubts and vague premonitions. Each time he thought of himself he winced like a man who has been in great danger and should be in synagogue giving thanks for his deliverance.

One thing was obvious. He, Itshe the tailor, had fallen on hard times in his old age. Having just spent eight hours pulling out threads in the company of monster machines, it struck him, first, that this was not what he had labored all his life for, and second, that nothing good could possibly come from such slopwork.

Aunt Malkeleh was alarmed by the sighs, grumbles, and oaths heaped by him upon the world.

She spoke to him gently. Yet when pressed for details, he began to shout like a madman:

"You stupid cow, it's a clothing factory without clothes!"

"But how can that be?"

"Go ask that damned merry-go-round!"

Presumably he was referring to the conveyor belt, which grabbed collars and sleeves from all hands and made off with them to some damned place where they were turned into ladies' coats.

"A lady's coat calls for vision!" Uncle Itshe proclaimed.

Who would have thought that he, who had always had time for the problems of others—who had crept like a boy beneath Uncle Zishe's window for a look at his brother's non-Jewish son-in-law—who, time and again, had cheerfully gone, almost danced, to take Tsalke down from the hangman's rope—who had even attended his own son's weddingless wedding feast for the sake of a glass of schnapps—who would have thought that he would make such a fuss over a little thing like working in a factory?

It was a black and bitter day.

Before going to bed, Uncle Itshe began to shout again, this time that he needed an alarm clock to wake him up for work.

Silently the room filled with mutely sympathetic Zelmenyaners come to watch him undress and fall asleep. Aunt Malkaleh put up pots of water to boil—why, unless she did it out of sheer befuddlement, nobody knew.

Finally, Uncle Itshe dozed off. His old chin lay stiffly on the blanket with the remains of its beard while his big, fleshy Zelmenyaner nose jabbed the air with profound annoyance at the world.

◆ ◆ ◆

The last tailor is gone—the old Jewish tailor with the little beard, the thin, amused brows, and the dry-as-dust fingers.

Gone is the barefoot potato wolfer and fecund progenitor who reproduced like grass, doubling and redoubling himself.

Gone is the merry Jew who needed only a bowl of sorrel soup to make him sing the world's wonders.

The last tailor is gone, and with him the Singer sewing machine shop, and the tall Polish salesgirl in its illuminated window. Gone is the Singer agent, the Socialist Revolutionary with the blond goatee, that jesting philosopher who did numbers from *The Luria Brothers*[*] and *The Tsvi Family*[†] for the whole town on Saturday nights.

Gone is Yankev Boyez's only daughter, who played the piano, knew Russian and Hebrew, and brought Grecian beauty into our Jewish lives with her charm.

Gone is the last tailor, and the little house, and the No. 8 lamp, and the Hebrew teacher from the Land of Israel with the black hat and heavy pear-wood walking stick, that quiet, neglected-looking man who surprised us all by going on foot all the way to the Slonim Rebbe's before killing himself one night.

Gone are the Socialist Revolutionaries, and the Bund,[‡] and the young man who sang "Yomme, Yomme, play a song for me . . ."

---

[*] *The Luria Brothers*—a play by the Yiddish playwright Jacob Gordin (1853–1909).

[†] *The Tsvi Family*—a play on the theme of pogroms by the Yiddish playwright David Pinski (1872–1959).

[‡] **The Bund** (the General Union of Jewish Workers in Lithuania, Poland, and Russia)—a secular Jewish Socialist party founded in Vilna in 1897 and active in the U.S.S.R. until 1920.

Chapter 10

WINTER

The winter evening lay hard and clear beneath a blue sky, as if chiseled from a lump of sugar. The snow-draped posts and beams gleamed in the windows of the tranquil yard.

The moon hung over the yard like a cold coin.

Tonke was still awake by her green lampshade, performing measurements and calculations and jotting down neat columns of figures on sheets of paper.

Her fatherless child lay in bed, the clucking sounds that it made in its throat oddly like the ticking of Uncle Zishe's clocks on the wall. Gradually, it fell silent and sank back into the sticky slumber into which all are born.

Tonke's shadow crept up to the rafters, then bent down to a plate on the table to take a bite of bread and cheese.

Uncle Zishe's old grandfather clock struck ten.

Cautiously, the glass door of Tonke's room opened, and several women, led by Aunt Gita, stepped inside. Even before they crossed the threshold, an air of piety and gossipy secrets preceded them.

Tonke's shadow rose again to the rafters and stooped for a sip of tea from a glass left on the table to cool.

"Good evening," said all three visitors at once.

It was clear they had come for a purpose. The first to speak was a woman with a mealy face, a high bob of hair, and a black shawl on her head.

"It is most difficult," she said, "for a simple soul like myself to find the words with which to address a well-educated lady like you. Not that we, too, didn't have some schooling in our day, but the travails of motherhood have made us gray before our time . . ."

"Can't you talk in plain Yiddish?" said Tonke.

So Tonke said. The woman in the black shawl, however, was not accustomed to plain Yiddish. She was Esther the penmanship teacher. Having taught a generation of housewives the elegant art of stylish writing, she found plain speaking foreign to her nature and vocation. Though now retired, she still loved the imperishable beauty of words.

"Even among us old women," she said, "I know of no other mode in which to express myself."

Things went on in this awkward vein for quite a while. Surprisingly, although education was pitted against education, no progress was made.

She was a vulgar lot, Tonke was.

Inasmuch as she was, though—seeing, that is, that she was a pifflehead—a change of tactics was called for.

And so the wife of the beadle of the old synagogue said, "We were wondering who the father of your child is."

"Were you?" said Tonke. She appeared to be losing her temper. The women exchanged piously worried glances.

"But how could we not be?" asked clever old Aunt Nekhe. "We need to do something to calm your old mother."

Tonke regarded her in silence.

"So tell us, what's the problem?" Aunt Nekhe asked sympathetically.

Tonke spoke up at last:

"The child's father is a good Bolshevik. He's shot more than his share of Jewish speculators."

"Look here, my child, what's gotten into you?" Aunt Nekhe wondered out loud. "Just because something happened, does it have to be a tragedy? In the old days, in our village, the priest's daughter once had a bastard; she was married off to the first comer, and that was that. Not that that's so easily done with you modern types, but we'll think of something. Somewhere there's a young man who'll agree to have you.

It's not the end of the world. Why tell everyone that the father is a Bolshevik who shot people? Why create problems? So tell me, who is he, a goy?"

Tonke nodded.

"Goy, shmoy!" laughed Aunt Nekhe. "You're a silly girl. Since nobody knows him, you can just as well say he's a Jew. And not just a Jew but a good Jew. Don't you see how you're shaming your mother?"

Now it was Tonke who laughed. She rose from her chair and took Nekhe's hand.

"You seem a decent, honorable woman," she said.

Aunt Nekhe was touched. "You see," she said, turning to her companions, "she's not the hussy she's made out to be. Tell us, what's your daughter's name?"

"Juliana."

"Juliana, Shmuliana! That won't do at all. Listen, my dear. Since nobody knows it, you can just as well say it's Soreleh or Leyinke. Or Goldetske, if you prefer. And that you had a proper wedding with lots of guests and food. Why tell everyone that your child was born out of wedlock? That's something no one needs to know."

"Not a soul!" said Esther the penmanship teacher, clapping a long, pen-weary hand to her mouth.

The women went on speaking to Tonke in low tones, presumably about a woman's duties. There was talk of baking challah, of the lighting of Sabbath candles, and of something else that made Tonke turn red.* Though her visitors, who were all talking at once, had clearly devoted much thought to it all, she rose again and interrupted them.

"You know what, ladies? I think I'd like to be left alone."

Just as things were beginning to get interesting, a man walked into the room. This was Uncle Yuda's son Tsalke. He stumbled through the door half-asleep, his necktie yanked to one side and his ashen face still smoldering with the embers of his thoughts.

The women fell silent. Then Aunt Nekhe had an idea:

---

* **Something else that made Tonke turn red**—the women are whispering to her about the laws of ritual purity (*niddah*) that govern the behavior of a married woman during her menstrual cycle.

"Listen, my child," she whispered in Tonke's ear. "Maybe you'll give him a chance. He's a fine young man, Uncle Yuda's son, a tad on the bookish side, it may be, but here a bit, there a bit, and he'll shape up. What do you say, eh?"

Before Tonke could collect herself, Nekhe was shepherding the women from the room.

"Let's go, ladies. We'll leave the young people to themselves."

Uncle Zishe's old grandfather clock struck half past eleven. Aunt Gita, who had fallen asleep in her chair, excused herself and hurried off to bed.

Yet despite the late hour, Aunt Nekhe's other companions were in no hurry to be gone. Retreating to a dark corner of the outer room, they sat on a cold sack of potatoes to await developments.

Through the frozen blue window loomed the curving white shoulder of Reb Zelmele's yard.

The beadle's old wife dozed off. Aunt Nekhe followed suit. Even Esther the penmanship teacher drifted into troubled slumber.

Esther the penmanship teacher dreamed of strange Hebrew letters —twisted *gimels* with swollen bellies, *teses* girdered like towers, spinning tops of *lameds* with snakes' tails.

She saw a noble *alef* torn in two before her eyes.

It was turning into a nightmare. The penmanship teacher woke with a start.

The door to Tonke's bedroom was slightly ajar, admitting a trickle of greenish light. Esther heard every word of the two young people's conversation.

Uncle Yuda's Tsalel:

"The window of my room faces north. Lately I've noticed that the stars in the northern sky have changed position. Motion, it seems, is universal. All things are in transit, everything mutates. Only I, Uncle Yuda's Tsalke, remain in one place."

Uncle Zishe's Tonke:

"You haven't really remained in one place. The question is, Tsalke, whether you've grown. All is not well with you. You wanted to turn the world upside down with your thoughts, but it's you who are standing on your head."

Uncle Yuda's Tsalel:

"Look, it's the times that are to blame. The times are bad."

Uncle Zishe's Tonke:

"There are no good or bad times."

Uncle Yuda's Tsalel:

"Is that so? Well, since I know nothing about myself, Tonke, maybe you do."

Uncle Zishe's Tonke:

"There are two routes to the dictatorship of the proletariat: that of the worker and that of an intellectual like you. The worker takes the simple, organic route. The petit-bourgeois intellectual takes the route of crises —of the loss of faith, of skepticism, of self-denial and self-alienation, of having to be born again. The great battles of the revolution leave their wounded behind to recover on their own."

Uncle Yuda's Tsalel:

"You're telling me I'm wounded. Have it your way. But don't you realize that means my cries of pain are sincere?"

Uncle Zishe's Tonke:

"What good does your sincerity do you, Tsalke? A bourgeois craves honor, a housewife happiness, a young bookkeeper beauty, a wealthy dilettante wisdom, and a petit-bourgeois intellectual sincerity, sincerity, sincerity . . ."

Aunt Nekhe roused herself on her sack of potatoes, her nose full of dust.

"Esther, what's going on?"

"They're talking in the most gorgeous Yiddish."

"But what are they up to?" Aunt Nekhe asked uneasily.

"Passing their time in sweet dalliance, like two noble youths."

"What's dalliance, Esther?"

"Dalliance is the making of love."

Nekhe sat bolt upright. "They're making love?"

"I didn't say that."

"Then what are you saying?"

"I'm saying," Esther said, her eyes full of longing, "that it's beautiful."

◆◆◆ *Chapter 11*

MORE ABOUT WINTER

The city, cast in snow, traced a hunchbacked line on the horizon, framed by the large blue window of the sky.

On the telephone poles, the green porcelain insulators cracked from the cold. The air was pure alcohol. Gray icicles hung from the roofs of the yard as though from the beards of water carriers.

Uncle Yuda's roof alone had a festive touch, a three-toed trail leading up to its chimney, where a bird had left its tracks before sunrise.

Not a single fleshy nose was poked out-of-doors. Lying beneath their blankets, the Zelmenyaners had heard the last unrotted roof beam splinter in the night.

Bereh's dark little boy, a future polar explorer,* it would seem, had been breathing on the windowpane since dawn. Now, through the steamy circle made in the frost, he saw snow dust shower from a roof as though pawed by a cat.

Putting on his father's boots and pulling his hat over his ears, he announced:

"That's it! There's going to be a blizzard."

"Where, sillyhead?"

---

* **A future polar explorer**—a reference to the celebrated rescue of more than one hundred members of the crew of the SS *Chelyuskin*, crushed by polar ice in the Bering Straits, in April 1934. The crew's original purpose was to explore the possibility of navigating the northern maritime route in a single season.

Peering through the window, Khayaleh had a sudden memory. During her winter of love with Bereh, someone in the yard had predicted that the first child to emerge from her womb would be an astronomer with veins of ice.

"A blizzard!" the little boy repeated. "The wind's coming from the North Pole."

A few snowflakes drifted down from above. The wind pawed the roofs and sent snow flying. Silver dust sprayed from a cornice. Uncle Yuda's festive roof grew dark.

A fistful of snow flurried up from the street. The roofs gave a shudder. Snow chuted from above as though from a rent in the sky. The wind turned a corner, lunging and tumbling with a bitter howl.

The snow whirled round, clutching at the walls of the houses and blowing through the chinks in the attics. A thin, tattered fog swept in, smearing the world with bright dots. The houses swam out of focus, as if made from smoke.

The windows thawed a bit. Through their dull panes, the Zelmenyaners glimpsed a figure in the yard, groping its way in the blizzard.

It appeared to belong to a slightly built, asthmatic-looking young man leaning on a walking stick. The snow streaked his face and plastered his thin overcoat against him. He seemed to be looking for somewhere to catch his breath.

Just then, Folye's little wife came running to Khayeleh's apartment with startling news.

"Do any of you geniuses realize who that man is?"

"No, who?"

"It's the husband of the redheaded seamstress, the one who . . ."

In no time tongues were wagging that the asthmatic young man was looking for Falke, who had been sleeping with his wife, the redheaded seamstress. She was so in love with him, it was said, that she had stopped supporting her husband, who, accustomed to a life of comfort, had come to ask his wife's lover to have pity on him and—if it wasn't too much of an inconvenience—postpone the affair until the summer.

"A fine child you have!" said Folye's little wife, spoiling for a fight, to Aunt Malkaleh.

The Zelmenyaners kept mum, though all knew the seamstress had six children of her own. They just edged a little closer to their windows.

But the young man was gone. Before their eyes, the yard turned into a whirlpool, swirling with sheets of snow.

It took a while to make sense of it. In the end it was decided that it was a snow mirage, a phantom vision such as coachmen sometimes have when lost in a storm in the forest.

♦ ♦ ♦

Too bad about those bird tracks on Uncle Yuda's roof!

The yard looked swept by a cold fire. The snow spiraled like smoke, piling up in glittering heaps. A broken drainpipe hung from a roof, banging against a wall like the torn visor of a cap on the head of a young Zelmenyaner.

Its windows battened down and its vestibules deserted, the yard looked like a ship capsized in a storm.

Uncle Itshe's thinly shingled woodshed, which had more holes than walls, remained standing for the sole reason that the blizzard blew right through it. Protruding from the snow was the flapping end of an old wicker mat and what looked like a man's shirt on a stick. It fluttered in tattered strips, blowing with the wind.

It snowed and snowed.

Uncle Yuda's Tsalke stepped into the yard. Wearing a light jacket with its collar turned up, he shook from the cold.

Snowy sparks showered over him as though from a knife grinder.

The Zelmenyaners guessed he was answering the call of nature.

They guessed wrong. Uncle Yuda's Tsalel had risen from his books. All winter long he had been working on an article about the prose of Mendl Lefin, the author of *Kheshbon ha-Nefesh.** Although he already had a large amount of material, he wasn't sure what to do with it.

Tsalke had gone outside to air his thoughts.

It snowed and snowed.

---

* *Kheshbon ha-nefesh*—a Hebrew translation of Benjamin Franklin's *Poor Richard's Almanac* by Menakhem Mendl Lefin (1749–1826), which was later adopted by Israel Salanter (1810–1883) to become a key work of the Mussar movement, an ascetic trend among Lithuanian Jews that aimed at the ethical improvement of the individual.

At Aunt Gita's, all was quiet. On the table lay a plate of perch bones, an open envelope, and Ricardo's *The High Price of Bullion*.[*]

Aunt Gita was standing on a bench by the prayer book shelf, searching for some volume. She sometimes liked, as is known, to look at a religious book.

"Good morning, Aunt Gita," Tsalke said after waiting in vain for his aunt to turn around.

"A good morning to you," the pious woman answered with the thoughtful mien of her small-town rabbinical forebears.

It was so quiet you could hear a pin drop.

The mysterious baby girl in the cradle had a fat nose. Her hair was suspiciously blond. Could a blond gene from a long-lost grandmother have surfaced in Tonke's daughter?

All of a sudden, Tsalke caught a glimpse of a familiar expression on the little face. His heart skipped a beat, which was perhaps why he couldn't remember where he had last seen it. He went to the table and held the envelope up to his glasses. It was postmarked Petropavlovsk-Kamchatsky.[†]

Uncle Yuda's Tsalel hurried from Aunt Gita's to make the rounds of the other Zelmenyaners.

It snowed and snowed.

The storm grew fiercer. The foggy flurries stuck their white paws everywhere. Uncle Itshe's woodshed looked like a marble castle. The world was an airless, spaceless, colorless tomb. Crawling out of it as though from a well, Tsalke stumbled and lost his glasses.

"Shut the door!" someone shouted.

"Don't let in the wind!"

"He let the warm air out on purpose!"

Everyone at Uncle Itshe's fell silent. Aunt Malkaleh's cousin, the brooding bricklayer, sat by the window munching on something. Under his bed lay his metal-studded steamer trunk. Uncle Itshe's Falke

---

[*] **Ricardo's *The High Price of Bullion***—a work by David Ricardo (1772–1823), a British political economist, advocating the adoption of metallic currency over paper banknotes.

[†] **Petropavlovsk-Kamchatsky**—a city on the Kamchatka peninsula in Russia's Far East.

was sound asleep on the plank couch, begrimed with oil and grease. Falke, now an assistant machinist at the electric power station, worked nights and slept days. He lay under the blanket with his shirt open, on his sunken chest the graven image of an aging woman with a braid and frightfully large breasts. Even Uncle Yuda's Tsalel knew who she was.

"The Kondratyeva!"

"Sailors do it," the bricklayer explained.

When it came to being woken, Falke was a tough nut to crack. Tsalel yanked the blanket from him.

"Talk! Who does Tonke have in Kamchatka?"

"No one," said Falke in his sleep, turning his head to the wall.

"Then who's been writing her letters from there?"

"Who?" Falke could have been speaking from the next world. "It must be Borovke . . ."

He sank back into his unfinished sleep like an ax in water.

For all anyone knew, he was dreaming of the redheaded seamstress. Or perhaps of a certain Khanele, whom he had lately, unbeknownst to Folye's little wife, been taking to the movies.

Leaving Uncle Itshe's, Uncle Yuda's Tsalke paid calls on the other Zelmenyaners.

"Shut the door!"

"Don't let in the wind!"

"He let the cat out!" Khayaleh screamed.

But Tsalel heard none of that. He was out slogging through the snow again, vanishing in the maelstrom of the blizzard. Stumbling, falling, and picking himself up, he made his way from the yard with a single thought in his head.

Hadn't Borovke, on his way to Kamchatka, passed through Vladivostok?

♦ ♦ ♦

Darkness and snow.

From beyond a roof comes the crash of a collapsing snow bank, dimly lit by a swaying street lamp three streets away. Now and then a human figure, all buttoned up and wrapped in scarves and blankets, emerges from a back alley and limps through the blizzard like a slowly bouncing ball.

The wind howls through the streets. With a shudder, snow caves in over a fence, baring naked cobblestones.

For several days now, Tonke has failed to come home even at night. She's up late at a small desk, smoking cigarettes and dictating a report on the plenary session of the commissariat. The snow piles higher on the black windowpanes. Huddled in a coat, her fingers stiff from the cold, Tonke's typist has long despaired of going home.

The heavy, round clock on the wall strikes twelve. Somewhere the wind, moaning in the endlessly desolate chimneys of the office building, rips a tin sheet from a roof.

Suddenly, Tonke glimpses a long, gaunt, pale face pressed against the misty windowpane. Its eyelashes are crusted with snow.

Even minus his glasses, she recognizes Tsalke at once.

Tonke goes to the window. Springing back into the deep snow, Tsalke stumbles and crawls off on all fours into the blizzard. A new, painful thought occurs to him.

"Would you believe it? That girl's whole life is her work! She's just come home from the far end of the world and she's already at it day and night . . ."

♦♦♦ *Chapter 12*

THE ZELMENIAD

A scientific investigation into the material and intellectual culture, traits, customs, and other aspects of Reb Zelmele's yard, compiled and redacted from the notes of the young field worker Tsalel Khvost, himself the yard's native.

INTRODUCTION

The courtyard was founded in 1864 by Reb Zelmele Khvost, a lower-middle-class Jew of short stature who came to these parts from "deep Russia." It was he who settled the yard and laid the basis for its development while supporting himself as a petty tradesman. Set apart from their neighbors, the Zelmenyaners forged a distinctive lifestyle of their own in the course of the next generations.

There are clear indications that, in their struggle for survival, the Zelmenyaners created not only an indigenous technology but unique systems of medicine, geography, zoology, and botany, as well as a spoken dialect adapted to their specific needs.

Since it is our contention that the Zelmenyaners throw light on human existence as a whole, an outline of their material and intellectual activity is urgently called for.

The technological artifacts of the yard include axes, knives, saws, a plane, chopping bowls, mousetraps, shoulder yokes, shovels, a sewing machine, thimbles, spectacles, needles, lamps, crowbars, a watchmaker's eyepiece, graters, pliers, pokers, oven lids, frying pans, and pots.

The preferred metal of the yard is copper. A shelf beneath the ceiling displaying scoured copper pots and pans was once taken as a sign of worldly wealth. This curious phenomenon calls for further investigation.

Unfortunately, these shelves have been bare since the war.

♦ ♦ ♦

The dullness of axes, knives, and nails has its presumed psychological concomitants, the Zelmenyaners being characterized by dull stares, dull minds, and a dull, obstinate persistence.

On summer mornings at dawn, Reb Zelmele was in the habit of stepping outdoors in his long underwear to shovel manure. Uncle Zishe kept an iron crowbar. In the final analysis, however, the yard's most important implement is the grater, which is indispensable for the Zelmenyaners' renowned potato puddings.

A kerosene cooking stove can be found at Khayaleh's. The first to introduce such a device into the yard was Uncle Yuda's Tsalke. Originally, therefore, it was thought to be a masculine implement.

Nailed to the door of Bereh's apartment is a mailbox.

Uncle Folye has a silver salt cellar, which is kept locked in a chest.

Once, at Reb Zelmele's, a heavy bronze chandelier, like those of synagogues, hung from the ceiling by an iron chain. It must have weighed forty pounds. The Germans, however, made off with it.

Khayaleh has a chrome bed.

There is said to be a silver spoon somewhere, too, although no one has actually seen it.

Electricity was brought to the yard by revolutionary means.

Up to that time, No. 8 lamps had cozily lit the Zelmenyaners' tables and whole sections of their walls. In the cluttered corners of their rooms, they sat around on winter nights plying themselves with hearty glasses of tea and experiencing the weather, the night, and the flow of their heavy Zelmenyaner blood. Then came electricity, its cold, dead gleam like a glowworm's, and robbed life of its pleasures. The Zelmenyaners were illuminated to the point of transparency.

Thus began the Great Electric War.

To this day, the Zelmenyaners feel discriminated against. The rumor persists among them that the outskirts of town get the worst electricity, the dregs from the bottom of the boiler.

Radio was introduced by Falke.

Twelve heavy copper ladles have survived all upheavals.

Though unable, it is said, to count that far, Esther the penmanship teacher has two ladles of her own, as well as a chopping bowl.

II. MEDICINE IN THE YARD

The main remedy for illness is a hot compress.

Hence, in any emergency, pots of water are put on to boil.

Hot compresses are a cure for headache, toothache, stomachache, and heartache. The sole Zelmenyaner never to have been treated with them may be Uncle Folye, though he once had a toothache, too.

Hot water bottles are considered effective against indigestion, rheumatism, and fever.

Jam is reserved for special cases. It is taken, propped on one arm, with a small spoon from a saucer, which it is considered refined to hold with one's little finger protruding. It is thought to be good for fainting, childbirth, chest pains, and panic attacks.

White bread is used for influenza, childbirth, and scrofula.

Uncle Yuda's Khayaleh is scrofulitic. Her consumption of white bread is in fact low.

A boiled chicken is recommended for women in labor.

A plum or handful of cherries is administered to children who vomit, don't eat, or refuse to grow.

Honey cake is for weakness and gray hair. Old women dip it in brandy.

Hungarian wine is for childbirth.

An enema is a box attached to a length of rubber hose with a black spigot at one end. This piece of medical equipment was introduced by Aunt Hesye, who is said to have suffered from constipation. In general, she was reputed to be spoiled. Following her death, enemas vanished from the yard. So complicated a contrivance was deemed unnecessary for the treatment of minor maladies. The box is somewhere in an attic to this day.*

III. ZELMENYANER GEOGRAPHY

Nuyorek. Aunt Khaye-Matle and her husband have lived in Nuyorek for the past thirty years. Although their original destination was America, they settled there instead.

Vladivostok. A city on the seashore to which the whippersnaps went, it is believed to be more distant than Palestine, let alone Austria. The latter is where Uncle Folye was a prisoner. It's a German sort of place.

When she was young, Aunt Gita traveled with a deaf cousin of hers, a rabbi's wife, to see a doctor in Königsberg. This is where the best Germans live. The Germans are known for the elegance of their language.

Aunt Malkaleh claims to have been in Vilna as a child, where she saw the Vilna Gaon and a suit of medieval armor in a display window. Her memory of the Gaon is, needless to say, chronologically impossible. Most likely she saw a lesser rabbi in the company of some synagogue beadles.

Apart from all this, the world consists of the Hot Lands and the Cold Lands. In the Hot Lands are found elephants, oranges, palm trees, lions, gazelles, and black people. But all this is theoretical. Goblins, for instance, are assumed to be realer than black people. Love grass exists more surely than do elephants.

The best-loved land is "deep Russia." It's from there that the family's founder, Reb Zelmele, hailed.

"Deep Russia" is a blessed place in which it is always summer. Grain

---

* *Aunt Gita, who is a bit of a quack, has brought an entirely different medical regime to the yard. Her remedies include spiderwebs, cat fur, urine, and the like. They represent a school of thought foreign to the pharmacology of the Zelmenyaners.*

grows higher than a man, especially wheat. Once, long ago, watermelons arrived from there at Rosh Hashana time. In "deep Russia" live great grain and cattle dealers.

At bottom, according to the yard, the world has three peoples: the Russians, the Poles, and the Peasants.

The names of other peoples are difficult to keep straight. The difference between a baron and a Frenchman, for instance, is not quite clear. Zelmenyaners tend to confuse princes, counts, Germans, Frenchmen, politicians, Englishmen, kings, and so on and so forth.

Uncle Zishe once had dealings with a count, unless it's all a fairy tale. This story calls for additional research.

It is said to have taken place soon after Uncle Zishe's wedding. One winter night, supposedly, a sleigh drawn by three horses pulled into the yard with a tinkle of bells. Its occupants asked for a watchmaker. Before anyone knew it, Uncle Zishe had disappeared for two weeks.

In the middle of the count's mansion stood a large clock in a glass case, from which a golden rooster would emerge every hour to crow the time. Recently, however, the rooster had taken to malingering. This so distressed the countess that she fell ill, whereupon the count sent for a watchmaker.

For two weeks, Uncle Zishe crawled about inside the glass case as if in a room in which he was living. A man of great brainpower, he eventually discovered what ailed the rooster. At the stroke of twelve, it began to crow again.

The joy at the count's was indescribable. That night, Uncle Zishe was given a seat at the dinner table alongside all the princes and Frenchmen. Since the food wasn't kosher, he didn't touch any of it. The count got drunk and handed him a hundred-ruble note; then, getting still drunker, he handed him another. Had it not been for the intervention of the countess, Uncle Zishe might have ended up with the count's entire estate.

Not without reason did Uncle Zishe go about for the rest of his life thinking he was a cut above the others.

Another nationality is the Hungarians. These were two men with measuring tapes and knapsacks who dealt in tablecloths. Their race was extinguished during the war.

Gypsies are known in Reb Zelmele's yard, too. They are, however, considered a profession rather than a people.

IV. ZELMENYANER ZOOLOGY

Thirteen species of animal are recognized in the yard: horses, cows, goats, sheep, cats, dogs, mice, chickens, geese, ducks, turkeys, pigeons, and crows.

Pigs are deliberately overlooked

The story goes that Bubbe Bashe once kept a cow, but this, one might say, is prehistory. Pending further research, it must be considered a fantasy. Quite possibly it was imagined by the Zelmenyaners in the difficult period in which they had no milk for their kasha.

Because of a hen and a slaughterer, Aunt Hesye departed this world.

Hens, with their placid nature, are as integral to the yard as potato graters. At all hours of the day, Zelmenyaner hens can be seen pecking at the foundations of the houses.

By the time electricity arrived, it is said, Bubbe Bashe looked like a hen herself.

The number of mice killed in the yard has set a world record.

Uncle Itshe hurls blocks of wood at them. Although more often than not he only manages to break a dish, the revolting creatures live in great fear of him.

Uncle Yuda's Khayaleh has a different approach. Upon seeing a mouse, she climbs onto a table, beats her breast, and shrieks:

"Scat!"

No wonder she is so attached to her brindled cat.

On moonlit nights, the biggest mice come out and stand on their hind legs in the Zelmenyaners' rooms. They scoop up the moonbeams with their front paws and cram them into their mouths.

They are believed to eat them.

"Crow" is considered an appropriate term for any black bird.

There is yet another bird that frequents the Zelmenyaners' rooftops. Gray and plain looking, it is, like the air around them, ignored by

Zelmenyaners looking in its direction. Tsalke calls it a sparrow. Since no one has any use for it, no one else has a name for it.[*]

V. ZELMENYANER BOTANY

Birch trees.

VI. ZELMENYANER PHILOLOGY

The Zelmenyaners drawl their words slowly and thoughtfully. They pronounce their z's as in "azure." "Zero" is "zhero," "season" is "seazhon," "houses" is "houzhezh."

Ns and l's are never glides. Zelmenyaners say "kitch-in" rather than "kitchn," "fi-lim" rather than "film."

Zelmenyaners sometimes confuse their pronouns. They have been known to say of Khayaleh's cat, "Get them thing out of here." Or, in speaking of Tonke, "She and me get along like a man and a boil."

For undetermined reasons, the Zelmenyaners have modified certain words. For example: "fimble" instead of "thimble," "bamble" instead of "bramble," "humblebee" instead of "bumblebee."

"S" and "sh" are transposed. Zelmenyaners say "sipsape," "shishy," "shunsine," and "soeshtring."

Especially noteworthy is the fact that Zelmenyaners create their own vocabulary, such as "whippersnaps," "shmintselgessel," "pifflehead," and the like. Such expressions have spread beyond the yard with great persistency. Language is contagious. The western limits of the Zelmenyaner idiolect are just below Minsk, in the vicinity of Logoysk, Samakhvalovitsh, and Smilovitsh, while eastward it extends to the village of Seletz near Mogilev, and from there in a southeasterly direction.

---

[*] *Ogres, trolls, gremlins, mules, and mongooses are unrelated species, having nothing to do with the yard.*

Chapter 13

GREAT UNREST IN REB ZELMELE'S YARD

The blizzard hasn't let up for two weeks.

Snow is piled high by the inner doors of the vestibules. A chimney—and one in good condition at that—has fallen on Bubbe Bashe's roof.

The blizzard whirls about the yard as if trapped and trying to break out, wreaking havoc with the last rotting rafters and moaning all night in the double storm windows and snow-filled attics.

From the storm come bearers of ill tidings.

Uncle Zishe's Sonya is ill. A girl in a fur coat and high boots came to fetch Aunt Gita and take her to Sonya's bedside.

One night a frozen Jew, the custodian of the graveyard, came to tell Uncle Itshe that Reb Zelmele's headstone had been stolen.

It had cost a pretty penny.

Next, someone turned up from town with news of Bereh. This sent shivers down everyone's spine.

Bereh, it appeared, was in bad trouble. It wasn't clear if he merely had enemies or had actually been assaulted by them.

Now, the Zelmenyaners sat by their frosty windows, waiting for the blizzard's next complication.

Was it the end of Reb Zelmele's yard?

Early in the morning, a Jew turned up from the countryside. From afar, he seemed little more than a frozen bundle of clothes. He brought a letter from Uncle Yuda to his son Tsalke, asked for a glass of water, and disappeared before anyone could have a word with him. That's how it became known that Uncle Yuda was at death's door.

Although Tsalke's crazy father wrote about higher things and only let on to his illness in the letter's last lines, Tsalke wiped his glasses and shook his head.

It was something you could die from.

The letter lay on Tsalke's table. Zelmenyaners fought their way through the storm for a look at it. It was read by whoever had a grasp of higher things.

It said:

> To my dear son Betsalel from his father Yuda, also known as Yuda the carpenter:
>
> A simple man talks about simple things, because he knows nothing else. The upper crust, kings and princes, talk about fine wines and hunting birds and animals. But the philosopher talks about philosophy. He thinks of nothing else and has his opinions and even something to say.
>
> As for the God deniers, I want you to know, my son, that I will refute them as long as I have strength, because everyone knows they have gone astray.
>
> I have written a book proving there is no such thing as oxygen. Only a shameless generation would have the gall to say it exists when it doesn't. With God's help, I have demonstrated this. All the talk about candles going out under bell jars is a lie, because a candle is not a living thing that needs to breathe. That's common knowledge.
>
> You will ask, my son: Why then does the candle go out? It's perfectly simple. It goes out by itself. You don't need a bell jar for that. If a fire in a wood-burning stove is untended, won't it go out too?
>
> I have thought much about such things and couched my thoughts in plain parables that the common man can understand.
>
> I want you to know, my dear son, that I am working on many erudite matters. Right now I am considering whether men can live without kings. Reason says that they can't. Even Aristotle, the world's wisest man, held that kings were necessary.
>
> I have other important ideas too, but I must stop now, because I have to

run to the village soviet to see the doctor. They think I have cancer. No one lives forever.

From your loving father Yuda.

♦ ♦ ♦

Uncle Yuda's Khayaleh let out two screams at once: one for her poor, sick father wrestling with death and one for her husband Bereh in the police force.

According to Khayaleh, someone was out to get Bereh. He might even lose his job. And there was another worry, too, which Khayaleh had been keeping mostly to herself for several days:

"He's stopped bringing me my two buckets of water every day with the shoulder yoke!"

Seeing that Khayaleh was faced with more than a human being could cope with, the Zelmenyaners laid cold compresses on her head. Aunt Malkaleh even brought some jam.

"Here, give her a spoonful. It's exhaustion."

But who's to blame when a person keeps everything to herself? Khayaleh is never in the yard. If she opens someone's door, it's only to say:

"Has anyone seen my cat?"

That evening she went into town to visit friends. Soaked to the bone and half dead from the blizzard, she returned with news that was hard to believe. Porshnyev, the Party commissar at police headquarters, had called Bereh into his office and kept him on the carpet for hours. When her fine fellow came out again, he looked dragged through the mud.

"But why didn't the dunce tell anyone?"

"Do you call that nice? The whole yard is eating its heart out because of him and he has no heart at all."

That was said by Uncle Itshe.

"He's a crude type any way you look at it!"

♦ ♦ ♦

The dunce was kind enough to open his mouth only when Aunt Malkaleh's cousin, the bricklayer, blurted something at the dinner table. This was:

"As I recall, your Porshnyev killed Jews in Ekaterinoslav."

Porshnyev, in other words, was a murderer.

The bricklayer said this casually while eating. The whippersnaps, however, fell on him.

"Who is this slob?" Bereh asked angrily.

"Why doesn't he go back to the Ukraine?" Tonke wanted to know.

Falke asked:

"What's that trunk he keeps under his bed?"

The Jew was quick to size up the situation and fell as silent as a stone. Head propped on one hand, he sat chewing glumly.

There was great unrest in the yard. Snow piled up without and worries within. Uncle Yuda was dying. Sonya kept fainting. Reb Zelmele's headstone was gone. And here sat a quiet Jew, a strange Jew, reaching out for more bread. The devil only knew what he wanted from the Zelmenyaners. One night Bereh, appearing in the doorway as the bricklayer was about to slice a loaf of bread held against his chest, stared at him furiously.

"What's wrong?" the Jew said. "Have the kolkhozes stopped growing wheat?"

"Who here has been spreading rumors about Porshnyev?" Bereh demanded to know.

The Jew put down the loaf and knife and said with a shake of his gray beard:

"Not me."

He must have thought that would be the end of it. But Bereh wasn't letting him off so easily. All evening they sat at Uncle Itshe's while Bereh questioned the Jew about his life. In the end, his story passed muster. He was indeed a bricklayer, a workingman who even had some class consciousness.

"It's like this," said the Jew. "Ever since I can remember I've been a freethinker. When I was a young, I was a bit of a skirt chaser. I couldn't have cared less about religion and all that prayer-shmayer. I was also a bit of a boozer. But show me a poor man and I did my best to help, even with my last penny."

It was as clear as could be. A simple bricklayer. He broke off a piece of bread from the loaf, stuck it in his mouth, and allowed himself a last question about the collectivization campaign.

"I don't get it," he said. "Aren't they planting more grain than ever?"

By that he meant that his emptying the Zelmenyaners' larders shouldn't be a cause for concern.

Once, forgetting that he was a guest, he sat down at the table and began to eat like gluttony in person. This caused Uncle Itshe to rush out into the yard and exclaim with much wringing of his hands:

"Help, he's eating me out of house and home!"

A commotion broke out. Zelmenyaners came running to the rescue. Uncle Itshe, however, was too noble to name names. The bricklayer, for his part, did not take it personally. Preoccupied with stuffing his mouth, he said:

"I don't get it. What are kolkhozes for?"

Aunt Malkaleh suffered the most. In a moment of aggravation, she even confided to a trustworthy ear that her cousin the bricklayer was actually a butcher. At one time he had had a business driving beef cattle from the Ukraine to a military base in Smolensk. Back then, he hadn't wanted to know he had a family. Now that he was ruined, he had become a kissing cousin.

◆ ◆ ◆

There was great unrest in the yard. Snow piled up without and worries within. In the morning, Aunt Gita returned from visiting her sick daughter in a dark, silent mood. To judge by the manner in which she spat and said nothing, she must have been present at one of Sonya's coming-to parties. The Zelmenyaners were more curious than sympathetic. They wanted so badly to know what had happened that the Adam's apples bobbed in their throats.

"It's none of your business," some scolded.

"Then stay out of it yourself," retorted others.

In the end, it was Falke who broke the news about Bereh. The dunce had been accused at the last Party meeting of antiproletarian aloofness and Khvostism.

So said Falke.

Porshnyev, the Party commissar, had called Bereh in for a talk, shut the door of his office, and spent a good couple of hours with him. From the corridor, he could be heard saying:

"Berke, are you sleeping? Wake up!"

Bereh said nothing.

"Say something!" Porshnyev shouted angrily. "Anything! Tell me what's on your mind."

Bereh said nothing.

He indeed looked dragged through the mud when he stepped out of the office. What upset him most was his own sluggish mind.

It was getting dark out. Wet snowflakes clung to Bereh's hot cheeks. Then they turned to sleet.

Bereh stopped at a kiosk to buy a copy of *Pravda** and strode on home.

It was then that he forgot to bring Khayaleh her two buckets of water. All night until dawn, he sat by the window reading *Pravda*. A pot of cold potatoes stood on the table. A herring lay on the oil cloth. Neither had been touched. As soon as it was time to go to work, Bereh went to see Porshnyev.

"All right, then," he said. "I'm going back to the leather factory."

◆ ◆ ◆

It was sleeting. A stinging, frozen wind slapped scraps of wet air on the windowpanes in a dirty slurry. The shingles on the roof of Uncle Itshe's woodshed flapped in the wind like hairs on a balding head.

Uncle Itshe sat in his warm home, pouring hot glasses of tea down his gullet and feeling good about life in spite of everything. He had been, it was no secret, through hard times. Now and then he still groaned at the memory.

Everyone knew a low trick had been played on him.

Meanwhile, however, Uncle Itshe had become an ace worker at the garment factory. It wasn't anything he talked about, since who knew what the whippersnaps might think of next if they found out? Still, he

---

* **Pravda**—the leading Soviet newspaper and the official organ of the Central Committee of the Communist Party of the Soviet Union.

couldn't help bragging a bit. When Aunt Malkaleh began to lament his bitter lot as she poured him tea from an earthenware pot, he exclaimed:

"Malke, you're a fool!"

Uncle Itshe took a deep breath, as if trying to collect his thoughts.

"Ach, the things a poor tailor has lived to see! We live in times when the coats go around making themselves. It's a whole new world. . . . To think of the years I spent sitting at that old piece of junk, rattling away from morning till night . . ."

He broke off. Too late did Uncle Itshe realize that his big mouth had already said too much. He put down his glass of tea, took an odd little stroll about the room, and hitched up his pants.

"Don't get me wrong, Malkaleh . . ."

He took another deep breath. This time there wasn't a thought in it.

Fat flakes of snow danced before the dull windowpane and stuck there. Uncle Itshe leaned forward to peer into the yard and froze with a dull anxiety. Coming up the slushy, black footpath was Bereh.

Bereh's rolling gait was as placid as always. Yet he was wearing an ordinary jacket without his red epaulets, and on his head was the greasy tanner's cap that had gathered dust behind the stove for the past ten years.

No longer, it seemed, was Bereh a policeman.

The suddenly still yard stood glued to its windows. No one could tear himself away from the sight. All felt a pang for the once mighty Bereh, whose star had soared to the zenith following his astounding adventures in the war. Now, unexpectedly, it had set again with a tanner's cap and a rolling gait that said nothing.

Hands were wrung. "Are you sure that's Bereh?"

"How a man can fall!"

Even pious Aunt Gita shook her head and murmured:

"Woe to the eyes that have seen such a thing."

Talk of ingratitude! Until now it hadn't occurred to anyone what a wondrous glow Bereh had cast over the yard.

The first sounds came from the top story of the brick house. Uncle Itshe's Khayaleh had thrown herself on her bed and was screaming like a woman in labor. Yet having only recently given birth to a second child, she couldn't get away with such a trick.

"Listen," Bereh was told, "you'd better make her stop."

At first, he had no success. Then the screams died down all at once. This happened while he was lunching on a slice of dry bread.

"Cut it out, Khayaleh," he had said bitterly. "Cut it out or I'll leave you."

"I'll bet you will, you bit of bad luck!"

"I have someone. Her name is Leitshe."

He blurted it out all at once and turned red as a beet, so shamed by his own words that he stared down at the floor beneath the table. For ten years he had kept that name a secret, guarding it even from himself. Now, in a moment of madness—and in front of his own wife!—it had suddenly escaped him.

Beet red, he listened to Khayaleh sob into the cushions.

◆◆◆ *Chapter 14*

A MOONLIT NIGHT

That night the moon came out. The blizzard was over. The moon swam out from soft, feathery clouds that shone with a far-off light.

The houses of the yard slumbered, their low shadows huddled on the bluish snow. Here and there a gouge in the snow testified to the gale winds that had passed over it. The yard was sunk in that deep, second stage of sleep from which it is impossible to be woken.

An agitated Tsalke roamed the yard past the moonlit rooms. Was it in aimless sorrow for his high-minded father, the noblest of the Zelmenyaners?

Several times Tsalke approached Uncle Zishe's, reached as far as the entrance, and backed away.

You could hear the moon swimming through the sky.

Finally, he made it to the vestibule, pressed the door handle, and stepped inside.

Aunt Gita was sleeping in the front room, which smelled of prayer books and old hens. In the darkness, Tsalel groped his way to the glass door of Tonke's room.

The room was still. The light was gray enough to see in. A few moonbeams striped the floor. Tonke lay in bed by the wall, tossing in her sleep with her brown arms on the blanket. The white trim of her nightgown was bright against her warm shoulders.

Tsalke looked away in awe.

His heart skipped a beat. It pained him to have to steal into his beloved's room at night for a look at her.

Moonbeams striped the floor. He crossed them carefully to Tonke's bed, bent over her, and gave her a silent kiss.

Tonke tossed in her sleep.

He held his breath and tiptoed backwards, his head throbbing wildly. At the door, he murmured in rapture:

> Ich bin so krank, o Mutter,
> Das ich nicht hör und seh . . .

Aunt Gita heard the door shut. A draft blew through the room. Lifting her long scarecrow's body from where it lay, she asked the darkness in her bass voice:

"Zishe? Is that you, Zishe?"

It was not. Uncle Zishe had died for good and no longer paced the room on winter nights.

Only Uncle Yuda's Tsalel wandered in the moonlit yard. The young man, it appeared, had been driven mad by the snow and the moonlight. The night was hushed. The moon shone with a slanty blue light. The houses clutched their shadows close to them. Uncle Yuda's Tsalel stood with his head thrown back, swaying and singing a desolate Jewish melody to the moon like a whipped dog:

> Ich bin so krank, o Mutter,
> Dass ich nicht hör und seh,
> Ich denk an das tote Gretchen,
> Da tut das Herz mir weh.
>
> Heil du, mein krankes Herze—
> Ich will auch spät und früh
> Inbrunstlich beten un singen:
> Gelobt seiest du, Marie!*

---

* **Gelobt seiest du, Marie!** (German)—"Praise be to you, Marie!" from Heinrich Heine's poem "A Pilgrimage to Kevlaar." The full quotation is: "I am so ill, oh Mother, / That I can't hear or see. / I think of poor dead Gretchen, And so my heart hurts me—- / Heal thou my heart so troubled / And day and night for thee / I'll sing with true devotion / 'Praise be to you, Marie!'"

A few days later Aunt Gita told her friends in strictest confidence that she had personally seen Uncle Yuda's Tsalel, an educated young man by all accounts, standing in the yard in the middle of the night with a prayer book, blessing the moon.

"Trust me," she said. "I know what I'm talking about."

He indeed sang so loudly and with such a dismal wail that the whole yard was stricken with fear.

Although Aunt Gita was probably mistaken about the prayer book, her lady friends came away convinced that the young folk were more Jewish than they let on. Aunt Nekhe, who had the best head of them all on her shoulders, put a finger to her lips, meaning that the less said the better.

♦♦♦ *Chapter 15*

ABOUT UNCLE ZISHE'S SONYA
AND AUNT GITA

As for Sonya, it's like this.

She's left her job and even, it would seem, given up her union card. She stays at home and is always cold, no doubt because of the frozen rabbinical blood smuggled into the family by Aunt Gita. She's always sick, too. For that she can thank Uncle Zishe, who bequeathed to her illnesses of various kinds and degrees.

Yet there is a school of thought that maintains that Uncle Zishe's Sonya only pretends to be sick when her husband is at home.

The following is adduced in proof:

Sonya never eats in Pavel Olshevsky's presence, in which she drinks only tea with milk while emitting little sighs to signify that something hurts her. (Little sighs are deemed sufficient because her poor health is already public knowledge.) These are intended only for Pavel—who, in view of their ambiguous nature, never knows when to run for the doctor.

He is at his wits' end.

Uncle Zishe's Sonya acts innocent and lets out a second sigh more portentous than the first.

Once left alone in her room, she gets out of bed, powders herself before the mirror, does her nails, and busies herself in a corner with her toilette. Let there be a knock on the door, though, and she is under the blanket and sick again.

Uncle Zishe's Sonya no longer lives in the yard. She moved to town before her father died and occupies a room in a second-floor apartment on Soviet Street.

Walking down the street of an evening and noticing a pretty curtain on a window and the glow of a yellow lampshade on the sidewalk, a person feels compelled to stop and sniff. If there's a smell of medicines in the air, it's Sonya's building.

That's Uncle Zishe's doing. It was he who replaced the Zelmenyaners' musty odor of hay with the dilute pharmaceutical scent that Sonya is surrounded by.

Uncle Zishe's Sonya inhales from little bottles, rubs her temples with white stones, and puts a few drops of iodine in her drinking water—exactly as was done in her far city by Countess Kondratyeva, who still haunts the yard like a dream, a decrepit Queen of Sheba draped in thirteen veils.

This winter, Uncle Zishe's Sonya has not left her apartment even once. On good days, she gets out of bed and sits on the couch with a kerchief and an open book in her lap, complaining to her young next-door neighbor, the college student Stashko:

"Is it my fault if I want a bit of culture in my life?"

Or:

"Am I to blame if I can't stand dirty fingernails?"

Uncle Zishe's Sonya has even stopped looking out the window, since she doesn't like what she sees. There's lots to do in the house, such as rearranging the furniture, hanging new curtains, and moving the pictures on the walls. The minute Pavel comes home from work, she's back in bed.

Not that, weak and sick though she is, she hasn't the strength to tell him the latest news.

"Have you heard? Bereh's been sacked from the police."

"How come?"

"The dunce got drunk and let a thief get away."

Pavel sits at the table and eats cold food from a plate. He keeps his mouth shut while he chews, which can mean one of two things: either he doesn't want to lose a crumb of what he's eating or he's afraid to upset his frail wife with his table manners.

As he eats, Sonya gives him the latest rundown on each of the neighbors in the building.

The world, it seems, is thoroughly degenerate. The things that go on! Why, in their own hallway, right under their noses, there are women living with several men at once!

Should Pavel still be chewing his cold food, Sonya produces a letter from beneath a cushion. It's from a man in Moscow named Gontshik, who has written a woman in the hallway about the summer they spent together in Sochi.

That settles that!

From the cushion's other side, Sonya extracts a wired money order for eighteen rubles for Stashko the college student.

That settles *that!*

If Pavel is still unmoved by these revelations, she punishes him with a secretive little sigh while holding out the mail to him in an excessively white hand.

"Here. Return this to the hallway, please."

Pavel says nothing. Though he is none too pleased with his wife's reading the neighbors' mail, he humors her, opens the door, and nonchalantly flings the mail into the hallway. It's his way of letting the two of them know that it's nothing to make a big deal of.

Really, it's all so ridiculous!

At night, the yellow lampshade casts its halo on the table. The room is quiet and cozy. Sonya, having risen and powdered herself, smells of distant hay mixed with tincture of iodine.

The usual company is gathered around the table.

There's the pudgy professor, Dovnar-Glembotsky. Long the butt of his students' jokes, he's finally been relieved of his teaching responsibilities.

There's an old, over-the-hill actor and his wife. Sometimes they're joined by a blond beanpole of a Belorussian teacher.

They sit around the cozy table playing cards.

Sonya has a passion for cards, which doesn't keep her from cheating.

It's a chore for her to have to put up with the actor's wife, who is said to come from a family of servants, if not worse.

Naturally, this makes their friendship tepid, especially since Sonya dislikes women who are not servants, too. If she bears a grudge against Pavel, it's for his not using his connections to ensure that there are only men in the world—with the exception, of course, of a single female, Uncle Zishe's Sonya.

♦ ♦ ♦

On one such evening, Tonke dropped by. Tonke, it is common knowledge, is not well liked in Reb Zelmele's yard. No one knows what to make of her. A one-woman household with a child (a small and silent one, but healthy, thank God) whose father is a postage stamp from Kamchatka raises eyebrows. Tonke remains a foreign presence in the yard, which believes it's best to keep away from her.

She came to say hello.

Though under no illusion that she wanted to be dealt in on the game, Pavel Olshensky invited her to join it.

Sonya asked:

"To what do we owe the pleasure, my dear sister?"

"I thought it was time I looked in on you," Tonke answered.

"Well, now you've looked. I don't suppose you play cards yourself?"

As though stricken by all seventy-seven of her illnesses at once, Sonya flared like a match.

"As a matter of fact," Tonke said, "I sometimes do."

"Washed down with lots of vodka, I'll bet!"

Sonya moved to the sofa so as to have a place to faint.

Tonke smiled. She had not, she said calmly, come to talk about such things. She had come because their mother, Aunt Gita, had recently taken to vanishing from the yard.

Sonya took a few sniffs from her bottles, sprinkled something on her hands, wet her lips with something else, and asked in a changed tone of voice:

"And where has she been vanishing to?"

She was thinking less of her mother than of how she, Sonya, had of late been too bothered by others to take proper care of herself and the little health she had left.

Uncle Zishe's Sonya knew she had to fight her own battles.

She had not, needless to say, the slightest confidence in the Zelmenyaners, who had failed to understand even the simple ailments of her father, let alone her own disorders, which only someone of refined character could grasp.

Indeed, what did a Zelmenyaner know about illness? As far as the yard was concerned, you weren't sick if you could still move a single limb. Such feats of endurance were beyond Sonya's feeble powers.

The bricklayer, for example, lay on the plank by the oven when he was sick, covered by coats and fur wraps and drinking forty glasses of tea. He drank until vapors rose from the fur as though from a compost pile. Only then did Aunt Malkaleh breathe a sigh of relief, persuaded he was on the mend.

As if Sonya were remotely capable of such a thing!

In fact, she had reason not to take her mother seriously. Aunt Gita, after all, wasn't the young woman in her prime that her daughter was. An old woman like her had had a lifetime to get used to her troubles.

♦ ♦ ♦

The snow let up. On the sunnier, drier side of the roof, the cats yowled. The brindled one was Khayaleh's. Spring was in the air.

A new breed of Zelmenyaners appeared in the oft-patched storm windows that looked out on the sun-drenched yard, mostly baby boys with hard round heads and flat noses, nourished on last year's potato crop. Still more dependent on their bottoms than their legs to get around on, they were not yet perambulating the yard.

Verge-of-spring rivulets coursed in the gutters. Sunny patches of light played over the walls of the houses, which shed the slushy snow like birds shaking off raindrops—all except Aunt Gita's, whose crooked roof lay in shadow all year 'round. Right now, it was locked. Aunt Gita had vanished again.

Uncle Itshe walked by and peered through the window. There was no one in the gloomy room, where nothing stirred but the pendulums of Uncle Zishe's ancient clocks.

Everyone was worried about Aunt Gita. Even Sonya rose to the occasion and let the yard know that there was no need to panic, since Pavel had seen her mother in town in the company of some pious Jews. Tactful as always, he had kept his distance so as not to embarrass her.

A few days later, Aunt Gita was back with a brush and a bucket of whitewash. She removed the double panes from the storm windows and lit the stove. Then, while all watched, she took a straw mat and marched off to the bathhouse.

By then it was obvious that something was going on.

The following evening, it became clearer.

Uncle Zishe's house flooded the yard with light through its newly scrubbed windows. The dusted clocks ticked away on the walls, their pendulums swinging merrily and their hands revolving freely.

In the middle of the front room stood a table covered with a white cloth and set with napkins, plates, glasses, hard-boiled eggs, and a bottle of red wine. At the head of it, tall and stately, sat Aunt Gita in Uncle Zishe's old linen prayer gown. A pair of spectacles on her nose, she rocked back and forth while chanting vigorously from a book.

Abashed and dismayed, the Zelmenyaners stepped outside to stare at a house that had been a chronic source of their troubles.

Had Aunt Gita taken leave of her senses?

Little Zelmenyaners, their fingers in their noses, hung on Uncle Zishe's window, wide-eyed at what they saw. To judge from Aunt Gita's behavior, she could only be dying. Although they had heard about death, they had never been told how it was accomplished.

Someone was sent to fetch Tonke in the hope that she might know how to deal with her mother. No one had the least notion of what to do. It was a lucky thing that Uncle Itshe happened to pass by just then. He stepped up to the window, peered inside, coolly assessed the situation, turned back to the yard, and declared:

"Imbeciles! Can't you see she's having a Seder?"

The Zelmenyaners hurried to have a look.

Indeed, Aunt Gita was reciting the Haggadah, dipping her finger in wine and flicking drops of it on a plate for each of the Ten Plagues.

The yard turned black from so many Zelmenyaner heads.

A crowd formed outside Aunt Gita's window. Nearly as numerous as the Israelites who left Egypt, the Zelmenyaners argued about Passover, raisin wine, and the pyramids. Chattering like savages, they engaged in outlandish speculations.

Yet Aunt Gita, it appeared, was not just motivated by simple piety. Feeling called upon to chastise a decadent race of Jews, she rose from the table, opened the window, and called into the suddenly hushed yard:

"You, Itshke! Do you think it would harm you, God forbid, to celebrate Passover like a Jew?"

Though he had fought many battles in his life, Uncle Itshe could only hang his head. It took that bigmouth, Uncle Folye's little wife, to speak up for him.

"Aunt Gita!" she shrieked. "Leave him alone. He's a worker."

Aunt Gita turned in another direction and continued in her bass voice:

"And you, Malkaleh! Are you also too modern to be a Jew?"

It was a grave accusation. Aunt Malkaleh turned red with shame. The decadent yard suffered Aunt Gita's glare in silence. Seizing the moment, she proceeded to deliver a sermon in the language of a true woman of God.

"In truth," she proclaimed, "the fallen state of this yard derives from two vices. The first is worldliness—lusting after food, drink, and the other bodily pleasures. The second is falsehood—blinding your eyes to whence you come and who you are. Yet you come from a putrid drop and are but as worms while you live, let alone when you die. Look to your deeds! Would you were worthy of God's tender mercy and not of His harsh retribution! Don't you realize, you degenerates, what lies ahead for you? The four death sentences of the Sanhedrin, stoning, stabbing, burning, and choking, are nothing beside the punishments of hell!"

With holy wrath, she shut her window. It was indeed a shameful scene, a whole yard full of Jews and their wives who had cast off the yoke of faith and stood prattling by a window instead of celebrating the holiday at home.

The yard was dead silent. The only sound was the verge-of-spring rivulets gurgling in the gutters with a tinkle like glass.

Just then the bricklayer grumbled from his window:

"It's a black and bitter day when an old woman has to remind us that we're Jews!"

More darkly yet, he added:

"Why do the rabbis keep silent? Damn them all, those bloodsuckers!"

The brooding fellow seemed about to launch a lengthy tirade himself. Before he could begin it, though, Uncle Itshe turned on the crowd and shouted:

"What are you gaping at, you imbeciles? What?"

One by one, he drove the Zelmenyaners back into their moldy rooms as if shooing geese.

An iron shutter clanged shut to signal that it was time for bed. The yard let out a yawn heard half a block away. Here and there a Zelmenyaner stayed awake, too lustful for pleasure to go to bed without his supper, his wolfish teeth sinking into a piece of pickled fish and a hunk of bread.

Gradually, the yard drifted off to sleep. It took a while for its slumber to grow restful.

You could have bought and sold the whole lot of them without their knowing it.

♦ ♦ ♦

In the middle of the night, a sleepy Zelmenyaner stepped out into the yard. There he saw that, though the curtains were now drawn, the lights were still on at Aunt Gita's.

He stood listening. Several voices were operatically singing *Khad gadye.** It was all very strange. Suspicion fell at once on Uncle Itshe and Aunt Malkaleh. Rumor even had it that they had deliberately planned the whole thing so as to join Aunt Gita at her Seder.

Uncle Folye's little wife, a delegate to the regional Soviet congress, made the affair her business and looked into it at length. There were those who accused Tsalke of having taken part in the Haggadah reading, too. It was no secret that he had been seen blessing the moon.

Who knows what it might have led to had not an even greater event followed—and on an even more extraordinary night.

---

* **Khad gadye**—"One Goat," the name of a song traditionally sung at Passover.

♦♦♦ *Chapter 16*

AN EXTRAORDINARY NIGHT

It was said in the yard to have happened on the day of Tonke's daughter's birthday. Uncle Folye's little wife, on the other hand, claimed this was a fat lie, since the child, she said, was born in the winter.

One way or another, the yard had never seen the likes of it.

That evening a carton arrived, smelling of sweets, spices, and fruit. Aunt Gita, realizing at once what it portended, hid her kosher dishes and went to sleep.

Whether she actually slept no one knew, since she was equally talkative waking or sleeping.

"Aunt Gita, where's the ladle?" someone might ask.

"By the water bucket on the bench," would come the answer in her sleep.

As the evening progressed, unfamiliar faces appeared in the yard. One graying head even arrived in an automobile, a sedan with two round headlights that startled the little street.

The yard was agog. Men, women, and children, the whole taciturn race of Zelmenyaners, spilled from their rooms in astonishment to gather in the dark corners by Aunt Gita's, licking their lips like a swarm of flies by a plate of honey cakes.

They all milled around in the darkness. It was bedlam.

Uncle Itshe pried open the iron slat of a shutter and peered into the enchanted room. Dazzled by its glitter, he remained glued there until dawn.

This is what he saw at Aunt Gita's:

A white tablecloth set with gleaming glassware that rang with a brittle chime. White dishes, too: white on white. Tall, thin glasses full of light. China brimming with radiance. Nothing so crude as food was in sight.

And the guests? Who were the guests?

Whether Jews or Belorussians (it was hard to tell them apart), all struck Uncle Itshe as aging whippersnaps, piffleheads with graying tousles of hair falling over their foreheads.

He only wondered why they weren't all wearing white dickeys. Wouldn't that have suited the color scheme better?

And the girls?

Uncle Itshe liked the girls with their short hair, red ties, white teeth, and cherry-red pins on their blouses. He liked them especially because he would kiss every one of them after a few drinks. Uncle Itshe knew a thing or two about women.

Lovely youngsters!

The food was served. Uncle Itshe had a sharp eye. He saw at once that it wasn't the usual Zelmenyaner fare. It started with little tidbits served from tins, each barely enough for a lick and a bite.

What else was to be seen on the table?

Gorgeous yellow apples on a white platter. Round little tortes in cobbler dishes. Canned delicacies on white trays. A suckling pig, its lewd little head at one end of a trencher with its feet tucked beneath it and its tail curled like a cord at the other end. Tall, thin wineglasses with napkins folded inside them.

A lick and a bite!

A broad-faced, pockmarked young man said hoarsely:

"I good know Yiddish. I was work in Mozyr."

"It you speak perfect!"

So, in Yiddish, said Tonke, sticking out her tongue at him.

"Mind your manners!"

Tonke was drinking vodka while eating with her hands.

"Mind your own! Claws are for grabbing."

"Then why are all the girls holding their forks so nicely?"

But Tonke was already talking to someone else, and everyone was talking to her. She was worth listening to, because her Russian was a delight. Now she was laughing.

She was the life of the party, Tonke was.

"And with us she's as silent as a fish!"

"That's Zishke's sneaky blood for you!"

Not everyone grasped what was happening at Aunt Gita's. Now there was singing there. The sound filled the yard as the notes of a piano fill a room.

It was warm out, the kind of starry night that makes you want to dance with pretty girls.

Uncle Itshe's Falke stood fidgeting by Aunt Gita's porch. He was not his usual self. He had been waiting for Tonke to invite him to her daughter's birthday party. Hadn't he raised the child himself? Hadn't he stayed up nights making hot compresses for her tummy while she screamed?

But Tonke did not come. Clearly, he meant nothing to her. Rummaging through his pockets, he quickly left the yard.

The night was warm. It was the black time of spring, when the earth is still black, the trees are black, and the first shades of green have yet to appear. The black roofs nestled against the high, starry night. Seething with rumors and gossip, the yard bubbled like a pot.

And what, when you got right down to it, was Reb Zelmele's yard? It was nothing but a power loom for the weaving of rumors and gossip. Ears cocked, it stood outside Aunt Gita's, whispering furiously.

"Glory be, I heard she's dead drunk and dancing with everyone!"

"With that gray old geezer, too?"

"With that gray old geezer, too."

Falke, sweating heavily, returned to the yard with a bottle of Polish vodka and a plate of raw cabbage and went off to his room for a private celebration.

"Screw her!" he told Tsalke, shoving the cork back into the opened bottle.

Tsalke sliced a herring, poured salt on a piece of paper, and went to Aunt Malkaleh's to borrow some bread.

When he returned, they attacked the vodka.

"Cheers," Tsalke said.

"Here's to you," said Falke.

"Screw her!"

Falke spat out the sickening taste of the vodka.

"You know what?" Tsalke said. "I think she's in love. She must be madly in love with someone she's trying to keep secret."

"Fat chance!" Falke spat through the crack between his two front teeth. "An intellectual like her doesn't know what love is."

"How do you know?"

"I know."

"How?"

"Listen, lay off!"

In a foul mood, Falke drank glass after glass and was soon drunk. Tsalke sipped slowly without touching the food and begged to hear more about love.

"Hold on. She had a child with someone, didn't she?"

"What of it? An intellectual is an intellectual. I know a woman like her with six children."

"You mean she had a child with a man she didn't love?"

"Lay off, will you!"

In the darkness, laughter rippled through Aunt Gita's walls. The guests were dancing. Tonke was celebrating her daughter's birthday, and the Zelmenyaners, weak from thirst and hunger, roamed the yard with their tongues hanging out.

"God, wouldn't some of that vodka taste good!"

It was dark. The roofs were black. The first shades of green had yet to appear. Aunt Malkaleh, having spent the night searching the yard for Uncle Itshe, finally found him clinging to a shutter.

"Go to bed, you crazy Jew!"

Sleep was the last thing on Uncle Itshe's mind.

"Just a little while longer, Malkaleh."

"Look here, you'll be late for work."

"What's it to you if I am?"

The night was at least half gone. The Big Dipper hung from its handle at the north end of Reb Zelmele's yard. Only a few lights still shone in the yard's silent rooms.

Falke, sad to say, had fallen asleep in his chair by the empty bottle.

Tsalke paced aimlessly back and forth, trying to fathom how his dream of the seashore in Odessa had gone up in smoke. By now it was clear even to him that he and Tonke would never share any villas.

A light still shone on the second floor of the brick house. If Aunt Malkaleh was to be believed, Uncle Folye was up there drinking by himself.

The Big Dipper hung from its handle at the north end of the yard. It was dark. The earth was black. The roofs were black. The first shades of green had yet to appear. In the darkness, laughter rippled through Aunt Gita's walls. The guests were dancing.

Poor Uncle Itshe couldn't tear himself away from the shutter. So, long ago, the great rabbi Hillel had sat on the roof of a study house, eavesdropping on a lesson in the Law until buried by a snowstorm. Uncle Itshe's mouth was agape. Aunt Gita's room was as beautiful as a theater.

Tonke was dancing.

A single lamp shone from the ceiling. Tonke danced. Slim, in a dark dress, hands clasped to her breast and head to one side, she moved with soft, tapping little steps between the corners of the room.

The guests sat in shadow by the walls.

Moving to the room's center, Tonke glanced at them with a faint smile. She danced faster, tapping out her nimble steps, black shoes clicking one by one.

Her feet wrote sentences with the finest calligraphy.

The pockmarked young man, unruly hair falling over a flushed face, knelt before her and clapped with thick hands.

"Down on the floor, Tonya, down on the floor!"

He was oddly earnest. A connoisseur, he judged the time had come for a kazatsky.

Tonke dropped to her haunches and flicked prancing shoes that glittered like the black keys of a piano. All but levitating, she touched the ground with only the tips of her heels.

Tonke sat on air as a swimmer floats on water.

She danced. Lying in their beds, the Zelmenyaners listened uneasily to the soft taps coming from Aunt Gita's. They were one more stab in the heart, a tuneless new music shunting aside Uncle Yuda's ancient fiddle whose wedding wails had taught their hardened souls to shed a tear on the happiest occasions.

"It's some world, eh?"

Uncle Itshe snuck home, hugging the walls. The lights were out everywhere except for one second-floor window.

There, by the window, sat Uncle Folye. Next to him was a quart of vodka. He sat without moving, staring dully at the wall across from him. Then he patted down his mustache and poured himself another glass.

In the whole world, there was no one who enjoyed his own company as much as Uncle Folye.

But how could a Jew afford to drink so much?

♦ ♦ ♦

At Aunt Gita's, things had quieted down. Dawn was breaking. The peeling yard, its rooftops poking through the morning gray, looked like a ruined fortress.

From somewhere, the gray light kept spreading. Yet in the windows and the chinks of the attic walls, a deep black continued to prevail.

Not a sound.

On a fence fluttered a white rag—a diaper, so it seemed, that a Zelmenyaneress had forgotten to take in with the wash.

The last guests had departed. At Uncle Folye's, a last light was turned out.

Dawn was breaking.

Tonke was still a bit high. Biting into an apple, she stood in the middle of the room. One end of the tablecloth was stained with wine. An empty bottle had rolled beneath the table. Swaying unsteadily, she took another bite from the cool flesh of the apple and smiled.

Hadn't she danced the night away splendidly?

Her black curls bobbed against her cheeks.

Uncle Zishe's clocks could be heard ticking in the darkness of the next room. Slowly, the outlines of a stove and a shelf emerged from the gloom.

"Mama, where's the jam?"

"There isn't any," Aunt Gita said in her sleep.

Tonke smiled. She went to the front door and opened it. The dawn's rosy-gray air flowed into the room, as fresh as a song.

In the yard, head resting on a railing, stood Uncle Yuda's Tsalel, his face looking as tiny as a bird's.

A gray day.

In the sky, off to the left, a rosy bar had begun to gleam like red-hot iron.

"So what's up with you?" Tonke swayed a bit, her head inclined toward Tsalke.

"Nothing," he answered.

Tonke leaned over the railing, eyes roaming the yard. "Highly intelligent chain of proteins that you are, Tsalke, just what are you thinking of?"

"Nothing."

"You're not very pleased with life, are you?"

"No, I'm not."

"No, you're not. Not at all."

He actually thought he heard sympathy in her voice.

"Come over here!"

Taking him in her arms, Tonke looked into his eyes and kissed him on his thin, cold lips that had long ago despaired, not only of the villa in Odessa, not only of Tonke, but also of his own last rubles, now gone as though through a hole in a pocket.

Tonke returned to her room and shut the door behind her. Tsalke remained standing there. For a long while he stared at Uncle Zishe's doorknob as if it were a magic line in the sand that could never be crossed.

♦ ♦ ♦

At nine o'clock sharp, Tonke left for work.

The yard sprawled listlessly, wearied by rumors and gossip. The doors were all shut. On the second floor of the brick house, Uncle Folye's little wife was already up and about, looking disgustedly through the window at the departing debauchee.

Uncle Folye's little wife did an imitation of the way Tonke walked. Then she said to herself:

"You think you're so beautiful? There are better-looking corpses than you in the grave!"

◆◆◆ *Chapter 17*

MORE UNREST IN THE YARD

It was the spring at the start of the great collectivization campaign.

Reb Zelmele's yard reacted with a sullen face, with a cold wag of its beard, and with silence for Tonke and Bereh, who were in any case off in the countryside for weeks at a time.

The yard had thought it was done with revolutions.

In the synagogue, Jews clustered by the tallow candle. The formerly pampered grooms of once wealthy religious brides sat exchanging the latest news in their turned gabardines, each hair of their beards neatly combed. An itinerant young cantor, newly arrived from somewhere, agreed to lead the evening prayer for three rubles. When he came to the words "And rid us of all our foes," he sang them with a catch in his throat.

Everyone knew whom they referred to.

The synagogues came to life. Cultivated Jews of the old school, refined types, dropped in on them from all over. Reb Yankev Boyez, the frail ex–dry goods store owner who had all but managed to acquire his own kolkhoz, huddled by the stove despite the mild weather, looking like a man barely pulled from a fire. Things had gone badly for him. The collectivization campaign had brought the city from which he had fled to the green fields and villages, its spring tempest leaving him in the cold. Now he sat wondering how it was that he, the twice-well-off Yankev Boyez, had been ruined for the second time in his life.

Spring arrived with sleek, vernal nights. It arrived with warm mists in the fields, with brigades setting out from the cities for bewildered villages, with showers of sparks in rural smithies.

Spring came to the city, too. It arrived with a smell of fresh grass, with dozens of black birds in the tall poplar trees by the electric power station, with young botanists pruning the dead branches from trees in the public gardens, with construction workers carting away old bricks from fresh spring sand.

Spring! It arrived with a new generation of laughing girls, winter-ripened at home. It arrived with birdhouses high on stilts, with clear waters in the rivers, with blankets hung out on fences, with the first white blossoms on the apple trees.

It arrived with the removal of the storm windows in the yard, airing the old, moldy rooms.

Spring arrived with a clatter of horseshoes on cobbled streets, with a great thirst in the throat, with the bare feet of children, with black smoke from cauldrons of boiling tar, with squat street pavers crouched by piles of old bricks and soft sand.

At Uncle Itshe's, it was still chilly and dark.

Aunt Malkaleh's brooding cousin sat on his trunk and wrung worried hands. His thoughts were of an expropriated flour mill, of a lost pen of cattle, of its being nearly summer with him still no more of a bricklayer than he had ever been.

All winter he had passed for one while the yard, each time it looked at him, looked forward to better weather. Now winter was long gone, and the Zelmenyaners went around grimly poking one another.

"I'd like to know why he isn't paving streets."

"It's time that sad sack found a job!"

The Jew's gloomy glance wandered over the room and fell on Uncle Itshe's abandoned sewing machine. It stood in a corner, its crude iron ribs like the excavated skeleton of a prehistoric trade.

The Jew found himself thinking about it. He thought all day until Uncle Itshe came home from work.

For a while, the Jew regarded Uncle Itshe in silence, waiting for him to shake off the factory and readjust to the yard. When Uncle Itshe began to splash himself with water from the faucet, a sure sign that tomorrow was a day off from work, the Jew tried asking nonchalantly in his brooding voice:

"Tailoring, now. Would you call that a real profession?"

"What else would it be, an unreal one?"

"And it gives a citizen all his rights?"

"Of course."

That was all the brooding Jew wanted to know. As squat and heavy as a moss-covered rock, he sat stock-still on his steamer trunk.

◆ ◆ ◆

The room lay in darkness, thirstily gulping the night's sleep. Never had the moon ventured so deeply into the rooms of the yard.

Uncle Itshe lay dreaming with dainty, whistling sounds. Have we said that he was the only uncle who smiled in his sleep instead of shouting?

Suddenly, Aunt Malkaleh gave a start and sat up in a fright.

"Itshe, do you hear that?"

"What?"

"You don't hear it?"

In the darkness, the old machine was sewing by itself. Or rather, not so much sewing as clattering hoarsely with a broken needle.

Through a crack in Uncle Itshe's still sleeping brain crept the awful thought that his former life—his little workroom, the No. 8 lamp, the oven poker, all that old Jewish baggage—had come back to haunt him.

"Now we're in for it!"

Poor Aunt Malkaleh was barely able to strike a match. When she did, she saw the bricklayer in a dark, unbuttoned linen smock, hunched over the machine like a hairy ball of yarn while biting off a thread with his teeth.

"It's nothing," he assured her. "I was just mending some clothes."

Uncle Itshe jumped out of bed. As concisely as possible, he asked:

"Are you crazy or just out of your mind?"

The bricklayer didn't answer right away. It took him a while to get hold of himself and say calmly to Aunt Malkaleh:

"I won't even mention being a cousin. A cousin is no better than a dog these days. What I want to know is: Are you still Jews or not?"

He rose aggrievedly from the machine.

"Because if you are, I'm telling you I have to be a tailor!"

♦ ♦ ♦

It was a difficult night. Everyone dreamed of oven pokers, No. 8 lamps, and the yard's big cooking pots.

The day off from work started out just as badly. It was the kind of day on which a person felt so out-of-sorts that only the prospect of someone to fight with kept him from doing something even worse.

That afternoon, at exactly two o'clock, an automobile pulled into the yard.

There were three passengers. Two, hands in their pockets, looked perfectly ordinary. The third was an elderly man with a long, forked beard, a coat open down to his stomach, and a wrinkled engineer's cap on his head.

The driver was Tonke.

The three men tapped the rotting rafters of the rooms and went to have a look at the brick house. When they came to Uncle Folye's room, they sat down to write a report.

Tonke descended the stairs to the bewildered Zelmenyaners.

"It looks like they'll knock down the yard," she said.

"Why?"

No one could think of anything else to say.

"To keep it from collapsing by itself."

Everyone saw black. A distraught Uncle Itshe flew out of his room with a birch cane. Hatless and shirt unbuttoned, he brandished the cane at his hairy-headed fellow Zelmenyaners.

"Why don't you say something, you thieves? It's our yard, our father's sweat . . ."

The women took brooms and began to sweep the yard. All at once, Uncle Itshe threw away the cane, backed against a wall, and let out a sob. Clinging to the bricks of Uncle Yuda's, he blubbered like a child.

"Ah, Yuda, my brother, where are you? Are you still alive?"

His shoulders heaved. Aunt Malkaleh suddenly noticed that his bald spot had spread almost to his ears.

Meanwhile, the cooler-headed Zelmenyaners sought to salvage what they could. Aunt Gita closed her shutters and went out to the yard to collect boards and stones. To the disheartened women, she declared:

"Why are you standing there like statues? Save something!"

"Can't you see I'm sweeping, Aunt Gita?" Khayaleh protested.

The men were occupied with Uncle Itshe, surrounding him to keep him from doing something rash. He went on standing by the wall, beating his breast and shouting:

"I'll go see Kalinin* about this!"

Falke came down from the second floor of the brick house, where the meeting was still in session, and said sternly:

"Papa, calm down. Capitalism has been abolished."

"Get out of here before I tear you apart like a fish!"

Luckily, Falke was not afraid of his father's temperamental nature.

"Calm down," he repeated. "There's going to be a factory here."

"A fine proletarian you are!" Tonke added.

Uncle Itshe spun around to face her.

"You don't like it? Maybe you'd like to have me fired from the factory, too? Pork eater! Do you think we didn't see that pig on the table? Go drown yourself in vodka! I'm telling you all, she's to blame. She'll be the death of us."

"What else can you expect from the shameless mother of a bastard?" cried Folye's little wife in Tonke's face.

"It's Zishke's blood!"

"Out of the yard!"

"You'll never set foot here again!"

Their kerchiefs awry, the women formed a circle around Tonke, looking like a flock of old birds with broken wings. Luckily, Uncle Yuda's Tsalel came along just then. Protecting Tonke with his body, he pushed his glasses up on his pale nose and said:

"What's the big tragedy? Stop being so childish! You'll be given better apartments. What's so tragic?"

---

* **Kalinin**—Mikhail Kalinin (1875–1946), a Bolshevik revolutionary and the nominal head of state in the Soviet Union between 1919 and 1946. Perhaps because his speeches about the Jewish Question were translated and widely available in Yiddish, Uncle Itshe considers appealing to Kalinin about the family's predicament.

"Apartments-shmepartments. You can have them!"

"We want to live out our lives in our own yard!"

♦ ♦ ♦

The automobile beeped its horn, drove off, and disappeared around a corner, leaving behind a small cloud of dust.

How did the yard feel? The yard felt forlorn and abandoned, like a stone by the roadside. The Zelmenyaners trooped silently back to their homes and sat there mulling things over. The setting sun splayed yellow flecks on the windowpanes and on the one-hinged doors thirsty for paint.

Was the extinction of Reb Zelmele's race approaching?

Falke stood in his doorway and sniffed the air. He didn't like what he smelled. Putting two fingers in his mouth, he let out a whistle. Then he took a few strides into the dead-silent yard and shouted:

"All right, you Zelmenyaner counterrevolutionaries—break it up!"

The Zelmenyaners, pale and shaken, pressed their noses to their windows. Framed by the small windowpanes, they looked like the bearded portraits of long-dead ancestors. The rooms resounded with fearful oaths aimed less at Falke, who was in the end a big nothing, than at Tonke, the yard's true nemesis.

Uncle Folye's dark little wife opened a second-story window and shouted down into the yard:

"You can go to your seamstress, Count Kondrat!"

The Zelmenyaners decided to wear the bad news down with silence. A Zelmenyaner can spin silence as a spider spins a web.

Silent were the bristly, unkempt beards and disapproving noses. Silent were the bony arms in sleeves folded on silent chests. Silent were the roofs.

The Zelmenyaners arranged their faces, wrinkles, bones, and all, to fit as tightly as a neatly packed suitcase: mouths folded on themselves, cold noses tucked into lips, hard, silent heads, knotted jaws, dimpled cheeks, eyes like frozen water beneath the brows.

Silent were the spaces behind the stoves, the big pots, the corner-stones of the foundations.

No one turned on the electricity that night. It was generally agreed that that's where all the troubles had begun.

Chapter 18

(By telegram to the newspaper *October*)
The Bikhov Shoemakers Cooperative has fulfilled its first-quarter plan in its entirety.

Cooperative Chairman Polovetz.

◆◆◆ *Chapter 19*

COUNT KONDRAT, OR UNCLE ITSHE'S FALKE

Countess Kondratyeva with her thousand scents of iodine and cloves, her pink fingernails and crow's feet, had gradually faded like a puddle of moonlight on the floor. If her presence was still felt, it was only in the winter dreams of dour old Zelmenyaners whose wives gave them heartburn like a fiery onion.

Falke hardly even remembered what she looked like, although sometimes the red curtain of her fourth-floor window still fluttered before his eyes like a restless semaphore in a station no train stopped in.

It was over. A Queen of Sheba made of love and spices, she had cast a sleepy spell over him in the enchanted city of Vladivostok, from which Tonke had woken him with a glass of cold tea and a hard slap in the face.

About the redheaded seamstress, it was harder to be precise. There was even reason to suspect her of being an invention of Uncle Folye's little wife. It wasn't she, in any case, who had cured Falke of his great infatuation. And unknown to Folye's wife, Falke also had a little girlfriend, Khanaleh, with whom he was having a love affair. Not that a love affair between a young man and a young woman is worth gossiping about. Such things happen all the time.

◆◆◆

Khanaleh was seventeen. She had a round face, nice breasts, and heavy, plump legs.

In a nutshell, she and Falke were having an affair.

He took her rowing on the Svisloch River. They ate pastries from a paper wrapper and floated with the current. Behind the Communard Factory,* they kissed and promised to be true.

Khanaleh twisted a lock of Falke's hair around a stubby finger and asked:

"Falke, will you always be mine?"

"Of course."

"Do you swear?"

Falke hugged her tight and said:

"You swear first."

"I swear by my mother," Khanaleh said, "that I'll be faithful to you all my life."

"*Prekrasno,*"† said Falke.

The boat drifted downstream to Lyakhovka.

The Svisloch breathed heavily with the rotted bodies of dead cats on its bottom. The rainbow-colored water had a thin crust. On the sandy hills on the far bank were cottages surrounded by gardens. Red poppies bloomed there. A train flew by on a bridge. Off to the left rose the high chimneys of the factory, belching spirals of black smoke.

Falke rolled up his pants, waded into the thick water, and pushed the boat back into it.

"Steady does it, Khanaleh! Steady does it!"

By nighttime they were far downriver, under a willow tree. Through its sturdy new branches, moonlight dripped on the boat. A horse grazed in a meadow by the riverbank. It pawed the darkness with fettered feet and whinnied. Falke and Khanaleh kissed.

"Swear," she said.

"You swear first," he said, kissing her.

---

* **The Communard Factory**—takes its name from the word "communard," referring to someone who was a member of the Paris Commune of 1871; this event was considered an important historical precedent in the Soviet cultural imagination.

† **Prekrasno** (Russian)—"that's wonderful."

"I swear by my mother," Khanaleh said, "that I'll be faithful to you all my life."

"*Prekrasno,*" said Falke.

It was after midnight when Falke returned to the yard. He grabbed something to eat and ran to make the last shift.

Falke worked at the electric power station.

He sat on a bench, straining to tell the sound of his two machines from the dozens of other noises around him. If they creaked, he oiled them from a can while keeping an eye on their black dials. Whenever a bell rang, he released steam from the pipes.

Falke stuck his fingers in his ears to block out all the sounds. His machines were running smoothly. Nothing creaked, nothing rang.

He went to the corner of the work floor, where the head machinist was writing at a desk, bent down to his head of white hair, and shouted in his ear:

"Makar Pavlovitsh, I'm in love!"

"Must be a great girl, eh?"

"You bet."

So Falke shouted into the deafening waves of metallic noises before running back to his machines.

♦ ♦ ♦

Morning found the yard bearing up under a swarm of heavy silence that drifted over it like a sky full of clouds.

The yard was mournfully tight-lipped.

Falke, back from work and sleepy, went looking for an explanation. All he could get was sad shakes of the head.

He stopped Bereh's son, who was wearing leather boots that came up to his belly button.

"What's up?"

"Nothing much. Grandpa Yuda died."

Before dawn a Jew had arrived in the yard with a package and put it silently on Tsalke's table. In it were some copper-rimmed spectacles, an old prayer shawl, and a pair of boots.

That was all that was left of Uncle Yuda.

The Zelmenyaners filed silently into Tsalel's room, crowding around the table and staring sorrowfully at its human remains. Tsalke was pale. He sat aimlessly running a finger over the table, the lenses of his glasses misting over.

No one could help feeling a bit sad.

"Tsalel, would you like something to eat?"

"What are you thinking, Tsalel?"

"Tsalel, have you thought of sitting shiva?"*

This last question was put with great caution by Aunt Nekhe. As silent as grass, the Zelmenyaners sat around the table at a loss for something to say. Some had tears in their eyes.

Just then Uncle Yuda's Khayaleh burst in. Without a word, she snatched the package from the table and headed back for the door, throwing Tsalke an angry look. From the doorway, she faced the room and shrieked:

"What next?"

It was as if the corpse itself had been carried away.

Who could blame her? Poor Khayaleh clearly had more rights to her father's estate than did a shiftless bachelor like Tsalke.

Aunt Nekhe, on guard lest someone, God forbid, burst into crude laughter, turned to Tsalke and said:

"Look here, why be upset? Everyone knows that your father loved Khayaleh more . . ."

"No one knows any such thing!" Uncle Folye's little wife jumped to her feet, white as a sheet from the crime committed in broad daylight.

Tsalke sat dejectedly, head bowed. Standing in the middle of the room, Uncle Folye's wife pointed at him and cried with foam on her lips:

"There! That's the true heir!"

The menfolk, naturally, shushed the women.

Aunt Nekhe fell silent too, afraid of the little wife's big mouth. She hadn't reckoned on Tsalke's having such a powerful ally.

The only way to avoid a family feud being to cease mentioning Uncle Yuda's death, it was decided to pretend he was still alive.

---

* **Sitting shiva**—observing the traditional seven-day mourning period following the death of a close family member ("shiva" means "seven").

Yet how long can misfortune be stifled or a daughter's pain be suppressed?

Upstairs in the brick house, Uncle Yuda's Khayaleh set about performing the prescribed rites for her deceased father. Out of respect for the occasion, all work ceased in the yard.

The first thing Khayaleh did was faint. The yard was good and scared. Everyone ran back and forth with water dippers and jam jars until informed from the second floor that Khayaleh had come to.

Next, she had herself a good cry. Her orphan's tears would have moved a heart of stone.

In their rooms below, the Zelmenyaners sat with wet eyes. There were sobs of sympathy when Khayaleh wailed in despair, "Papa, how could you have left me?"

Next, she let out a great sigh.

The women of the yard followed the progress of her requiem in silence. It all went without a hitch. When the sighs began to rain down like soulful brickbats, they said with a knowing nod:

"It's really quite proper of her. You couldn't ask for more."

Next, Khayaleh fell into a pained silence. She was already feeling better. Slowly she got out of bed, shook her head a few times, and let her son put on his grandfather's boots. Watching the wintry stargazer from the window swagger about the yard in waist-high leather, she burst into tears again.

This time no one heard her. She was crying for a father, outlived by his boots, who had died like a stone by the road.

After which she said in a normal voice:

"Gershke, go ask your grandmother if she's seen the cat."

At that very moment, Tonke stood up from her sofa and opened the window to let in some light. She had always hated Reb Zelmele's yard and its ways.

Why on earth, she wondered, had she traveled thousands of miles to come back to this place?

"Rubbish!" she exclaimed and said to Falke:

"Go see if anyone's at your parents.'"

Falke reported back that no one was.

"Not even your mother's cousin?"

"No."

"So what is he?" Tonke asked. "A bricklayer or a tailor?"

They went to check on the Ukrainian Jew.

♦ ♦ ♦

The yard was in mourning. It was a mild spring day. The air was filled with the simple smells of chamomile and apple blossoms wafting over fences from Reb Yankev Boyez's old garden.

Little Zelmenyaners in cotton shifts splashed in the gutters and licked flakes of whitewash peeled from the crumbling brick house.

The two rows of houses cast their triangular shadows on the sunlit yard.

"Say, Tonke, is it true you've read Hegel?"

Tonke didn't answer.

Uncle Itshe's home was still a twilight, wintry gray, as if a former life were forever frozen there.

Clotheslines on which nothing hung crisscrossed the front room. Above a chest of drawers on the eastern wall a pair of shaggy, dark-red, embroidered deer pointed toward Jerusalem, a memento from Aunt Malkaleh's religious childhood.

There was also the bricklayer's own peculiar smell, the smell of a village threshing floor.

"Open the trunk," Tonke said.

"Take it easy, will you!"

"What for?"

Tonke threw Falke an odd look. They bolted the door.

For a while, Falke puttered with the lock. It might as well have been made of stone. Wiping the sweat from his face, he spat on his hands, reached for Uncle Itshe's dull ax, and attacked the iron-studded trunk from all sides.

It might as well have been made of steel.

Falke, losing patience, hacked away as though splitting logs.

"Watch out! You'll break it."

"Get out of here, you!"

He breathed the words with a lunge at the trunk, bashing in one side of it.

A hard, light-colored object protruded from the trunk's innards. Falke dug it out. It was a sugar bowl made of heavy silver. Turning it this way and that, he glanced at Tonke, unsure what to make of it.

"A speculator, eh?"

Stretching out on the floor, he reached into the trunk and pulled out a venerable object of uncertain nature. The black trunk had the musty smell of a village threshing floor.

Tonke bent to look.

Next, Falke extracted a potbellied bronze urn with a handle and narrow neck that looked like a church cruet.

Soon the floor was as littered with items as the counter of an antique shop. Alongside the sugar bowl lay a silk prayer shawl and two opened, velvet-lined boxes, in one a bracelet and in the other some gold rings; a pocket watch in a linen pouch; a sheathed slaughterer's knife; some silver spoons; a horseshoe; a Kiddush cup, and a woman's prayer book bound in brown leather with a bronze clasp.

"A kulak," Falke murmured. "We've caught a big fish!"

Out of the trunk, tied with a piece of cord, came a moldy green shoe as heavy as lead. Slipping from Falke's grip, it fell to the floor. Yellow tsarist imperials scattered with a hollow ring.

Falke jumped to his feet. The blood drained from his face. Only now did he comprehend the full dimensions of the affair.

"Gold! How low can a man sink?"

Although the two Zelmenyaners had studied the theory of gold (Falke with a flunking grade) from Adam Smith to Soviet economics, the bricklayer's shoe was, so it seemed, their first glimpse of the actual substance. Both had a vague dread of it that stemmed from something even more repellent—the hideous creature that crawled, writhed, and flashed its fangs under the name of capitalism.

"Go on, pick it up," Tonke said, trying to sound casual.

"You do it."

As if wading into deep water for the first time in her life, Tonke stooped to lift a heavy gold coin and studied its scruffy, double-headed eagle and yellow profile of a tsar. Falke stood beside her. He, too, had never been in so far.

Tonke threw the coin on the floor.

At that exact moment, the bricklayer appeared in the yard.

The story was later told that Aunt Nekhe, who saw all things in the yard as though through the clear waters of a stream, had run to get the Ukrainian Jew. It was she, it was said, who told him he was being robbed.

The bricklayer was running. Or rather, he was hopping on short legs like a kangaroo.

At first he tried opening the door. It was bolted from within. He rushed to a window, banged on it, and rebounded into the yard.

"Help! Bloody murder!"

Yet his cry was oddly muted. Equally afraid to shout and to be silent, he produced a barely audible blubber while performing more kangaroo hops. One second he was in the vestibule with his eye to the keyhole of the door; the next, his petrified face was pressed against the window as though against the bars of a cage, though he had the whole sunny yard to hop around in.

"Jews, they're skinning me alive!"

Just then Tonke opened the door.

The Jew rushed through it, swinging his elbows as though pushing his way inside and seizing the ax. An errant sunbeam streaked his nose and cheek. His eyes swept over his belongings.

"Hand it over!" he screamed as if certain that Tonke and Falke's pockets were filled with his gold.

Falke leaned his hands on the table and glanced at Tonke to see how she meant to deal with the big fish.

"I said hand it over, you thief!"

"Suppose I don't."

Knees shaking, Falke struck a heroic pose.

The Jew brought the dull ax down on the table.

Uncle Itshe's house, with its two little windows and Aunt Malkaleh's shaggy deer, did a somersault and landed on its head.

With a shriek Falke ran for the door, his bleeding hand held in front of him.

"A kulak!" he screamed. "We've caught ourselves a kulak!"

The table was sprinkled with blood.

The brooding Jew threw himself on the trunk, scooping up his imperials and old bric-a-brac while wailing voicelessly:

"My blood! My life's work!"

When evening came, he was still sitting by himself in the dark room. A colorless white sun set dully in the dark window panes.

Apart from old Uncle Itshe, not a male was left in the yard.

Clearly suffering from dementia, Uncle Itshe, hearing of the incident upon returning from work, took refuge at Aunt Gita's, where he locked the door to be safe, collapsed in a chair, and sat quivering all night like a leaf.

Aunt Malkaleh, as a matter of record, turned gray that same day.

Only Uncle Folye's little wife was unfazed by the tragedy. Loath to miss any of it, she took her supper down to the yard and sat eating from a bowl by the door of the brick house. Then she went to have a peek at Uncle Itshe's through the window.

The brooding Jew was still sitting on his black trunk.

Chapter 20

BEREH AND UNCLE FOLYE QUARREL
OVER THE NEW SOVIET MAN

It was a matter of different speaking styles.

Folye, as he once admitted, talked perfectly well but had nothing to say. Bereh had lots to say but couldn't talk. There are men who think they talk a great deal, though it later turns out that they haven't spoken to their wives in weeks.

Taciturnus vulgaris is a dangerous species. Women flee from it.

Would Porshnyev succeed in driving the silence out of Bereh? That was the question.

Porshnyev had agreed to Bereh's working in the factory in the hope that there, on the assembly line, shoulder to shoulder with his old mates from the tannery, he would grow with them and the work.

In fact, Bereh could feel this happening. Of all people, it started with Folye—who, not without a struggle, had finally come to terms in his own peculiar way with the mechanization of labor. He now brushed his teeth with tooth powder.

Folye, it must be said, had played no small role in the antimechanization resistance. On the factory floor, he sometimes had to be whipped into line. While he could be quicker than others to adjust to a new method introduced by some engineer, he could just as well get it into his thick head to make such trouble that drastic measures had to be taken.

Uncle Folye was something of a fruitcake.

It was clearly a bad idea for him and Bereh to work on the same floor. Yet being old vat rats, both were employed in the wet hides division.

Folye was happiest in the vats. Naked to the waist, he stood with his long-handled scraping knife on a board above the ooze, currying the slippery hides that hung from their scaffold of beams and dripped on him a greenish fluid that smelled of dead, pickled horse.

Without it, that smell, he lost his concentration and fell asleep at once.

For years Uncle Folye had worked in the vats, lugging the wet hides up to the beams. When the management decided to modernize, its first step had been to replace him with a mechanical lift.

This got Uncle Folye's dander up. Taking a big swig of vodka, he went to the technical department.

"We don't need a lift!"

"Why not?"

"Because I'm the lift around here."

He pounded his chest with a fist.

The technical department looked Folye over and saw no reason to overrule the management. The Second Engineer, a man with a thin, blond mustache, patted Folye on the back and declared that the whole point of the revolution had been to relieve him of the need to be a lift.

Uncle Folye thought this a lot of hot air. The mechanical lift, he believed, would spell his doom. In desperation, he told the union representatives:

"I want you to know I'm not leaving the vats."

It was then that he was promoted to scraper.

Once it turned out that the pay for scraping hides was higher than it was for lugging them, Folye calmed down. Yet not for long, because next came the incident of the Smorgon tanners.

The Smorgon tanners were known far and wide for their philosophical minds. They even managed to prove, in defiance of human reason, that pigs have no hides.

This happened when the factory switched to tanning hog hides. The Smorgon tanners complained to the management that this spelled their demotion. Master artisans though they were, they were horse and cattle specialists who would never stoop to stripping pigs' bristles in their old age.

At the factory meeting convened that night to discuss their case, the Smorgoners were in a fighting mood. Pushing their caps back on their heads, they proceeded to demonstrate the hidelessness of hogs.

"Hogs," declared their spokesman, "have pork below, lard in between, and bristles on top."

"Then where's their hide?" asked the Third Engineer.

"That, Comrade Engineer, is the very thing we're asking."

"If you don't watch out, Comrade Workers, you'll soon be tanning crows."

"And white hens too, I'll bet!"

This last remark came from Khemeh, a religious old Jew with spectacles on his nose.

Uncle Folye sided with the Smorgon philosophers. Seated in a corner with his inseparable sidekick Trokhim, he took a few digs at the triumvirate of engineers and at the wiseasses, as he called the young Komsomols, who would even tan crows if they were told to. "Not that pigs are all bad," he sighed in conclusion, "because there's nothing like pork with vodka."

He wiped his mustache with his sleeve.

On one of the following mornings, carloads of philosophically refuted hog hides were delivered to the factory.

The Smorgon tanners leaned on their long-handled knives and played dumb. A young wiseass rubbed his eyes as if brushing away a dream and declared:

"Well, well, you Smorgoners! What have we here if not a shipment of hog hides?"

The Smorgoners hunkered down on their scaffold. The indomitable Folye answered fearlessly from his board:

"Don't call that shit hides!"

The shipment was accepted by the factory and wandered for fourteen days from one work floor to another before ending up by silent agreement in the dry hides division.

One afternoon the three engineers and the union representatives came to the vats and presented the Smorgon tanners with a handsome black pelt, elegantly crosshatched with crocodile patterns.

The silent Smorgoners tapped the soft skin and shrugged with resigned shoulders. Folye alone stuck to his board like a nail and refused to join them. He claimed he had too much to do.

◆ ◆ ◆

It was at about this time that Bereh returned to work in the factory. He did so with the grand notion of making up for something that had eluded him.

The factory greeted him with strong, sharp smells, with youthful memories, with the cool, greenish gleam of the vats, with thousands of fetid rivulets that trickled from the walls into gutters and then down the drains in the stone floors.

His first job was stripping pig bristles.

From afar, Uncle Folye threw him cautious glances, full of cunning suspicion. Although no one could say why, Uncle Folye regarded Bereh as a shmintellectual who had returned to the factory out of ulterior motives.

"Get a load of him!" he said to Trokhim.

He didn't say a word to Bereh all day. In general, following his victory in French wrestling at the athletic club, Uncle Folye had kept away from the other Zelmenyaners to avoid being scolded for his dissolute ways.

◆ ◆ ◆

Undoubtedly, Bereh had come back to the factory for the best of reasons. To the local Party leaders he confided that he was looking for a "serious social challenge." He even signed up for the Polytechnic Club.

A few days later he sat squirming at a factory meeting, trying to decide whether to speak or not.

Bereh was sure that this time he had something to say, since it was more a matter for the police than for the tanners.

On the agenda was the question of a flask.

The factory manufactured glue from its waste products. The process called for an ex-shopkeeper named Shimshe to arrive at the last moment and sprinkle several drops of a secret formula from a flask into the boiling cauldrons.

It was Shimshe's formula that turned the waste products into glue.

Shimshe, who had been making a living from his formula for several years, refused to reveal it to anyone, even his own wife.

The meeting had been called to debate the matter.

The engineers presented their case. Shimshe's flask, they argued, was unnecessary for the production of the glue. The workers who tended the cauldrons, on the other hand, insisted that nothing would work without the formula.

"It's ridiculous to say we don't need it. How can anything turn into glue just by being boiled?"

Bereh wanted to speak.

He had a suggestion to make: let the flask be confiscated from its antisocialist owner and analyzed for its contents. Yet his habit of silence so weighed on him like a stone that he doubted whether he could get the words out.

In the end, he rose to his feet and went to the podium.

Folye was sitting in the front row. A hunk of skin and bones with jutting joints, quivering whiskers, and jug-handle ears, he sprawled in his seat and laughed at the engineers who thought mumbo jumbo from books could make glue without Shimshe's formula.

"This," he said, giving them the finger inside his jacket for Trokhim to see, "is what they'll get."

Bereh stood on the podium. For a moment, until he saw that the chairman was still waiting to press the timing bell, he thought he had already begun to speak. Getting a grip on himself, he took a step forward and declared:

"Comrades! You are attending a meeting called by the Bolshevik Party to consider how best to build socialism for all the workers. Today, in the capitalist countries, there are sixty million unemployed. They go around with no work, rummaging in garbage pails, though everyone knows they have sweated for the bourgeoisie and had their blood sucked, not just by heavy industry, but by the banks and stock markets, too . . ."

Uncle Folye was struck dumb with wonderment. How did Bereh

know so much? Enviously, he looked around at the tanners and at the men on the podium—none of whom, however, seemed to be in the least bit impressed by Bereh's rhetoric. From this, Folye deduced that it was a lot of baloney.

"You can say what you like, Berke, but first learn to put two words together!"

So Folye shouted. There was, he thought, laughter in the hall.

Bereh was taken aback. Quickly recovering, he pointed at Folye.

"There he sits, comrades, an old worker, Folye Khvost, sticking out like a horse's rear end. He also happens to be an uncle of mine. Comrades, I say to him: 'Folke, open a book, because it's time you learned a thing or two yourself.' But no, he doesn't want to, he'd rather French-wrestle. He won't even look at a newspaper. All he does is sit on his porch to see whose wife is pregnant and whose isn't. He is, comrades, a foreign element who wants everything handed to him and won't lift a finger to help."

"I've been a worker longer than you, you moron!" shouted Folye, his whiskers quivering.

Bereh lost his temper and doffed his cap to Folye with a bow.

"Bravo! I thank you kindly. And you've been making goddamn shoddy goods, too!"

The chairman rang his bell. The old workers laughed so hard at the Zelmenyaners that tears rolled down their eyes.

Bereh was so pleased with himself that he only realized on the last step down from the podium that he had forgotten all about the secret formula.

Like any accomplished orator, he didn't dwell on his oversight. Wiping the sweat from his face with his sleeve, he took a seat.

Later he asked one of the glue makers:

"When does this Shimshe show up?"

It seemed that it was always late at night.

♦ ♦ ♦

Two nights later, Bereh brought Shimshe's flask to the Party committee. It was a squat, handsome little bottle with a round body, a glass stopper, and a dark, dull red liquid.

"What difference does it make how I got it? Take it."

That was all Bereh was willing to say.

The engineers took the flask to the laboratory. They spent all night investigating its magic formula, heating it over a flame, licking it with their tongues, straining it through absorbent cotton, and dyeing it different colors until the First Engineer wrote down in a notebook:

$Ch_2On + COH + Ch_2On$

The Second Engineer went on dipping his finger in the liquid and tasting it. After a while he wrote down:

$C_2H_{12}O_6$.

The Third Engineer arrived at a different result. He wrote:

$C_6H_{12}C_6$.

They couldn't all have been right.

The engineers wrangled all night. In the morning they emerged sleepless, ties disheveled and nerves on edge, with the surprising announcement that the Jew was a swindler.

The factory was agog.

The flask, it turned out, contained a concoction of glycerin, molasses, and cherry brandy.

Every summer the Jew had distilled a bottle of homemade cherry brandy and made a handsome living from it. Now, however, no one being allowed to make a living any more, the poor man had to leave town in a hurry and abandon everything he owned.

♦♦♦ *Chapter 21*

ENOUGH BIRDSONG FOR THE
AVERAGE ZELMENYANER

The blood stains on Uncle Itshe's table were scraped away with a knife. A dull dent from the ax remained in the wood.

The bricklayer was gone.

In the yard it was said that he had merely sat there and shrugged. There was not much, after all, that he could have said. A person might have thought he didn't know who Falke was. Unless, that is, it was all the invention of Uncle Folye's little wife.

Why would she have done such a thing?

Presumably, to widen her net of gossip, into which most of the Zelmenyaners had already fallen like flies in a spider web.

Now, since early morning, Falke has been standing in a corner of the yard, his bandaged hand in a sling.

Falke has a medical certificate releasing him from work. Convalescing in a sunny spot, he breathes in the summer smells of Reb Yankev Boyez's old apple orchard three courtyards away. He has an earnest look and feels, after his clash with the bricklayer, like a battle-seasoned soldier.

It's summertime.

Falke blows on his fingers and warms his bandaged wound in the sun. Yet not only, behind his back, is the yard indifferent to his pain, it's out to blacken his newly enhanced reputation.

Bad blood simmers among the Zelmenyaners as it does among thieves.

"Wait and see," they say. "Before long the redheaded seamstress will turn up here, too."

They are alluding to the fact that, during the commotion over the bricklayer, a Jew in town told some other Jews that the yard was in an uproar because a seamstress's husband had killed a young Zelmenyaner.

"The lowlife was carrying on with his wife."

Everyone in town, it seemed, had heard something, though just what was hard to say.

Uncle Folye's bad-mouthing little wife seized on this gem of a tale and spread it around.

"Didn't I tell you crazy people that the seamstress's husband would make him pay for it?"

The Zelmenyaners held their tongues. At first, no one argued. Some even assumed that Uncle Folye's little wife may have been right, since the story sounded perfectly reasonable. Not only that, the seamstress's husband, Folye's wife added, wanted Falke to share in the upkeep of their six children. Since they weren't his anyway, he deserved compensation from someone.

But you couldn't put a swindle like that over on Uncle Itshe.

"God almighty!" he said, tapping his head. "You'd think it was the husband who chopped off Falke's finger, not the bricklayer."

The bad-mouth gave Uncle Itshe a cold-blooded look and turned her back on him, though not before saying:

"And suppose it was the bricklayer? Next you'll be wanting compensation, too!"

Dismissing Uncle Itshe with a bitter smile, she went on telling her version. By now no one could prove her wrong, even if, apart from some oldsters whose names no one had remembered to erase from the Book of Life, few Zelmenyaners were convinced by her.

The stories about Falke's dissipated ways and errant love affairs were particularly prized by Aunt Gita and her circle.

◆ ◆ ◆

Summertime.

The flies clung to the walls, doing nothing.

It was the placid sort of day on which Aunt Gita and her friends, sitting by the cold oven with their spectacles pushed down on their noses, liked to take stock. On one side of the table, Aunt Nekhe was peeling potatoes. On the other, Esther the penmanship teacher held her white hands in her lap—the very hands to which so many Hebrew letters owed their delicate curlicues.

The women were discussing Falke's hard life—the life, that is, of the bandaged young profligate standing in a corner of the yard with his body inscribed like a tombstone, who would be made to sweat blood, it was said, for sins that weren't even his own.

"I'll wager," said Aunt Gita, "that she gave him a potion of love grass."

"Who did?" asked Esther.

"The pale-browed one who shines with devil's moonlight," Gita said.

Although the pious woman spoke in riddles to avoid mentioning the forbidden name, she was thinking of the Kondratyeva. The Queen of Sheba in her far-off land had given Falke love potions, and the poor fellow would now go around falling in love for the rest of his life.

It was said that her image had broken out on his chest, right over his heart, like a rash.

The worst part of it was that Falke's malady had no cure. Take the case of the religious Jew who drank a whole glass of such a brew and proceeded to fall in love ninety times. The crazy grasses made him blind, though not so blind that he didn't run a hundred miles to get to every woman in heat.

A man sinned and sinned and ran a hundred miles to sin some more. That's how it was with Uncle Itshe's Falke.

"They say it happens to sailors," declared Aunt Nekhe, who wasn't quite sure what a sailor was.

Early summer.

The houses on either side of the sunny yard threw their triangular shadows. Although the yard had no trees, this didn't mean that nothing grew in it. Uncle Yuda's roof bloomed with a delicate green, velvety mold. In the little windows stood potted plants that for some reason were known as aloes. There was also a pole in the yard with an old chamber pot at the top of it, braving the elements. With better care it might have made something of itself, perhaps even a tree.

It was just one of the yard's missed opportunities.

On Aunt Gita's roof stood a sulky sparrow with drooping wings, chirping a tune that was neither pleasant nor annoying. It was enough birdsong for the average Zelmenyaner.

One day Uncle Itshe's Falke brought a letter for Tonke and laid it on Aunt Gita's table. Handed to him by the postman as he was standing in his corner, it bore a heavy black postmark stamped Petropovlovsk-Kamchatksky.

The women in the room regarded the young invalid with a worldly wisdom born of their knowledge of love. Aunt Gita even broke her perpetual silence to engage him in a serious conversation.

"You must hanker for far places, my boy."

"I'll say I do!"

"And what is it that you hope to find there?"

"What's it to you?"

Aunt Gita rose from her chair, deep in thought.

"Tell me, Falkele. Right now, what would you like to do most?"

"What's it to you?"

"Tell me one thing."

"Right now? Ride a bicycle."

If truth be told, Aunt Gita was not very satisfied with this answer.

"What else?"

"What's it to you?"

"Tell us, son. Don't be ashamed. We're all old women here."

This came from Aunt Nekhe, who thought it advisable to put in a word of her own.

"I'd like a bottle of beer," Falke said.

The women sighed, their old faces screwing up with displeasure. Pulling herself up to her full buttoned height, Aunt Gita said in a voice deeper than any man's:

"And what else?"

"What's it to you? Do I have to sit here and give you a list?"

Falke was getting annoyed.

"Yes, a list, you lowlife, a list!"

If it was possible to shriek in a bass voice, this is what Aunt Gita did.

Only now did the cunning Falke grasp what Aunt Gita was up to. She, the descendant of rabbis, wanted to wangle a pious declaration from him for her friends—to get him to confess, for instance, that he wanted nothing more than to study a page of Talmud. Being a lowlife, however, he ran his left, uninjured hand through the mop of hair on his forehead, stepped right up to his tall aunt, and said:

"Aunt Gita, do you know what I'd most like to do?"

"Yes?"

"Kiss every pretty girl I can get my hands on."

There was no longer any doubt.

Her friends' wordless glances confirmed Aunt Gita's diagnosis. The young man was an incurable lecher.

Silently, they returned to their potatoes, the conversation ended. Yet seeing that Falke lingered in the room as if waiting for a clue to what it was all about, Aunt Gita serenely turned her stern, priestly face to him with its many blue-blooded lines, folds, and wrinkles.

"Go, Falkele," she said. "Go ruin the lives of a few more good Jews in this world."

Falke winced. You had to feel sorry for him. Red with humiliation, he stood with his tall shoulders pulled back. Now, at Aunt Gita's, he had acquired something of the hard, lumpy look that was had by such older, rock-bound Zelmenyaners as Bereh and Folye. For the first time in his life, he felt deceived and surrounded by strangers.

In his anger, he grunted something under his breath in Russian that does not bear repeating.

Falke's hand hadn't hurt as much as this did. The bricklayer, after all, had dealt him a fair blow in broad daylight. It was far harder to have to swallow the poison of old wives, administered with blind, loving religious reverence.

The great, pious love of old wives! In the Middle Ages, it burned heretics at the stake.

Falke slunk toward the door. On the threshold, he made a fist with his good, left hand. Shaking it at the women, he said

"You'll see! I'll have you eating dirt yet!"

He was gone with a slam of the door. The murderer! Having done in the bricklayer, he was now out for the blood of the last noble souls in the yard.

The yard was still.

Through the window, the frightened women watched the lowlife hurrying toward town—to his little Khanaleh, they supposed, or to the redheaded seamstress, or even, perish the thought, to the Kondratyeva.

Just then, the first wagonload of bricks pulled up in front of Bubbe Bashe's.

The yard grew black with Zelmenyaners. The simple peasant wagons bore a grim message. Although even the women at Aunt Gita's had known the yard was doomed, not a heart failed to sink.

A flash of pain ran through Reb Zelmele's old, low, warm yard, in which love grass grew silently and at night, by the light of the moon, the Queen of Sheba appeared from out of the past in the guise of the ethereal Kondratyeva.

♦ ♦ ♦

The letter lay on the table. Tsalke, quick to arrive on the scene, ascertained that it was indeed postmarked Petropovlovsk-Kamchatksky.

All afternoon, while Tonke was away, Juliana had screamed with a tummy ache. Returning in the evening, Tonke was informed that the yard's demolition was about to start and that there was a letter from her husband asking her to join him.

The yard, it seemed, could make out a letter's contents from its postmark.

Tsalke kept to his room. Pacing in its shadows with the lights turned off, he peered outside to see if the green lampshade was glowing at Aunt Gita's.

Tonke's window was dark, though she had been home for quite a while.

Soon word spread that she was crying.

First she cried in the darkness. Then she cried by the green light of the lampshade.

It was Falke, it was said, who had switched on the lamp for her.

"You don't say! She's still crying? It serves her right!"

"It's nothing to worry about," the cynics said reassuringly. "A good cry never hurt anyone."

"It builds character."

Next, the rumor spread that Tonke had been widowed. Her husband, so the Zelmenyaners were given to understand, until now no more than a few thick postmarks from Petropovlovsk, had cashed in his last rubles in a river thousands of miles away.

The letter came from Tonke's friend, nearsighted Nyute. Both women, it turned out, had been in love with the drowned man and now mourned him together, one at one end of the earth and one at the other.

According to Falke, Tonke's husband had been a good fellow—that is, another whippersnap. Yet when the yard ran to ask whether he was also the father of Tonke's daughter, Falke said:

"Mind your own business."

Plus:

"No one asked you to stick your nose into it."

Even a death, it seemed, was nothing to stick one's nose into.

Tonke went on crying. Through their open windows, the women thought they heard her sobs. She was said to be sitting with a handkerchief, grieving for her lost youth. Who would have her now, a woman with a child?

The Zelmenyaners held their tongues, letting one another know with winks and nods, which merged like pieces of clothing on a conveyor belt, that the drowned man's death was no accident. However you looked at it, drowning was a punishment for scoundrels—and speaking frankly, hadn't a harmless bricklayer been ruined for no good reason?

It was an opportune moment for Uncle Itshe to speak words of comfort, which he did by giving the women his first Torah lesson. Unfortunately, there were so many f's in it that it whistled through their ears like an ill wind.

It went something like this:

"*Fukh mukh leyfatfukh, veyfafoykh leyfafoykhe!*"

In Hebrew this was supposed to mean that every drowner would be drowned and the drowners of drowners drowned, too.

Although at first, unaccustomed to his new role, Uncle Itshe blushed, he soon grew aware of his importance. The women stared, amazed to discover such hidden erudition.

Uncle Itshe stepped into the yard. Tonke's lamp was lit beneath its green shade. For a while he wandered here and there, stopping by the pile of bricks to hitch up his pants and shake his head at someone invisible. Finally, he came to a halt outside Tonke's window. Slumped on the old sofa, she held her child in her lap and stared at the wall across from her. There seemed to be tears in her eyes.

What didn't pass for mourning these days!

Returning home, Uncle Itshe thought:

The husband is no husband, the tears are no tears, and this world is some world.

Falke ran off to send a telegram.

♦ ♦ ♦

That night, Uncle Yuda's Tsalel went to see Tonke—or more precisely, to pay her a condolence call. Wan and silent, he sat with his glasses on his nose as a certain Eliphaz the Yemenite had once sat in the presence of a certain Job. The glow of the lampshade fell on his pale, thin hands resting on the table.

He sat for a long while without a word. There wasn't a thought in his head, because he had already done all his thinking long ago. He glanced at Tonke. Curled up in a corner of the sofa, she was writing on a pad of paper, though she hardly had any light.

All at once Tsalke asked:

"And if I died, would you cry too?"

Tonke gave him a thoughtful look and said nothing.

"Not even a sigh?"

Tonke said nothing.

"You're a bad one!"

So Tsalke said, going to the sofa to hold Tonke's hand.

♦ ♦ ♦

It was supper time in the yard. The little windows blazed with their electric flames, glass panes shimmering merrily, though there was nothing to be merry about.

Through one of them Uncle Itshe, his jacketless sleeves rolled up, could be seen bent over a bowl from which he ate with a wooden spoon—a sure sign that the meal was dairy. Uncle Itshe was busy doing two things at once: eating and grieving for the yard.

Up above, in the brick house, the windows were open. Sounding close to exhaustion, several voices, some old and some young, sang a long, slow song with Zelmenyaner rapture. Its melody drifted over the yard.

Chai pila,
Samovarnichala,
Vsiu posudu perebila,
Nakukharnichala.*

The hoarse voice of Uncle Folye's little wife joined in the chorus. To be honest, it was better than hearing her gossip, even if it was a bit much to be singing in the yard on a night like this.

The Big Dipper hung over Aunt Gita's. At that exact moment, Tsalke started up the yard's ladder.

He scaled it briskly, his movements sure and nimble like a thief's. Due less to its color than to the thin curve of its sadness, his dark silhouette stood out against the deep blue of the night. Soon he vanished through the opening of the attic.

Above him, the rotted roof was patched with pieces of starry sky. In the darkness he groped for the rafters, which were covered with a cold, damp mold. His feet crunched over rotted rags, old junk, and mousetraps.

Tsalel threw a rope over a rafter and found something to stand on. Then he kicked it away.

Something snapped in the roof. As he plunged downward, feeling a sharp blow to his neck, the frightful thought crossed his mind that he, Uncle Yuda's Tsalel, had at last, by a stroke of good fortune, successfully died.

The singing stopped all at once. The wearisome song of the weari-

---

* **Chai pila** (Russian)—"I drank some tea, / I put on a samovar, / I broke all the dishes, / Such a wonderful housewife I am!"

some Zelmenyaners was cut short. Faint with fear, half-naked bodies leaped through the windows.

"Good lord, what was that?"

"The yard's on fire!"

"It's nothing. Part of Uncle Yuda's roof caved in."

Overhead, a pair of rafters stuck out against the starry sky like crippled bones. Beneath them, the bare, ghostly darkness of the attic yawned like a grave.

It wasn't the cold that was making teeth chatter. The yard's days were clearly numbered.

"Look at that! The yard's falling down by itself."

"What kind of person can't patch his own roof?"

"Ay! They'll drive us out of here like dogs!"

Just then, Tsalke was spied in the opening of the attic, dangling from a rope, one long leg reaching out for the ladder.

The benighted Zelmenyaners finally grasped what had happened. A hush like a graveyard's descended on the yard. The first to recover was Uncle Folye's little wife, who screamed:

"It's time he learned to hang himself properly!"

"Look what you've done to your father's roof!"

"You big carcass! What did we do to deserve you?"

One old woman was weeping.

But Tsalke, so it seemed, heard none of this. He descended, God help us, from the ladder, singing something without words. Most likely, he was already climbing ladders in the World to Come.

On the ground, he surveyed the dumbfounded Zelmenyaners with misty eyes and lifted a hand as if to say:

"Let's have some quiet!"

Needless to say, there was quiet. Holding the rope around his neck, Tsalke addressed the crowd in a husky voice with a clarity never had by him before.

"Our revels," he said, "now are ended.* These our actors, as I fore-

---

* **Our revels now are ended**—from William Shakespeare's *The Tempest* (act IV); in Kulbak's original, part of this quote appears in English transcribed in Yiddish letters.

told you, were all spirits and are melted into air, into thin air; and, like the baseless fabric of this vision, the cloud-capp'd towers, the gorgeous palaces, the solemn temples, the great globe itself, yea, all which it inherit, shall dissolve, and, like this insubstantial pageant faded, leave not a rack behind. We are such stuff as dreams are made on, and our little life is rounded with a sleep. My old brain is troubled. Be not disturb'd with my infirmity!"

Uncle Itshe had tears in his eyes.

"What a man can come to!"

♦ ♦ ♦

What might the yard have been compared to that night?

The yard might have been compared to a stagnant old pond. A green scum covered it beneath the drooping branches of the trees. The air was dank and malarial. Even the golden carp that sometimes wriggled in the slime left only a fleeting wrinkle in its thick, green crust.

The next morning Uncle Yuda's Tsalel was found dead. He had hanged himself in his room, from its western wall.

Chapter 22

UNCLE FOLYE'S DOWNFALL

Mende the tanner's original pair of tar-papered houses on the river-bank, which resembled two garbage bins, had accumulated around them a quarter-of-a-mile-wide yard with large buildings, a sky-high brick chimney, a network of narrow-gauge railway tracks, electric and telephone wires, an automobile perpetually parked by the front office, a summer garden, workers clubs, libraries, laboratories, engineers, and a whistle with its own phlegmatic tanner's voice.

In the early hours of the morning, when factory whistles sounded all over the city, the still-sleeping tanners made out their steady foghorn, discernible by its low, ample drone like a bassoon in an orchestra.

That was when the lights flickered on in Uncle Folye's window. Soon afterward, the electricity came on at Bereh's, too.

In early morning, as a gray dawn broke, the stars ceased their singing. In Reb Zelmele's yard, a polyphony of sirens took their place.

♦ ♦ ♦

The leather factory stood like a whole new city on the banks of the Svisloch River, whose drab waters that flowed to the gray fields of Belorussia seemed to originate there.

There were old tanners, especially among the Smorgon philosophers, who had never known a time when every limb of their bodies—hands, bare feet, heads, shoulders, even tongues—had not been meant to cure hides. Now, surrounded by mechanical skivers, fullers, and stretchers, they felt cheated and wandered yawning about the work floors as though suffering from indigestion. Sending the wiseasses to run the machines, they, the old tanners, clung to their vats, where they could at least still scrape a hide with a knife.

Khemeh the tanner, a clever sixty-year-old, was promoted to quality inspector in the trimming division. The machines stood by a row of gray windows. All day long, in the dull light of the work floor, Khemeh watched the naked, kneaded shoulders of the trimmers silently stretching the green hides. His glasses on his nose and his head in one hand, he sat at a table piled high with hides, waiting for the next delivery as Jews in a synagogue wait for the rabbi to finish the silent prayer.

It was getting the poor man down.

♦ ♦ ♦

In the vats, it was wet. A dark green light fell from the clerestory windows. Seen through the damp, greenish air, the workers appeared to be standing at the bottom of a deep river.

Uncle Folye's bony, knotted face was cactus green. An unmechanized holdout, he stood on his board with his scraping knife, the same Folye as always. A swab of the hide with his rubber glove, a few swipes of the knife, and he was already stretching the next hide on its beam. A heavy, dense smell hung over the vat like a cloud. Without it, Uncle Folye could never have done a stitch of work.

Once, a young woman from some committee came for a visit. She stepped onto the vat floor, clutched at her throat, and gasped:

"What's that smell?"

Uncle Folye looked around, took a few sniffs, and said:

"What smell?"

He winked at his sidekick Trokhim. A smile creased their faces, and thousands of tiny wrinkles webbed their small eyes. All it took to make a man grin was a young woman's first smell of the vats.

Uncle Folye was a shrewd customer.

◆ ◆ ◆

A moonlit night. Soft light trickled through the branches of the willow trees onto the Svisloch. Flowing past the short, knobby trees, the sleepy water inhaled the cool moonbeams and exhaled a sweet warmth onto its banks. The Svisloch, too, lived by nature's laws.

Something splashed in the water not far from the leather factory. A bony figure with a sack on its back rose from the Svisloch. It was not a mermaid stepping onto the silent, moonlit shore—no, definitely no mermaid, unbraided hair let down, come to cast a spell on passing tanners. It was Uncle Folye wading across the Svisloch with a stolen hide. His hard mustache bristled on his pale face.

A narrow footpath ran into the grass, winding back and forth across the marshy ground like a long rope before climbing a hill on which stood several small houses.

Folye started along it, the sack on his shoulder.

The rumor that Bereh had been fired from the police for turning a blind eye to a thief was, it seemed, quite unwarranted. He had in fact been keeping an eye on his cunning uncle for some time.

How could a Jew afford to drink so much?

The moon sprayed the damp bushes by the riverbank. The cool air stretched for translucent miles to the horizon. Shadows. Air. Smells. Folye halted, glanced back at the shadow behind him, and left the path to cut across the fields.

The shadow man was still there.

Folye made for the railroad tracks, tightening his grip on the sack. He crossed a bridge and headed for the woods.

The shadow man was still there.

With bitter foreboding, Uncle Folye doubled back to the fields and took a roundabout route to the city, drenched in sweat. The man behind him walked calmly, matching him step for step. Folye, the moon, the sack, and the man were a single composition.

A brittle silver light lay over the fields. The few trees looked etched on air. There was not a sound, not a stir.

The man was still there.

They could all, Uncle Folye thought, go to hell. For half the night he had tramped through the fields with his sack and crept through the back streets of the city. Now, more dead than alive, he turned into Reb Zelmele's yard.

The little windows twinkled beneath the scaffolds. The yard looked like a disassembled watch. Uncle Yuda's roof had caved in. At the back, by the brick house, someone sat by a small fire—the watchman of the construction site. Mesh nets hung on the walls; mounds of fresh sand stood behind them. Bathed in moonlight, troughs of lime lay between piles of lumber.

Fenced off by boards and littered with bricks, ladders, and metal pipes, the moonlit yard with its rotting roofs and patchwork windows looked like an excavated catacomb.

Uncle Folye stepped over the troughs and disappeared with his sack into the dark recesses of the brick house.

The fire crackled, catching on the dry wood. You could hear the smoke rise to the sky. You could hear the crickets sing their last song in the yard's moldering walls. You could hear the moon stir in the glass panes of the crooked, ramshackle windows.

The next thing the watchman knew, a crowd of Zelmenyaners was running to the brick house. Women wrung their hands. Never had the yard been so hushed, so null, and so void. The moon spun its spiderwebs over the rooms and trickled soundlessly into the dark vestibules.

From the top floor of the brick house came the crash of a broken windowpane. For a while, furious shouts were heard. Then they stopped. The watchman got to his feet. On the top floor, he was sure, the Zelmenyaners had fought to the death.

Uncle Folye's was jam-packed. Men jostled each other and shook their heads at Folye for letting his little wife make a thief of him. Stiff and mute, he arched his broad, bony back over the sack in the middle of the room with dull Zelmenyaner obstinacy. Coldly, Bereh grabbed him by the waist and flung him off it.

That was when Uncle Folye hauled off and gave Bereh a haymaker. What happened next was about as clear as a punch in the eye.

Over and over the two men tumbled in a narrow space with no room to breathe, fierce thuds coming from on top and on bottom at once, as when a stake is pounded into the ground. It was hard to tell who was astride whom and whose knee was jammed into whose chest.

Uncle Folye, it stands to reason, was mostly on bottom, since the sounds of the ensuing free-for-all reached him from afar as though having nothing to do with him, apart from a hand thrust into his face, the clawing fingers of which made a mishmash of his nose.

About Uncle Folye's nose, the less said the better. In the state it was in, his soul's only way out of his body would have been through his gasping mouth.

When it was over, he was doused with a bucket of water. His stomach heaving and his long arms and legs twitching aimlessly, he lay like a fallen horse.

By the door stood Folye's dry-eyed little wife, her hands folded over her belly. In a strange voice that seemed more like a mechanical doll's than a human being's, she wailed:

"Why are you murdering him? Who murders his own uncle? Who murders anyone like that?"

Afterward, Folye tried convincing the Zelmenyaners that the hide had been given to him for safekeeping by someone who then disappeared, his only crime having been to be thought a trustworthy guardian. No one believed him.

A few days later, he suddenly remembered that he himself had skinned the hide from a dead horse he proceeded to bury. He just couldn't remember where.

Uncle Itshe, for some reason, went around insisting that Folye was innocent. He even let it be known that Bereh, his own son, would no longer be allowed to cross his threshold.

But things had gone too far. In the end, even Folye stopped trying to explain his inexplicable behavior. He merely shrugged, which was taken to mean that he was so amazed by what he had done that he attributed it to supernatural causes.

♦♦♦ *Chapter 23*

THE GREAT TRIAL

During the trial held at the Workers Club, a thoroughly downcast Folye, accused of theft, sat silently on the podium with his head hanging and his long hands on his knees. All seven hundred employees of the factory were in attendance. Reb Zelmele's yard, the jackets of its hairy denizens in need of patching at the elbows, sat on the front bench, trying to hide the disgrace in their beards while feeling it was not so much Folye as the entire yard that was on trial. Folye's little wife had brought him his supper in a basket, from which she passed him bits of food from her place near the podium in the hope of reviving him.

The judges, three veteran factory workers, sat at a table covered with a red cloth. Partly concealed by wreaths of smoke was a fourth man with a rugged, close-cropped skull. It soon became known that this was Porshnyev—the same Porshnyev who was a legend in the yard. He sat smoking a cigarette with his elbows on the table and his chin propped on his hands

The Zelmenyaners stared at him with a mixture of fear and astonishment. It was hard to believe. What had always seemed a winter night's dream, an apparition of the yard's moldy rooms, had now become a real person.

Uncle Itshe reached a marveling hand beneath the bench and pinched Aunt Malkaleh's knee.

"I hope you realize who you're looking at!"

Aunt Malkaleh realized. It was the same Porshnyev who had been Bereh's good fortune in the war—whose specter had burst into the yard one winter night with a blizzard, making the bricklayer quail and driving Bereh from the police to the factory—who had caused the yard's walls to tremble.

"He looks just like anyone else."

"Don't be a dumb cow!"

Old factory hands were called as witnesses. The first was Vincent, the hoary-headed head of the chrome department, who testified that Folye was a backward element. Then came Vishnyevsky the trimmer, who laid the onus on Reb Zelmele's yard for its petit-bourgeois atmosphere that had wormed its way into Folye's consciousness. Then came old Khemeh the inspector. Khemeh put on his reading glasses, the better to hear his own clever remarks. As he saw it, Folye had only himself to blame. This he demonstrated with some fine parables, the best of which concerned a young bride and her mother-in-law. These were especially well received by the Smorgon tanners, it being widely acknowledged that all Smorgoners spoke in parables. Then came Trokhim. Mumbling a few words from his seat in the audience, he twisted his cap in his hands and ended by declaring that whatever the judges decided would be fine. You could see he was trying to wriggle out of it. What else could he do when he loved Folye more dearly than life itself?

Then came short, stout Shimtshik, who played in the factory orchestra. He too spoke out against Folye, although his tongue kept getting caught between his lips, the result of too much trombone playing. Then came Konye the smith from the machinists' division, tapping his foot as if working a bellows. Then came Mitchulikha the vat rat, who had soaked like a hide for twenty-five years in Mende the tanner's solvents until the last tooth was gone from his gums. Mitchulikha asked the court to show Folye mercy.

It was then that it happened.

The Zelmenyaners were shaken to the core. Their runny noses in the ground, they stared up at the crowded club with fat tears in their eyes through which they saw nothing at all.

"What a disgrace!"

A young woman, Uncle Zishe's Tonke, had taken the witness stand. With oddly cool venom, she told the judges all the yard's secrets. It was beyond belief that the yard's own flesh and blood should harbor such hatred for it. Probably because of her elegant Russian, the Zelmenyaners failed to understand all she said, but what they didn't hurt just as much.

"The Zelmenyaners," Tonke declared, "wished to cover up Folye's theft. They thought it unbecoming, though it's in fact precisely what they've become. For what, at bottom, is Reb Zelmele's yard? The yard, even when it doesn't steal, is potentially stealing all the time. True, it only pilfers odds and ends. That's your Zelmenyaner thief for you. (Not that the bricklayer didn't try to get away with a whole trunkful!) The yard is a bottomless pit of such things. I know a Zelmenyaner woman with a single silver spoon because of which she doubts that she belongs to the proletariat. She thinks she's too good for it. For generations, the Zelmenyaners have collected bits of this and that and built their world from it. The yard has a bit of vanity, a bit of mendacity, a bit of larceny, a bit of sycophancy, and is in fact composed of nothing but bits. The Zelmenyaners own no banks or grand estates, but they do have eighteen trash bins, twelve copper ladles, a chamber pot, a fur muff, and plenty more. Always up to something, a Zelmenyaner leaves, like a moth, only holes behind him, but these are holes of the darkest stupidity. Uncle Folye thought he could be a mechanical lift! Their benightedness is so great that reality is transformed by them into a dream, while conversely, rumors and tall tales come to life in the yard as though they were real. Such is the case of a machine operator from Vladivostok who haunts the yard to this day in the form of a countess. The yard subsists on leavings and scrapings, on the remnants of superstition and religion, on naïvely distorted scraps of scientific knowledge. Alongside Komsomols and Pioneers, the Zelmenyaners' rooms spawn hidden saints, Yidls with fiddles who dance on electric wires and deny the existence of oxygen with dialectics. Even as electricity was being installed in the yard, the grasses of love potions kept sprouting magically in its dank crannies. Its inhabitants go about in a stupor, talking in their sleep, their ears not hearing what their mouths say. That's Reb Zelmele's yard—and yet there are those who make of it an ideal, a philosophy, even a science. Ah, our Zelmenyaner intellectuals, who would prove that the yard has its own distinct culture, the culture of bits! Tsalke, an educated young native of the yard, spent so long investigating its uniqueness that he hanged himself out of sheer spiritual poverty . . ."

Those were her very words.

Uncle Itshe wiped eyes wet with shame. The Zelmenyaners might as well have been stripped naked in the street. He felt embarrassed in the presence of his own nose.

A tumult broke out in the clubroom. If truth be told, there were workers who doubted whether, so near their factory, there could exist a yard whose residents lived as though in an enchanted castle. Folye's sidekick Trokhim was the most indignant. A regular visitor in the yard, he swore that it was not like that at all. The Zelmenyaners were simple Jews, working people, and Tonke was nothing but an anti-Semite. He raised his cap to Folye from the audience to convey that his friend needn't worry.

The judges cross-examined the defendant.

Silent until now, Folye was no more intelligible when he talked. Because of a flayed horse, he claimed, he had become a tanner, not a watchmaker, and because of a flayed horse he was now not long for the world. His line of defense was to convince both himself and the judges that flayed horses were his destiny. In this, he did not succeed. As for Tonke, he had to admit that he was too dull-witted to understand a word she had said. Still, it was his opinion that she was blowing smoke in the judges' eyes.

"Do you promise never to steal again?" they asked.

Folye rose and declared that there would be no more stealing once he moved to a new apartment.

"Does that mean," asked the judge Vasilyev, a machinist from the gelatin division, "that your petit-bourgeois environment is to blame?"

Folye debated how best to answer and replied:

"I won't steal anymore."

The court adjourned to consult. The clubroom was rank with smoke and sweat. Porshnyev came down from the podium. Eager to know what he thought, the audience crowded around him. He brushed it off and made for the Zelmenyaners, extending a hand to Uncle Itshe. A wave of emotion they had never expected to feel for Bereh and his mates swept over their hard, bony faces.

Porshnyev smiled.

He was, it turned out, well informed about the Zelmenyaners and even asked Uncle Itshe how much he earned at the garment factory and inquired about Uncle Yuda. He also knew of Tsalke's suicide. Of Bereh, he appeared to be quite fond. He was, in a word, a down-to-earth type with a straightforward grasp of things and certainly no one to be afraid of.

Clever Aunt Malkaleh took advantage of the opportunity to set him straight.

"When it comes to the Zelmenyaners," she said, "things aren't what they seem. We may be simple folk who aren't cut out for much, but we're honest in all our dealings, and our word is a word. Even Folye, despite his coarse character, being a man who never wanted to educate himself, wouldn't touch a hair of the factory's property, because he had fine, upstanding parents. And as for Tonke," Malkaleh said, "no one knows what she wants. Of course, she's had a hard life. She and her husband weren't meant for each other and didn't get along. She's unhappy and said things she shouldn't have. But she has a noble character. You could leave a bar of gold with her and she'd never lay a finger on it."

Porshnyev let her go on.

Aunt Malkaleh plucked up the courage to declare that, in her opinion, the yard should not be taken away from the Zelmenyaners, since if nothing else, it was a shame to waste so much money on it. With a glance at Porshnyev, she waited for his answer. He laughed, patted her on the back, and said:

"What can't be helped can't be helped."

Aunt Malkaleh laughed politely along with him.

♦ ♦ ♦

It was late at night when the Zelmenyaners trooped home from the trial. The night was cool and starry. In front, gnarled like an old billy goat (Itshke the Goat!), strode tall Uncle Itshe, leading his flock. Behind him shuffled old Zelmenyaneresses, bearing the yard's dilapidated lanterns.

All was now clear.

Reb Zelmele's kingdom, which had endured for seventy years and several generations, had come to an end. Not only would it never see the fulfillment of its founder's dream, the well from which it could drink its own water, it was doomed to be wiped from the earth with its little houses, fences, sheds, and even its brick building that had been the incomparable pride of so many Zelmenyaners.

Ultimately, the yard was guilty of theft. But the real crime was not the theft but the trial, which had yanked off every last flimsy coverlet, probing the yard's innards and holding them up to the light. For all their glorious past, the Zelmenyaners, it turned out, had not a stitch left to their name. Reb Zelmele, may he rest in peace, had built on sand, and Uncle Itshe, the last princely scion of the Zelmenyaners, had lost his precious crown in the mud like all great monarchs.

Uncle Itshe felt faint.

Tonke was standing on the corner. She had been waiting for the stolid Zelmenyaners, always so calm, phlegmatic, and cold. Uncle Itshe strode at the head of them, bringing the condemned yard back home.

They filed past her without a word, in deadly silence, their wooden clogs clopping on the bricks. Then, as Tonke stepped toward them from the sidewalk with a look of surprise at not being recognized, Uncle Itshe turned a glowering face toward her.

"Jew hater! Get out of our honorable family!"

"Out, you damned slut!"

The women let loose a volley of frightful oaths. Tonke quickly about-faced and disappeared around the corner. She hurried down another street, perhaps never to see the yard again, her blood boiling at the wasted lives that had trickled away for seventy years as though into a dark puddle at the base of a wall.

She didn't turn around to look back.

Chapter 24

KHAYKE, WHAT DID YOU DO WITH
THE KOSHERING POT?

The last days of the yard went by like smoke. One thing after another swam before the Zelmenyaners' eyes, and nothing remained in their memory. The main recollection was of a still-wet, newly built brick wall whose fresh red color cast a pall over the tumbledown houses. The Kommunarka Candy Factory had begun to rise from the scaffolds.

The Zelmenyaners closeted themselves until the last minute in their old rooms, into which not a ray of light shone anymore. From time to time, voices called from somewhere among the scaffolds:

"Khayke, what did you do with the koshering pot?"

"Hey! Where's the koshering pot?"

There was a major problem, so it seemed, with a koshering pot. Unaccustomed to moving, the yard was addle-brained.

On that hot summer day, Zelmenyaner looked pleadingly at Zelmenyaner, begging to be told what he was doing in the dark rooms beneath the scaffolds. No answer was forthcoming. Zelmenyaners did not want Zelmenyaners knowing their business.

Chests of drawers stood tied with rope. Tin buckets were stuffed with pillows.

On a stove, alongside two pieces of stuffed cabbage, burned a Zelmenyaner fire, a wearisome flame cooking potatoes with onions.

♦ ♦ ♦

Uncle Yuda's Tsalke had a memorable funeral.

This young man, who wrote the history of his life on water, was buried with the rest of Reb Zelmele's yard.

The young Zelmenyaner was carried out from the scaffolds in a red coffin. Soon the funeral procession was heading down the side streets. Not a single passer-by inquired who was in the coffin. Tsalel, the last noble youth of the yard, was dead.

The sun beat down. The chestnut trees on the sidewalk, aflame with summer light, watched the handful of bearded men pass on foot, followed by a carriage with Uncle Zishe's Sonya and Aunt Malkaleh. Sonya, naturally, leaned her head on the breast of her aunt, who inexperiencedly proffered little bottles to her nose.

Slowly, the red coffin with its silver bells went by, the hairy coachman in the driver's seat looking like the Angel of Death.

Needless to say, the sorrow was great.

The Zelmenyaners were silent, not so much out of respect for the dead as because there simply was nothing to say.

On a fence in a narrow street near the cemetery stood a bird without a name, though Tsalel had fought all his life to have it called a sparrow. While its tedious chirp was no substitute for Chopin's funeral march, the nameless bird was sufficiently educated to declaim from the fence several well-known lines from the collected works of Heine, vol. I, p. 457:

Keine Messe wird man singen,
Keinen Kadosch wird man sagen,
Nichts gesagt und nichts gesungen
Wird an meinen Sterbetagen.*

A pair of drunken Jews performed Tsalel's last rites. No one tipped the gravediggers, though they stood by their shovels looking sharply at the mourners. It simply didn't occur to anyone.

Old Uncle Itshe wiped away his tears with a large handkerchief. Although he had barely ever exchanged a word with Tsalke, he wept all the same as a token of good breeding so as not to embarrass the corpse.

---

* **Keine Messe wird man singen** (German)—"Not a mass will be sung for me, / Not a Kaddish will be said, / None will say or sing a service / On the day that I lie dead"— from Heinrich Heine's poem "Gedächtnisfeier" ("A Memorial Service").

It was a hot summer day.

High overhead, a small white cloud drifted over the cemetery. The air was so clear that it seemed nonexistent. Not a leaf stirred on a tree.

After everyone had left, Esther the penmanship teacher went on standing by the tree-shaded grave. She was wearing her best black shawl, and her eyes glittered hotly in her long, mealy face. Late at night she was still standing there, wringing her white, pen-weary hands over the sorry pile of sand.

She let a tear drop.

Esther the penmanship author thought in all seriousness that she was standing by the grave of a fellow laborer in the vineyard of knowledge, of which she was one of the planters.

It was late summer. Down below, in the valley beneath the cemetery, the potato plants were already in bloom.

♦ ♦ ♦

This is what was salvaged at the last moment from Reb Zelmele's demolished yard:

Twelve copper pans, eight large copper pots, sixteen cast-iron pots, three copper jugs, five earthenware ones, six iron pokers, four oven sweepers, seventeen graters, eighteen chamber pots (including four large ones), a shovelful of flour, a box of Vissotzky tea, a jar of blackberries, a doormat in good condition, a bolt, a fur muff, a stewing pan, a hard hat left behind by Uncle Zishe, may he rest in peace, some dried lemon peels bound with string, one felt boot (the other was given up for lost), an inkstand, brass scales with weights, a white tile for chopping herring, and a birch bobbin. Uncle Folye ripped from a wall a porcelain electric fixture, and Aunt Gita, a mezuzah from a door. Perhaps, in the new apartments that awaited them, there would be a place for it.

One corner of the yard was dark with people.

"How about those Zelmenyaners? It looks like they're getting some swell apartments."

"And for free!"

Observant Jews, the yard's boarders, stood with their walking sticks and handsome beards, discussing things from all angles. Some thought the Zelmenyaners were being treated high-handedly. Any Zelmenyaner emerging from the scaffolds was quickly surrounded like a man coming from a sickroom.

"So, what's the latest? Not so good, eh?"

The Zelmenyaners were sparing of words. Regarding the circle around them with a superior look that signified they knew everything and weren't talking, they retreated back among the scaffolds to resume their secret work—in all likelihood, pulling nails from the walls.

Thus the Zelmenyaners made off with the yard piece by piece, scuttling quietly behind the wooden boards like a band of mice, packing everything into chests and carrying it away like threads plucked from an old, tattered coat. Surrounded by the brick walls of the factory, the little houses had nothing left in them but a glimmer of cobwebs and the bare ribs of what had been. In the middle of the night, a young voice could be heard calling in the yard:

"Khayke! What did you with the old koshering pot?"

"Hey! Where's the koshering pot?"

It was all over. A glare of electric lights lit up the yard. Dozens of pickaxes rang out. A crane creaked high overhead, lifting bricks to the top floors. A luminous glow bathed the sky above the old roofs that lined the forsaken street. It was reflected back by the little windows of the low houses, whose sleepers heard without waking the sound of the yard's last rafters falling.

About White Goat Press

White Goat Press, the Yiddish Book Center's imprint, is committed to bringing newly translated work to the widest readership possible. We publish work in all genres—novels, short stories, drama, poetry, memoirs, essays, reportage, children's literature, plays, and popular fiction, including romance and detective stories.

whitegoatpress.org
The Yiddish Book Center's imprint